MISS
BURMA

CHARMAINE
CRAIG

Grove Press UK

First published in the United States of America in 2017 by Grove/Atlantic Inc.

First published in Great Britain in 2018 by Grove Press UK, an imprint of
Grove/Atlantic Inc.

A portion of this novel originally appeared in *Narrative* magazine.

For everything that they have given to me and this book, my deepest thanks go
to Ellen Levine, Peter Blackstock, Andrew Winer, and Arthur and Judy Winer.
—C.C.

3 5 7 9 8 6 4

A CIP record for this book is available from the British Library.

Grove Press, UK
Ormond House
26–27 Boswell Street
London
WC1N 3JZ

www.groveatlantic.com

Hardback ISBN 978 1 61185 624 8
Export Paperback ISBN 978 1 61185 507 4
Ebook ISBN 978 1 61185 940 9

Printed and bound by CPI Group (UK) Ltd, Croydon, CR0 4YY

'Like many o   n its time and
place, while also laying bare timeless questions of loyalty, infidelity,
                                        ation the   lly perpetuated
un   le

'*Miss Burma* serves as a much neede. ... ration of history, one
that redresses the narrative imbalance by p acing other ethnic, non-
Burmese points of view at the center of its story . . . By resurrecting
voices that are seldom heard on a wider stage, Craig's novel . . . brings
one of Burma's many lost histories to vivid life.'
— *New York Times Book Review*

'[An] epic new novel . . . The sweeping, multi-generational story of
a family belonging to the Karen ethnic minority, *Miss Burma* charts
both a political history and a deeply person 1 one – and of those
incendiary moments when private and publ c motivations overlap'
— *Los Angeles Times*

'Charmaine Craig wields powerful and vivid prose to illuminate a
country and a family trapped not only by war and revolution, but also
by desire and loss. Both epic and intimate, *Miss Burma* is a compelling
and disturbing trip through Burmese history and politics.'
— Viet Thanh Nguyen, Pulitzer Prize–winning
author of *The Sympathizer*

'*Miss Burma* is a book which resonates with meaning, of how we are
all actors in our histories and the histories of our nations, it disrupts
our settled sense that the past is the past, and shows how it reaches
forward to touch the future. It is a powerful, moving and important
novel.'   — Aminatta Forna, author of *The Hired Man*

'A sweeping novel of Burma and its complicated history, told from the
perspective of people whose voices have been systematically erased
from the official record. Charmaine Craig writes about war and exile
with an exquisite mix of tenderness and intelligence. A brilliant book.'
— Laila Lalami, author of *The Moor's Account*

Also by Charmaine Craig

The Good Men

In memory of my mother, Louisa;
and her parents, Ben and Khin—all born in Burma

And for Andrew, Ava, and Isabel

Look at the history of Burma. We go and invade the country: the local tribes support us: we are victorious: but like you Americans we weren't colonialists in those days. Oh no, we made peace with the king and we handed him back his province and left our allies to be crucified and sawn in two. They were innocent. They thought we'd stay. But we were liberals and we didn't want a bad conscience.

—Graham Greene, *The Quiet American*

Prologue

There she is, Louisa at fifteen, stepping onto a makeshift stage at the center of Rangoon's Aung San Stadium in 1956. *Give yourself to them,* she thinks. And immediately one hand goes to her hip, her head tilts upward, her awareness descends to her exposed thighs, to her too-muscular calves, now in plain view of the forty thousand spectators seated in the darkening stands.

Give them what they need, her mother told her on the way to the stadium. And Louisa understands that her mother meant more than a view of her gold high-heeled sandals (on loan from a friend and pinching her toes), more than the curves accentuated by her white one-piece (copied from a photo of Elizabeth Taylor). Her mother meant something like a vision of hope. Yet what is Louisa's appearance on this garish stage, during the final round of the Miss Burma contest, but a picture of something dangerous? She is approximately naked, her gleaming suit approximately concealing what should be private. She is approximately innocent, pushing a hip to one side, close to plummeting into indignity.

A tide of applause draws her farther into the light. She pivots, presenting the judges and the spectators beyond them with a view of her behind (ample thanks to her Jewish father, who sits with her mother somewhere in the stands nearby). Before her now are the other finalists, nine of them, grouped in the shadows upstage. Their smiles are fixed, radiant with outrage. "The special contender," the government paper recently called her. How strange to be dubbed "the image of unity and integration," when she has wanted only to go unremarked—she, the mixed-breed, who is embarrassed by mentions of beauty and race. "We never win the games we mean to," her father once told her.

She pivots again, crosses the stage, moving through a cloud of some nearby spectator's smoke, her eyes landing for a moment on her parents. Daddy is slumped away from Mama, his balding head slightly turned, his docile look catching hers. Though under house arrest, he has contrived special permission to be here. It is even conceivable that he has somehow arranged for the pageant to be fixed. Beside him, Mama, with her demurring aspect, appears anxious, overly engaged in the proceedings. She seems to lift off the edge of her seat, her eyes alight with pride and accusation and something resembling anguish. *Move!* she mutely cries from her perch, as though to avoid capture by Louisa's recriminating glances.

And Louisa does move—past her parents, downstage, to face a view of the smiling judges and the rows of eyeglasses glinting up at her, the rifles in the hands of the soldiers manning the stands. It feels nearly benign, the applause that gives way to a flurry of coughs; almost sweet, these whiffs of someone's perfume, of putrefying garbage and dampness beneath the field; even liberating, this offering of herself, of her near nakedness. Aren't they all compromised in Burma? They have been through so much.

Several minutes later, before the crown is placed on her head, it occurs to her that the spectators could be worshipful congregants—or penned beasts—and she has the instinct to escape.

But here is a sash being slung across her shoulder.

Red roses shoved into her hands.

A camera flash.

"Miss Burma!" someone cries from the far side of the stadium, as if across the darkness of what has been.

PART ONE

Conversions

1926–1943

1

The Pugilist

When, nearly twenty years earlier, Louisa's father saw her mother for the first time, toward the end of the jetty at the seaport of Akyab—that is, when he saw her *hair*, a black shining sheath that reached past the hem of her dress to her muddy white ankles—he reminded himself, *God loves each of us, as if there were only one of us.*

It was a habit of his, this retreat from cataclysms of feeling (even lust) to the consolations of Saint Augustine's words. Did he believe them? When had he felt singularly loved, when since he was a very young boy living on Tseekai Maung Tauley Street in Rangoon's Jewish quarter? Even his memories of that time and place were unsatisfying: Grandfather reciting the Torah in the Musmeah Yeshua Synagogue, Daddy behind the register at E. Solomon & Sons, and the wide brown circles under Mama's eyes as she pleaded with him, her only child, *Be careful, Benny.* Dead, all of them, of ordinary disease by 1926, when he was seven.

Be careful, Benny. Mama's terrified love had kept him safe, he'd felt sure of it, until there was nothing between him and death, and he was shipped off to Mango Lane in Calcutta to live with his maternal aunties, daughters of that city's late rabbi. Their love was nothing like Mama's. It was meek and bland and threw up little resistance to his agony. So he took to throwing up his fists, especially when the boys at his new Jewish primary school taunted him for his strange way of speaking, the odd Burmese word that decorated his exclamations. His aunties' solution to "the problem of his fists," and to the

3

way those fists brought other boys' blood into their house ("*Jewish* blood! Jewish blood on his hands!"), was to pack him off again, to the only nearby boarding school with a boxing program, Saint James' School, on Lower Circular Road. The location was a comfort to his aunties, who mollified their anxiety about the school's Christian bent by insisting that no institution of serious religious purpose would ensconce itself on a road whose name sounded, when said briskly enough, like Lower *Secular*. "And no more Jewish blood on his hands," they reminded each other with satisfaction.

And they were right. Over the next five years on Lower Secular his fists found everything *but* Jewish blood: Bengali blood, English blood, Punjabi blood, Chinese blood, Tamil blood, Greek blood, Marwari blood, Portuguese blood, and Armenian blood—lots of Armenian blood.

Poor Kerob "the Armenian Tiger" Abdulian, or whatever his name was. In a swollen gymnasium that reeked of feet and stale tea and wood rot, seventeen-year-old Benny fought him for the crown in the Province of Bengal's Intercollegiate Boxing Championship, and never had one young man's face been so rearranged physically in the name of another's metaphysical problems. Before going down in the first round, the Armenian took a left to the chin for the loneliness Benny still suffered because of his parents' deaths. He took another left to the chin for a world that allowed such things to happen, and another just for the word "orphan," which Benny hated more than any anti-Semitic slur and which his classmates cruelly, proudly threw at him. The Armenian received a right to his gut for all the mothers and fathers, the aunts and uncles and grandparents and guardians—colonized citizens of the "civilized" British Empire, all of them—who banished their young to boarding schools like St. James in India. But none of these jabs could vanquish the Tiger. No, what sent the Tiger to the mat and all the spectators to their feet was an explosion of blows brought on by something Benny glimpsed in the stands: the entrance of a young, dark St. James' novice called Sister Adela, to

4

East Renfrewshire Culture and Leisure
Giffnock Library

Customer ID: *****9883

Items that you have checked out

Title: Miss Burma
ID: 11075589
Due: 13 July 2022

Total items: 1
Account balance: £0.00
Checked out: 1
Overdue: 0
Hold requests: 0
Ready for collection: 0
22/06/2022 12:46

Contact:
Giffnock.library@ercultureandleisure.org
0141 577 4976
www.cultureandleisure.org/libraries

whom Benny had hardly spoken, yet who—until today—had arrived precisely on time for each of his fights.

He took her presence at his matches as some kind of exercise of devotion on her part—to him or to the school (and by extension God?), he wasn't sure. Now, as the referee began to shout over the collapsed Armenian, Sister Adela positioned herself in her white habit near a group of students whose raucous display of support for Benny only illumined her stillness, the alertness of her black gaze presiding over him. But when the match was abruptly called and Benny struggled to free himself of the spectators flooding the ring, she slipped out of the gymnasium, unnoticed by all but him.

That evening, the proud schoolmaster hosted a feast in Benny's honor. Leg of lamb, roasted potatoes, trifle for pudding—those were the Western dishes that Benny could hardly taste because he was directing all of his attention to the tip of Sister Adela's fork, which she repeatedly used to probe her uneaten dinner while stooped over her corner table with the other nuns. Only once did she meet and hold Benny's gaze, her focus on him so sharp and accusatory that he felt every flaw in his face, especially its swollen upper lip, the result of the one right hook the Armenian Tiger had managed to land. Was she *angry* at him?

As if to deprive him of an answer to that question, her father came to take her away the next morning. She left in a deep pink sari that clung to her hips and set off the impossibly black strands of hair falling from the knot at the base of her neck, the most elegant neck Benny had ever seen. A queen's neck, he told himself over the following few weeks, as he tried and failed to assert himself in the ring. Remarkably, his desire to fight had followed Sister Adela right out of the stands.

A month later, a letter from her arrived:

Dearest Benny,
 Do you remember when I came across you sitting in the library talking to yourself? I thought you had become one screw loose because

5

of all the pummeling your head receives. But no you were going over the lecture on Saint Augustine and you were saying God loves each of us as if there were only one of us. Well you were saying it with a good amount of mocking but I have seen from the start that you are a very sweet and immensely gentle being. And maybe you were thinking what I have come to. That sometimes it is necessary to go without human love so God's love can touch us more completely. It is true that no human love can be as untroubled as God's don't you agree? Try as I am trying to think of God's love whenever you are blue. Oh I know you will do the opposite! Well let this be a test and a reminder that true rebels are unpredictable. I told myself I COULD NOT FACE your match when I learned my father would come for me but then I changed my mind. Did you have to be so hard on that boy? You can't imagine how very very very very happy it made me when you beat him so happy I am crying all over again. Oh Benny. Pray for me. Your very dearest Sister Adela is now a wife.

In faith,

Pandita Kumari (Mrs. Jaidev Kumari)

He sailed for Rangoon later that year, in June 1938, when a cyclone crossed the upper Bay of Bengal and swept his steamer into its violent embrace. With each pitch and lurch, he leaned into the wind over the upper deck rail, purging himself of his choked years of loneliness in India—years that had ended with his rebellious proposal to his aunts that he convert to the faith of Saint Augustine (whose God he truly hoped loved him as uniquely as a parent), followed by their retaliatory proposal to perform his death rites. By the time the cyclone passed and he caught sight of the placid mouth of the Rangoon River, he nearly felt dispossessed of what had been.

At the wharf, he was met by an employee of B. Meyer & Company, Ltd., a lucrative rice-trading house based in Rangoon and run by one of his second cousins. The employee—a young Anglo-Burman called Ducksworth—was chattier than any fellow Benny had encountered. "They didn't mention you were a heavyweight!" Ducksworth exclaimed when Benny insisted on lifting his own trunk into the carriage drawn by two water buffalo (he'd had the fantasy of being met by an automobile, and stared with some envy at one idling on the road). "Mr. Meyer should have put you to work hefting bags of rice instead of pushing a pen! Not a hopelessly boring job, being a clerk—nor a hopelessly low salary. Enough to live respectably, to take care of your board and lodging at the Lanmadaw YMCA. Well, you wouldn't want to live anywhere else. A lot of jolly fellows, many of them British officers, half-whites. You're . . . half Indian?"

Before Benny could answer, they were caught in an afternoon downpour, and Ducksworth busied himself with helping the driver raise the rusted metal roof of the carriage. In any case, Benny thought, better to avoid the subject of his race. He wasn't worried about bigotry—Mr. B. Meyer was a shining example of Jewish success—but he was tired of wearing a label that no longer seemed to describe him. His Jewishness was like a feature lost to childhood; it had been part of him, to be sure, but he saw no recognizable evidence of it in who he had become.

Ducksworth was eager to take him under his wing—just as eager as Benny soon became to take flight from anything constraining his newfound freedom in Rangoon. Over the weeks that followed, Benny discovered that if he did his job well, if he worked very hard at pushing his pen, and then was adequately polite to the fellows at the YMCA (where he was the youngest boarder and roundly liked)—if he rewarded Ducksworth with a few generous smiles or minutes of attentive conversation, he could escape into the city on his own. And so every evening after supper he found a way to flee down Lanmadaw Street to the Strand, where, amid the grand official structures and residences built by the British, his pace slowed and he drank in the evening air. He was thirsty, desperately in need of replenishing himself with the kind of sights he'd missed while shut up at St. James'—sights that had become so foreign to him he felt

7

himself taking them in with the embarrassing curiosity of a newly transplanted Brit: the men sitting on the side of the road smoking cheroots, chewing betel, or singing together; the Indians hawking ice cream and the Muslim shopkeepers reading aloud from their holy book; the stalls advertising spices, canned goods, and umbrellas varnished with fragrant oil; the clanking workers in the passageways; and the buses, the trishaws, the bullock carts, the barefoot monks, the Chinese teetering past on their bicycles, and the women in their colorful, tightly wound sarongs, transporting sesame cakes or water on their heads and even meeting his shamed eyes with a grin. How closed in he had been on Lower Circular!

Painfully, it struck him that his aunties had stopped routinely inviting him to Mango Lane long before his talk of conversion, and that the intoxication he felt here was partly due to his burgeoning sense of belonging. In truth, he knew little more about Burma than what he'd learned in history classes: that the region had been set-tled centuries (or millennia?) ago by a medley of tribes; that one of the tribes, the Burmans, had dominated; and that the problem their domination presented to everyone else had been solved by the British, who'd taken possession of Rangoon nearly a century before and who continued to rule by staffing their civil service and armed forces with natives. The very names of these tribes bewildered his ignorant ears: Shan, Mon, Chin, Rohingya, Kachin, Karen (these last pronounced with the accent on the second syllable, it seemed to him—*Ro-HIN-gya, Ka-CHIN, Ka-REN*), and so on. He could no lon-ger speak more than a few phrases of Burmese—English had always been his language (though he could make his way with the Bengali and Hindustani coming out of the odd shop). But as he passed the people gossiping in their impenetrable languages and playing their energetic music, he felt seized by a powerful sense of understanding. It was something about their friendliness, their relaxed natures, their open courteousness, their love of life, their easy acceptance of his right to be among them, elephantine as he must have appeared in their eyes (and hopelessly dumb, miming what he wanted to purchase). He had the sense that wherever they had come from (Mongolia? Tibet?), however many centuries or millennia ago, they had long ago accepted others' infiltration of their homeland so long as it was peaceable. Yet he also had the distinct impression that they'd never forgotten the dust of homelessness on their feet.

"Damnable citizens," Ducksworth often grumbled at the Lanmadaw YMCA, where every night after dinner the fellows would gather in the close, teak-furnished living room and fill their glasses with cognac (purchased, Benny learned with a pang, from E. Solomon & Sons, where his father had worked). Invariably, they would begin a game of bridge, and as they played and smoked and drank into the early hours, they would talk—about girls, about politics, about the splendor of the British Empire, the great Pax Britannica, which kept this country running with the ease and beautiful regularity of a Swiss clock.

"Unlike China," Ducksworth cut in on one of these nights, "with Manchuria overrun by Japs. What the devil do you think Hitler's up to by favoring the Japs, anyhow?"

There was something distasteful about Ducksworth, Benny thought. He was too eager to laugh, to lose himself under the annihilating influence of tobacco and drink. The fellow would never bloody his fists for anything, had he even the mettle to believe in more than a decent pension and a decent meal and a decent-enough game of bridge. No, his lightness appeared to be how he survived, how he sat so easily with not treating anyone but a white or a Burman quite as a man—and how he managed to get away with championing the imperialism that more and more of the Burmans were beginning to revolt against.

Just the other day, Ducksworth had been taking a break for tea at the firm when he'd revealed the shallowness of his convictions to Benny. They'd been alone in the office; Ducksworth had put his feet indecorously up on a chair, raising his teacup to his pursed lips; and Benny had decided to broach the subject of the law student, a Burman fellow at Rangoon University—someone by the name of Aung San—who'd begun raising a ruckus about the British presence. "A solidly anti-empire nationalist sort," Benny had added rather breathlessly. "They claim he's starting some sort of movement, saying the Burmans are the true lords and masters—Britons be damned, and everyone else along with them." By "everyone else," Benny had meant people like B. Meyer and him, and also the Muslims and Indians and Chinese and, well, the natives who'd been here for centuries, some *before* the Burmans. "It's not anyone *else's* country," his new friend had disdainfully replied, reminding Benny that Ducksworth, born to a Burman mother and an English father, had a uniquely dominating perspective.

Yet Ducksworth was habitually unwilling to go so far as to side with the Burmans; it suited him better to sink into the plushness of the Pax Britannica. Indeed, during their conversations, each time Benny came close to the point of pressing him on political matters, Ducksworth would slip away into the haze of his tobacco-drenched musings about the fine pleasures of British tea (which he bought from an Indian) and British cut crystal (which he hadn't any of) and British manners (which he rarely displayed). And, generally speaking, Benny had to admit that British rule did nurture a spirit of tolerance that appeared more to benefit than to harm many of Burma's citizens. Certainly there was a kind of caste system, by which the white man was on top and the Anglo-Burmans just beneath them; certainly the British had the deepest pockets; but there was also freedom of religion, an equitable division of labor when it came to British civil and military service, and, for the most part, a general prospering of every sort. From the little Benny had read since landing back in Rangoon, he understood that the Burman rulers whom the British had conquered had shown no such charity (even of the self-interested sort the British practiced) to those they'd overthrown.

"I say, Benny," Ducksworth said on this particular night, when no one rose to his question about Hitler's favoring of the Japanese. "Have you put in that application?"

They'd begun to play the cards he'd dealt.

"What application?" said Joseph, one of the others who worked at the firm and lodged at the Lanmadaw.

"Benny doesn't take our work seriously, Joseph—too 'stifling,' too—"

"Well, it is!" Benny said, hiding behind his hand.

"What application?" Joseph repeated.

"To His Majesty's Customs Service," Ducksworth answered. "It does have a distinctive ring, doesn't it? You're too bloody lazy for that sort of thing, Joseph—but not Benny. And wouldn't he look dashing in a white uniform?"

Was Ducksworth mocking him? He'd been the one to urge Benny to apply for a junior position, so impatient was he to convert Benny to his chosen faith of imperialism.

"What's the point?" Benny said. "The English will be out soon enough."

For a moment, Ducksworth only peered at Benny over his cloud of smoke. Then he said, "Your problem is that you believe in right and wrong. Don't you know evil will find you no matter what?"

It happened now and then in Benny's wanderings that he caught a glimpse of a cheek, neck, delicate hand, or sweep of black hair that could have been Sister Adela's. One evening in November—when the rains had fallen off and he'd wandered beyond the city limits—he noticed a girl walking swiftly along a deserted side street, tripping in her fuchsia sari as though her attention were on something higher than the procession of her feet. Up the steep hill leading to the Schwe' Dagon Pagoda, he found himself shadowing her, until he was sure she had become as sensitive to his presence as he was to hers: two tuning forks, each dangerously setting off the other's vibrations. The ground leveled off, and she scurried along a concrete path toward the pagoda, glancing back at him as she fled up a dilapidated set of stairs. Instantly, he saw that her terrified eyes were nothing like Sister Adela's, and the spell was broken. She disappeared into the golden entrance, set between two enormous griffins covered with horrifying pictures of the damned.

"Are you a fool?" he heard. When he looked back at the entrance, he saw an Indian man facing him. The man's long lax hands, hanging against his gaunt frame, were not a fighter's, nor was the fierceness in his amber gaze. Rather, there was something wounded about him, ruined. Benny felt awfully ashamed, awfully sorry. "Are you a fool?" the man said again, in an English thickly accented by Bengali.

"Just foolish," Benny responded.

"Where does your father work?"

"Forgive me, sir—"

"I insist that you take me to your family!"

Now the man descended the stairs and drew close, so that Benny could smell the tobacco on his breath.

"Are you stupid?" he said more quietly. "Terrorizing a child who only wants to light a candle for her mother? You should be honoring the dead yourself. What do you imagine they think when they look down and see you behaving this way?" His questions seemed to chase one another out of his throbbing heart. "Don't you know that when no one is present to be strict with a man, he must be strict with himself?"

Benny hadn't intentionally avoided his parents, or the Musmeah Yeshua Synagogue in whose cemetery they lay. A few nights later, he ventured to the Jewish quarter, where the bazaar was still in full swing. His eyes flicked over the flares of the vendors' stalls, up to the rickety buildings' timber balconies, which his father had predicted would be burned down one day. (*"You wait and see, Benny. Careless, so careless with their flares, these street peddlers."*)

Farther up the road he soon found E. Solomon, shut up for the night and somehow less commanding than it had long ago seemed. He peered through the dusty window of the dark store at the rows of liqueurs and whiskies. Whenever he'd managed to keep his hands off the merchandise, his father had rewarded him with a bottle of orangeade. How he'd loved the way the marble in the bottle's little neck gurgled as he swallowed down the sparkling, syrupy drink. Daddy had been head cashier at E. Solomon, which provided the British navy with drinks and ice from its wells on the riverbank. (*"The navy keeps us safe, Benny. And how do you imagine their sailors relieve themselves from the press of this heat? Our ice! Our fizzy drinks!"*)

At the corner of Tseekai Maung Tauley, he stared up at their old second-story flat, from which Mama had peered down on him while he'd played here with the other boys. She'd never been a doting, fussing type; no, her love was more even-keeled than that: a stroke on the cheek, a brush of warm lips on his brow. But her counsel had lavished him with love, with attention and praise. (*"You must not just think of yourself, Benny. Only animals just think of themselves. The worst sin is to forget your responsibility to the less fortunate."*) She had seemed to carry her sacred separateness from man's lower impulses in the hollows of her frail, perpetually melancholy face; in her slow movements; in the way she watched him, as if already from the remove of eternity. Generosity and charity—those had been her trading posts. How often had she packed a basket of fruit for the less fortunate? How often had she plaintively prayed for the sick before the candles forever being extinguished by fretful Daddy, who had lurked around their flat almost deferentially? Mama had loved to sing—quietly, unassumingly—and her voice had drifted from the window down onto the graced street. And then . . . silence.

Benny's feet fled to narrow Twenty-Sixth Street, where he found the dark outline of the menorah and the words "Musmeah Yeshua" over the archway of the grand white synagogue. Musmeah Yeshua—"brings forth salvation." The meaning came back to him along with his grandfather's counsel that he must not hesitate to flee to this refuge in times of darkness. He couldn't remember where any of his loved ones were buried in the cemetery, but again his feet discovered the way, along a path through the overgrowth, to the tree under which they lay. As he knelt, he touched the cold headstones inscribed with Hebrew he could no longer read, and then he pressed his forehead to the rough stone of his mother's grave. "*I am right here beside you, Benny*," he could almost hear her say.

The world of the dead was something he could reach out and touch; he had only to give it attention, and it reached back out and met him.

For a long time, he sat with his head against the grave, his mind quiet, attentive, sensitive to the wind and the birds and the life in the overgrowth. It must have been a few minutes past dawn when one of the synagogue's caretakers saw him asleep, and Benny woke with a view of light-suffused clouds before a rock hit him on the cheek. "Indian!" the caretaker shouted at him. "Tramp! Scat! You'll find no sanctuary in this place!"

2

By Sea

Khin had seen him before, the young officer (an Anglo-Indian?). She had noticed his hands, strong and clenched by his sides, and the restless way he charged from one end of the seaport to the other, as if he were trying to expend something combustible stored within him. One afternoon, she had watched as he'd ridden a launch out toward a ship anchored in the bay; he'd stood at the bow, leaning into the wind, arms crossed over his chest. Was he so sure of his balance? she wondered. Or did some part of him hope to tempt fate, as she sometimes darkly did when she ventured out to the very edge of this jetty, where she stood now, in September 1939, with the boy who was her charge.

She had come to Akyab four months earlier to work as a nanny for a Karen judge, who made a practice of hiring people of their own persecuted race, or so he said. His six-year-old son often drew her out to the port, where from the jetty they could look out over the fitful water and watch the beautiful seaplanes landing and taking off. She loved the planes as much as the boy did, loved their silent sputtering grace—though her love was distressed. Sometimes she saw a plane swerve and imagined it falling like a bird shot out of the sky.

The boy pointed up to the silvery body of a plane ascending toward a cloud, and she shuddered, drew him sharply from the rotting end of the planks giving way to the sea.

"Time to go," she told him.

"I want to watch until we can't see it anymore," he said.

He hadn't been told that Japan was at war with China, that Germany had invaded Poland, or that France and Britain had declared war on Germany. His innocence made her feel guilty, as though by encouraging his fidelity to the planes she were somehow betraying him. But she was being silly, she knew, imagining that *these* planes were doomed. "War will never come here," the sessions judge had told her, after listening to his nightly English radio program. "It's Malaya the Japs want. There's no penetrating our territory but by sea, and when it comes to the sea the British are unsinkable."

"I have a surprise for you at home," she lied to the boy. She shielded her eyes from the glare and tried to give him her most convincing smile.

The boy studied her for a moment. "What surprise?" he said.

"I'll tell you when we're there."

There was no surprise, of course, and as they stumbled back toward land over the splintered planks (as she stumbled away from the unbidden image of her body slipping into the shivering waves), she kept her eyes on her feet and searched her mind for some small treat the boy might deem acceptably unforeseen. He was already beginning to doubt her reliability. Perhaps the maid had bought a few cream puffs from the Indian who came around on Wednesdays.

She was halfway to the shore again when she looked up and saw the officer watching her intently from the other side of the wooden gate leading to the jetty. His white hat cocked to one side, he leaned against the rickety gate as though to block her path back to land. Even across the distance, she could see he didn't hesitate to scrutinize her hips, her hair. If any other man had stared at her in such a way, virtually *eating* her with his eyes, she would have—well, she would have *laughed*.

The officer suddenly shouted at her, coming out with a confusion of English words of which she clearly caught only "*not*"—something he said with great emphasis and at least twice. He was surely instructing her to steer clear of the jetty (the way he further cocked his head and pointed away from the water told her as much), and his loudness and directness should have offended her; yet there was something mellifluous, some kindness, in his baritone voice.

She stopped five feet from the gate, taking the boy's warm hand in hers, and steadying herself against a fresh assault of wind and sea spray. The officer's gaze narrowed now on her eyes, and she felt herself blush as she absorbed the full force of his face—the heavy jaw, the mouth too full to be truly masculine, the ears that stuck out beneath the brim of his hat. There was nothing extraordinary about his version of handsomeness, about his large features (though he did have something of the elephant about him!); there was nothing unusual about his authoritative claiming of the port (all the officers seemed to claim Burma, as if they were not also subjects of His Majesty the King of England). But she had to admit that he was more striking than she had imagined him from afar. What was so very unforeseen (what she must have noticed without noticing) was the expression of meekness in his eyes, markedly in contrast to his obvious physical strength. Even the smile that he now leveled at her own lips, and that she unwillingly returned, seemed aggrieved.

"Are we in trouble, nanny?" the boy asked.

"Perhaps," she said quietly.

Again, the officer began to speak, to express something to her in English, while beside them a seaplane revved its engine.

"Look!" the boy said, pointing to the plane that started to skip over the waves.

For a moment all of them stood in mute wonderment, watching the plane lift off into the vivid blue sky, where it banked and peaceably headed northwest, as though a war were not raging somewhere beyond the horizon.

"Beautiful," she heard the officer say over the whistling wind.

He had stepped back from the gate. And when their eyes met again, she felt so embarrassed that she yanked the boy forward, yanked open the gate, and hurried past the officer and his spontaneously stricken face.

That the officer had taken an interest in her was something she found both agreeable and unsettling—unsettling just because it reminded her that she had been avoiding taking an interest in herself for fear of discovering something distinctly disagreeable inside.

She could remember moments of tranquillity from her youth, when her father still had his land and life, when her mother still had her smile. There hadn't been the features of what others might call an easy childhood. She and her younger sister had never attended school, but worked their orchards from the start. Yet there had been ample time to climb and run and play, to bathe on the riverbank, to sit as Mama braided their hair, and to sing.

Singing—that was their ease, their art, their prayer, their lesson. They sang to the Karen god Y'wa, who, she had been taught, was also the Christian Creator. Stretching out under the mosquito net at night, they sang to the spirits of the orchard. And then, as she and her sister fell into sleep's embrace, they listened to Mama sing their people's story. *Long ago,* the story went, *we came here along a river of sand. We came upon a fearsome, trackless region, where, like waves before the sea, sands rolled before the wind. We came to this green land, to the sources of the waters and the lakes above. Until we fell among the Siamese and Burmans, who made slaves of us. They took our alphabet and holy books, but our elders promised the coming of our Messiah. White foreigners would bring a holy book, they said. Give thanks exceedingly for the coming of the white men. Give thanks, sons of the forest and children of poverty, for before their coming we were poor and divided and scattered in every direction.*

Before the white men, we lived on one stream beyond another, and the Burmans made us drag boats and cut rattans. They made us collect dammer and seek beeswax and gather cardamom; weave mats, strip bark for cordage, pull logs, and clear land for their cities. They demanded presents—yams, bulbo-tubers of arum, ginger, capsicum, flesh, elephant tusks, and rhinoceros horns. If we had no money to give them, they made us borrow and thus become their slaves again. They made us guard their forts, act as guides, and kidnap Siamese while they tied our arms. They beat us with rods, struck us with fists, pounded us for days on end, till many of us dropped down dead. They made us march carrying rice for soldiers, so that our fields fell fallow and great numbers of us starved. They kidnapped us, so that we sickened with yearning for one another, or begged for mercy and met with immediate death. We fled to the streamlets, to the mountain gorges, so they could not take our paddy or our women. But they found us and took from us again and forced us to assemble near the city, where great numbers of us perished.

And in our turmoil we prayed beneath the bushes. "Children and grandchildren," the ancient sayings of the elders went, "Y'wa will yet save our nation." We prayed as the rains poured and the mosquitoes and leeches bit us. "If Y'wa will save us, let him save speedily. Alas! Where is Y'wa?" we asked. "Children and grandchildren," said the elders, "if the thing comes by land, weep; if by sea, laugh. It will not come in our days, but it will in yours. If it comes by sea, you will be able to take breath; but if by land, you will not find a spot to dwell in."

"And how did the white foreigners come, Mama?" she sometimes sleepily asked from her mat under the mosquito net.

By sea! By sea! Mama's song replied, yet Mama sang it like a lament.

The following evening, she was in the kitchen of the sessions judge's mansion with his boy, feeding him his rice and soup at the table, when she looked out the window and saw a black car crawling to a stop before the house. Soon the officer was emerging hesitantly from the rear, while she was taking the boy into her lap and hiding her face in his soft neck.

"What's the matter, nanny?" the boy asked. "Are you sad?"

"Shall we hide?" she found herself murmuring to him.

There was a knock and the familiar squeak of the sessions judge standing up from his mahogany chair. "Someone's here!" the boy exclaimed, darting from her lap out of the kitchen. Since his mother's death two years earlier, such social calls had become rare.

Khin listened with all of her attention to the rise and fall of the muffled conversation in the other room—the judge's halting questions and pronouncements, the deep force of the officer's disclosures, muted, she thought, by nervousness and respectfulness. Only a few English words—"girl," "port," "sun" (or "son"?)—leaped cooperatively to her ears, and the conversation's opaqueness increased her sense that she was being temporarily shielded from a confrontation with her fate.

"Khin!" the judge called to her.

She stood with a jolt and then proceeded to the living room, where she found the officer seated calmly in the judge's chair, his hat in his hands, his dark hair smoothed down in brilliantined waves. He sought out her eyes at once, nodding politely to her as though silently beseeching her for something, and she looked sharply away—to the judge, who assessed her from the settee across the room while the boy rested against his knee.

"Do you know this young man, Khin?" the judge asked in their language. There was nothing insincere about the question, nothing pejorative. The judge's kind, graying eyes told her that he simply wanted to hear from her.

"I have seen him before," she confessed.

If the judge heard the tremor in her voice, he made no sign of it. "And do you care to see him again?" he asked. A soft smile passed over his mouth. "He very much would like to see you," he went on. "You will think it funny, but he has already decided to marry you if you will have him."

She glanced back at the officer, whose ears—without the cover of his hat—appeared to stick out even farther from his head, and whose long-lashed eyes pitiably batted at her, all of which struck her as funny indeed. And as if she had downed a cup of rice beer, she felt abruptly dizzy, delighted, delirious . . . Her lips began to emit an odd, barely audible twittering laugh, which only redoubled in force when the officer looked at her with an enormous sheepish grin (sheepish because he thought that she and the judge had exchanged a joke at his expense?). She held her fingers over her mouth, commanding herself to stop, thinking she would weep if she didn't, but for some reason the boy began laughing, too, and then the judge chuckled, and even the officer joined in—and what a resonant, kind, innocent laugh he had!

"The thought pleases you then," the judge said to her when their laughter had run its course.

She caught her breath, composing herself. "No," she said quietly to him.

"No?" he asked.

"I mean to say yes."

"Yes?"

The officer looked between them, clearly as mystified as she was by her responses. Then, after a long moment of silence, he startled her by tumbling into what sounded like a series of half-sung professions of devotion and regret. Again, his eyes lavished her with attention, even as they admitted a suffering that she couldn't comprehend.

The judge raised a diplomatic hand and interrupted the officer with a few English words of his own. Then he turned to her. "What he has just expressed to you, Khin," the judge began, "is that he is in Akyab for only the month, after which time he will be transferred back to Rangoon. He says he was so taken by your beauty, he followed you and Blessing from the port, for which he begs your pardon."

"He is a white Indian?" she found herself asking.

The judge looked displeased by the question, yet turned to the officer and began to query him. At first the officer responded in hardly more than a whisper, though when the judge continued to press him, his answers became more forthright, it seemed to her, more emphatic and even impassioned.

"He knows nothing of our people, Khin," the judge explained to her at last. "Doesn't even know the difference between a Burman and a Karen, though he was born here. He is a Jew. I told him you are a Christian, that your mother would very likely require you to be married in a Baptist church, as you no doubt would like to be. Oddly, the prospect doesn't deter him. He says, rather, that it endears you to him more, that he is, for all intents and purposes, half Christian." For a moment, the judge appeared to be lost in thought, then he continued: "I imagine many of us Christian Karens are also half spirit-worshippers or half Buddhists when it comes down to it."

But not me, she wanted to tell him. Oh, she was enough of a spirit-worshipper and a Buddhist, but she had secretly renounced her Christianity years ago—after what had happened to her father. No, the judge had misjudged her, and she must not allow herself to mislead any of them a moment more. Here she was, permitting a conversation about marriage to a man from whom she'd had the impulse to hide, a man whose language she could not even understand!

The boy stood up from his father's knee and began tentatively crossing toward the officer, who, she saw now, was holding out a silvery object to him—a harmonica. The officer's eyes lifted briefly to meet hers, and he flashed her the quickest, most natural smile. Then he lifted the shining thing to his mouth and blasted out a tune so absurd, so childishly playful and loud, they all began to laugh again, she with more sorrow than terror this time around.

"Can I play it?" the boy asked, holding his hand out.

The officer wiped the harmonica on his sleeve and presented it to the boy as a gift.

"Leave us, Blessing," the judge told him.

The boy scampered off with his new treasure. In his absence, the officer's question—what he had come for, his yearning for her—became almost unbearably conspicuous. She tried to wrest her eyes away from his, but something about his gaze claimed her again. *My life is already yours,* it seemed to say. When had she ever experienced such simple, undiluted feeling or desire?

"You needn't feel pressured, Khin," the judge said now. "This is just a first visit. I can tell him you need time. Perhaps we can send for your mother."

"Where did he learn to play it?" she said. She supposed she meant the harmonica, though, again, her question surprised her.

The judge, looking vaguely exasperated, relayed her inquiry to the officer, whose eyes closed while he answered, as though he were searching through the recesses of a dark past for some scrap of lightness.

"He says he doesn't remember," the judge told her with more feeling now. "But he believes it was his mother who taught him. He says his mother wasn't a particularly talented singer or musician, but that she made the most of her gifts, something he has tried to do now that he's on his own. He says her voice was the only one that deeply mattered to him."

She couldn't speak for a moment, could hardly breathe or think clearly about what she ought to do.

"Hear me now, Khin," the judge persisted. "I've seen terrible things in my profession. I consider myself a good judge of character. And looking into this man's eyes, I see someone who is sincere. You owe him a sincere expression of your feelings, even if it's just to tell him that you sincerely want him to leave you in peace."

To be sincere would necessitate knowing herself, having a self that wanted to be known, having an instinct for life, rather than for death.

"Shall I tell him I'll write to your mother then?" the judge said. "Or should I tell him to leave?"

She looked back at the officer, at his proud young features radiating longing. It suddenly seemed to her that she could see through to his marrow. That language was irrelevant. That he had no one else to turn to in the world.

And who was she to argue that the world was any different for her?

3

Something About
the Karens

The marriage was at first a respite of a kind that neither of them could have anticipated—at least it seemed so to Benny.

To be sure, there had been the awkwardnesses of the wedding, conducted entirely in Karen, in a bamboo-floored Baptist chapel at the heart of the village where her mother lived not far from Rangoon. Khin was, as ever, beautiful in her long white traditional dress, with her hair swept up in a chignon that accentuated the endearing roundness of her face, her milk-white skin and shining dark eyes, and the yellow flowers tucked behind her ears. Yet she had seemed rather aloof here and there, rather distant, as if periodically floating farther and farther from his side at the head of the chapel, before all at once returning to the moment and gazing at him in an upsurge of warmth and reassurance.

True, her mother and sister had never smiled at him. The preacher was an effeminate, bespectacled type, whose fiery sermon seemed to warn against demons, against damnation (twice Benny thought he caught a reference to "Satan"); and the mother and sister absorbed his admonitions with such unblinking gravity that Benny found himself miming his terrified incomprehension of the sermon to lighten their mood. Khin, he thought, was too distracted to notice, whereas the rest of the congregation greeted his gestures with spontaneous laughter. Everyone, that was, but the mother and sister, who appeared concerned, though not necessarily about his fitness to marry Khin. Yes, something in their eyes, something about the recriminating way their gaze flicked over the figure of Khin beside him, told him that the person they stood in judgment of was his bride.

"You belong to her now," the mother said to him, via the grinning preacher, who interpreted for him at the outdoor feast immediately following the ceremony.

"I'd be damned if I didn't!" Benny gushed, trying to see beyond the coldness in her eyes, the flat line of her mouth. Even after the subsequent strained bout of translation, that mouth never wavered. Perhaps, he thought, she hadn't understood him.

Like the ceremony, the festivities that followed were attended by a flurry of tittering village women and stony-eyed men, all of whom seemed continually to mock and admire him, and just as often to remark on his dimensions. (Could it be that they were laughing not only at the extent of his height and muscle mass relative to theirs, but also at his penis, which, in his trousers, was more pronounced than it would have been if he'd worn a sarong as their men did?) There was a certain bawdiness in their mirth, like nothing he'd encountered in life, which both won him over and caught him off guard. All the while, they were mindful of the specter of Khin's missing father, to whom they often referred, yet with a worried detachment that only increased Benny's sense of being an outsider and alarmingly ignorant of his new bride's history and culture. "Very sad, but the way life is," one man muttered in reference to the father and his presumed end. "He was a drunk and that is what happens," another said. "Didn't stand a ghostly chance," the preacher more charitably offered, as he ate a plate of curry with his fingers. "Out of nowhere, dacoits!"

Dacoits, Benny knew by now, were one of the problems the British had long faced here. Burman bandits who roamed the countryside armed with sharp swords and faith in tattoos and magic, they were notoriously merciless, notoriously without conscience. "It's a good thing you're not signing up to be a police officer," Ducksworth had once told him. "Knew one when I was a kid, a friend of my father's, and the man was forever tormented by dacoits. I remember hearing him describe what a band of dacoits had done to a baby—pounded it into a jelly with a rice mortar right in front of its mother's eyes." "But *why*?" Benny had said—meaning, What in God's name did they have to gain by that?—to which Ducksworth had merely laughed, as though to imply that Benny was ignorant of a seething darkness that would someday come blindingly to light for him. And to a certain extent, all *was* still a darkness for Benny as far as the dacoits were concerned; their ruthlessness seemed to come indistinctly from the same source as the Burman nationalism now taking the country by storm, claiming anticolonialism as its cause. In the weeks before the wedding, when Benny had returned to Rangoon to set up their new flat on Sparks Street, he had been repeatedly confronted by the news that the former law student Aung San—the one who'd risen to the top ranks of those protesting with the rallying cry "Burma for the Burmans!"—had cofounded a new political party, which opposed backing Britain's war with Germany, called for Burma's immediate independence from the yoke of imperialism, and, for all Benny could see, emphasized the supremacy of the ethnic Burmans, thereby aligning itself with the master-race ideals of the Nazis (who, Benny learned from a recent radio program, had monstrously decreed that Jews over the age of twelve must wear an armband with a Star of David). Benny was only beginning to understand that to be *Burmese*—meaning, to be one of Burma's natives—but not to be *Burman* was, in Burman terms, to be distinctly undesirable.

And he couldn't help thinking of just that word—"undesirable"— toward the end of the festivities, when he and Khin stood side by side before the chapel, she now donning the red-and-black sarong of a married woman, her lips splashed vermilion with betel juice. He hadn't been permitted a taste of those lips. Karens, he was learning, showed no affection—at least of that kind—publicly. No shortage of attractive girls had taken Khin by the hand or squeezed her soft forearm in solidarity and tenderness; even the men strolled about the muddy square in front of the chapel with their arms around one another. But for Benny? Not so much as a touch from Khin. And now, posed with her before the chapel, he was told that they must ritualistically pay off a string of villagers blocking the boulder-strewn path that led to his Buick and by extension their new home, that private sphere created for the very purpose of satisfying their desire for closeness.

"Part of our culture," the excitable preacher explained as he gestured toward the line of villagers. "You must give them your rupees." Benny sought out Khin's evasive gaze, and then took her hand and pressed into it a clutch of coins that she received with a calmness appearing almost burdened by effort, such that her serenity suddenly struck him as the effect of a tremendous harnessing of will.

Yet laughing lightly, she began to toss the coins in bright arcs to the merry villagers. And Benny chided himself for not being merrier, for feeling so very undesired, so undesirable, even as he made a show of pulling his pockets inside out to indicate his anxious poverty, to the general jollity of the villagers (why was he playing the imbecile again?). *God loves each of us, as if there were only one of us,* he reminded himself, and then he pushed the phrase out of his mind because it embarrassed him to seek such shelter from his loneliness with his new bride smiling beside him.

Yes, the wedding and its aftermath had presented him with a series of thorny disappointments. But then.

Then.

He had made all the arrangements for the flat on his own, selecting a few mahogany and teak pieces including a glass-fronted cupboard and a dressing table, on which he'd placed an artfully shaped, fragrant sandalwood comb. It was to this comb that Khin was initially drawn on that first night together, after he led her through the small living room to the bedroom, where he set down her bags. Immediately, her eyes searched the dim room—not in a panic, not for an escape route, it seemed to him, but to take in the proportions of what life had offered up to her. She lingered over the sight of the comb, then crossed to the dressing table and picked the comb up.

"For you," he said, and she seemed to understand. She ran her finger over the comb's scalloped edge, and he watched her in the act of perceiving it. Here he was, with a generous and utterly exclusive view of her engaged in this private moment of perception. He now had permission to watch; the last time he had been permitted that closeness was in the presence of Mama and Daddy, who'd expected him to study them as living examples of how to be human.

She didn't smile, but the comb clearly touched her, and he saw her relax. The change was slight, starting somewhere in her shoulders. Not a forced loosening, but one he thought arose from her finally being apart from everyone else's eyes but his own.

Without sitting, she turned to the dressing table's mirror, set down the comb, and looked at his reflection behind hers. He watched her in the yellow lamplight, watched her watching him watching, watched his own astonished eyes, taking in the new and ancient pleasure of feeding another's desire to be watched. He could see now, for the first time, what they looked like side by side: as physically different as human creatures could be from each other—he at least a foot taller than she and nearly twice her width, with features that appeared the inverse of hers (he'd never noticed how elongated, how tapered his face was, a perfect contrast to her flat, square-jawed one). The difference excited him, daunted him; he felt blood flow to certain places even as it drained from others, and he wanted to go to her, to watch her doing just this and just for him.

For a moment, her gaze lowered, and she pulled gently at the waist of her sarong. It fell instantly along with the lace petticoat beneath it, and he saw (because she'd worn no underwear!) the white curves of her backside and ample hips, and, reflected in the mirror, the generous thatch of her black hair. Swiftly, she raised her arms and removed her black embroidered top, and he saw the pucker of fat around her waist, the surprisingly heavy breasts, each focused on a petite dark areola. Now her eyes returned almost impassively to meet his—as though to communicate to him that she was in familiar territory, and expected that in this she had the upper hand. *And did she?* My God! This was not the nervously giggling girl he had encountered at the sessions judge's house in Akyab! This was . . . a gift so unsurpassable, he was sure it would be abruptly retracted, that she would come to her senses and hide herself again in the sarong.

A shy smile tremulously lit up her face as she continued to watch him, pity and feeling passing like shadows over her eyes. She seemed suddenly vulnerable, suddenly afraid, as though she would cry, or as though this were in fact all new to her and she had only been fumbling for how to start.

In one sure step, he went and knelt before her and turned her around, and then he pressed against her damp warm scent, looking up past the pendulous breasts at her frightened, waiting eyes.

"Are you happy?" he asked.

She couldn't answer, but she held him with her eyes. *It is enough that we are here,* she silently communicated.

He was twenty, and she was eighteen. And they had discovered in each other a reprieve from loneliness beyond measure.

And yet their new intimacy was not perfect. Khin, he learned, spoke nearly fluent Burmese—the language of the Burmans (utterly distinct from the Karen language, he was learning, though apparently of the same tonal family). Soon he discovered that if he put some effort into cultivating his memory of Burmese, which had wilted after his Rangoon boyhood ended, whole branches of its syntax sprouted up in his mind. But it had never been his native language any more than it was hers, and there was something pathetic about the way he used it to draw closer to Khin, something disturbing about even their most harmless verbal exchanges. "You like?" he thought she asked one evening, when they were at the table and he started to wipe his nose and eyes while enjoying the smoky, spicy soup that she called *ta ga poh*—a mélange of rice, meat, greens, and bamboo shoots. "Tasty!" he chimed. Tasty. Like a Burman child. How he hated his swallowing, grinning self at that moment. As if to compensate for the deficiency of his words and praise for her, she pushed forward a little bowl of fermented fish paste (which she called *nya u htee*, but which he clumsily kept referring to as the similar Burman condiment *nga pi*). Instead of helping himself to the savory paste, he took her hand, feeling alone and afraid he'd hurt her feelings. *We will get through this*, her steady, kind gaze seemed to communicate.

But would they? "I have been . . . move up!" he stammered some days later, meaning to tell her of his promotion to the grade of senior officer in the customs service. "Very good! Very . . . happy!" he caught her reply. And "We . . . baby," he understood her to say a few weeks after, when he had returned from the wharves exhausted and she came to him in joy and timidity. Her hair was loose, and she had powdered her face, penciled in her eyebrows, and put on the small sapphire earrings that had been his wedding gift to her. "We . . . baby." In Burmese. It was almost as though she were telling him that the pregnancy, the child, was already inadequate. "Very good. Very happy," he found himself parroting. He had wanted to say *everything*. Instead he kept repeating "Very good. Very happy," as he held her just inside the doorway, and she laughed without making a noise.

Their sputtering exchanges never failed to leave an aftertaste of disappointment in his mouth. Not that he was disappointed with *her* precisely. He was still surprised by her mysterious beauty, and his admiration for her as a manager of their new household increased with every passing week. With the salary that he turned over to her, she purchased a few handsome pieces to complete the flat, filled in their wardrobes, and even arranged for a neighbor's servant to help her clean. She was an excellent cook and seamstress, and a truly gifted nurse (once, when he returned from the wharves wretched because of some bad fish he'd eaten, she spent the entire night by his side, washing his mouth, rinsing out the spattered porcelain, ignoring him when he waved her away in shame). In short, she was more capable and dignified than he could have anticipated. Yet gazing into her sweetly peering eyes, he often felt locked out of a place to which he'd never be permitted entry, because she was Karen, and he never could be.

He began to wonder about the secrets she might be keeping, such as what exactly had happened to her father at the hands of the Burman dacoits, what toll that had taken on her, and why her mother and sister had looked at her with such blame. And also: How sexually experienced *had* she been before their first encounter as man and wife? Her nightly abandon with him, so in contrast to her demure (enforced?) tranquillity by day, both fed and poisoned his peace of mind. While away from her at the wharves, he had vivid fantasies of her undressed and entertaining some old Karen flame. And at the same time, he became increasingly sensitive to the differences between his Burman and Karen underlings—how the former tended to fly into a rage when slighted, while the latter tended to smolder, even when treated to a generous dose of the former's sense of supremacy.

He had hardly considered the matter of race when spontaneously determining to marry Khin, his only consideration being his embarrassing lack of awareness of how the Karen were distinct from any other people among the Burmese. Perhaps this had been his privilege as a "white"—though olive-complexioned—citizen of British India. If he was very honest with himself, he understood that he had distrusted the notion of race to begin with. His aunties' clannishness reeked of false comfort, even of superiority, no less than Ducksworth's claiming of his Anglo blood reeked of latent self-hatred. But now he felt cornered by questions pertaining to race. Was it a *Karen* trait, Khin's preference for the quietness he sometimes found stifling? Had she been *taught* never to impose, to avoid eye contact, to fold her arms across her chest in conversation, to duck when passing others congregated on the street? He wasn't at all sure that her habit of refusing his offers to purchase her some tidbit (a coffee, a trinket from a stand) wasn't in fact a Karen form of modestly *accepting*. Nor was he certain that the concerned glances she cast him when he asked something of her directly (say, that she use a tad less chili in his lunchtime curry) weren't in fact meant to be reproving. She very visibly forced herself not to comment when he offended her sense of propriety (as when he walked with a heavy step or shut the doors with a bang). And the few times he lost his patience with her (generally because he was fed up with having to read her mind), she seemed to be on the verge of packing up to leave.

"Leave them, *please*," she beseeched Benny one afternoon when they were walking along the Strand and a pack of runts began shouting crass words about her clothing (because of the unseasonable heat, she was wearing a native tunic rather than one of the fitted and buttoned Burman blouses that she'd come to favor since moving to the city). Benny ignored her pleas, charging over to the runts, taking one of them by the sleeve, and asking him in an English that was meant to put the kid in his place, "Do you *know* what you are doing?" But, of course, only Benny was stunned by what had just been done to his wife.

And as 1940 progressed and Khin became resplendently pregnant with his child, Benny's sense of what he didn't know about Khin and her people seemed to take on the dimension of Burma's problem—what with a warrant issued for Aung San's arrest for conspiring to overthrow the government, and the Burman elites and masses, helmed by this de facto leader, attempting to turn the pressure of the wars at large into a domestic opportunity by demonstrating, rioting, and striking. For that matter, Benny and Khin's troubles seemed to be magnified by the scale of the *world's* recent problems—Japan's capturing of Nanning in China, the Soviet attack on Finland, the sinking of a British destroyer by a German submarine. True, Khin continued to appear mostly secure in their marital arrangement and her life as a member of a minority, just as the British continued confidently to frequent their Rangoon clubs in their ascots and evening gowns, insisting that their hold on Singapore—"the most important strategic point in the British Empire"—was safe, that the Japs were armed with no more than a fleet of sampans and rice-paper planes. But in more ways than Benny could count, he felt threatened. And, without ever admitting as much to himself, he started to ready himself for a fight.

> There have been so many unfortunate, and disagreeable, and regretable things in connection with our annexation of Upper Burmah, that whatever pleasant features there are should have full prominence. And one of the most pleasant features has been the remarkable loyalty to the British Crown of the little nation of Karens. It is a nation almost unknown at home here, and is frequently misunderstood and misrepresented, even in India; but it is one with such marked idiosyncrasies and of such peculiar suggestiveness, that we have thought it would be of interest to our readers to set before them a few facts . . .

That was Charles Dickens Jr., in December 1888, in an essay Benny had very nearly neglected to read. He'd first heard mention of the piece several months before meeting Khin, when the inspector above him at the Rangoon wharf, a Briton and recent transplant to the country, had mentioned casually over tea that it was the son of the great author who had first introduced him to the Karens (or the "little people," as he'd called them). "Wrote a marvelous little musing on the Karens," he'd told Benny. "Can't say I remember the title . . . In the *All the Year Round* series, it seems to me."

Now Benny ransacked more than fifty mildewing volumes in the series, the bulk of which sat neglected on the shelves of the officers' club library, before opening volume XLIII to the contents and, under the chilling listing "JEWS, SLAUGHTER OF, IN YORK," finding what he was searching for: "KARENS, SOMETHING ABOUT THE."

There are times when time is revealed as a mockery. It was as though Dickens were in the musty room alongside him, pulling him by the sleeve, leading him to the worn leather armchair in which the ghosts of Benny's predecessors had pondered their papers; it was as though Dickens were pushing him down and prodding him to leaf through the volume, thrusting his finger at Benny, and crying with all the reproach of the unheeded: "See what my son saw! Over half a century later, and you people are still living in ignorance! My God, man, do something!"

The article was more comprehensive than its unobtrusive title suggested, covering everything from the term "Karen" (a broad one, if Dickens Jr. was right, and referring to several tribes sharing linguistic and ethnic traits) to the geographic (the Karens of Dickens's time were spread out from the hills abutting Siam down to Tenasserim and as far to the west as the Irrawaddy Delta) to the topic of origins (drawing on the publications of several of his contemporaries, Dickens Jr. advanced the theory that the Karens had originally lived on the borders of Tibet, then crossed the Gobi Desert into China and journeyed south, although "why they migrated," he stipulated, "and when they first came to Burmah, remains a mystery"). What was most immediately fascinating to Benny, however, was the article's meditation on the Karens' faith, whose traditions the author's son described as having "a singularly Jewish tinge"(!) with "accounts of the Creation, the Fall, the Curse, and the dispersion of men . . . startling in their resemblance to the Mosaic records":

> But now we come to the most remarkable tradition of all, held absolutely identical by each tribe of the Karens, and enabling us to understand the success which the American missionaries have had among them, and their devotion to the British alliance. After the Fall, they say, God gave His "Word" (the Bible) to the Karens first, as the elder branch of the human race; but they neglected it, and God, in anger, took it away and gave it to their younger brother, the white man, who was

35

placed under a promise to restore it to the Karens, and teach them the true religion after their sins had been sufficiently expiated by long oppression of other races.

"Oppression." The word was one pole of an axis around which Dickens Jr. seemed to pivot, the other pole being "loyalty," as in: "their loyalty to the British Crown is beyond question," and "their loyalty and courage have been in refreshing contrast to the dacoity and unfaithfulness of the Burmese." Were not oppression and loyalty, Benny wondered, the twin forces that still kept the Karens in a kind of limbo—caught between outright destruction and advancement of any meaningful kind? Even in Dickens's time, the Karens had "rendered signal service" to the British government, which had received their loyalty with "only scurvy acknowledgement"—so much so that they were "not even known at all" in England. The Karens: the chronically oppressed loyalists spinning continually in the void of an apathetic realm.

On a March morning several weeks later, Benny was introduced by the inspector at the wharf to a new colleague and fellow officer named Saw Lay—"Saw," Benny knew by now, being the Karen for "Mister."

"This chap was a national football hero until recently," the inspector raved. It was fitting, Benny thought, that the inspector had hired a Karen to fill in for the recently transferred Indian, but also curious that a Karen could rise to national stature as an athlete. Perhaps the British domination of the Burmans had allowed for such a shift in the order of things.

Saw Lay was a serious sort, the same height as Benny, though leaner, lankier, less apt to meet others in the eye. He spoke English impeccably, and was terribly unimpressed with his renown—"It's only football," he liked to say. If it weren't for the nimble way he leaped up onto the launches, Benny would have doubted his football prowess, so unassumingly did Saw Lay stride up and down the wharf each day. And yet, there was nothing passive about him. His every infrequent look, his every measured word, burned with intelligence and intensity—and rage. A steadying rage, Benny thought, just the opposite of his own explosiveness.

The new officer had taken a flat across from Queen's Park, which abutted the Sule Pagoda and the colonnaded municipal office in Fytche Square, and often after work they would stroll through the gardens, seeking shelter from the heat under a variety of blooming trees, Benny asking questions and then retreating into silence while Saw Lay began to speak.

"You must understand," Saw Lay explained as he and Benny walked one evening in April. "The loyalist bond we share with the Brits . . . what made it stick was our mutual security. Their takeover of the country wasn't easy. It happened over time, with several wars. We welcomed them because we'd been persecuted by the Burmans for centuries, we'd been their slaves—our villages perpetually attacked, our people perpetually preyed upon, stripped of everything from our clothing to our lives. There is a reason that we are characteristically afraid. Our tendency to be shy, to be modest, to avoid confrontation, to be cautious—all of this comes from our long history of being intimidated. And the Brits, well, they made use of that history. It didn't hurt that we populated strategic territory. It behooved them to make nice with us, as they say. And, well, it behooved us, too. We're not shy about referring to the missionaries who brought many of us our faith as 'Mother,' just as we're not shy about referring to His Majesty's government as 'Father.' Why shouldn't we? Like a good father, the British government rescued us, taking us out of our long state of slavery and subjugation."

They stopped to sit on a bench under a shade tree, and for a few moments Saw Lay fell quiet, as though sinking into the recesses of his vast mind. He sighed, looking up at the intricate white facade of the municipal building.

"Is that why there are so many Karens in the army and the police?" Benny ventured. He'd learned in recent weeks, with some surprise, that of the four battalions of the Burma Rifles—the regional regiment of the British army—two were made up exclusively of Karens.

A melancholy shadow passed over Saw Lay's eyes, and he looked up again, above the municipal building to the white clouds poised above the city. "Without us fighting by their side," he said, "the British couldn't have won the wars against the Burmans, couldn't have annexed one piece of the country after another." He glanced at Benny, in one of his rare moments of meeting another's eyes. "The Burmans rose up, rebelled—sometimes in the smallest, the ugliest of ways, with dacoities, armed robberies. And the Brits didn't hesitate to use us as police, as troops, to suppress these rebellions. If you were a Burman, wouldn't you therefore hate the Karens as viciously as you hated the British?"

Benny didn't immediately answer, and the silence into which Saw Lay fell again silenced him further—he had the sense that even a single word might disturb the calibrations of thought vitally taking place in his new friend's mind.

"The problem—" Saw Lay went on, with the caution of someone vigilantly staking his claim, "the problem is that the Brits are more favorably inclined toward the Burmans when it comes to issues of administration—no doubt because of the Burmans' centuries-long rule over this country. You would think that, knowing the Burmans' tendency to subjugate, our Father would limit their power, politically speaking. But our Father has always behaved very strangely in this regard. Even as we've continued to serve loyally, militarily, we have had to suffer being governed by Burman subordinates. We have a Burman prime minister, a Burman cabinet, a legislature dominated by Burman nationalist parties . . . And now with their strikes, their riots, our Father has been giving them greater and greater self-government. You can understand why we Karens are apprehensive, fearful. Has our Father forgotten our needs, our acts of loyalty? Surely he must ensure the fulfillment of our right to a measure of self-determination, to a separate administrative territory or state that we can call our own, and to some sort of guarantee of representation at the national level."

Now Saw Lay looked straight at Benny, his intelligent, perspiring face suddenly frightening for its startling openness. "If our Father abandons us, Benny, everything—*everything* will come undone. Don't you see?"

4

Burdened by Choice

His hands swept over her body whenever he made love to her, as though he couldn't quite believe that this—her body, this closeness—were real. And sometimes Khin felt unreal. Sometimes, even in this, she felt herself drifting away . . . Benny's pants had to be taken in at the waist, she might remind herself. Obviously, the food she was preparing for him wasn't rich enough. Or: Why had he yelled at her after dinner and then denied it? Was he so tone-deaf he couldn't hear the difference between a frustrated and a loving pitch? Her sense of drifting might all at once vanish: she would catch a glimpse of Benny's arms—how strongly beautiful they were, and how lucky she was to be held by them. Then she would be drawn back to her body, to the moment, to the fortunate reality she shared with this man, who like her had been so lonely before their union.

But the happenstance of that good fortune could strike her then with unbearable force. How arbitrarily they had landed in this bed together! How arbitrarily their child, expanding right now in her womb, had come into existence! Had she and Benny not each been sent to Akyab—had the neighbor in her village not been a cousin of the sessions judge—had her mother not wanted to tear her away from the only Karen boy whom she'd managed to care for—had Mama not found her and that boy talking by the riverbank, only talking, only sharing some rice candy . . . Even while Benny seemed to strive to restore her presence of body in their bed, her mind would leap to the original chain of arbitrary events from which she had never really recovered: had Daddy not become a drunkard—had he not lost their orchard—had they not moved into a borrowed hut—had the dacoits not broken into *that* hut—had her sister not been raped—had Mama's hands not been smashed—had Daddy's abdomen not been sliced open so that his intestines spilled out over the floor . . . If Daddy hadn't been drunk, would he have been able to fight the dacoits off? If she had managed to save him, rather than stuffing his intestines back inside and holding him together while he choked, would Mama still despise her? If she had been raped like her sister? If she had been murdered like Daddy? "Unscathed," Mama said of her. "The only one to walk away unscathed."

Benny was correct to remind himself of her reality while they made love. As if from a distance, she would watch the way that he, like their unborn child, determinedly knocked against her; and she would find herself grabbing his flesh in panicked desire, longing alternately to lose herself and to protect this passion that they'd accidently discovered from some unimaginable menace beyond their door.

She was seven months pregnant when Benny brought Saw Lay home to meet her. All through the dinnertime visit, she listened in astonishment as, with Saw Lay translating, Benny revealed his past to them—describing the death of his parents, his years in Calcutta, his near conversion, the pain of having been hounded from the Rangoon synagogue's graveyard where he'd come to mourn the dead. "Imagine if I'd been recognized, embraced," he said at the table with alcohol-induced vigor. "Imagine if it'd gone another way—the return of the prodigal son. Might have married a pretty Jewess. Might have never accepted the temporary post in Akyab. Might have never spotted my girl, the girl with the beautiful hair."

How lightly he spoke of their accidental love, as though he had no reason to justify it—whereas all evening this Saw Lay had been stealing strange glances at them, perhaps because he didn't approve of the union that had led her to abandon her village and their people.

"Do you miss your Judaism?" she asked Benny through Saw Lay now. She was standing at the table, pouring coffee into the guest's cup, and in the candlelight she could feel Saw Lay retract from her outsize belly (because he was repelled by the reminder of her procreation with Benny? Or merely afraid that she would pour hot coffee all over his lap?).

"I suppose I miss the sensation of being in a community," Benny said, some kind of pain flooding up to his lips. "But I'm sure that describes many happy childhoods. And I'm sure that we have something like that together, my darling."

He reached across the table for her free hand, as though to reassure her, yet his fingers were weak with loneliness.

Two weeks later, she brought Benny's lunch to the wharf at an hour when she knew he was likely to be absorbed with work. She found him with Saw Lay in the offices and told the latter casually in Karen that she would be waiting to speak privately with him at the coffee stall up the Strand. Now Saw Lay looked at her in outright fear, but after forty minutes he appeared nervously at the counter and ordered a strong coffee with condensed milk.

When she explained what she wanted from him, he blinked at her in confusion, then began to laugh—a result of his relief or the outrageousness of her request, she wasn't sure.

"I mean to honor my husband," she said quietly.

"Then why not go *through* him?" he countered, his amusement already dissipated. "Benny is my friend, and much as you think you'd be serving him by—by reintroducing him to his own, I can't help thinking he'd take all this as a gross violation of our confidence!"

Nevertheless, he did as she asked, setting up an appointment for the two of them to meet with the rabbi of the Rangoon synagogue, covertly informing her of the time and date of their engagement, and then showing up at the appointed hour on Twenty-Sixth Street.

Inside the bright pillared building, in an office strewn with papers and books, they sat across the desk from the hunched rabbi, whose countenance spoke to her primarily of skepticism. Saw Lay wouldn't look at her, even as, with perfect elegance and straightness, he began to translate into English the case she shyly presented to the learned man: how she felt her husband would benefit from a reintroduction to his people—community being the thing they were so lacking in now, orphaned as Benny was, and alone as they were in Rangoon.

"You don't mean Joseph Elias Koder's grandson?" the rabbi blurted out. At her first mention of Benny's full name, the rabbi's eyes had clouded over with sullen confusion, but now his bushy eyebrows lifted and he went very pale.

"Yes—he—him," she said, in an English the rabbi clearly had to strain to understand. She recognized the grandfather's name, which Benny had repeatedly thrown out when listing relatives on the night of Saw Lay's visit to the flat—thrown out as though he were throwing lines back into the sea of his past, trying to catch pieces of himself that had been swept irretrievably away from him.

All at once, the rabbi began rummaging through the piles on his desk, launching into a speech. "He says," Saw Lay translated for her, "that he assumed—they all assumed—that Benny was lost to them . . . He says he has a letter here somewhere . . . from Benny's auntie. A letter for Benny." Having clearly not found what he was looking for, the rabbi started flinging open the drawers of his desk. "He says that she also wrote directly to him asking—" Saw Lay continued, "*charging* him with the responsibility of finding her nephew, who was lost to the Jews."

The rabbi emitted a sound like a bark and held up a thin envelope with a flourish, a gleam in his pale eyes. But his smile faded when he fixed his face on hers, as if, one problem having been solved, a new, greater problem had surfaced—and *she* was that problem: she, the living manifestation of Benny's having been forever lost to the Jews. Was it not a problem she could fix?

The now wilted-looking rabbi seemed all at once reluctant to part with the letter he'd just found. He set it squarely in front of him and tapped it heavily with a forefinger as he began to speak again—this time in melancholy complaint, she thought, with moans and shakes of the head.

"He says it's not so simple as being welcomed into the community," Saw Lay said, turning to her worriedly, a new pity washing over his face. "To begin with, your condition and Benny's marriage to you, presumably in a church, present obstacles . . . Theirs is a traditional community, and they abide by many ancient laws . . . They all must live in this neighborhood, for example." The rabbi gestured to and fro, the letter now clutched in one of his fists. "And they must exclusively obey Jewish elders. They must study a good deal, study their holy book, keep kosher . . . Surely Benny no longer keeps kosher, with separate dishes and pots for dairy and meat . . . And their women—he says they must wear less revealing clothing than our Karen sarongs or fitted Burmese tops."

The rabbi's eyes narrowed on hers as Saw Lay went on. "But the bigger problem—the insurmountable problem—is that you are not a Jew, Khin. And he says that you can't simply *become* a Jew. Apparently, you must be born Jewish, which means being born to a Jewish mother. And so you see, Benny's child will not be Jewish, not unless you and the child convert—something that he is required by his holy book to try to dissuade you from doing. Not that you would ever consider conversion."

Of course she knew what the word "conversion" meant; it immediately conjured the image of members of her village surrendering to their icy river in baptism, and reminded her chillingly of the falseness of her own faith. That falseness wasn't as simple as her having begun to doubt the existence of a higher power after the dacoits incident; such would have been a cheap form of doubt, because faith, she had come to feel, derived its meaning from difficulty. Rather it seemed to her that baptism was a desperation to submerge doubt in the rescuing waters of belief, a desperation to wash away aeons of suffering with the promise of salvation. To her mother's and sister's satisfied dismay, she had many times refused the village minister's attempts to lure her down to the riverbank to be reborn—but now, in the face of this rabbi, who peered with such grave concern at her (and at the problem of Benny's having gone astray), she longed all at once to be saved.

"Is it so hard to convert to Judaism?" she asked him.

As the rabbi turned expectantly to Saw Lay, no doubt awaiting his interpretation, the latter gazed at her in reproachful panic. "It isn't a matter of walking into a river and accepting the faith of Jewish elders," he whispered to her, as though all along he'd been reading her mind. "I can't believe you know what it means to be a Jew."

"It means not believing that Christ is the Messiah," she found herself replying. The words had come from a deep, as yet untapped well within her, and she suddenly had to swallow to prevent herself from sobbing. Strictly, it wasn't that she doubted Christ was the Messiah, but that she didn't believe in anyone's capacity to *know* that he had been—that, ultimately, she didn't believe in sure-footed belief. Faith without belief—that's what she wanted, something that seemed suddenly, irrationally possible in this realm of her husband's ancestors.

Idiocy! Saw Lay's eyes seemed to reflect back to her, before he turned his gaze away and stared out the small window facing the barren cemetery. "To be a part of this—this—" he said, gesturing to the expanse of the surprised rabbi's office and beyond, "you would have to shed your very skin, shed your past and every last thing you were taught to believe in—all your customs, the teachings of our elders, the realms of the spirits, the Christian parables!"

For a moment, no one said anything. Then the rabbi's head fell into his hands. He seemed to be praying, or summoning some higher wisdom. When at last he raised his eyes to them and began speaking, it was with newfound grief and calm. And as if steadied by his words, or as if steadying himself to translate them, Saw Lay breathed deeply.

"In the Jewish faith," he said to her finally, "one needn't become a Jew to find one's place in the coming world."

It wasn't that this rabbi had spoken to her as a Burman might; anytime a Burman engaged with a Karen, it was with the posture of superiority—intellectual, spiritual, racial. No, this rabbi hadn't condescended to her, but he had treated her as something alien. He was fighting to preserve his people in a country, it so happened, that was ceaselessly obliterating hers. And she saw that much as she wanted to find someplace to take root with Benny, she would never *not* be a lost Karen. She would never not be wandering in the desert, homeless, unwanted—except by some of her own. Except by equally rootless Benny.

Abruptly she burned for her husband, and she pushed back her chair and stood. "Please thank the rabbi for his time," she told Saw Lay. "Thank you," she said to the rabbi in English.

Neither man immediately responded. Then the rabbi smiled at her, the light of defeat shining in his eyes. He slid the letter across the desk, saying something to her that, despite the roughness of his voice, struck her ears as almost loving. "One of man's injunctions is to strive to live joyously," Saw Lay translated. "In the face of these terrible wars abroad, when our very peace is threatened, we must find a way to rejoice in our circumstances. We must find a way to do more than endure."

She summoned the courage to tell Benny about the clandestine meeting a few weeks later, in September 1940. Rather than being enraged, Benny was touched and took her in his arms, ignoring the letter from his aunt that she held out to him. They must invite Saw Lay to the flat to discuss the matter openly, he told her in his increasingly fluent Burmese. And they must wait to open the letter until Saw Lay could join them.

She would never forget the night when they did open the letter, just days before their child was born. They had sated themselves on a

variety of dense Burmese dishes, which she had been preparing recently
to fatten Benny up—pork and coconut milk noodle soup, deep-fried
squash, and curried meat stewed in sesame oil—followed by cake and
cigarettes and generous tumblers of Scotch for the men; and when
they moved into the living room, Benny belched and, in an English she
could just understand, said, "Looks like it's about that time, don't it?"

He sat heavily on their cane sofa, taking his spectacles from the
coffee table while she brought him the letter and the small opener he
preferred. She and Saw Lay sat across from him, and she noticed how
much older Benny had become, the new spectacles poised on the tip
of his nose as he worried the envelope open with the knife. Only in
his twenties, and already his hair lightly graying, his upper body—in
spite of her efforts to put weight on him—losing a measure of its
massiveness. He set the opener on the coffee table and extracted a
single sheet of folded paper from the envelope. "Let's see. Let's see,"
he said, as he unfolded the thing and leaned back into the sofa. He
began to read, his eyes squinting with the faintest frown.

"Well then?" Saw Lay said.

"Benny?" she said, frightened for him.

He looked up at her then, letting the letter fall with his hand
before he removed his spectacles. "Do me favor, darling?" he said to
her in Burmese. "Burn it in stove for me."

He held the letter up, shaking it slightly, gesturing for her to
take it, to be rid of it. And when she did, sadly, he caught her by the
hand and smiled into her eyes and said something that Saw Lay later
rendered for her in Karen: "One mustn't make the mistake of judging
one's relationship to a person by how that relationship ends. No, one
must look at the entire canvas. When I think of the woman who wrote
this letter, my auntie Louisa, I think mostly of my childhood. I think
of the kindnesses she showed me after Mama and Daddy died . . . She
was a warrior in her way, Auntie Louisa—did you know that's what
her name means? 'Renowned warrior.' And was she ever a fighter!
I think if it had been acceptable, she would have pummeled me for

every schoolyard fight . . . If we have a girl, we shall name her after her. Louisa. Renowned warrior."

And what a warrior little Louisa turned out to be. Khin gave birth to her—with the aid of a midwife at home—in total silence, and Louisa's immediate and unrelieved cries seemed like an argument against Khin's practice of stoic submission to pain. She had Benny's thick hair and Benny's angry fists and Benny's unremitting need for Khin's body, for Khin's breasts. Yet how furious Louisa was when digestion caused her discomfort! How piercingly she screamed! And how thorough were Khin's tears for her baby, whose slightest suffering seemed to her as weighty as all the agony the world had ever seen. Louisa screamed when she woke and Khin was not immediately in sight. She shook if Khin was more than a minute rushing to her side. She stuck out her bottom lip—even at two weeks!—when anyone but her mother or father approached, as though she were keenly aware of her unjust vulnerability and mustering any line of defense in her personal command.

At two months, Louisa began, pathetically, trying to speak, emitting a series of plaintive, songlike, rounded sounds meant evidently to communicate deep layers of hurt. What past atrocities had she suffered? Khin wondered. What lives had her death destroyed? Khin had expected the child to be a salve to her own death-tainted spirit—but this baby! She might have been a general who had failed his men, a grandmother who had survived the slaughter of every last grandchild. And the only salve to *her* inherent anguish appeared to be Benny. Certainly, Khin's breast quieted the girl (at least, until the agonies of digestion set in); Khin's arms soothed her for a time, as did Khin's songs of their people's centuries of suffering. But only Benny could unburden her of the weight she'd come hobbling into the world under. He would stride up in his half-interested, half-distracted way, cooing and babbling English terms of endearment— "turtle dove!" "precious angel!" "Daddy's little darling!"—and, astonishingly, Louisa would gurgle; she would smile, like the most ordinary of babies. "Da!" she said to him at three months. "Want Da-da!" she said at twenty weeks. ("Is it normal for a baby to speak so early?" Benny proudly asked Khin. "Strange," Khin's mother reprovingly commented about the girl's blabbering during her only visit to them in the city.)

To escape the heat that seemed to be rising in parallel with Louisa's powers of articulation, Khin often strolled with her down noisy Sparks Street all the way to the Strand, where they could catch a breath of river breeze. Something about the river cast the child into a contemplative frame of mind. "Want another boat," she was soon saying, with her chubby little index finger pointing at the ships docked in the harbor. *Want another boat,* in Karen to Khin and in English to her daddy when he and Saw Lay had a moment to greet them on the wharf. Benny would tip his hat to Louisa, telling her that he would do what he could to gratify her desire.

"You think she's the smartest baby in all of Burma?" he repeatedly asked Saw Lay, who stood shyly aglow beside him, peering down into Louisa's wide-set eyes.

"She *is* remarkable," Saw Lay never failed to say—his admission a cocktail, Khin thought, of one part compliment to two parts worry. Oh, yes, it was clear as day that Louisa was remarkable—but remarkable in a sense that doomed her to the glories or the miseries of greatness? "Don't think I've ever seen such eyes" was another of Saw Lay's refrains. And it was true: Louisa's eyes were astonishing. Not just for their unusual shape—a hybrid of the doe's and the snake's. Not just for the way they were spaced, floating almost luridly over her porcelain cheeks. What made them astonishing was the way they seemed, disarmingly, to confront one, to penetrate one, to demand something of one in a nearly menacing way. Yes, they were eyes that made you want to run and hide.

* * *

And was that just what they ought to do—run and hide?—Khin wondered toward the end of 1941, when Aung San reportedly went underground to receive support from the Japanese, and Benny's fellow officers started to stream through the flat as though to find an outlet for the troubled eddies of their conversation. It was possible, some of these officers said, that in the Japanese the Burmans had found their potential liberators—not that the Anglo officers would admit to fearing for their own security in the East. Not even when Pearl Harbor was soon bombed and the Japanese went on to do the impossible—landing in northeast Malaya—did these Anglos find reason to mitigate their professions of optimism: Singapore was safe, and war would never reach Burmese shores. "Why trouble with banalities like air-raid warning systems and shelters and adequate air defense and ground troops?" Benny privately mocked them. "Why forgo supper and dancing and the pleasures of club life when the hostilities are so far away?" True, the British were now at war with Japan, the Anglos said, but Churchill was said to have dispatched four unsinkable destroyers to the Indian Ocean. Did the fact that two of those destroyers swiftly sank along with nearly a thousand men not constitute a threat to the great Pax Britannica? Khin reasoned.

By then, she was pregnant for the second time; Louisa was confident in her mobility and willingness to be charmed by strangers; and Benny . . . Khin couldn't help thinking that the new fatigue spreading like a mask across his features was the manifestation of a terror seizing him more with every passing day. It was as though the external pressures of the war had possessed him and were exerting their force on him from the inside out. And as long as he kept those pressures contained, their little family would be safe—from external strife and also from trouble within.

That trouble began one night when a man called Ducksworth was visiting. Benny had run into him on the street and invited the sallow, too-talkative fellow to come home with him for a drink. As they chatted over cognac (their "old favorite," according to Benny),

Louisa ran between them, and Ducksworth looked at the child crookedly, plainly displeased by her repeated claims on Benny's attention.

"They say Aung San's reemerged in Bangkok," Ducksworth broke out, as though to break through to Benny, who bounced Louisa on his lap while tickling her under her chin and redoubling her glee. Ducksworth had spoken in English, but Khin knew too much of the language to be excluded from the conversation (at least, from understanding it; she rarely found the courage to speak). In fact she was seized by Ducksworth's disclosure before Benny appeared to be; a moment passed before his knee went still and Louisa began to complain.

Khin rose from her chair to scoop up the child as Benny, still immobilized by mistrust or disbelief, watched his friend. "Aung San, you say?" he said slowly.

"Sure as day," Ducksworth went on—too cheerfully, a sly smile playing at the corners of his mouth. "Been in Japan all this time, training with the Japs, his would-be liberators, the little runts. They say he's become a genuine samurai. And now he's enlisting anyone he can get into his pro-Jap Independence Army. You can bet dacoits and all the other political vermin are lining up."

"And when will you go?" Benny said now.

At first, she thought he'd meant to slight his friend, meant to suggest that Ducksworth would be lining up alongside the vermin. Ducksworth, too, looked momentarily blindsided. He fixed his stunned eyes on Benny before relaxing into an overfriendly smile, followed by a bout of forced chuckling.

"No need to flee," he murmured, and tossed back the remains of his cognac. "I've never been the one to doubt in the British."

The only sign that Benny was offended or distressed was the slight wrinkle on his brow. By the next morning, though, on Christmas Eve, he was racked with emotion, storming from one end of the living room to the other, cursing Ducksworth—"the Britons and Burmans be damned"—and arguing that they should listen to common sense and flee the country. "If the Japs make it here—or if

Aung San's army invades—we're sunk," he called to Khin, who was preparing Louisa's morning meal in the kitchen. "Not only everyone who worked for the British—not only the whites. Everyone the British favored. Everyone the Burmans hate."

Khin worked away steaming and mashing yams, and then sat Louisa down at the table off the living room to spoon the concoction between the baby's lips—all as a way to slake her own urgent need for Benny to stop speaking. She had the sense that he was forcing her closer to a precipice beyond which lay perpetual homelessness, perpetual misery. "What a mess!" she teased Louisa, whose happy, smeared cheeks seemed to support her cause: that if they could just persist in the everyday, the clouds of danger might pass uneventfully.

"Are you listening to me?" Benny said, all at once appearing before her. "Because I have the sense that you're not taking any of this seriously."

She had the sense—or her Karen ears did—that this last profession reverberated with unvoiced shouts of frustration. There was certainly accusation in his tone, as if the threat they faced could somehow be attributed to her unwillingness to acknowledge it.

What she wanted all at once was to throw down the baby's spoon and run away. Instead, she grabbed a napkin and began roughly wiping Louisa's yam-coated mouth.

"Listen to me," Benny said—no less firmly, but with less indictment of her, she heard with relief. "My mother was from Calcutta. If we go there, my aunts can't turn us away."

"The same aunts who wanted you dead if you became a Christian?"

"I'll *be* dead if the Japs make it here."

"Then you should leave." She didn't know quite what she was saying as she turned from the now-fussing baby to his startled eyes; she knew only that something about his effort to save himself, to save them—reasonable and wise as it may be—felt like a betrayal of . . . of what she wasn't sure exactly. But it was a betrayal she longed to make him feel the sting of.

"You don't mean without the two of you?" he said.

"Yes, of course," she replied, ignoring Louisa's rising complaints. Those complaints gave voice to what she was feeling inside. "Don't you trust me to be faithful until your return?"

His astonished features drew together. Until this moment, he'd had no reason to distrust her faithfulness. But in hesitating to flee with him, in raising the subject of trust, she had injected distrust into his heart—maybe so that he could suffer doubt, as she did. He now had reason to doubt in their marriage, just as she had reason to doubt in his sureness about it.

"This is foolishness," he said. "You must go because you will be a target, too—don't you listen?"

"You think I'm a cheap woman," she pressed on, lured by the seductive waves of self-destruction. If an end to this period of accidental love must come, she would hasten them toward it; he wanted to save them, but she would sink them first. Hadn't she struggled to save her family as well as she could in the presence of the laughing dacoits, only so that they could spit on her as she'd held Daddy together while he died? All her subsequent years, she had paid for that effort. It would have been better to submit, to die. "A cheap Karen. A woman of weak race—"

"Stop," he said.

"Why didn't you marry a white?"

"I said stop—"

"Don't you know that Karens are so stupid their loyalty can be bought for the price of two cows?"

As if to stop her forcibly—or as if to stop himself from doing something he would regret—he lunged for Louisa, who somewhere along the line had fallen silent in her chair and begun to watch them with her frightening, assessing eyes.

"Come on, my precious darling," he murmured as he pulled the child into his arms.

Louisa clung to his neck, smearing the remains of the yam across the shoulder of his white jacket while he headed for the door. "Where we going, Daddy?" she asked him.

"Where *are* you going?" Khin cried.

He flung open the door, then slammed it shut after his retreat. A few minutes later, she heard him crossing the flat roof overhead, where they kept a few toys and a tricycle that Louisa still could not ride.

In shame, Khin sank down to the floor and stared into the geometry of her sarong, as though it might yield up a reason for the wretched way she had just behaved. Was it really as simple as her wanting to lie down and die? Shouldn't she be desperate to live—if only for the child's sake? Perhaps part of her wanted to stay put in order to end the same arbitrariness that had landed her here with this man and this child. Again, her mind played its tricks, its guessing games: If Benny stayed with her and were killed . . . If he left and she stayed and died . . . If the child were orphaned . . . If they all fled together to India, a place where she was sure to be even more of an alien than she already was here . . . The more she thought, the more she understood that if Benny were the only one to leave, she would be exonerated of the burden of choice—whereas if she left with him, she would be his burden; and if he remained, he would be hers. She had pushed him away, told him to go without her, because she wanted fate alone to hold the burden of their deaths, and their lives.

As she was thinking of this, and remembering all the sorrows that fate and choice had delivered to her door—as she was grasping the extent of all she had already lived through and suffered and received in her twenty years—she heard something strange. A wail, but not human in origin. A cry so piercing, it sent a shudder down her body.

"Benny?" she said quietly, knowing he wouldn't hear her, knowing it was already too late to protect him and Louisa from whatever menace the noise was bringing. It was a menace coming from the air outside.

Across the living room, a single window faced Sparks Street. She couldn't see the street from her vantage point on the floor, but she stood now and crossed to the window, dimly aware of confronting the fate that she had been so eager to entrust with her life a moment before.

As the undulating moan took hold of her again, she reached the window and was blissfully relieved to see the usual pandemonium below—not a panic, but the cheerful disorder of a barber clamoring for a customer, of children playing a game with a ball and sticks amid a flock of strolling monks. No one seemed to hear what she could. Then a woman pushing a cart pointed in the direction of Sule Pagoda's pinnacle, and Khin lifted her eyes to see, flashing through the still-unknowing sky, at least fifty planes flying in formation toward her—toward them all.

How oddly beautiful the vision was, set against the cry of what her ears now clearly heard as an air-raid signal—like nothing she had ever seen, and yet precisely like what she had been preparing to witness all her life.

5

Grace

From that moment, until the war was finished, Benny noticed beauty only in the unexpected. In the waters off the wharf, roiling with iridescent oil slicks and debris. In the winged statues on the arched roof of a corner municipal building, all at once ascending over the rubble on the street. In a doll's head that Louisa found in the stairwell ("Poor baby," she cooed, clutching the head whose ice-blue eyes rolled open crookedly). In the startled voices of British wireless announcers, who promised that Rangoon would be held at all costs, even as news came that the Japanese had begun a land invasion along with Aung San's Burma Independence Army ("The enemy is currently occupying all three major southern airfields, and now the city of Moulmein"). In the broken glass glinting up and down Sparks Street, which suddenly seemed worthy of its name, and which lit the way for families optimistically fleeing with all of their trunks and laden coolies (and, conveniently for Benny and Khin, leaving their stores of tinned food behind). In Louisa's serenity amid the blasts, and the way she covered her ears during moments of peace (as though to assure herself of her capacity to drown out noise should she please). And in the too-crimson, smoke-choked evening skies that gave way to tremulous nights, to ardent acts that Benny committed on increasingly pregnant Khin ("*Leave*—save yourself," she pleaded with him. *Not without you*, his fervent silence replied).

Rangoon was a virtual ghost town by the time Singapore fell in mid-February, and then the British lost the Battle of Sittang Bridge in southern Burma, all but relinquishing Rangoon to the advancing Japanese army. Nearly all the "foreigners"—the Jews and Indians and Chinese and Anglos—were already en route to India; and nearly all the "natives" had already taken shelter in the countryside. But now, at last, came the official evacuation signal—a signal that at first seemed to relieve Benny of the burden of choice: he was given nine months' severance pay and permission to leave the country; yes, he and Khin agreed immediately, they would follow the hundreds of thousands over the Arakan Yomas to India—their path was virtually mandated. But as they were preparing to vacate the flat in the middle of the night, Saw Lay appeared like a specter in their doorway, throwing choice back at them.

"We thought you'd gone on, my friend," Benny said, taking Saw Lay into his embrace. They hadn't seen him since late December, and he seemed to have lost a third of his weight, and just as much of his life expectancy, so worn was the skin clinging to the bones of his face, so haunted were his eyes, so racked was his body by tremors of the kind one sees in only the very aged or sick. They warmed him with blankets and the last of their brandy, and, as Louisa slept, pulled their chairs very close to his in the living room. Every unforeseen intimacy threw into relief for Benny the possibility of its loss; they seemed to be holding on to the final moments of their time in the history of humankind.

Slowly, very slowly, in a thin voice occasionally overtaken by fits of silence, Saw Lay began to speak of having volunteered to assist the refugees walking over the mountain passes between Burma and India. He had heard that the British were organizing stations to feed and hydrate the refugees, but when he got there ("merely to man a tank of chlorine with a rifle"), he found many tens of thousands already succumbing to malaria and cholera and dysentery. "One almost becomes accustomed to stepping over fallen bodies, human remains," he said softly. "Amazing how butterflies descend on the dead—have you ever seen such a thing? Thousands of colorful wings, flitting about over the bloat and the stink. I still can't shake the sight of it from my eyes."

The territory, he said, was largely unmapped; all each man had was the man (or the woman or child) in front of him to lead the way, forming an interminable progression of the dying. And those who made it across the border were divided into camps by race. "You have the Anglo camp, of course. And then the Anglo-Indian camp. The Anglo-Burman camp. The Indian camp—that's fouler than any of the other three. Even in their own country, they're third-class citizens, the Indians." He seemed to be describing one of Khin's arguments for avoiding India; if Benny would be protected there by the British, far less certain was her and their children's fate.

"Meanwhile, Aung San's army is marching northward, westward, swelling with Burmans, with dacoits," Saw Lay went on. "You can be sure they've already started targeting Karens." His eyes lifted and met Khin's forcefully, Benny noticed, then fell to her protruding belly. "It won't be safe anywhere here for our kind."

For three days, as Saw Lay recuperated on a mat laid out on their living room floor, Benny and Khin were plunged back into the darkness of indecision. Breaking reports over the wireless had more than half of the five hundred thousand refugees dead, many succumbing to the Japanese troops now blocking the southern Taungup Pass leading to India. It seemed like madness to flee to their likely demise—particularly for Khin, in her state, and for Louisa, so vulnerable in her youth. But they were also plagued with indecision about things increasingly too dangerous to face: the value each of them accorded to their togetherness, to their race, to their place in this country. She, who had evidently been momentarily eager to sink into Benny's Jewish identity, could not now conceive of herself as anything but a Karen in Burma; and he was unwilling to conceive of himself as a young man again alone and homeless in the world. And yet they each now argued emotionally on the other's behalf: she, that they must find another escape route into India; he, that they must hide in a Burmese village that wouldn't become a target of Aung San's army—one whose inhabitants weren't staffing the British armed forces.

Then came word that the Japanese were fifteen miles from Rangoon, that everything would be set fire to or demolished in the retreating British army's wake—the docks, the government buildings, the post and telephone offices, the refineries. Within an hour, still not knowing if they meant to land somewhere in Assam or the Shan division, they were crammed on an airless train bound north for Katha, their terror momentarily muted by the thunder of the carriage clanging down the tracks. Khin perched on a stranger's trunk, Louisa jostling on her lap, while Benny—the only "white" aboard—crouched by Saw Lay, to be repeatedly stepped on and kicked by others' feet. "Is he a British spy?" one man hissed, scowling down at Benny. "He's jeopardizing all of our lives!"

"Dearest Father," Saw Lay said, leading them in prayer that first night as Louisa slept on Khin's knees, "we ask not to be favored over any of your other children, but that you might show us the wisdom of your grace. That we might make the right decisions, and trust and forgive according to your higher judgment." At this, he paused, and his silence seemed to tremble with doubt. "We remember tonight," he went on quietly, "all that our British Father has saved us from, and we ask for faith that in his present retreat from our capital he has not forgotten us, as fathers sometimes forget even their most devoted children."

How to reconcile the ordinary discomforts of the body—a pinching in the lower back, a stiffening neck, the thickness of a parched tongue, the unpleasant constriction of clothing—with the extraordinary discomforts of remaining crouched in one place all day and all night, bathed in sweat and the reek of others' unseemly shapes, in temperatures sometimes exceeding 115 degrees? How to reconcile the ordinary comforting sights of the breaking day—the milky-green meadows, the villages rising on stilts from the mist, the flash of a gilded stupa, or the smoke from someone's fire—with the ominous black clouds now billowing on the horizon?

"It's the oil fields," Benny told Khin. "We're burning them so the Japs can't use our oil."

"You mean our Father is burning them," Saw Lay said. "Scorching our earth as he leaves."

The early monsoon had started by the time the train pulled into Katha the next evening, and they learned that the roads to the Tamu Pass leading to Assam, to the northwest, were now swarming with Japanese. They dared not pause, but, taking turns holding Louisa, they walked east for hours through sodden paddies and along undulating muddy paths toward the mountains of the Shan. Only when they reached the cover of a forest did they stop to build a fire and take out the cans of nectar and sardines that Benny had stuffed into his pockets.

"I want you to look at this," Saw Lay told them as Khin rocked Louisa. He smoothed the map that he'd been carrying in his pocket over a log by the fire. "You've been talking only about the Shan State. But if we go just north, beyond Bhamo, in Kachin State"—he pointed to the hills bordering China—"my sister's husband was from a village here—a little Karen village, called Khuli."

"You don't understand," Benny told him with impatience. "We can't hide with the Karens. They'll be the targets, as you said. Aung San's army—"

"No one else will hide you," Saw Lay said sharply, and he folded up his map before suggesting that he take the first shift keeping watch while the others slept.

The next dew-drenched morning, about fifty feet from where they had camped in the cold, they discovered a family of slaughtered Chinese. They had just packed up their few things and begun to walk off, Louisa strapped across Khin's back, when they saw the family through the mist: the naked husband and wife, bound to facing trees, his penis amputated, his abdomen sliced open and disemboweled, one of her breasts sliced off, sticks impaling her vagina and anus, their heads dangling at odd angles, and, between them, in the undergrowth of the trees, three decapitated children lying side by side amid a pile of their parents' traditional clothing.

The meticulousness with which these people had been made to suffer. The particular attentiveness to their genitals. The passion behind that. The personal ferocity. So incomprehensible was the scene that Benny found himself clinging to his only respite from it—the thought that at least this family's worst nightmare was past them, that in death they had arrived at the completion of suffering toward which we continuously strive.

"I didn't want to tell you," Saw Lay whispered. "Always like this, the Japanese."

It was very difficult for any of them to leave, with no one else to witness that family's untold suffering. Khin hid with Louisa under the shelter of a nearby tree, and Saw Lay began to pray: "The Lord is my shepherd. I shall not want. He maketh me to lie down in green pastures. He leadeth me beside the still waters . . . Yea, though I walk through the valley of the shadow of death, I will fear no evil, for thou art with me . . . Thou preparest a table before me in the presence of mine enemies . . ."

The mandate to survive forced them to keep moving. And for a time, God—or circumstance—did provide, even in the face of the mutilated bodies they continued to confront along the way. The war's unfathomable brutality could not vanquish the startling reality of their ongoing lives: The steep gorges through which they trekked along the placid Irrawaddy River. The warm soup and wool blankets unassumingly provided by the strong Kachin villagers who took them in. The wind whipping through those villagers' mat walls. The dizzying sunlight of Bhamo's scorching alluvial basin, its swaying rice fields edged by limestone and distant snowy Himalayan peaks. Then the simplicity of the Karen village called Khuli, a thicket of stilted huts under the clouds. And its inhabitants' swift construction of a hut in which they were invited to live, to stay. Even Louisa's diarrhea, Benny's first bout of malaria, Khin's pre-labor pains—each a bodily battle to purge a foreign element more pressingly present than the Japanese or the complicit Burma Independence Army.

Within a week of their arrival in Khuli, Saw Lay announced that he would be leaving for Mandalay to help with some of the refugees. "They say the entire city is burning," he told Benny.

It was evening, the worst of the parching heat already spent on the day, and Benny had left the hut for the first time since his bout of malaria. He and Saw Lay sat by the thin stream that wound from the village down to the Irrawaddy, a bit of fresh breeze coming through the forest, bringing with it the scent of something floral.

"I should be strong enough to come along in a day or two," Benny said.

It was a lie, or a partial lie. Not that Benny couldn't have summoned the strength to join his friend or even to join the British army. God knew their side needed reinforcement; rumor had it that an all-out British retreat from Burma was inevitable. But a strange malaise had taken hold of Benny. For all his life in the tropics, he'd never lived outside the city; and now, with tigers and pythons in close range, with the threat of the enemy looming in the silent caverns of the forest—here, in hiding, when he ought to have been tenser and angrier than ever before—he felt oddly at peace. He could hardly feel his fists, let alone summon the energy to want to wield them against his opponent.

"The first bout of malaria is always the most vicious," Saw Lay said, and took a stone in hand and cast it slanting across the stream. "Like the first soldiers coming through enemy territory. You'll need more time." He fell silent and looked up at the strange clouds assembling in the darkening sky. "It will be easier for me to pass through without you, in any case. Hard for a Jap to distinguish a Karen from a Burman. You'd be marked as a target immediately."

"And if the Japs come here?" Benny said. "What will happen to these villagers who've sheltered me?"

Now, at last, Saw Lay looked at him again, a kind, impatient frown pinching his eyebrows together. "Let me tell you something about the Karens," he said. "Part of our culture is to take strangers into our home and care for them. This is odd, when you think about it, because part of our culture is also to be slow to trust, slow to take a person into our heart." He paused, looking down at the stream. "Once we've put a person in our heart, though . . ."

He fell silent again, and for a while Benny watched the reflection of light on the water play against his eyes. *It is enough that you should stay and take care of yourself and your wife and your child, you who are so dear to me,* Benny felt him silently go on, with his absolute surrendering of anything approaching envy.

"You must allow them to do what comes naturally," Saw Lay said. And two days later, he was gone.

What soon came naturally to Benny was a life in which he and his family members slept on mats rather than beds. A life in which they took shelter in a home without walls, a home entirely open to the damp and the night and the sound of others chattering and washing and singing over the riot of creatures in the trees. A life in which men to whom Benny could hardly speak worried about him being lonely, and came visiting and were content to sit with him and smoke *moh htoo* or share a cup of strong homemade *htaw htee*. A life in which privacy held no quarter, because—because it was a life in which there seemed to be nothing to hide. Each villager was so accepting of others (Benny had never witnessed such routine and unabashed public spitting and belching, and yet everyone was exceptionally clean, bathing twice daily down by the stream) that there was little reason for anyone to retreat from view. Astonishing, Benny thought, how linked the value of privacy was to that of personal (rather than collective) betterment or gain.

He began to wear a sarong, which more than once fell to his ankles, to the village women's hilarity, and which he rather enjoyed plodding in down to the stream, along with naked Louisa, to dump buckets of icy water over their heads each evening. He began to rely on the soothing babble of women visiting with Khin as he drifted into sleep each night. He even began to laugh at others teasing him about his routine *mee ga thah thaw* (his snoring, which apparently projected across the village, waking even the roosters in the morning). Their teasing struck him as a kind of spiritual practice—an insistence that none was above being teased. As did the stunning specificity of their frequent obscenities—*"Aw pwa lee!"* ("Eat vagina!"), or *"Na kee poo thoo!"* ("Your asshole is black!"). Even the marital bond between these Karen villagers (literally, as he had it, "the strings that tie a marriage together"), though utterly strong, seemed to leave space for responsibility for others in it.

"Come to me," Benny still whispered to Khin in the darkness, and she did come to him, and yet wasn't entirely his, as she had once been. Her ears were pricked for others in need, her face turned to the night.

And as the knot of their intimacy vaguely loosened, she seemed to thrive in this highly democratic community, establishing herself near the top of its particular system of hierarchy. Here, the elders were revered, the young expected to serve anyone older or perceived to be a leader—a teacher, say, or a minister, or a military adviser. Because Khin's months in Akyab and Rangoon had taught her about sanitation, about the importance of sterilization, she—in addition to never hesitating to instruct teenage girls on how more vigilantly to tidy their hut or cook their supper—was soon being referred to as *tha ra mu* (teacher) and asked to heal others' sick children, even to assist with others' difficult deliveries. Sometimes she would wake in the middle of the night and murmur the names of herbs of which she'd dreamed, and in the morning she would leave him with sleeping Louisa in order to hunt for the plants, muttering about how she was sure the cooling properties of such-and-such would bring down so-and-so's fever. When he asked if this was something she'd done before—healing the sick, having premonitions about medicinal herbs—she blinked at him as if to ask, *Is any of this something* you've *done before?* Their easy adaptation to the present made him almost question if they had ever had a past to leave (something emphasized uncannily by the absence in Karen language, he now realized, of a past or future tense; "In the era of yesterday," someone would say, "heart disease takes my wife away from me").

Yet the past did encroach, particularly with news that trickled in—along with the occasional English-speaking Karen soldier—of the destruction of four hundred Karen villages ("not villagers, *villages!*") within the span of a few days by Aung San's army. ("Man, woman, child—no matter. They shot them and pushed them into heaps—eighteen hundred of them just in that one place.") News of Karen retaliation. Of race wars. Of a total British retreat to Assam. Of emptying prisons, and escalating murder rates, and thousands of released dacoits joining Aung San's ranks. Now and then one of these reports would break through to a distant part of Benny, and his fists would almost tighten (once he very nearly used those fists to thrash a good-looking soldier, no more than a kid, whose flashing glances kept alighting on Khin's engorged breasts while she flirtatiously touched her hair). Sometimes Benny even felt prodded to action by Khin's nearly imperceptible expressions of disappointment in him, expressions that sounded an awful lot like praise ("I'm glad you're not like Saw Lay—he'd never have it in him to commit himself to a family over a cause"). But then he would glimpse Louisa contentedly making pots out of the muddy clay beside the hut, or Khin's swelling belly, and his family's immediate need for him to keep living would lure him into the stupor of idleness, if not indifference, again.

* * *

In June, Khin noiselessly gave birth to their second child, a perfect wailing boy named Johnny. Benny leaped around the village, passing out fistfuls of cheroots, and the villagers smiled at him in their pleased, puzzled way, for the birth of a baby was also part of the natural order of things. Their silent absorption of baby Johnny into the body of their community found its counterpart in Khin's tired, quietly happy, quietly anxious eyes, and in Louisa's easy claiming of "her" new baby (as if Johnny had been there all along). Even Johnny's insistent need for milk and burping and caresses seemed to contend that this present was their only reality. Benny almost believed it would never cease.

And then, one day, it did. That July morning had been like any other in the heart of the rainy season, beginning with a light drizzle as the village children scampered across the square to the schoolhouse, and brightening by ten o'clock, when Benny often accompanied his family members on a walk before the worst of the heat set in. He took tremendous pleasure, during these morning sessions, in watching Louisa observe the intricacies of the forest, with whose features he, too, was becoming acquainted: the berrylike cones of the dwarf junipers, the rhododendrons' eruption of colorful flowers, the clutches of mushrooms that Khin told them were edible, and the sultry way the earth steamed after a shower. Then came the gathering storm clouds and the children scuttling back across the square before the afternoon showers began, when Benny and Louisa would huddle together inside, sipping plain tea and nibbling on the sweet Khin had managed to scrounge up. Today, it was golden-brown jaggery candy, and he was soon following Louisa to the edge of the hut, from where they watched the earth's soaking, the excess of water running off in rivulets across the angled square. Those rivulets seemed to jostle one another, didn't they? he remarked to Louisa—"Look how each of the fellows tries to get ahead?"

"Daddy," Louisa said, holding her wet piece of jaggery candy in her fist. "Which fella is that?"

"Which fella?" Benny said, crouching down, captivated by her tender cheeks, by her impossibly deep, thoughtful eyes. He rested in those eyes—and in the astounding thought that they reflected a soul entirely unique from his own. Only after a time did he follow them back out to the view of the rain and to the sight of a Japanese soldier, standing three feet from their hut and staring right back at him.

For a moment, Benny was so dazed, so disbelieving, he could note only the peculiarity of the soldier's snug helmet, like a dome, with a startling yellow star sewn into the fabric above his forehead. The soldier was drawing a sword from his waist and then pointing it at Benny's face. And all at once Benny became very aware of that face, of its fleshy foreignness, of the nozzle of its nose and the thickness of its lips, parting and gasping for breath, even as he feigned calmness. The last thing he should do was run, intuition told him. If he remained composed, if he was honest with the man—if he explained that he was no longer a British officer—

"Kuro," the man said very coldly, drawing the staccato word out—*kkurrro*—as he stared with revulsion at Benny.

And suddenly a thought came to Benny, very simple and clear: *He is a soldier, trained to kill.*

"Go to Mama," he told Louisa quietly, understanding that if he so much as raised a fist this child and her brother and mother would be slain.

And, almost involuntarily, he stood and stepped down from the hut into the mud, his hands held up in surrender. He registered the soldier's instant bewilderment, and then—from a distance, it seemed—he watched the man lower his sword and lunge toward him, watched his own body fight off a wave of revolt and allow itself to be carried down by the arm clamped around its neck. Another soldier appeared above him—Benny caught glimpses of the sweat trickling down this other stranger's cheek, of the lips pursed in concentration, the yellowing teeth, the attentive, disconcerted eyes. "Not a British spy," Benny heard himself saying in Burmese, before he choked on the arm dragging him by the neck through the mud into the trees. They were shouting to each other, the strangers—and somewhere above the din, Benny heard the village rousing to the crisis, Khin crying out, pleading over Louisa's cries. What he could see, apart from his legs kicking strangely to be free, even as he forced his fists to be still, was a blur of blue in the clearing sky, over the green branches of the sheltering trees. And then he was out of range of the village, being dragged down an embankment, his back suddenly pushed up against the solid mass of something—a tree trunk, the bark of a pine, its every irregular surface reminding his neck and wrists and cheek that he was still alive. They might have been Karen, these men, the thought came to him. They were so ordinary, so familiar, these faces that contorted with exertion and fury as he was fixed to the pine. But no, the thought flashed through his mind. These were not men any longer. They had passed somewhere beyond the bounds of manhood, had become something other, imbued with a conviction so unfaltering it was dehumanizing. They withdrew their long swords and began to slice them through the air under the darkening sky, screaming insults or questions while behind them a dripping magnolia tree seemed to weep for Benny's particular life, bidding him good-bye. *God loves each of us, as if there were only one of us.* Suddenly he wanted to apologize—to Khin, to Louisa, to Mama—who had pleaded with him to take care, to stay safe. Too late to use his fists now—they were tied behind him, halfway around the trunk of the tree. And as his animal self spread out across the pricked surface of his skin, as his heart clamored for life wildly, the tips of the soldiers' swords whirred over his head, and he closed his eyes, all at once flooded with grief.

* * *

"It was very strange, the silence then," he told Saw Lay, seven months later, in February, when the weather had begun to parch again, and his friend had returned to Khuli for a breath before his deployment to the front lines. Saw Lay had joined up with the Karen levies leading the effort against the Japanese from the eastern hills, and was acting as the makeshift colonel of his irregular unit, which expected to receive more weapons by way of British airdrop any day. "I thought it was the silence of death," Benny continued, finishing his story about how he had come to be released by the Japanese. "Or—no, that's not quite it. I thought it was the silence of the *anticipation* of death, the muting out of everything but that awful expectancy, when one knows the end is very near."

Saw Lay looked at him out of the corner of his eye. They were sitting down by the stream in the evening, just as they had been before Saw Lay had left for Mandalay, and, again, Benny watched his friend take refuge in finding stones with his fingers. There was a certain shyness about him, Benny thought. A reservedness about speaking directly, about meeting another's exposed eyes. Could it be this was why his friend had never found it in himself to take a wife?

"When did you first become aware of them?" Saw Lay asked now. He sent a flat speckled stone over the surface of the stream.

"I'm not sure," he answered. "I remember thinking the silence had gone on too long. Being afraid to open my eyes. And then the shock of seeing them, in a kind of ring around the Japanese and the tree where I was bound. All of the Karens—the entire village. And Khin with the children at the front—Johnny over her shoulder, Louisa pressed to her leg, with her gorgeous curls and deep eyes. And that terrifying expression on Khin's face."

"Describe it to me."

The nakedness of Saw Lay's request made Benny look at him with a start. Had he imagined something personal, a long-dormant urgency, in his friend's tone? "It's that way she sometimes looks," Benny began tentatively, but also almost frantically, as though, now that he had picked up a thread, he must rush to discover where it would lead, for fear of losing it again, or for fear of losing his courage to pursue it. "That look where she seems to be acknowledging that you are about to do something to break her heart. But there's a defiance about it. As if she's daring you to go ahead and break it. Or as if she's telling you it's already beyond breaking—so shattered is it already. Anyone else would have thought that she felt nothing at the moment, because her features were very relaxed. But her eyes . . . rage and longing were behind them. I couldn't tell if she was bidding me good-bye or pleading with me to stay brave."

Saw Lay smiled softly, looking out at the glistening stream. Then the light in his eyes seemed to fade, as though he had become impossibly sad.

"I'd have died if it weren't for her courage," Benny said, staking his claim on Khin—on the claim she'd made on his life by rescuing it. Only in the days after the Japanese incident had he pieced together, from the villagers, that she had summoned them to follow her through the forest to the tree where he was bound, and where the soldiers were slicing their swords over Benny's head, in preparation to scalp him. When Benny's eyes had opened and he'd looked at her beseechingly, she had stepped forward and explained to the soldiers that they were making a mistake. She had spoken in Burmese, and it wasn't clear if the Japanese—who were said, generally, to have learned a smattering of the language from Aung San and his comrades—understood a word of what she meant to convey. But they became very still, the Japanese, listening to her as she went on to explain that the man whom they had captured was not a British spy. That he belonged to her, that she was his wife.

"Why do you think they listened to her?" Saw Lay asked. He was still focused on the stream, strangely purple in the dying light.

It was a question Benny had often asked himself. Was it the fact that she was holding a baby? Was it Louisa's obvious relation to him, with her curly hair and Eurasian eyes? Or was it Khin's startling combination of meekness and strength—a combination that dared the soldiers to defy her. If they had defied her—if they had strung her up beside Benny and mutilated her in the villagers' plain sight—they would have proved the point that they were above showing and being shown mercy.

"She is unexpected," Saw Lay said quietly, before Benny had the chance to answer his question, and then a flock of parrots suddenly screeched overhead. For a moment they sat back, watching the beating blur of blue and red passing by.

Benny wanted to say something then, to ask a question that he couldn't quite bring to the forefront of his mind. But something about his friend's eyes, about their persistent sadness, told him to hold his tongue, to still his brain. Saw Lay was five or six years older than Benny, nearing thirty, and whatever he'd been going through recently had aged him significantly. Watching him—the way he sat with one knee bent, his serious eyes, the sheen of perspiration on his forehead—Benny thought, *He's passed out of his youth at the very moment that his dignity is deepening.* And he realized, with a warm wave of feeling flooding his chest, that he'd never loved a man as he did Saw Lay. It seemed to him that his friend was largely above human concerns, above even the primary concern to fight first for one's own life.

"Let me ask you a question," Benny said, surprising himself. "If a person should want to become a Jew, the process is really very circumscribed—certain guidelines must be followed, certain steps."

Saw Lay turned to him now with a certain flat caution, a hint of something like defensiveness in his eyes.

"If one wanted to become a Christian," Benny went on, bumbling, "well, there is baptism."

"And?" Saw Lay said.

"And—" Benny rushed on, afraid his friend might be misunderstanding him—the question of faith wasn't actually on his mind. "If one wanted to become Karen—say, if one wanted to take on a Karen identity, how would one go about it?"

Now Saw Lay looked at him in plain astonishment.

"Would that even be possible?" Benny asked.

"To become Karen?"

"Yes."

The question seemed to hang suspended over Saw Lay's widening features. Then all at once those features contracted, and he broke out in a fit of full-bellied laughter that sent him falling back onto the dusty bank. Benny had never seen him so stripped of the armor of his poise.

"As if anyone would want to become a Karen!" Saw Lay heaved, barely getting out the words. "As if anyone would willingly . . ."

He looked so foolish, Benny couldn't help laughing along with him, first in reluctant spurts, and then fully, relievingly, half sobbing as he fell back beside his friend and they laughed together, laughed until all their laughter was spent, and they lay smiling side by side.

"It's the simplest thing in the world, my friend," Saw Lay said finally. Benny heard him inhale the night, then release himself back into it. "All you have to do is want to be one."

PART TWO

Revolutions
1944–1950

6

Buy That Dream!

In April 1944—more than a year after he had laughed with Saw Lay on the riverbank—the Japanese secret police came for Benny. He and the family had recently moved in with Saw Lay's brother in Tharrawaddy, a town on the plains where many Karens were seeking sanctuary, not far from Rangoon. First the secret police took him to their headquarters at the local American Baptist Mission High School and strung him up to a pillar in a classroom. Using their swords to nick his scalp again and again so that blood streamed down his face into his eyes, they threatened him with death and charged him in English-crossed Burmese with espionage—"espionage activities" was the exact phrase they kept repeating. They stripped him of his clothes, thrust a pipe down his throat, and poured water down the pipe until—with him retching and choking—his stomach ballooned and water burst from his nose. Then they pulled out the pipe, thrust it up his rectum, pumped water into his bowels, and smacked his penis when he tried to urinate. And the strange thing was that when they replaced the pipe with a sharp stick, increasing his agony so much that he truly wanted to die, he began to hear the voice of Ozzie Nelson, whose orchestra had made such a hit with "Dream a Little Dream of Me" in the 1930s. Was he dreaming? That voice, the brass, the strings—it all seemed to come to him from a great distance. From an even greater distance, Sister Adela appeared before him in her white habit, clutching at her wimple as if to pull it off, or as if to hold it down, and staring at him with those anguished eyes. It occurred to him that Saw Lay's eyes had something similar about them. And he seemed to see Saw Lay stealing glances at Khin from across the kitchen, and then Saw Lay taking Khin in his arms and beginning to dance with her . . .

But no . . . no, he realized, as his bruised eyes blinked open. He had been dreaming. The whole thing had been a dream. Except there, in the bright empty room adjoining the one in which he was bound, were two of the Japanese who had tortured him. He had the confusing impression that they were dancing, that behind them a peeling gramophone was plaintively giving voice to the old tune he had been hearing again and again in his dreams. He heard the hiss of a record. The jaunty horns. Ozzie Nelson singing. Could it be? He had to strain to see, but yes, sure as day, his tormentors were dancing, alternately serious and smiling, their arms guardedly locking their bodies together as they skittered through the morning light.

It was Khin who answered the door several days later, when he showed up at the house in Tharrawaddy. She drew him inside with trembling hands, and four-year-old Louisa looked at him with elation and then horror, her eyes moving to the slits crisscrossing his now bald head while little Johnny hid behind Khin's leg. Then Saw Lay's brother led him to the back room and laid him down, murmuring something about Saw Lay having just left, about Saw Lay going back to the hills to get them, to get them all, to murder every last one of them himself if it came to it. Benny was beyond words by then, beyond the instinct to put suffering into sentences. There was just the relief of no longer being apart from his loved ones, and a new, animal awareness that a cavern of misunderstanding had opened between Khin and him.

It didn't help that, before Benny's recent apprehension, Saw Lay had been sweeping through this house, bringing stories from

the front lines of wasted survivors, exploding shells, scorched villages, and the agonies and heroics of the fallen. It didn't help that
during these visits Saw Lay's eyes had seemed most eager to seek
out Khin's, or that, whenever he'd spoken, Khin had paid him the
kind of attention she no longer lavished on Benny. How many nights
had Benny watched her listen to Saw Lay while she worked over the
stove, flushing with horror, with gratitude, with—with something
more?

Now, as he lay shivering on the mat in the back room, she un-
buttoned the torn shirt he had managed to put on when the Japanese
had abruptly released him (with the warning that they would have
their eyes on him, that he would die the moment he involved himself in British affairs). She laid her hands on the tender skin of his
abdomen, and he felt her heat. Then she lifted his buttocks to draw
down his sarong. She did not gasp, but the expression that came over
her intent features made him conscious of what she must be seeing:
the oozing welts along his penis, the blood caked with the residue of
excrement between his inner thighs—images that had appeared to
him in flashes throughout the seven days and that had melded with
his piercing sense of foreboding about her, about Saw Lay. He felt
with his fingertips for a blanket, but Khin stilled his hand, pressing
his fingers tightly.

"I won't rest until you tell me," she said, struggling for breath.
"What happened, Benny? Don't lie to me."

Each of them had been made a sharp-eyed creature by the war;
what he'd been through had to be roughly evident to her. But why
mention *lying*?

As though to nurture the seed of her doubt in his ability to be
honest (and as though to punish her for the falseness she'd mentioned), he found himself lying to her in response—lying in the most
obvious of ways. "Nothing," he said in a voice small and hoarse from
the repeated ramming of the pipe down his throat. An irritated voice.
Nothing.

And then he said what had been on his mind since his return here, maybe since he'd had those visions while being tortured: "What happened with Saw Lay?"

Her eyes hardened on him, and he could almost feel that hardness spreading around the soft center of her ache for him. "I will make you soup," she said, and she called for one of the children to sit by him.

Over the following days, she fed and washed and slept by him, waking at his slightest sound, dressing the wounds he didn't insist on tending to himself. He couldn't bear for her to know the extent of his humiliation as a man. For him to be able to make love to her again, for him to find enough fire to take her (here he was, just back from the brink of death by violation and already thinking of the necessity of possessing her), he'd have to heal without being infantilized by her motherly familiarity with the details of his torture. But there was something else: even as he realized he didn't *want* to know if she and Saw Lay had assumed he was as good as dead and had found it impossible not to take comfort in each other, he instinctually wanted to punish her for precisely what he didn't want to know—to punish her by depriving her of the intimacy that she now so desperately needed.

"I can see you want your privacy," she told him about a week after his return, when he'd begun to prop himself up and manage his bedpan. She put his breakfast on the table beside his bed. But rather than sitting down to feed him, she went on: "Saw Lay's brother is here if you need anything else."

Something about her manner, or the quality of her voice, begged him to question her, to ask where she was going. But he said, "That will be fine."

He'd hurt her—that much was clear. Yet the expression that came over her face also seemed to tell him that she accepted his unwillingness to count on her. "Then you won't mind," she said quietly, "if I begin to volunteer a little at the hospital. I was back there for your medicine, and they're short on help."

"Of course," he answered, forcing himself to keep his hard gaze on hers.

A word from you, that gaze of hers now silently pleaded with him, *just a word of tenderness, and I'll be yours again.* "Benny," she stumbled, "when you were gone, I tried—"

"I know," he cut in. He couldn't bear it—couldn't bear the naked need and regret in her eyes, which reflected back to him only his own enfeebled position. He reached for the bowl of rice and egg on the table, as though to dismiss her, to disprove her powerful hold on him. Still, he felt her questioning face hovering above, the light of hope—or whatever it was that had brought her into the room— shining a moment longer over him. "Let's never speak of it," he said with a bite of food in his mouth.

That was the extent of his ability to help her bring out everything that had been damaging them from within.

If he had become a sort of nonparticipant in life with the start of the war, now—as Khin began to spend a portion of her days away from the house—he also became a distant observer of his family members, whom he saw with newly objective eyes. Something had been chiseled into Louisa's winsome face, something that made her seem ferociously determined—as though she were intent on keeping a secret or forgetting something.

"Did Mama tell you to forget what happened while I was gone?" Benny asked the girl one evening, about a month after his apprehension, when she ventured into his room for a cuddle. "Maybe Mama said to forget something about Saw Lay."

He wasn't quite sure what he wanted to know more about—the state of his daughter's soul or his wife's capacity for deceit.

Louisa looked up into his face, her pretty eyes darkening with recollection, he thought—or with the effort *not* to recollect. "Saw Lay was sad," she finally admitted.

CHARMAINE CRAIG

"He was?"

"He cried."

"I see."

"Mama didn't tell me to forget."

She'd made this last declaration almost to shame him, it seemed to Benny. And over the following days, she began to escape the house with toddling Johnny, as though to evade something unpleasant. From the bedroom window, Benny watched her and Johnny disappear into the far thickets of trees on the plain and then reemerge covered in mud, with wildly transported looks in their eyes. They could have just communed with the trees, or been touched in the shade by some higher, redeeming light.

"Where are your shoes?" Khin demanded of Louisa one evening, when the girl and Johnny returned after a long day out, and Benny found the strength to limp to the kitchen to greet them.

Louisa stood barefoot within the doorway, gripping Johnny's hand. "I gave them to a little girl who didn't have any," she replied—so boldly Khin slapped her across the cheek. But Louisa didn't cry; she didn't repent of her generosity. As Johnny held up one foot at a time to display the shoes he was still wearing, Louisa stood resolutely glaring at Khin with a kind of wounded pride that made Benny's heart break all over again.

By June, though, they had all mostly recovered. Khin sold one of her rings, and she and Benny decided to buy a plot of land to till in a nearby valley. With Louisa and Johnny between them, they planted peas and avoided involvement in the war and each other's eyes. Avoided each other's touch, too. Only after Khin came to him one night and tried to straddle his weak thighs did he become aware of her metamorphosing body, of the hardening under her belly button and the slightest swelling that did not allow him to harden and swell toward her.

The child was born to them in January, after they had begun to harvest and dry the overabundant peas, a portion of which they sold

80

to some of the gentler Japanese who began to infiltrate Tharrawaddy, one explaining to them with a chuckle that it was now assumed by the Japanese secret police that Benny was part Negro—part black, part *kuro*, the fellow chided him, pointing to his twists of hair. (Wasn't *kuro*, Benny wondered, the word he'd been called by the soldiers who'd apprehended him in Khuli?) The child was a girl, and they named her Grace, because even the most painful life is still life, still inexplicable and blessed. And they never spoke of how she had come to be. He loved the little girl. She had Saw Lay's placid eyes. Saw Lay, who had disappeared into the hills after giving a piece of himself to them, and for all they knew died soon thereafter.

The loyal are fully capable of deceit. That was something Benny told himself four months later, in May 1945, after the last of the Japanese had evacuated Rangoon and more than twelve thousand of their troops had been killed by Karen guerrillas supplied by British airdrop. Those Karens—a network of more than sixteen thousand by the end of the war—had not been the only irregular forces to resist the Japanese, Benny learned. Among the other intelligence and paramilitary groups working separately in Burma in support of the Allied cause were Kachin Rangers, Chin levies, Communist Party cadres, socialists, and even, in the final weeks of the campaign, Aung San's renamed Burma National Army. (Benny heard that when a British military commander had quipped that Aung San changed sides only because the Allies were winning, Aung San had told him, "It wouldn't be much use coming to you if you weren't, would it?") They had all fought the same enemy, yet what they had been fighting *for* apparently diverged widely. Thus, with the Japanese exodus, the alliances and promises that had been made or received (alliances and promises supporting individual causes, and leaving the future free in all the details) couldn't be kept. Benny was distressed to learn that the same British and American intelligence and military officers who during the worst had guaranteed the "loyal" Karens their own state, or had convinced Kachin leaders of their support in a liberated Burma, appeared far less invested in the country and its peoples now that the Burma Road had been regained and the pipeline to China thus restored. And Benny could only shake his head when Aung San began preparing to fight the British as soon as they'd helped him oust the other imperialist enemy. Mutual effort gave way to mutual chaos, to widespread distrust, even before the war at large had formally been won.

Benny was so wasted by the breaches of faith near and far, he found himself turning his back on making any kind of sense of it all. Instead, suddenly liberated from the threat of the Japanese occupation, he found himself setting his sights on the future—a future in which he needn't be a victim of others' disloyalty or self-interest or viciousness, but could become a force to be reckoned with, a pugilist. Yes, a pugilist once more! A man prepared to fight for his share of the dream in Burma's remaking, prepared to prove that he was still the kid who could counter life's blows and make something of himself!

And so, as the Allies trooped through the country from May to August, installing units of both British forces and Aung San's Burma National Army to "mop up operations" and restore the peace, Benny chose to look past the madness (was anyone *less* qualified to broker peace than the Burma National Army, whose leaders had ushered in the Japanese, and whose throngs of dacoits had raped, pillaged, and slaughtered those most loyal to the British effort?). He chose to look past what any of these deserters owed the Karens in particular (the Karens, who, when all was said and done, did more damage to the Japanese than any other irregular military force during the war). Instead, he seized the moment to extract something concrete from the British army: a food contract. With the earnings from the sale of dried peas to the Japanese, he'd doubled the size of his tillable land and hired several Karens to help him sow a new crop. It was really quite simple, in the postwar pandemonium, to convince a British quartermaster that his forthcoming pea yields would be excellent.

The problem was how to transport to the Brits the almost obscene amount of peas he soon harvested—a problem that worked to Benny's benefit when those Brits decided to scrap many of their old lorries, and he took advantage of the old bookkeeping skills he'd acquired while pushing his pen back at B. Meyer. He bought a fleet of three hundred junkers, mostly three- and five-ton trucks capable of years of service once they'd been overhauled by a flotilla of mechanically inclined Karens from Tharrawaddy. Then, over the following few months, he sold half the trucks—to civilians wanting to get on with their own lives, for the most part. With the stunning profit, he hired his mechanics to transport not just piddling peas, but all the supplies and foodstuffs the army posts needed—even posts in China and India once the war was done with. Sure, a few Chinese soon got into the same racket, but with the partial profit-sharing plan Benny put into action, his well-paid, loyal employees soon made his the biggest postwar transportation company in Southeast Asia.

Within ten months of the Japanese retreat, he wasn't just supplying the British army; he was hauling teak and rice back to long-dormant export companies (such as good old B. Meyer) in the Rangoon port of his youth. That sector of his business became so explosive he almost couldn't keep up: he bought another fleet of lorries and a parcel of land eight miles from the port, where on a hill overlooking the Karen village of Thamaing he built a sprawling house, several cottages to house his personal assistants, a gas station to fill his trucks, and a machine shop and garage to service and station them. The problem was that many of his new trucks, though stuffed with supplies for export on their way to the Rangoon wharves, were wastefully empty going north. Then one day he remembered that E. Solomon, where his father had worked as a cashier, used to provide ice to the British navy. He was at the port, keeping an eye on a couple of workers unloading one of his trucks, when it occurred to him that a stone's throw away on the Strand his father had pointed to a British navy ship and first illumined for him the essential concept of supply and demand. *("And how do you imagine their sailors relieve themselves from the press of this heat? Our ice! Our fizzy drinks!")* Hadn't Benny's drivers moaned that if there was one thing civilians and soldiers needed in the outposts, it was ice to prevent their food from rotting?

Turned out there were no ice factories anywhere near the outposts from which he was hauling supplies; turned out that if you covered ice with palm leaves and stored it in a metal compartment, it lasted for up to two days; turned out E. Solomon's abandoned ice factory was still standing—albeit in utter disrepair and need of upgrading; turned out, what with economies of scale and the onetime cost of shipping refrigeration machinery from Britain, it made more sense to open *two* ice factories simultaneously—one to serve Rangoon and its outlying communities, the other stationed farther north in Tharrawaddy, where he could rely on his Karen contacts. This new venture, launched well before the first anniversary of the war's end, he named Aung Mingala Refrigeration Company. He just couldn't help referencing the claim to success made by the Burman military ruler and self-proclaimed lord—*aung* being the Burman word for "succeed," *mingala* being a Burman bastardization of the Pali word for "auspicious." He couldn't help referencing it because, truth be told, he'd done nothing openly to express his dismay at an evolving slew of negotiations between Aung San and the Brits, the latter of whom had put forward white paper plans to ease Burma toward self-governance (even as they supposedly wanted to ensure the "Frontier" peoples' involvement in the country's political future), while the former was sticking to a hard-nosed Burman agenda and encouraging the imperialists to make a prompt exit from the scene. Theft, dacoity, mass strikes . . . If Aung San didn't precisely incite them all, neither did he seem to be seeking a way to forestall the collapse of peace; and the spent British—helmed by Attlee's Labour Party, which had trumped Churchill's Conservative Party by a landslide earlier that year—were backing away.

But how successful Benny felt with his own expanding business empire—and at just twenty-six! How reassured he felt by the vast metal buckets tipping blocks of ice over the conveyor belts in one of his factories. There was something so undeniable about the ice and the relief it brought others; it quenched a parched place within him and restored his vitality. "Careful not to get your hair stuck in the belt!" he'd call to the children (*his* children—and how handsome all three of them were, how bright and articulate and charming). Their delight in the machinery, and in their new proprietorship of something, was his delight; their pleasure in the long tubes of flavored sugar-water, frozen especially for them by the workers, was his pleasure. Even Khin looked on with vague relief at the chugging machinery, pleased, he tried to convince himself, by the reliable creak of the rollers, by the clunk of ice dumped again and again and again onto the belt. Something else—*someone* else—had taken over her burden. Yes, for the first time in his life, he truly felt like a man.

And that man got a kick out of renting space in the same building as B. Meyer and putting his name on the office door. That man enjoyed the things money could buy—the Steinway concert grand and the Packard and the private schools for the kids; the chauffeur and servants and membership at the old British Rowing Club, where he took up billiards and also bridge again. That man became reacquainted with the Western music they'd mostly missed out on during the war. How he loved belting out love songs (so many about dreams, now that he thought about it) while little Louisa plinked out the melodies at the piano—"Sweet Genevieve," "Charmaine," "I'll Buy That Dream."

And, bloody hell, did he buy that dream! A large part of his time was now spent cultivating and keeping business contacts, and if at the many parties he attended and hosted he took certain privileges with women, if he did more than allow his eyes to luxuriate in their coconut-oiled hair or kohl-lidded eyes—if he sometimes left Khin's side to slip some sweet dame a business card, what of it? Hadn't he earned a certain right to flaunt his freedom? None of it *meant* anything. None of it had the slightest thing to do with what he *refused* to entertain—thoughts of the war years (and what he'd suffered, what *they'd* suffered). And if he doubted his decency now and then, if he questioned the authenticity of his renewed bullishness, if he was ashamed about his lack of involvement on the political scene, if he noticed the return in Khin's eyes of a disappointment that she'd only just begun to shed—he threw it off with the thought that his wife was back in his bed, back in his corner, and *he* was back in the ring, fighting as never before.

But several things happened to rouse him from the dream he'd bought. The first was that, in May 1946, when he was twenty-seven, he had the hubris to think he could saunter unscathed down to the old Jewish quarter to drum up some new business. He'd been reflecting on his father and the man's modest station as head cashier at E. Solomon. His memories had taken him back to the fizzy drinks Daddy had often rewarded him with, and he'd thought, I'm damned if I can't still feel the cool shape of those bottles in my hand, still taste that bit of sparkling orange sunshine—why not bottle the stuff for everyone to enjoy again? No one else in the country had gotten it together to start up a domestic bottling plant after the war (idiocy, given that drinking water had to be boiled for three minutes minimum). He seemed to remember a pair of ginger-haired brothers, Jews from the neighborhood, whose father guarded secret recipes for several aerated sodas. E. Solomon hadn't reopened after the war, but wouldn't Daddy be proud if one of the Jewish grocers stocked drinks from his son's very own bottling outfit? Mingala Waters—that's what he'd call it, because the idea had bubbled up from the same well of auspiciousness that hadn't yet slaked his thirst.

It was near dusk when his car pulled up on Dalhousie Street, where E. Solomon had stood, and where he remembered the ginger-haired brothers living in an overstuffed flat—something between a fleapit and a magician's lab. He knew this was Dalhousie—his driver and the sign at the corner reminded him as much—but his soul refused to believe it. Where the rows of rickety buildings had been, there was . . . nothing, a stray dog hunting for food on refuse-riddled mud, a few abandoned pieces of decaying furniture keeping company with the weeds swaying in a gentle wind. (*"One of these days, it'll all be burned up. You wait and see, Benny."*) From behind a distant heap of rubble, an isolated bark rang out. He had the frightening impression that the dogs had finally achieved their dominion. Then he noticed, down the empty street, a pair of indolent armed soldiers, Aung San's henchmen—the star of the Imperial Japanese Army on their caps gave them away. They loitered on a corner, smoking, sporadically eyeing his car, as though positioned there to keep out the place's past occupants. Hadn't Benny known that nearly all the members of this once flourishing community had fled after the invasion because they were targets, many perishing en route to India and hardly more than a handful returning to set up shop again? He'd known it, and yet he hadn't been able to fathom it.

"Take me home," he told the driver.

When they passed Tseekai Maung Tauley Street, where he'd spent his first seven years, he kept his eyes averted. He had the chilling sensation that his mother was watching him now from their timbered balcony—watching him in all his greed and cowardice. (*"You must not just think of yourself, Benny. Only animals just think of themselves. The worst sin is to forget your responsibility to the less fortunate. Thank God you are a good, noble boy."*)

But though he left the Jewish quarter, along with the fleeting dream of Mingala Waters, he could not evade the memory of the woman who had once showered him with dignity. And over the following few weeks, as the worst of the hot weather blew in with the southwest monsoon, he felt drowned by an awareness of having abandoned Mama's God when he'd felt most abandoned during the war.

If he was angry with God, if he had lost his faith, he didn't know it, because somewhere along the line even the thought of faith, of God, had become too much. And what about his faith in man?

That June, Benny was obliged to make an appearance at a British embassy party. The banquet hall was one of those airy, suddenly eerie residuals of colonialism, all gleaming teak and mirrors and candlelit chandeliers. Looking past the rim of a tumbler of pink gin at the blur of chattering, gulping, ogling, richly dressed partygoers, he seemed to see their every anxious bead of sweat. The room and its brightness all at once struck him as a glaring denial of the dark fright brewing within each of them.

Like every one of the guests, he had clawed his way to the top and to what he had imagined was his freedom by insinuating himself into the good graces of the powers that be—principally those in the upper ranks of Aung San's Anti-Fascist People's Freedom League, the nationalist party formed during the war and presently involved in exclusive bilateral negotiations with the Brits. Benny had done so with a kind of willful disregard for these men's machinations—a cold, albeit largely unconscious calculation that if they were getting their lot, he would get his. And now, swallowing down his gin, and watching a pair of flirtatious wives pretending not to try to attract him, he wanted to cover his face in shame.

He was just about to make his escape when Aung San's right-hand man suddenly approached the bar in his Japanese-inspired military uniform. He leaned into the counter a few feet from where Benny stood and barked out his drink order, his mouth hanging open as if to better display the full prominence of his mismatched buck teeth and disturbingly sensual lips. Benny had never met the man before (and everything about his posture suggested it would take more than the usual pleasantries to get him to pay attention to anyone whom he didn't care to meet), but he knew that this general had been an underperforming university dropout before joining up with Aung San in the We Burmans Association and then becoming one of the "Thirty Comrades" to receive military training in Japan. Like his comrades, the general called himself *Thakin*, Burman for "lord" (the thinking being that the ethnic Burmans, and not the British, were the natural lords of their country), and he'd chosen a nom de guerre: in his case, Ne Win, or "Radiant Sun." The only thing about him that was remotely radiant, however, was his perspiring brow.

Without a glint of graciousness, he accepted a drink from the nervous bartender and turned to survey the crowd. He could have been a schoolyard bully who didn't want to be caught showing kindness to flatterers or the powerless. "One blood, one voice, one leader"—that was the slogan that he and his bully friends had recently been chanting from their parapets of power (how many times had Benny heard the slogan broadcast over the wireless since the conclusion of the war?)—and there could be no doubt that what they had in mind was a country overrun by their values, their culture, their language, their military. That military had "liberated" the country from its captors, according to their spokesmen, from "aggressors," whom they sought to repel by rousing Burmans to continue to strike, to create bedlam.

"How have the negotiations been going?" Benny found himself sputtering loudly in his English-inflected Burmese. He meant the negotiations with the British aggressors, of course. The negotiations for independence. But it wasn't clear at all if Ne Win had heard him.

A moment passed before the general turned to him with an inconvenienced stare. Then a bizarre smile rose to this sensual mouth. "You're the Jew," he said, disconcerting Benny to the point that he couldn't quickly come up with a rejoinder. In all Benny's days in Burma, no one had ever accused him of *that*. Being Jewish here simply wasn't—or hadn't been—something to slight someone for, unlike, regrettably, being Indian. "The rich Jew," the general went on. "The Jew who is so good at making mountains of money."

"Is that what they say?" Benny laughed, trying to match the general's touch of theatricality.

The man's eyes cast around the humanity before him again, as though he wanted to be sure of having been observed while making his cutting point. Indeed, the women who had been pretending not to flirt for Benny's benefit had fallen into the false notes of forced conversation. They were listening, all right—on alert for Benny's fall from the general's favor.

"Tell me," Ne Win said now, with a seriousness that caused Benny to stiffen. "What do you make of what they did to all those Jews in Europe?"

For a while, Benny just stood with his emptied tumbler in his fist, staring into the unhappy eyes of the man who was now breaking into a stupid grin. He felt as if he were looking at the unsightly reflection of his own inability to confront what had happened halfway around the world. And he hated himself. Hated himself as much as he hated this man who had stooped to threatening him with the unspeakable suffering of others. He set his tumbler down and forced out his hand, half expecting the general to touch fists with him, to declare the start of their fight to the end. But Ne Win wouldn't touch him.

"Saw Bension," Benny said. "You'll have to excuse me." And that was how he came spontaneously to invent the new moniker for himself, one that was still Jewish but unmistakably Karen.

Two days later Aung San's party held a public rally. So many thousands showed up to hear the Burman leader speak that the entire city shut down—all the Rangoon shops and the roads whose impassability would no doubt cause the ice blocks in Benny's idling trucks to melt. The rally was relocated from overfull city hall to Fytche Square, where, on the cloisters near the Sule Pagoda, across from Queen's Park, a platform was erected and the usual banners unfurled (INDEPENDENCE WITHIN ONE YEAR! GO BACK! BURMA IS OUR LAND, BURMESE OUR LANGUAGE!).

With a pang, Benny saw his old friend's flat, still standing at the edge of the gardens in which, a lifetime ago, they had strolled under the fragrant blooming trees, getting to know each other.

At last Aung San took the stage and the tide of humanity surged toward the platform, pulling Benny from the periphery of the square into the crowd. Even if Benny hadn't been a head or two taller than the others, he would have understood immediately that the leader had the luminosity and magnetism that was utterly deficient in his fellow lord, Ne Win. There was Aung San's chiseled head, for one, close-shorn and angled slightly toward the tops of the nearby thicket of coco palms. There were his eyes that stared unblinkingly down at the crowd. And then, as soon as he had opened his mouth, there was, if not what one would ordinarily call rhetorical talent, a meticulousness of conviction that at once lifted him toward the gods and insisted on his place among the ordinary populace—a populace that had been victimized by more than just imperialism. "*Capitalism* has called forth irreconcilable antagonism between man and man, race and race, nation and nation!" the man broodingly announced. "Even before the war, most people in our country were poor, while only a few—chiefly *Europeans* and *foreigners*—were rich. Place this alongside the havoc wreaked by the war . . . We need to take money out of the keeping of the rich, fix prices of essential commodities, and curb the activities of profiteers and hoarders!"

Listening to this chastising yet effervescent young man, Benny felt himself shrink into the crowd, as if Aung San were targeting him in particular. After all, Benny had been amassing a good amount of money of late (a disconcerting amount that just might be plain unfair, much as he had also pulled some eight hundred employees out of the postwar economic wasteland along with him, not to mention the dockworkers, the export outfits that relied on his trucks, the citizens near and far whose perishables lasted a few days longer on his ice), and for several seconds he nearly convinced himself that, in Aung San, this beleaguered country had indeed found its solution to people like *him*.

He was all but ready to slip out of the crowd in shame when the leader suddenly called for a nationalism that, to Benny's ears, sounded like nothing less than a denial of difference. "What is *nationalism*, anyway?" Aung San asked, almost as though to dispense with the question by raising it. "It's having to lead one common life. Sharing racial or linguistic communities, traditions that make us conscious of oneness and the *necessity* of oneness. It's the *unity* of the entire people. What's important isn't that parties other than ours exist or not, but that they refrain from partisan activities detrimental to *national* interests."

There wasn't evil anywhere in the man's face that Benny could spot. There was anger, ancient anger, to be sure, and the focused ferocity of someone who would stop at nothing to free Burma's people. But as Aung San suddenly absented himself from the platform, leaving the crowd too momentarily stunned to respond, Benny couldn't help wondering exactly what menace Aung San was seeking to free his own people of.

At last, a delayed applause thunderously rolled over the park, followed by an eruption of cheers for the same old "One blood, one voice, one leader!" And Benny, feeling dazed, turned and spotted a familiar face twenty feet off, a face so unabashedly swept up— so transported, so expressive of something appearing like amorous love—that a moment passed before he realized it belonged to Ducksworth, the Anglo-Burman Pax Britannica apologist, who had been so besotted by his British inheritance. Now, riding the trajectories of history, Ducksworth appeared to have recast himself as another chosen one—as a Burman, maybe even a Thakin. There he stood, slightly apart from the throng of his countrymen: clapping exultantly, red-cheeked, aglow with righteousness, ready to claim his rightful place in a Burma reborn.

While the crowd dispersed, Benny dejectedly angled for the street that would lead him to his office, and took one last lingering look at his old friend's flat. That was when, by what initially seemed like an implausible second coincidence, he saw another ghost from his past—Saw Lay, standing on his stoop, smoking a cigarette. Benny was still so disoriented by having spotted Ducksworth, and so accustomed to imagining that he had glimpsed Saw Lay here or there—at the wharves where they'd met, or in this neighborhood where Benny often was brought on business—that at first he didn't believe his eyes. As the departing rally-goers jostled him, he stopped about fifty feet from the flat, luxuriating in this specter of his old friend. Only when the man on the stoop dropped his cigarette and stiffly stubbed it out with the toe of his boot did Benny begin to trust that he was looking at Saw Lay in the flesh.

Saw Lay caught sight of him while Benny was closing the distance between them. He seemed about to step back, to disappear behind his door, but then he braced himself on the rail by the stoop and stared at Benny with a kind of painful tenderness, as though he were steeling himself to face an affection that was almost more than he could bear.

"I didn't know . . ." Benny said, when he was at the foot of the stoop.

"Will you come in?" Saw Lay answered.

Inside, Benny waited in a chair while Saw Lay put on the kettle and rolled himself another cigarette. Saw Lay hadn't smoked before the war, and as Benny watched him put the burning thing to his lips, he was moved, and saddened, by how much had changed about his friend. Saw Lay's hair was almost all white now, and there was a kind of secret on his face—some evidence of struggle beneath the quietness of his aspect, which itself had lost much of its polished elegance. He'd suffered, no doubt. But he would never speak of it; no, Benny knew from the way his friend sank into a chair across from him and closed his eyes when he inhaled, only sporadically looking at Benny without apology or shame or resentment, that whatever had happened in Saw Lay's personal past would remain there.

"You've been back . . ." Benny started.

"Oh, a few months now," Saw Lay cagily confessed. "And how . . . how are the children?" he asked with a sincere smile. "Louisa must be very aware of her own superiority to the rest of us by now."

Benny chuckled as tears came to his eyes. If he was sad, it was because he identified with Saw Lay's despair. And he was reminded for some reason of his mother, and how protected he'd felt by her against the inevitability of loss and pain. He had meant always to protect this friend from pain, but instead they had brought pain on each other. *This is my wife's former lover,* he thought. *This is the progenitor of my own little daughter.*

The kettle began to scream, and Saw Lay stubbed out his cigarette and limped to the kitchen—he'd been wounded, Benny observed. When he returned, it was with a single cup of milky tea, which he foisted on Benny, and an open bottle of beer for himself; perhaps he needed Benny to stay sober as much as he personally needed to be loosened.

"I want to ask you something," Saw Lay said, sinking back into his seat as he took a long swallow of beer. "Do you suppose that the British—that any of the Allies—would think it would be reasonable for the Jews to trust the Germans again? I mean to live peaceably under the Germans, under their government?"

"Don't be ridiculous," Benny said. If he'd been short, it was because Saw Lay's question had struck his ears—and his heart—as a latent insult, because it presupposed that Benny was so much an outsider that a comparison with the Jewish condition had to be drawn in order for him to understand that of the Karen people. But there was also something painful about how easily Saw Lay had started down the path of political discussion, as if picking right up from where they'd left off years before—painful because it had been so absent from Benny's life.

Saw Lay sipped his beer without meeting Benny's eyes. "You probably haven't heard," he said quietly, "that we wrote a memorial of sorts, a letter, to the British secretary of state before the war was even over."

"We?" There it was, the excluding "we."

"The Karens leading the effort against the Japs," Saw Lay said, putting his beer down. "We wanted to remind the British of the slaves the Burmans made of us before they came here, of the huge role we played in the British army and police forces all along."

"And did you ask for something in return?"

Now it was Saw Lay who became very sober, staring at Benny as he might at a fool. "The creation of our own state, of course," he said, but there was no conviction in his words, and his eyes seemed to follow the dispirited train of his thoughts as he looked to the window that faced the park and the place where Aung San had stood. "No response," he said quietly. "And with every one of Aung San's rallies, with every one of his mass strikes, the Brits come closer to all-out capitulation. How can they expect us to trust the Burmans after what's been done to us?"

"You don't think Aung San has . . . reformed?" Benny ventured.

Saw Lay gave him a sidelong, disbelieving look.

"You don't think it's possible that he actually wants something like democracy here?"

"Democracy," Saw Lay said, his tone full of contempt. "Yes, this is the word that makes the British sit a bit easier with themselves now. One of the things they don't seem to understand—that no one outside Burma seems to understand—is the duplicitousness of most Burmans, even those who are highly educated and who seem to have the 'Frontier' peoples' interests in mind. How very Western to trust the word of a man who speaks fluently, intelligently, even brilliantly. How very Western to trust that he has the same code of honor. How naive to think that because he makes one sweeping gesture toward Western democracy he couldn't possibly at that very same moment be plotting a systematized form of inequality—a state in which one 'dominant' race rules and is sanctioned to discriminate

against others—against 'minorities'—minorities that together make up half of the population, though no Burman would ever admit that!"

The alcohol and tobacco had done their work, relaxing Saw Lay's agitation so that he openly seethed as he spoke. Benny wanted to say something to soothe him, but he sensed any speech would only further incense his friend.

"I'm so tired of their story that we're only minorities!" Saw Lay cried, jumping up from his chair and going to the window. The sun had finally begun its descent, bringing with it a breath of cool air, which Saw Lay loudly inhaled as though gasping for life itself. "We Karens are a national group on a given territory that is our *homeland*," he said. "*They* were the invaders. We were here centuries before—"

"Isn't what you're speaking of, Saw Lay," Benny interrupted him gently, "a kind of tribalism?"

Now Saw Lay turned to him with outright reproach in his eyes.

"What I mean to ask is," Benny carefully went on, "isn't Aung San correct in a sense—that the best thing would be for us to form a perfect union, as the Americans put it? We could, after all, rise to the top in such a union, instead of always being the outsider, the other."

If Benny had felt excluded by Saw Lay's "we" before, the frostiness that came over his friend now left him entirely out in the cold. Saw Lay went to the table where he kept his tobacco and mechanically rolled himself another cigarette, which he lit and held to his lips. "You surprise me, Benny," he said, after he had exhaled. "Aung San's talk of unity . . . Surely you know 'unity' is just the word tyrants use before heads begin to roll . . . But very well. Let us take your American example. I'll pass over the very obvious case of the American Indians, who have been incorporated into that perfect union with such stunning success—"

"Saw Lay—"

"Suppose—" the man persisted, but with a trace of his old politeness, "suppose that your Americans suddenly found themselves being overrun by Japs. Say Hiroshima never happened and so on. Say that we had lost the war, and suddenly America is overrun. Americans are no longer permitted to speak English in any governmental setting; their children must learn their lessons in Japanese, learn a 'history' that mocks their 'minority' perspective. Say that in theory their children can rise to the top rungs of the social and political ladder—but only by adopting Japanese values, a belief in the superiority of Japanese blood, and even a disdain for American primitivism. American religion—be it Christianity or anything else—is, if not formally stamped out, labeled crude, 'aboriginal.' Or say something more radical happened . . ." He had begun to pace, and as Benny watched him, as he listened to him, he felt drawn into an old comfort: some slip of his old cautious friend had reappeared, had survived after all, in spite of the setbacks. "Say that these Japanese rulers institutionalized handicapping Americans by cutting off their hands if they were found with reading materials or writing implements, so that before long—without a written language, without a written history, without access to education—Americans were as ignorant as the Japs said they were. If, instead, these Americans refused to relinquish their writing and language and values and culture and history so easily, would that be 'tribalism,' as you call it?"

"But—" Benny started, and Saw Lay held up a hand to silence him.

"But," Saw Lay went on with a fanatical gleam in his eyes, "in the better of these two scenarios, these Americans would have the right to speak their own language and practice their own religions in private, you argue! Why should they insist on educating their children in English, and on practicing a form of government that coheres with their American cultural tenets?"

"That wasn't going to be my argument! You've conveniently chosen an example of a group not bound together by racial sameness! Not to mention the fact that the Burmans made slaves of the Karens hundreds of—if not a thousand—years ago."

"And so what? It is time for the Karens to accept their lot—like the American Indians? Oh, yes, I know how this argument goes . . . It's the history of the world, one group invading another's territory, swallowing them up. But we're still here! And you're conveniently forgetting that our problems were largely resolved for a century under the British—resolved until a mere five years ago! This is a critical juncture! When, for all intents and purposes, we won the war for the British in Burma, and thereby aided the Allies' overall effort in the Pacific—and therefore have a right to expect something in turn. And you're absolutely incorrect that the Karens are racially homogeneous—there are more subgroups and dialects of Karens than I care to name. Black Karens, White Karens, Red Karens—Muslim, Christian, Buddhist, animist—all Karens with a shared vision of self-determination. You, for example, are Karen and racially different from me."

This last point, delivered with a smile, had the effect of making Benny smile unexpectedly in turn, of disarming him at precisely the moment that Saw Lay proceeded to discharge his most explosive point.

"Mark my words, Benny, with or without Aung San, the Burmans *will* try to wipe us out. And Aung San's insistence on a union will lead to Burma's destruction. Which is why, with or without the British, we are forming our own union. The Karen National Union. If London truly wants to secure future peace, the only course is to divide Burma into autonomous nation-states."

For a moment, Benny couldn't respond. "And if that doesn't happen?"

Saw Lay crossed to his chair, picked up his bottle of beer, and drank at length. When he set the bottle down, he put his bloodshot eyes on Benny again. "What you've done for the Karen people is no secret—what your business smarts, your money smarts, have done. If it should happen that the British concede everything to Aung San— you see, we need to prepare."

"You're talking about—about armament?"

"How much could you give us to help?"

All at once, Benny wanted to tell Saw Lay that everything had been forgiven, that he loved him as innocently as on the day they'd last sat together on the Khuli riverbank; but that would have been a lie: if it was too late for a peaceful union of Burma, it was also too late to recover the peace they had once shared. What had been done would go on finding its ways to wound them.

"I reinvest almost everything into the businesses," Benny stammered, but already he felt himself weakening—waking to some ancient instinct to resist injustice, to come out swinging . . . "I don't have much in the way of capital," he stammered on. "Money's always going in and out."

"We have some men who've robbed some banks upcountry—"

"My God, Saw Lay!"

"We could mix the money in with yours—"

"You're talking about *laundering*!"

Now Saw Lay laughed with all the ugliness of the condemned. "Fools rest easy on the ground of easy labels and easy morality, Benny. If you're going to be a goddamned fool, at least be a fool on our side!"

7

Polished

When, several months later, in September 1946, Louisa woke from a nap on the afternoon of her sixth birthday—that is, when she was woken by her white Scottish terrier, Little Fella, whose nudging paws and licks demanded tea—she had the sensation of having emerged from something frightening. It was a feeling she often had on rousing in the bright, airy room hung with ivory Chinese draperies and strewn with her dollies. Little Fella (who, as Daddy said, "just happened to be female") pushed the nub of her wet nose into Louisa's ear so that she laughed, though their pre-teatime ritual mandated that she scowl in complaint. "You remember that Saw Lay is coming?" she scolded the dog. It was possible to believe that Little Fella was enchanted, that she possessed the ability to comprehend Louisa's every word, and that she bristled with excitement not just because of the forthcoming tea, with its two spoonfuls of sugar, but also out of a love she shared for Saw Lay, who had been visiting them of late.

The dog followed her out to the landing to peer down at the lower floor of the house, already busy with preparations for tonight's party in honor of Louisa's birthday. Several employees were moving the living room furniture in order to make way for an orchestra and dancing, while gardeners were bringing in armloads of Mama's flowers and two men from Daddy's brand-new bottling company were unloading crates of fizzy drinks. Little Fella nosed Louisa toward the staircase, but a sound made them turn—the sound of Daddy's voice—and through her parents' open bedroom door Louisa saw her father sitting at the window. They lived in a southern suburb of Insein—itself a suburb of Rangoon—and Louisa knew that Daddy had designed the window to look out over their hillside estate and the Karen village of Thamaing, past the highway. It was for the village, he frequently reminded her, that he'd chosen this spot on which to develop this compound that was always humming with Karen employees. "They didn't forget me, the Karens," he told Louisa, "and we must never forget them."

It could have been any late afternoon now, with Daddy just bathed, his curly hair just washed and wrapped in a handkerchief tied tightly around his head ("nothing flattens the hair like a handkerchief!"), with him dressed in his white suit and beginning to speak aloud to the window. His afternoon sessions in prayer, his "grand exercises in gratitude," he liked to say—these were the only times Louisa would see him so still. He was such a big, quick man, with such noisy steps, such strong features, such a booming voice. But something about the way his eyes gazed upward reminded her of the darkness of her dreams, and she had the thought that maybe there was no God, that maybe Daddy was like a little lost boy.

Little Fella prodded her down to the kitchen, and there they found Mama already enjoying her own tea. Mama always preferred to dine with the servants, as if she didn't like spending time with her family. "Have you practiced?" she asked Louisa, casting her a look of having been disrupted.

Louisa was supposed to give a short piano recital at the party tonight, but she hated practicing. Maybe to save her, one of the cooks handed her a cup of tea, which Louisa poured into the dog's bowl before spooning in generous helpings of sugar. Only when boiled milk from the stove was floating in the tea did Little Fella lap up the frothing drink. "Your father will be embarrassed if you play poorly," Mama persisted.

The truth was that *Mama* would be embarrassed. There was so much about Louisa she seemed not to like. "As far back as when she was the tiniest thing, she'd come home crying because another child didn't have something," Mama would complain. Or: "She knows too much"—as though what Louisa knew were Mama's secrets. (And Louisa did remember things meant to be forgotten: the cuts on Daddy's scalp after he had returned to their house in Tharrawaddy, the way he'd kicked while being dragged off by the Japanese in Khuli. She seemed always to have understood that it was better to pretend to forget, to not mention remembering. It all left her feeling forgotten sometimes.)

"Here you are, bitch," the cook said with a grumble, doling rice and curry into the dog bowl. Little Fella licked the gravy, then stared up at the cook, who smiled at her with charmed eyes. A yap and a dismissive wave of the hand followed, and then the cook took her time opening a jar of brined limes, kept next to the pickles on the counter. "Hold your tongue, and show some gratitude for once," the cook said. "I haven't forgotten your condiment." She forked a lime out for the dog, who seized it and immediately began to tear off a pungent piece of rind.

"You remember it's my *birthday*?" Louisa broke in, her voice catching slightly.

For a moment, the adults stared at her. They seemed to be preparing for one of her "moods." Then they broke out laughing—at her, Louisa realized, feeling the heat of humiliation on her cheeks.

"Silly girl," Mama said, and reached out and hooked her hand around Louisa's waist.

Louisa leaned her hot face against Mama's cool, powdery one, breathing in the earthiness of her scent and sandalwood comb. These moments of Mama's attention and affection were so rare and bewildering.

"You think I would forget you?" Mama murmured into her ear. "I've made you something special to wear tonight."

The last time Mama had sewn Louisa a dress they had still been in Tharrawaddy. Then, Mama had used her own petticoat, and

Louisa had loved the dress's lace zigzag hem and the blue ribbon at the waist—had loved the dress so much she'd suddenly been willing to take a more generous view toward being a big sister to her second younger sibling, whom Mama was then expecting, and who would turn out to be Grace. That memory—of the dress, of baby Gracie— was a happy one, wasn't it? But why did it make Louisa want to hide her stinging eyes in Mama's soft neck now? (Why did it bring to mind certain other memories of the war? A Japanese soldier cutting off the top of an old man's head. Johnny's sweaty hand in hers as they ran for the trench. Daddy hiding in the back of the house in Tharrawaddy. Learning how to disappear with Johnny into the trees. You put your fingers deep into the moist earth by the roots so that you could hear the trees drinking, and you were very quiet, so quiet you were erased, and the only sound was the tree sucking, and then the tree began to speak—)

"Boo boo."

Louisa lifted her eyes from Mama's stiffening neck and found Saw Lay in the kitchen doorway, a sheepish grin on his face and that familiar, yet comforting look of sadness in his eyes. He was wearing an oversize polka-dot cravat that Louisa had never seen. It made her want to laugh, to leap into his arms.

"Boo boo," she told him. As far back as she could remember, they had welcomed each other that way.

"I thought I would come early," he said to Mama. "I did promise to teach Louisa how to swing dance before the party, if it's all right . . ."

"Why wouldn't it be?" Mama said, hiding her eyes in her tea.

But when Louisa went and took Saw Lay's hand and tried to pull him away, he turned back to Mama as though to apologize.

"This isn't swing!" she cried in the living room, after Saw Lay had cleared away the servants and put on one of Daddy's records that he said would be "just the thing"—Glenn Miller's "Fools Rush In."

The servants had polished and powdered the floor so that it shone like a mirror, and for a few minutes it was just them, laughing and pressing cheek to cheek while Saw Lay bent down in his silly way—all to that song that he kept dashing back to the Victrola to play and that Daddy had once described to Louisa as so sad and so assuring. "We can swing dance to this," Saw Lay kept saying. "See? We're swinging."

But then Johnny and Gracie, woken from their naps, barged into the room wanting to join in—Johnny with his seriousness even in play, and thin Gracie with that constant smile of hers despite the fact that she was always the loser in their games. Louisa could see the way Saw Lay hesitated to swing Gracie around with the same abandon.

"What's this? The party already started?" came Daddy's voice. He had entered the room with an enormous wrapped object in his outstretched hands, and now he stood looking muscular and ruddy, beaming at Saw Lay.

"Why not?" Saw Lay said, already retreating to the bar as though Daddy had just offered him something. "Will you have one?"

Daddy looked confused as Saw Lay poured out some brown liquor. These days it was often this way between them, Daddy pressing his too-eager smile on his friend, Saw Lay sinking into the shadows and complaining of headaches. Yet eventually the two of them would disappear into Daddy's study, where they held meetings with other men, and where the children were forbidden to enter.

"Is no one interested in what I have here?" Daddy said as he lifted the enormous gift up to his ear, giving it a shake, and making Gracie giggle and Johnny look on with interested alarm.

And that was all it took to rescue Louisa from the worried wanderings of her thoughts. Soon they were all pulling at the wrapping paper, revealing pleated layers of cloth—the bellows of something—of an accordion, Louisa realized, exclaiming her pleasure while Johnny instantly asked to have a shot at playing the thing.

Daddy threw off the remains of the paper and gave the accordion a few tugs. "My mother used to play one of these," he said. "Doesn't it make you happy? You can't listen to it and not feel compelled to smile . . . See? And the marvelous thing—the really marvelous thing is that you can take it with you wherever you go."

"Where are we going?" Louisa said. There it was again: the sting of spontaneous tears behind her eyes.

"We're not going anywhere," Daddy assured her as Saw Lay looked on, and then one of the servants came to whisk the children away to be bathed.

The party was more wonderful than Louisa could have hoped for, with her "very fine" performance at the piano, and the beautiful new dress that flared out whenever she twirled, and heaps of ice cream, and a show by a snake charmer (terrorized by Little Fella), and so much swing dancing—all the lamps in the house aglow, all the doors flung open to let in the cool night air. For hours after Louisa was sent to bed, she sat in her nightgown at the top of the stairs, watching her parents and their guests, the silks and flashing jewels. Daddy danced with Mama, staring into her eyes as though this—as though she—were the thing he needed most.

It was all almost enough to make Louisa forget how unhappy Saw Lay had been throughout the evening. Before going upstairs, she had found him smoking out on the veranda and gazing back through the open double doors at the couples gliding by. "Boo boo!" she had said to startle him out of his thoughts and make him smile, and he had looked at her—not crossly, but without joy. "Boo boo," he had told her after a pause, quietly. And only after another moment had he smiled and touched her cheek and asked if it wasn't already time for her to be in bed dreaming.

Now he was by the front door talking sternly with one of the servants, as though to grumble about something. Yet a moment later, he left the servant's side to charge through the guests toward Daddy, who was still holding Mama on the dance floor. He put a hand on Daddy's shoulder, and when Daddy nervously stepped aside, he bent toward Daddy's ear, and then the two of them headed off toward the hall leading to Daddy's study.

Louisa had never spied on adults before. She had listened, and she had looked, all her senses attuned to the signals they put out, signals she kept recorded somewhere deep inside. Maybe, though, because it was her birthday and she was no longer a very little girl—or maybe because of the way Mama remained out on the dance floor, as if lost—she slipped down the stairs and darted down the hall unseen.

The door to the study was shut, and when she pressed her ear against it, a moment passed before she could hear anything but the thudding of her heart. Then the muffled sounds coming through the wood gave way to voices, to words.

"Could it have been one of the guests?" Saw Lay was saying.

"Goddamn government," Daddy told him, "poisoning meat to kill off stray dogs."

"And stray men . . . What about Louisa?"

"I'll tell the sentry to bury it. Better for her to think the dog wandered off."

Before she could quite formulate the thought that she had lost track of Little Fella after going up for bed—that Little Fella had to be buried—the door opened, and Daddy stood breathless and blinking back at her, a curious, startled look on his face.

Behind him, Saw Lay watched her with an expression of regret, and she felt a tug of shame for having put him in the position of discovering her. Then she noticed, in the dim light of Daddy's lamp, the stacks and stacks of rifles on the dark floor. More rifles than she had ever seen.

8

Saw Lay's War

The sense of having missed an opportunity to *prevent* something was one Saw Lay had experienced as far back as the time he had met Khin, before the war, when Benny had invited him over to their flat on Sparks Street, and he had sat across from her at a table laid with her aromatic Karen dishes. On the surface of things, there was nothing special about Khin's face, but the candle on the table, flickering down to a stub over the course of the night, had emphasized to Saw Lay what seemed to be an unusual introversion and sweetness in the woman's eyes. Then there was the way that she had strained to speak to Benny through him. Saw Lay had been left that first night with the impression that Khin valued her husband more greatly for the difficulty loving him entailed, yet also that the bravery of her love went unnoticed by the object of its interest. And he knew, with a kind of pain, that Benny was doomed to inadvertently hurt her, to misunderstand and undervalue her difficult devotion to him much as he adored her, and that the only chance that he, Saw Lay, had of protecting her had already passed, because she was already Benny's.

This feeling of regret soon enough became something more potent, though Saw Lay hadn't known that until it had already done its damage. What happened was that the moment Benny had been captured by the Japanese secret police in Tharrawaddy, Khin had sent word to him through their network of Karen friends, and Saw Lay had just as reflexively, though stealthily, rushed to her, along with three of his junior men. The problem was how to rescue Benny without compromising the greater Karen underground effort—something Saw Lay and his brother and soldiers had debated for nearly twenty uninterrupted hours. "You have to understand," he finally confessed to Khin with exhaustion at the kitchen table, "if it were merely a matter of risking getting shot in order to save Benny, there would be no question." The problem was what the Japanese did to those they captured. Saw Lay didn't trust himself to endure that without leaking a word about his unit's covert operations. It was an impossible situation: the willingness to die, the desperation to save, and the cold confrontation with the limits of his own strength.

"I made a mistake calling you here," Khin finally said to him. There was coolness in her tone, scorn for his unspoken conclusion that one man must not be valued over their shared cause. Yet the pain in her eyes—issuing from a deeper, warmer place—cried out that one man's wife and children could be a cause all their own, worth sacrificing even a war for.

Well, Saw Lay was also a man, and as the others crumpled around the kitchen fire and slept, it was the man in him who faced her. "Promise me you'll never mention a word of this to Benny," he said. When she didn't immediately answer, he repeated, "Promise me." Then he told her, "Khin, it should have been me." Even as he spoke, he wondered if he meant he should have been the one taken into captivity, or the one whose life was uniquely tied to hers.

But she didn't question him. She went to him at the table and cupped his face with one of her hands, and that was all it took to unclench him. Soon he had her supple shape in his own hands, which had a will all their own, and minutes later—just out of view of the kitchen—he had what he'd never allowed himself to want. And the bewildering thing—the first of many bewildering things—was the distinct pitch of ease he detected underlying what they wordlessly, frantically did. Not just then, but again and again through the night, until she drew the blanket up over her full breasts and said, "We must rest," before adjusting her head on the pillow and thanking him, as though for the comfort she'd found in him. And, just like that, she fell into a sleep so deep it seemed untroubled by anything remotely approaching terror or regret.

For the next two hours, as day dawned, he lay watching her, amazed by the miracle of their sudden familiarity, by the illuminating vision of her closed eyes and bare arms, by the rise and fall of her breath, more sweet than acidic. He felt graced by that breath, which emanated from a soul whose beauty he was only beginning to fathom. But the depths of his own soul were also revealed to him: he had been devoted to her all along, and more steadfastly for her steadfast devotion to her husband. If he loved her, it was paradoxically for the very nobility and loyalty that he had just sabotaged. And he knew that, the better to love her, the better to *serve* her, he must spare her his newly revealed self. He must run.

For most of the following year, then, after he'd heard word that Benny had survived the capture, he'd run from one mission to the next, hiding his wounded heart among the remains of his fellow men—all of them stinking and soaked to the bone, and many rotting alive as they slashed through the jungle, gasped in the mud, evaded the bullets and mortars that ceaselessly fell around them. And when the Brits at last celebrated their successful recapturing of the capital, he threw himself into what they called Operation Character, by which the loyal native troops were to ambush the retreating Japanese as they fled. Often during these final weeks of war, he had to engage in hand-to-hand combat, and once at the bend of a river found himself being grabbed by the throat before he was able to get the upper hand. He held his assailant under the limpid current, squeezing the stranger's neck as though to intensify his pain or more quickly extinguish it, staring into the man's startled eyes while it came to him, like a wave of grace, that he had nothing anymore but compassion for him, and nothing left for himself but cold hatred. And weeping blindly, wondering what he was putting out exactly—a life or his own right to life—he released the man, half prepared for him to jump up and do

109

him in. But the man's glassy eyes were unchanging beneath the water, and Saw Lay tramped back to shore amid the shots and shouts of the surrounding battle, knowing only that it was too late, that too much had happened, that in some sense he, too, was finished.

And nothing revived him—not even his effete efforts to organize the Karens politically at the conclusion of the war. Nothing, that was, until the early evening in 1946, when, after the Aung San rally in Fytche Square, he spotted Benny from his stoop and was immediately seized by a painful, begrudging, remorseful love that seemed physically to shake him back into life. It was a sensation—of being sharply resuscitated—that only intensified the next day, when Benny sent a car for him, and he was driven in a downpour from the capital to the nearby suburb of Insein, where the rain fell off and the sun reappeared and the car all at once ascended a glittering, lush hillside toward a sprawling house in which she—in which *they*—still existed.

The entire family met him at the door, a baby in Khin's arms, and tough little Johnny half hidden behind Benny's wide stance. Only Louisa stood a step apart from the group, and he was immediately taken by the ethereal prettiness of her face, by her wild black ringlets and deep, mysterious eyes, which she raised to meet his with an open defiance crossed with expectancy. How could he have left them? she asked silently but unmistakably. And how could he have taken so long to return? She must have been five already. Saw Lay stooped before her and held out one of the flowers he'd brought.

"Boo boo," he said. He held the bright pink bloom farther out toward her knowing glance.

"Boo boo," she said after a pause. At last, the impression of the old child emerged in her face, and she smiled.

"Are you unwell?" he heard Khin ask.

"Khin!" Benny corrected her. "For God's sake! What a greeting! Here our poor friend is still recovering from the harrowing things he's seen . . ."

Only now, as Saw Lay stood and took in the husband and wife, did he recognize the overlay of shame in Benny's rebuke, as though he were embarrassed not just by what Khin had said, but also by the person she'd become, by her diminished youth and beauty. True, she was altered, but not all for the worse. Her new status had hardened her, glossed her up, and the sheen of her silk garments along with the tightness of her hairstyle matched the new angles in her cheeks. Yet something burning in her eyes suggested hardness's counterpart: the liquid heat of restlessness, of longing—of worry for him? In spite of a note of caution now sounding in his chest, he lowered his eyes to the child on her hip.

If Louisa's fierceness had been drawn straight from Benny's pugilism, this baby—happy and hapless, poor girl—had a dullness, an easily pleased, conciliatory disposition that was as much a denial of Benny's paternity as was her slight Karen nose, her fine black hair and Asiatic eyes. He held a finger out to her curious, outstretched hand, whose clasp set his heart beating, so that he found himself flashing the baby girl an oafish, quivering grin. There was no question. No question. No need for speculation.

"I am changed," he said, in response to Khin's question, he supposed.

"As we all are," she said, drawing the baby closer to her breast. Yet the desperation with which she quickly glanced at Benny told him that nothing had changed about her loyalties.

Over the next months, they almost fell back into their easy prewar camaraderie.

At great risk to himself, Benny started up a bottling plant called Mingala Waters and another business called the Karen Trading Corporation—the first to generate cash and the second to launder it (the idea being to purchase and stockpile arms in case the Karen National Union had reason to revolt). But Benny couldn't yet give up on the British, and Saw Lay soon went along with his plan to send a delegation of Karens to London in order to plead the Karen case ("A 'goodwill mission'—that's what we'll call it. A goodwill mission to London, during which *you'll* sit shoulder to shoulder with Atlee's men"). In London, Saw Lay did what he could to play into British sympathies, even loosening up to the extent that he was able to share a few inebriated hours in entertaining talk about his favorite British authors and actresses with the likes of the Labour Party's Lord Pethick-Lawrence at the luminous Claridge's Hotel. But Atlee's buttoned-up ministers—who listened politely enough to his (pained) words of thanks for how the British had delivered them from the Japanese, and to his (too emotional) reminder of how the long-loyal Karens needed an autonomous state that he hoped might exist within the British Commonwealth even if Burma itself gained independence from it—ultimately distanced themselves from their predecessors' protectorship of the Karens. ("We're terribly grateful for what you have done," one particularly sympathetic minister said as he escorted Saw Lay to the door. "Without you, Aung San might never have come around. But I can't imagine how our officers thought they had the right to promise you statehood in exchange for your service. They overstepped. Yes, they overstepped. Very unfortunate.") In the end, they were advised to throw in their lot with the Burmans.

That betrayal seemed only to redouble the tenuous bond being forged between Benny and Saw Lay again (just as Louisa coming upon the rifles in Benny's study soon drew them together in their guilt). Together they smarted from the sting, in January 1947, of Aung San being invited to Buckingham Palace ("Even Churchill is in disbelief," Benny noted, reading a dispatch from one of his London contacts, "saying—listen—'I certainly did not expect to see U Aung San, whose hands were dyed with British blood and loyal Burmese blood'"— meaning Karen and Kachin and Chin blood—"'marching up the steps of Buckingham Palace as the plenipotentiary of the Burmese Government'"). Together they chafed at Aung San's victorious return to Burma and his hubristic assertion that he alone had determined the country's fate ("And was it not *I*," the ruler proclaimed, "who pulled Burma out of the stage in which she was held in regard by neither men nor dogs, to a stage in which her affairs have attracted the attention of the world?"). Together they argued against a naive faith in Aung San's "principle" of Frontier rights, prompting the Karens to walk out of the conference that the Burman leader soon staged at Panglong, at which Shans, Kachins, and Chins agreed to terms that some argued paved the way for a future Burma of semiautonomous ethnic states ("But read the fine print," Benny made the case to anyone who would listen; "what he wants to give us is *minority* rights"). And when, in April, Aung San publicly and repeatedly threatened to "smash" anyone opposing his national objectives ("We will allow freedom of speech, freedom of press, and freedom to agitate," the leader asserted, "but if the opposition abuses these freedoms they will be *smashed* . . . Try whatever tactics you wish to take over the power that is now in our hands, but we will *smash* anyone resorting to tactics that hurt the people and the State . . . Go on and agitate, but agitate unfairly and you will be *smashed*"), they felt jointly sickened and justified.

Still, Saw Lay had the sense that, for all their political unity, he and Benny were avoiding the treacherous terrain of something that still lay between them: not the subject of Khin, precisely; not even the truth about what had happened between Saw Lay and her one night; but something more proximate—Saw Lay's singular devotion to the mother and child. It was very possible, Saw Lay knew deep down, that the only thing keeping him fighting for the Karen cause, with which he felt himself becoming more disenchanted every day, was the chance it gave him to be near Khin and the baby.

For her part, Khin seemed to retreat with each passing week further into a world made up exclusively of the children and the servants, and further into a silence, whenever she was around Saw Lay, that anyone else would have taken for aloofness. There were whole days when the only glimpse he had of her was when he ambled into the kitchen ostensibly in search of something to eat or drink; even if he found her alone at the table, she seemed to struggle to speak a word to him. And he understood that her reluctance to address him was an expression of her desire to keep the peace between them, even as it admitted to some war still going on within her. Not that she gave any sign of wanting him. But his presence clearly aroused her anxiety.

And the more time he spent in the house, the more sure he was that this anxiety extended to the other family members in a mysterious way. Sometimes, when he happened to be sitting with Benny and Khin together after dinner—listening to the same rain outside, drinking the last drops of the same sherry, being moved by the same plaintive or jubilant music drifting off the gramophone, watching the older children stage a play or read aloud from a book of English poetry—he would catch a glimpse of Khin looking up from her knitting needles at Benny, or gazing mournfully out the window at the mists rolling down the hillside while Grace napped in her arms, and it would come to him that nothing had been resolved between them. That they were merely holding their breath, like everyone else in the country. And that even the children, with their fierce love of play and ever-watchful eyes, and Benny, with his reassuring glances and swaggering ways, were uncertain, and that their uncertainty was the measure of hers with Saw Lay.

Then it came: the break in the peace, theirs and the country's.

On the nineteenth of July, in that year of 1947, sirens began to wail over the radio, and a shaken and tearful broadcaster announced, "At ten thirty-seven this morning, our leader and liberator, General Aung San, was tragically martyred during a cabinet meeting at the secretariat, along with eight others. He leaves behind a nation in mourning, a wife, two boys, and a daughter."

Immediately, rumors spread that the assassins—figures in fatigues who had burst out of an army jeep into the secretariat before

114

opening fire and escaping through an exit on Sparks Street—were agents of some Western party wanting to shut down what progress Aung San had made with the minorities. But that made no sense, Saw Lay and Benny agreed. Indeed, evidence was soon unearthed linking one of Aung San's Burman political rivals to the murders. And in short order, the rival was tried and convicted of conspiracy to murder, making way for another Thakin to lead Aung San's party, one who had professed great resistance to the idea of semiautonomous ethnic states, and who, unlike his predecessor, hadn't switched sides to join the Allied camp during the war, but had retreated with the Japanese. It was thus doubly heartbreaking when, some months later, around the time that Burman veterans descended on Rangoon incanting the refrain "We want to eat Karen flesh," Attlee signed Burma over to this successor Thakin, U Nu, and the country was granted its cruel independence.

Or triply heartbreaking, because this was when Khin revealed something about Benny that shattered Saw Lay's faith in his friend's nobility. Many evenings around this time, Saw Lay would show up at the house expecting to find Benny, only to be told that his friend was still out at his office or one of the factories, and that Khin, pregnant again, was resting upstairs, and he would find himself playing with Louisa and Johnny, or, reluctantly, with little Gracie (he somehow felt it was a betrayal of both Khin and Benny to do so out of their sight). But on this night, Saw Lay was finishing up the paper and a drink alone in the living room, steeling himself before his return home and another lonely stretch of fitful sleep, when he heard Khin's step on the stair.

He stood, dusting the ash from his lap, and saw her enter the room. She didn't seem at all surprised to find him there, but rather relieved and expectant, though for several moments she just stood by the door, looking at him and clutching her thin fingers over her small, swollen abdomen. Her black hair—always worn tautly back in a chignon—was slightly mussed so that several pieces fell down around her face, giving her a softened look, as though she had just woken, or were coming undone.

"Is there something you need?" he found himself saying uneasily.

The question clearly surprised her, and she glanced around and shut the door, sealing them into the room alone. "Need?" she said. "No. No." She could have been speaking to herself, so lost in thought did she appear. "Only"—she made a little motion toward his package of cigarettes on the table, also sprinkled with ash—"may I?"

He'd never seen her smoke, but he took up the package immediately and held it out to her. The awkwardness with which she approached and then accepted a cigarette and a light touched him, and for a moment he stood bashfully watching her fumble with the thing and take a few meager puffs.

"Has he said anything to you?" she said finally.

"Benny?"

She peered at him with such apparent feeling that he feared she was on the verge, after all these months together again, of speaking about what had happened between them. Instead, she said, "About where he goes every night."

"I don't know what you mean," he bumbled. He'd never thought to wonder about Benny's comings and goings, but the question had him feeling suddenly implicated, guilty.

She took another mouthful of smoke between her lips. "About other women," she said softly.

For a moment, he couldn't speak—her revelation brought up too many contradictory things inside him—and his lapse in composure was enough to cause her to withdraw, both within herself and to a bank of windows on the far side of the room.

"Some nights, he doesn't even bother to return . . . It's not what he does with them that troubles me anymore. It's the question of whether or not he lets himself go. Whether or not it's cost me something, diminished me in his eyes. I keep wondering, is there romance? Talk of love?" Now she hiccupped, or laughed, or choked over a sob, and suddenly became aware of the ash she was scattering over her sarong and the floor. "I'm helpless," she said. "Hopeless."

"Let me," he said, crossing to her, but she hardly seemed to notice when he took the cigarette from between her fingers and went to the table and put it out.

"You think I'm silly." Without anything to occupy her hands, she had begun to wring her beautiful fingers. "Of course there's romance. Of course he tells the others what they want to hear. Of course he believes what he tells them. When Benny gives, he gives everything!"

"Khin—"

"Do you know," she said, her eyes ablaze, "one time I found an address in his pocket? And the next day, while he was away, I took the bus to the capital—I didn't dare have the driver take me. On foot, I found the flat—not at all a dingy corner of the city. Very posh. But I didn't hang my head. I didn't cower. Me, a farmer's daughter." Suddenly, she looked proud in all her glowing shame. "Sometimes I wonder what I would have been capable of if I'd had an education. I could have had my independence, if that's what I wanted—"

"Is it?" he interrupted her, but the question seemed only to annoy her, as though he'd missed her point.

"I rang the bell," she said. "And when a servant came to the door, I asked to be taken to her mistress. She had a very pretty face, the lady of the house. A fair, thin face. A wide mouth with too much lipstick. She was writing some letter at her desk, and if she hadn't looked so startled I would have thought I'd made a mistake. She motioned as though to tell the servant to take me away, but I said, 'Please. Please, just let me talk to you. I don't blame you.' And I meant it. She didn't know me—what I'd been through with Benny, everything I'd given him. 'I'm not here to insult or blame you,' I said. 'I only want to know what happened. I want to understand. Is it—is it romantic?'"

Khin blushed, shamed all over again by her question, it seemed to Saw Lay, or by the vulnerability it betrayed.

"Do you know what she said to me?" Khin stared at Saw Lay almost hostilely. "She put down her pen and straightened herself in her chair—she never stood to greet me—and she said, with a voice so low it might have been borrowed from a monk, 'That is for him to tell you.' And she said, 'You must find the trust to be honest with each other.' The bitch."

Khin's mouth was trembling, and she touched it with her fingers as though to silence it. But she wasn't done. "I wanted to say, 'Do you think *you* can trust him? Do you think he isn't having his way with some other girl—with me practically every night? He's the worst kind of liar!'"

With these last words, she threw her hands over her face, and he stood looking in bewilderment at the slope of her curved back and thin shoulders. How alone she was, even as she held another life within the contours of her body—still supple, though aging, and crying out to him to be held.

"Don't hate him, Khin," he said.

"Why shouldn't I?" he heard her say from behind her hands.

Because we have done the same to him. Because we began what he has continued. "Because you love him, and that trumps disloyalty," he said.

Now she raised her eyes to his. "It's you I love," she said with a frankness that startled him.

And a moment passed, as he stood catching his breath, before he grasped the meaning of that frankness, which spoke of steadiness, and not of passion's restless doubt and urgency. She might have said: *On the arduous path of life, it is you—you whom I have never wanted—who has not failed me.*

From there, their descent into war was steep.

Khin seemed to hide from the glorious final phases of her pregnancy by busying herself with domestic tasks and ceaselessly knitting (though she must have known that the little sweaters and socks and caps she turned out could never shield any of her children from pain). For his part, pugilist that he was, Benny fixated on the injustice that had become his rallying cry, taking the helm when the Karens orchestrated a peaceful and ultimately useless nationwide demonstration that called for an avoidance of civil war, an end to violence, equity among all ethnic groups, and the immediate creation of a separate Karen state. In some sense, too, Saw Lay was guilty of losing himself to the call of history in the making, to the intoxications of being pressed up against the shifting political face of the country. Yet he understood that their cause was also a distraction for him—from Khin, from Grace, from the chances he'd lost at love.

And a distraction from what he was increasingly noticing about Benny—about his unfaithfulness to Khin, which could rear up in the most unsullied corners of their lives (even in the *nursery*, for God's sake, where Saw Lay spied Benny eyeing the jiggly rear end of the nanny—a plain, plump Karen girl named Hta Hta, who couldn't have been more than nineteen, and to whom Gracie was particularly devoted). Saw Lay held his tongue about these lapses. Oh, he held his tongue, much as he knew he couldn't forever hold off having it out with Benny.

Amid the rising mayhem across the country, Benny's own capacity for avoidance (of anything to do with what should matter to him personally, thought Saw Lay) seemed to consolidate. After dinner each night, when the children had been excused from the table, Benny would drink tea and ask Khin about her day and watch Saw Lay defiantly quell his agitation with Scotch, and then he would say something cryptic about the dangerous state of affairs for their people. And Saw Lay would think: *Better to draw guns and finish one another off! Anything but this painful constriction of friendship, anything but this politeness!* He wondered how the man could stand never saying a word about raising a child he must have known wasn't his. Then it would come to him that Benny's silence was an expression of his nobility, for by means of it he avoided the trap of laying blame.

119

In June, Khin gave birth to her fourth child, a girl called Molly, and though Saw Lay was relieved that both the mother and the child came through the ordeal unscathed, he was wounded by the further evidence of Benny's claim on her. And when rumors swept through the streets of an alleged Burma Army operation—Operation Aung San—calling for "the elimination of the Karens first and then other hill people," he told himself that it was only a matter of time before it would be too late to redress either the wounds he suffered or those that marred his friendship with Benny.

Though not one of the rifles stockpiled around Benny's compound was yet fired, Saw Lay knew the violence they would do was already inevitable. Still, he and Benny, in solidarity with the Mons, approached Nu about the question of a separate Karen-Mon state. The government responded by arming Burman irregulars, who proceeded to fire on Karen neighborhoods unprovoked. Then on Christmas Eve, while the congregated inhabitants of two Karen villages were singing carols at midnight, Burman policemen launched hand grenades into their church, fired on the survivors, and torched every last structure.

Hundreds more Karens were murdered during the first weeks of 1949. Had the time come for armed revolt? Together, Saw Lay and Benny insisted that Karen leadership request another meeting with Prime Minister Nu, and a date was set for the thirty-first of January. But on the thirtieth, Nu named Ne Win "Supreme Commander of All Defense Forces and Police Forces," thereby removing every last military impediment to Burman xenophobia; and that same night shots were fired across Benny's compound into the Karen village of Thamaing, while now eight-year-old Louisa shook with fever, and Khin—unable to bring down the fever with paste—pleaded with Benny to fetch a healer from the besieged village.

"Let me," Saw Lay said as Benny threw on his coat in the dark entryway.

"She's my child—" Benny countered, and a spasm of contrition instantly passed over his face.

"All the more reason to stay with her—with them. Don't risk it, Benny. I can be down and back with the healer in a quarter hour—"

There was a thundering blast from the bottom of the hill, followed by a clap of light that briefly illuminated the lifelessness of the room behind them. The children and staff were hiding with Khin among the rifles on the floor of Benny's study. But as if in that clap of light Benny had seen a vision of a world deprived of the family he'd forgotten to cleave to, he became very still, riveted by horror. "I'll have to take them away," he told Saw Lay finally, "to Khuli or Tenasserim . . ." He didn't continue: *And will you come with us?*

"Of course, my place will be on the front lines," Saw Lay said after a pause. He had the feeling of falling, of the overstretched thread that had drawn their spirits together all at once snapping. *So this is the end,* he thought.

And how strange that it had come at the very moment the revolution had begun.

9

Into the Trees

I n February—while the Karen revolution entered its first tragic
weeks, and the Kachins joined in the revolt, and government troops
mutinied, and major towns including Mandalay and Prome fell to
various "insurgent" armies—Benny hired an airplane to transport
the family, along with many Karen civilians, to Thaton, the capital of
an old Mon kingdom on the Tenasserim plains in southern Burma,
and a cease-fire area.

If Louisa sensed something of her past in the house they rented
in Thaton, a house that stood on tree-trunk-like pilings over beaten
earth—if the stench of the moldering ground under this house took
her back to the murky days of Daddy's capture in Tharrawaddy—if
this escape reminded her vaguely of the earlier one to Khuli—she
pretended not to have a care. Beside the house was an ancient city
wall overgrown with weeds and vines, and beyond it rose a steep hill
topped by a white-and-gold pagoda, and every day she and Johnny—
liberated from the constraints of regular baths and piano practice
and school hours—played marbles and dug for yellow clay, or else
raced after their new Mon friends to the pagoda's pinnacle, where
they kicked off their shoes and imagined they were birds about to
catch a breeze. On a breeze, the lumps in their throats could melt
away.

Daddy had insisted on bringing along Louisa's accordion, and at
night he roared with laughter as she wrestled with the clunky thing,
squeezing out melodies that were alternately jarring and jaunty. She

understood in her way that his laughter was as desperate as her need to provoke it, and she longed to keep playing, to keep laughing, to keep outrunning misery and Mama's reproving eyes.

It was Ducksworth, finally, who caught up with them in April— "Mr. Ducksworth, my dear old friend—excuse me, *Lieutenant* Ducksworth," Daddy said after the pale man in Burma Army garb showed up by the foot of the stairs of their rented house, with a strange profusion of apologies and a handwritten letter from Prime Minister Nu.

That letter, Daddy explained to the children while Ducksworth waited outside and Mama packed Daddy's traveling bag, was a request that Daddy meet Nu for a tête-à-tête in Moulmein—"So we might bring this mayhem to a right end and get on with our lives," Daddy said. "This is wonderful, wonderful—no?" (Wonderful, but why could Louisa see fright in Daddy's eyes? And why had Mr. Ducksworth's breath given off the smell of guilt—why in that man's eager, aggressive smile had she seen the look of lying?)

Mama shivered as she dropped long bamboo tubes of steamed sticky rice into Daddy's bag and asked Hta Hta—the only servant they'd brought along—to press a pair of Daddy's trousers for the journey.

"Khin," Daddy called to her. "Come."

When Mama wouldn't stop fussing with the eggs she was boiling, Daddy went and took her by the hand and pulled her into a circle with the children—all of whom, Louisa noticed, had become very silent, absorbed in listening for signs of imminent menace.

"There's hope, you know," Daddy said quietly to them, as Mama began to cry. "There's more hope than ever before. We're very fortunate that nothing terrible has happened to us so far—that we're here together. I'm not afraid, Khin."

Usually Mama and Daddy clung to their own languages, to their own friends and their own lives. But now Mama fell against Daddy's neck and clung to him.

"I'll kill that man when I grow up!" Johnny shouted.

"Don't say that," Daddy scolded him. "Mr. Ducksworth is only doing his job."

Why were they speaking as though Daddy had been captured already? Louisa felt apprehension darken her own smile, a smile she pressed upon her siblings, upon Daddy, because it was possible— wasn't it?—to keep him safe with her joy. "How will you get to Moulmein, Daddy?" she asked lightly.

"Well, I imagine by airplane."

"And how long will you fly in it?"

"Not long—a few hours at most."

"Will it be very big—or small—the plane?" Johnny chimed in. Yes, talk of planes was a means of evading their alarm and even the permanent darkness that waited for them all.

"When I return, I'll tell you about it," Daddy said, trying to smile back at them. "Now don't look as I leave—don't watch me. I don't want to glance back and see unhappy faces. I want to go with the vision of these shining eyes in my mind . . . There, now even Gracie is smiling!"

And little Gracie—the most vulnerable of them in every sense— suddenly broke into soundless sobs and clung to Louisa's neck.

All that night, as the silence deepened around her—the silence of Daddy's absence—Louisa lay on the floor of the room she shared with her siblings and concentrated on Daddy's journey to Moulmein. She saw him sitting beside Ducksworth in the shuddering plane, the descent through a sky shivering with rain, and then sunlight as Daddy disembarked by the turquoise sea. But try as she might, she could not stay the vision of what came next: soldiers rising up out of that sea, surrounding Daddy like a wave, and Ducksworth helplessly standing by.

She was woken the next morning by a fearsome moaning surging through the streets. Mama rushed into the room and roused the others before gathering them together on the floor of the dark room. There was a look of dismay on her face as she told them that the Burmans had broken the Thaton cease-fire. "Betrayed," she kept saying. "We've been betrayed." Already, the Burmans were invading the city.

What did it mean for Daddy? Louisa wanted to ask.

But Mama said, "You will die if you make a noise. From now on, you must not cry out, you must not complain. If you are hungry, find a way to feed yourself. If you are thirsty, find a stream. If your body is tired, ignore the tiredness. If you are hurt, let your tears fall only inside." And then, with tears in her own eyes: "God bless you, children."

Right away, they crept out to the bushes behind the house, where they stayed for hours, and when baby Molly complained, Mama suckled her, and when a scream penetrated the woods at their backs, the servant Hta Hta covered the children's ears with the edge of her sarong. Toward dusk, Mama left them, but then she returned with a small sack and some oranges, which she peeled and fed to the older children, and even to Hta Hta, slice by slice. Only at night, when she motioned for them to crawl out behind her and they drew themselves out of the bushes, emerging like shadows under the black dome of the sky, did Mama speak again: "I will try not to lose you, and you must try not to lose me."

How would Daddy find them? Louisa kept the question tucked inside her mouth as she trailed Mama in the moonlight.

"I'm thirsty, Mama," Johnny dared to utter.

Immediately Mama stopped and picked up a stick and whipped his backside. Johnny's lip trembled, but he didn't cry.

"We will find something as we go," she said in an uneven voice.

A man with a horse carriage was waiting for them down the empty road. He took all of them, including Hta Hta, as far as the Thaton train station, which they found heaving with Karens wanting to flee. "Three Karen families were beheaded while trying to escape," one woman on the platform said, and Louisa watched how Johnny and Grace encircled Mama, turning their mute faces up toward hers, as if seeking reassurance that those faces were still attached to their beings.

Near dawn, as blue light washed the sky, they caught a current onto the only train to appear. Wedged as they were among hundreds of other evacuees, Mama's body gave off a warm wave of relief, telling Louisa that now at last, in the shelter of the train's thunder, she might feel free to speak a few words.

"Will Daddy come find us?" she asked.

Light seemed to pass over Mama's features, but then she closed her eyes and sank into her thoughts for a time. "The minute he can," she said in a voice that was not hers.

The train refused to roll past Bilin—a town, Mama explained anxiously, less than thirty miles north of Thaton, and also overrun the previous night by Burman troops. Soon they found themselves carried by tides of refugees along muddy streets littered with bodies and broken glass and burned bricks, to the banks of the Bilin River, the other side of which hadn't yet been breached.

Louisa had assumed until now that Karens were unvaryingly charitable, that whatever a Karen had was what he had to share. But the rafts crossing the Bilin were being controlled by Karens with rifles, and the family had no choice but to wait for the teeming bank to be cleansed of the armed. That first evening, Mama took a small pot from her sack and told Hta Hta to boil water for them to drink—there hadn't been time for her to pack more than a few biscuits and pieces of fruit, which they had already eaten. She asked a family, also waiting on the west bank, if it would be possible for her children to have the crust on the bottom of their pot of rice and chicken curry, and the father bitterly peered into Mama's eyes, pried out the crust, and tossed it into the river.

Louisa knew better than to speak of her hunger that night. But Johnny—when they were huddled in a heap by the fire, trying to sleep alongside the moonlight glittering across the river—broke out all at once, "You shouldn't have asked for their crust, Mama!"

Usually Mama suffered no complaint, though tonight she allowed the gurgle of the river to speak for her awhile. Then she said, "It is better to be in a position of having to ask for charity than to be in the position of never having to ask, children." Her voice was filled with sorrow and deep reserves of tenderness for them. "Most people think it is the other way around—that one is at an advantage having everything." She didn't need to remind them, Louisa knew, that they had recently lived in a world built on such false advantages.

"I would rather have chicken curry!" Johnny cut in.

Mama laughed, along with Hta Hta, and drew Johnny very close to her body, causing Louisa to feel a stab of envy.

"No," Mama said, still laughing. "Ordinary people think of things that way. Don't look down on them for it—they've never been taught differently. They can't imagine that it would be to their benefit spiritually to have to ask for something, to have to become acquainted with their meekness, and to find tremendous strength in it. Why do you think monks beg for alms?"

It was the first time Louisa could remember sleeping under the exposed sky, and as the sounds of war—of shots and snarls and wailing—drifted toward her from the city, she blinked back at the staring stars, and comforted herself with the rustle of the river and the cool water-scented breeze tipping her closer to sleep.

"I know of a root we can search for when dawn breaks," she heard Mama say as she drifted off finally. "It is soft and sweet, and we can mash it with a stone into a delicious cake to be baked over the fire . . . No, don't be jealous, children . . . And don't feel small, even when you have to ask for rice."

The next day, when the west bank was nearly empty, they boarded a raft and crossed the river—on the other side of which, Mama explained, they would make their way over the mountains to a place called Kyowaing, a teak reserve whose governor was a Karen leader and one of Daddy's trusted friends. "We will ask him for shelter," she said. "And until then we will try not to linger."

For three days they hiked upriver, stopping only to forage for edible greens or to gnaw on roots or to collapse into the mud at night. And for three days they were hungry. But the farther they trekked from the fighting frontiers, Louisa noticed, the farther they seemed to stray from cruelty and greed. On the fourth evening, they came to a bamboo hut owned by poor mountain Karens whose table was a carved wooden pan and whose evening meal was salted watery rice. The juices from the rice flowed to the edge of the pan, and Louisa ate with relish, shyly saying it was the best meal of her life.

Through bursts of rain then, they continued up a mountain and crossed some of the most breathtaking terrain Louisa had ever seen. Villages shrouded in mist in the early-morning sun, and always a clear stream running by. Hill plantations where rice stalks grew side by side with marigold flowers. The people inhabiting these places had never encountered a car, Mama informed them. The rice they ate came from their fields, vegetables either grown or gathered from the bounty of the forest, fish from the stream, meat from their traps. Their clothes were made with their own looms, dyes from nature. Unmarried girls wore woven white dresses adorned with red strands that fell down to their ankles. Marrying, they donned long tubelike sarongs and short tops woven in black and decorated in the traditional patterns of their village. Their lives were serene, harmonious, and brief. "They know of no artifice," Mama said.

"What is artifice?" Louisa asked her.

"The way one tricks oneself into forgetting that death is nearby."

Sometimes the six of them would sleep in a monastery. Once they sank into sleep on a pile of stinky fruit in someone's storage shed. When their teeth became unpleasantly dirty, Hta Hta searched for a special twig that, when broken, foamed with natural toothpaste.

And when the day was hot, they cleaned their bodies in the cold, clear streams, washing away their old life.

"Where is Daddy?" Grace asked one morning, as they prepared to descend the mountain. Grace gazed down at the thin river, which wound its way back toward Bilin, with the longing of someone who could see, not precisely what she was looking for, but only that it was something she had left behind.

Johnny shot her a punishing look, and the poor girl nearly broke out in sobs again, but then a flock of parrots rose up before them and flew east, transporting Louisa's thoughts to the vaporous distance beyond grief.

As long as they were walking, moving toward the distance, their bodies stayed strong. But when they arrived in Kyowaing, with its British-built brick-and-wood houses and its teak plantation that spread out under the shadow of a far-off pagoda, they immediately fell down and became sick.

The Karen overseer of the plantation, called the "Forest Governor," lived with his wife and their two teenage sons on top of a hill overlooking the teak fields, and while the man himself showered them with fondness—turning a room over to them and bringing them soup that first night—his wife seemed wary and distracted by the silk of Mama's torn, muddied sarong. "Where did you find such fabric?" the woman asked.

The embarrassed Forest Governor gently reprimanded her: "Don't you know this is Saw Bension's wife? He is very rich! The richest man in all of Burma!"

"Not so rich," Mama murmured, and Louisa felt suddenly ashamed of their wealth.

For many days, the children were ill with dysentery, and Louisa also with malaria, and as they languished in their room, Louisa had the sense that they were hiding from the wife, who, unlike her husband and smiling sons, never came to check on or help them (though Mama and Hta Hta hardly slept, and at one point expressed genuine worry for Gracie's life). Hta Hta grew weepy, wondering aloud if her soldier brothers had survived the battles surrounding Insein, and Mama became strained and short-tempered. "Remember what I told you about not making a noise!" she snapped when Louisa and Johnny bickered.

"I can't breathe!" Johnny protested—the close air in the room *did* reek of illness.

"Nevertheless!" Mama scolded him. She was trying to determine their next step, Louisa knew, and in the meantime nearly drowning in stagnation.

One night, they woke to the wife shouting, accusing her husband of being a sinner. Satan was trying to wedge her out of the house! she cried. The children stayed quiet, listening to the woman's evil words. But baby Molly—as if understanding every one of them—screamed in fright, and would not be consoled by Mama's breast.

"Don't worry, children," Mama whispered in the darkness. "Sometimes it is like this between a husband and a wife."

The next morning Mama woke them early. She looked very proud, Louisa noticed, almost as though she were pretending at pride, and had drawn in her eyebrows with ash, powdered her face with rice flour, and washed and mended her sarong. Even her blouse had its pink color back. She led them out of the sleeping house into the fresh open air, and for a time they simply stood on the hilltop, waking up with the day and the view of the houses scattered below. A sleepy stream wound around the enchanted village, which seemed to have settled itself placidly in the mist, tucked into the folds of the slim, still mostly barren teak trees.

"With the first monsoon rains," Mama said, "the new foliage is emerging. Soon the trees will flower and bear fruit."

"Can we eat it, Mama?" Johnny asked.

"Better not," she told them. Then, with a strange sadness on her face: "Better do only what they tell you to until I come back."

Now there were new questions for Louisa to hold in her mouth. Where was Mama going? And why *without* them? And would she be safe? And would *they*?

"You are almost strong again," Mama said. "What is more, Bilin is now in Karen control." She lapsed into silence, and when she spoke again it was in a voice broken by sorrow. "There is not enough room for me in this house," she said. And then she explained that she had brought along several pieces of her jewelry, including her star sapphire earrings, which she would sell in Bilin in order to establish their new life. She would come for them in short time—and they wouldn't have to walk back to Bilin, she would see to that. And in the meantime, Hta Hta was here to care for them, to ensure that they were treated with kindness.

"Why can't you ask them for help a little longer?" Johnny asked. "Isn't it better to be in the position of having to ask?"

"Not when one can help oneself," Mama said. "We can't depend on others forever—we mustn't."

"How will Daddy find us if you are there and we are here?" Louisa found herself asking, and straightaway the question put hurt in Mama's eyes.

"He will know we have gone to friends," Mama said after a pause. "Don't be afraid."

A few minutes later, a group of Karens going down to Bilin came for her. Louisa, whose legs were all at once weak again, stood in a huddle with her siblings on the front steps of the Forest Governor's house to watch her leave.

How elegant and vulnerable Mama seemed, in her petal-pink blouse, her head held high as she walked away from them into the trees.

10

The Cause of Her Need

Saw Lay had been a mistake, though as Khin picked her way down the muddy path leading away from Kyowaing—away from the children about whom she couldn't, even for an instant, bear to think—she wondered if she would ever feel the way she had with him again.

"Khin," he'd said on that appalling night, when he'd failed to rescue Benny from the Japanese in Tharrawaddy, "it should have been me." His sureness about what should have been, in a world in which nothing seemed as it should be, had touched something deep within her. Suddenly, she had become sensitive to the grief in his lamplit eyes—grief that sought a relinquishment that she could provide, if only temporarily. She had gone to him and taken his face in her hand, still nearly innocently. And she had seen for the first time that he had such a fine, well-made face, with such a distinguished jaw—a Karen jaw—and such a vulnerable mouth that parted in the shadows as he looked up at her, and then moaned as she pressed his eyes to her breast. She had still been half expecting a simple consoling caress between them, yet nothing surprised her about the press of his wide hands grasping her buttocks, about his urgent unleashing need to be touched by her and to touch her.

Would she ever be touched that way again? she wondered now, stumbling toward the stream where the group of Karens whom she was following had stopped to rest. In this escape from the Forest Governor's house, it would be easy to believe that she was also essentially innocent, this time merely the victim of another woman's jealousy. But the Forest Governor's quiet interest in her could not be denied, and she had found herself vulnerable not to him (in fact, she had gone out of her way to avoid the man) but to his recognition of her as a woman worth being recognized, worth being wanted even in her deprivation. His stifled yearning for her had pushed her back to the memory of what had happened five years before, when she had melted, during a moment of desperate need, into what had felt like perfect understanding. With Saw Lay she had escaped not just her fear for Benny's life, but also all the agitation that came with loving a man with whom she had never easily been able to speak in her first language, and to whom her Karen tendencies too often had to be explained. She had not known how *very* Karen she was until there was Benny—boisterous, belligerent Benny, who bigheartedly trampled all over her preferences for gentleness and humility and silent attunement to others. And she had not known how isolated she had felt with him until there was Saw Lay.

It will pass, she had reassured herself in the joy of Benny's return from the hands of the Japanese in Tharrawaddy. But then she had seen the extent of his wounds, and the wound that had just been created in her bled all over again. That Benny suspected something had "happened with Saw Lay" and yet wouldn't reveal what he himself had just been through seemed a confirmation of the fundamental condition of their shared isolation in marriage; that he then proceeded not to touch her, not so much as to raise an eyebrow when she became heavy with child, plunged her into despair. Well, as far as he was concerned, the child was his, she inwardly argued. Hadn't they lain together in the days before his capture? Then the child was born, and every day the likelihood of its being Saw Lay's molded itself onto Grace's pretty little features, and Benny's silence enslaved her, Khin, to her original sin.

She had felt trapped within her mistake, hurt and increasingly bitter. When Benny's philandering soon began, she had submitted to his renewed sexual interest in her as she would to a sentence—degradation being the means by which she would pay for her mistake. Oh, she'd profited from the explosion of wealth that his business initiated, but she'd silently judged his foolish faith in what that wealth could buy them and the Karens. And she'd begun to disdain his assumption that he could champion a cause that called for revolution with unbloodied fists. If she had loved Saw Lay—loved him even when he'd reentered their lives and when she'd rebuffed his tentative glances so as to keep her mistake a thing of the past—if she loved Saw Lay still, it was not just for his blood, but for his feeling that he was no better than the cause they rallied around, that he had no more right *not* to fight than the poorest peasant. And if she'd shut herself in with the servants more and more, it was in stoic revolt against the trappings of a world that her children had come to assume was comfortable and secure.

Now, the thought of those children made her stand up from the bank, and she turned, as though to turn her back on them. She was twenty-eight and had already tolerated so many sorrows, so many terrors. She could not now confront another. She must only find a way for her family to endure. And as she followed the Karens, who had begun to wander down the darkening mountain again (doomed, as all Karens were, to wander and wander), she moved swiftly through the gnarled landscape with a feeling of unburdening herself of her load.

The Bilin River was peaceful and green in the fading light when she arrived at the west bank, where a makeshift camp—with temporary barracks and a mess—had been erected for the soldiers and refugees. Exhausted, she gratefully accepted a bowl of rice and fish paste, then went out to sit alone under the trees bending with the breeze on the bank; she couldn't yet pretend to be comfortable visiting with others, even when she gleaned the extent of their further suffering. Such visiting still felt like a betrayal of those she'd left behind, and of Benny.

But as she was raising the first mouthful of warm rice to her lips, she glanced up the bank and saw a soldier she'd last seen in

Khuli. He was sitting alone beside a campfire, playing a harmonica. Lin Htin—or Lynton—that was his name, she remembered. He'd been passing through Khuli on his way to join the Karen levies in the war effort, and for some reason several men in the village had questioned his allegiances. Even then, she'd found his quick, sure manner and laughing poise to be riveting. He was also troublingly good-looking—and at least a few years younger than she was.

As if sensing her stare, he all at once stopped playing and glanced up at her. It was very straightforward, his stare—it made her blush, though she doubted he could see the evidence of her embarrassment from twenty feet away. She gave him a little reluctant smile and looked back down into her bowl of rice, which she suddenly felt self-conscious about consuming alone. The harmonica started up again—to cry out the first part of a Karen ballad she hadn't heard since childhood—then stalled.

"Join me," she heard his relaxed voice call to her.

How ridiculously false her response, of surprise, of bewilderment, of hesitation. Soon, she was plodding toward him with her bowl, through the mud and a swirl of mosquitoes, the echoes of self-recrimination droning in her ear. Why was she coming, like a good puppy, at his first command, when all she really wanted was to be left alone? He continued to stare hard at her (there wasn't a trace of Karen modesty about him, was there?), smiling broadly when she sat. And his smile only increased her sense that she must untangle herself from the situation as quickly as she'd ensnared herself in it.

"Just who I was hoping to see," he said, but the comment was directed at someone else—at a soldier, a doughy, thick-lipped, smiling boy who lumbered up to the fire with a bulging sack and a pot of water.

Lynton picked up his harmonica and proceeded to puff out the sad tune again, thoroughly ignoring her and the boy, who went about making his senior's supper, measuring a finger of rice, putting the pot down to boil, pulling an array of mushrooms, bamboo shoots, and fiddle-leaf fern from his sack, along with two small birds. Well, she *had* wanted to be left to her thoughts, hadn't she? And there was something comforting about the respite that this togetherness allowed her. She relaxed into a state of merely eating and listening and observing as Lynton played and the boy plucked and cleaned the birds, and then scattered the charred wood, moved the pot to the embers, salted and skewered his finds, stoked the fire, and—with forked branches that he drove into the ground—constructed a stand on which to set Lynton's dinner.

Only when the birds began to drip and the mushrooms were sizzling did Lynton speak again. "You'll have some of Sunny's delicious cooking, won't you?" he said, putting his harmonica in his pocket while Sunny, the boy, smiled sweetly at her. Sunny held out his hand for her bowl. When she gave it to him with thanks, he prodded a bird and some vegetables onto her leftovers.

For a while, they ate in silence as Sunny dismantled the stand and headed off to bathe in the river. It was ridiculous, but the juiciness of the meal (more decadent than any she'd had since leaving Thaton), the way its oils coated her fingers, made her self-conscious all over again, and she felt her color rise with Lynton's eyes, which expectantly met hers.

"Do they know what has happened to your husband?" he said, jolting her. She was suddenly afraid of losing her composure.

"Not as yet." She put her bowl down, her appetite all at once gone. "Is it known—by everyone—that he was supposed to meet with the prime minister?"

Lynton set his own bowl aside and felt for something in another pocket—his tobacco and paper, she saw. He silently rolled himself a cigarette, which he held out to her with a questioning look, and which she refused—and quickly regretted refusing. Then he put the cigarette to his lips, lit it, and fell into his thoughts, as though forgetting her question. In the flames of the fire, he seemed to see something painful; but his eyes drifted up to the deepening sky, and all the pain behind them instantly vanished.

"Generally speaking," he said at last, his face cast up to the emerging stars, "the *everyone* of whom you speak is utterly stupid." He took a deep suck of his cigarette. "Of course, the higher-ups in our disorganized mess of a military have heard of U Nu's supposed summons of your husband, and they say it was naive of Saw Bension to assume the meeting would ever happen."

"Why do they assume my husband assumed that?" she said quickly. The truth was she had struggled with her own private judgment of Benny's unquestioning trust in Ducksworth's—and Nu's—word. Yet it had seemed *possible* to her that Benny knew Ducksworth could be leading him to his end, and that his reluctance to resist was a willful one, meant to spare her and the children, just as his reluctance to defend himself with the Japanese had been.

Now Lynton took measure of her with the cigarette between his lips. "A drink?" he said. When she nodded, he pulled a bottle of whiskey and a metal mug from behind a nearby log, and poured out some of the whiskey for her. "There is something courageous," he said, removing the cigarette from his lips, "about Saw Bension's trust, no? Maybe it takes an outsider to trust the Burmans. Someone whose ancients haven't been bitten by them again and again."

A cold wind blew in from over the river, carrying with it the memory of the mountain that she had traversed with the children. She shuddered, and Lynton's eyes narrowed on her again.

"Drink," he commanded her.

She did as he said, gulping the heat down, but the alcohol only further agitated her. "Is it true what they say," she spat out, "that you spied for the Japanese?"

Now *he* seemed to have been stung. He laughed—a brief, defensive chortle—and bowed his head, inhaling from his cigarette and then stubbing it out on a rock. "Who told you that?" he said finally.

When she didn't respond—she'd forgotten who exactly had spread the rumor to her—he went on: "Our people are too simple. Their trusting nature can make them untrustworthy."

Without another word, he reached for some of his things behind
the log, put on a brimmed hat, and threw down a jacket like a makeshift blanket. Then he took a rifle in one hand and stretched out his
long body, tilting the brim of the hat over his eyes.

"You might want to watch for the python," he said sleepily, hat
still over his eyes. "At least fifteen feet long. Before dinner, I saw it
slither out of the water and swallow a rat Sunny had his eye on."

Something in the reeds rustled, and she gave a little yelp, causing him to chuckle.

"Why don't you sleep in the barracks?" she asked angrily.

"I don't like the reek of the group."

"And you're not fighting *for* the group?"

"Good night, Khin."

That he knew her name—had known it all along—set her heart
beating hard.

And for a moment more, all she could do was glare down at
this undeniably beautiful young man, bound for battle, with only the
dying fire by his side to warm him.

Bilin's Burman residents had fled along with their soldiers, and in a
vast brick split-level, amid the ghosts of a family with at least three
or four children, Khin quickly—if temporarily—established herself.
She used the proceeds from the sale of her jewelry to purchase a
hand-crank sewing machine and to hire three Karen women to help
her run a tailoring shop (now the only one in town). The women
were unskilled in the sewing arts but quick learners; soon she had
trained them to operate the sewing machine and to embroider, cro-
chet, and knit with the needles that she crafted by burning the point
of bamboo sticks in ash. In exchange for vegetables or rice or peanuts
to be ground into oil, she and the women began to turn out not just
hemmed sarongs and men's shirts, but also dainty dresses for girls

and even festive sweaters—turquoise with orange designs, scarlet with violent streaks of purple.

I will get the children, Khin said to herself with every passing day; but then another day passed, at the end of which she plunged hollowly into sleep by the embers of the kitchen fire (she couldn't bear to sleep in any of the family members' beds). *The children are safer beyond the river,* she thought. Or, *I might hear of Benny's whereabouts and need to go to him. If the children are here, I will have to leave them again.* Her instincts told her that, much as the children might be suffering with the Forest Governor and his wife, they were better off without her— because her circumstances were unreliable, and because something inside her had become equally unreliable, even as, with every hour, she reliably put together a semblance of another life.

And she *was* always searching for Benny—writing letters to Karens near and far, never failing to ask passing soldiers if they'd heard of his whereabouts or seen Saw Lay, who was supposed to be somewhere close to the delta leading a brigade. About two months after she'd set up the shop, one of her customers came rushing to tell her that a white Indian had been admitted to the Bilin hospital and that people were saying it was Saw Bension. She fled to the hospital, nearly more frightened of finding Benny than of continuing to live in the unknown. That unknown had allowed her to keep on soldiering through, hadn't it? Yes, she realized, when she saw—instantly, and with enormous relief—that the balding, blood-drained, mortally wounded man who lay unconscious with a gaping mouth was not Benny. A sudden vision of her husband's or children's suffering would have been the end of the hope that allowed her to work on their behalf. She had the sense that, separated from one another, and unaware of one another's fates, they were all in a kind of indeterminate state, a kind of limbo, where they were just managing to escape outright disaster.

And as though to widen the limits of that limbo, and to avoid her confrontation with fate itself, she added to her daily burden in Bilin by starting to spend half of nearly every night in the hospital, ministering to the wounds that reeked of rotten meat and that fouled her mind with fear for Benny and the children. A teaspoon of Dettol in a gallon of water: that was the antiseptic mixture she used to clean the wounds and sterilize her thoughts. But not every man whom she treated survived, and not every man was purified by his suffering; many seemed to have been poisoned by suffering itself, reduced to nothing more than a shattered limb, blinded eyes. And, absorbed in the small task of aiding them, she became tainted, too—almost fatalistically resigned to her separation from Benny and the children.

Then one night a stretcher with a dead child was brought in and another with the gravely injured mother, who wouldn't allow Khin to nurse her and wouldn't trouble anyone with her loss. She must have been around forty, the mother. One of her legs had been blown apart by a mortar, and when the question of amputation came up, she merely held up a hand and waved it across her face, as though to wave away the question and her life along with it. Khin crouched down beside her, while the woman took her in with a strange recognition, as if to acknowledge the torment Khin must be enduring having to go on in this world. Yet in her final, fitful hours the woman was racked by terror of further suffering, and the difficult death drove such fear into Khin that she determined to go for the children right away.

But as she was preparing for the journey the following night, tidying the shop after her hires had gone—her body seething, close to dropping along with the heat and the last light—*he* showed up. Lynton. Eleven weeks had passed since she had last stood in his presence, and he was more beautiful than she had wanted to remember him being, so unblemished, so relaxed, she had to wonder if he had simply been loitering and avoiding life all this time. He stood in the front doorway of the house, his hands in his pockets, his eyes radiant and refreshed in the lamplight, giving her the impression that war was serving him, rather than the other way around.

"You don't remember me?" he asked.

She heard the rumble of an army truck down the road, and then silence, and then her heart banging in her chest. "I am going for my children."

"Alone?"

"You don't think I can manage?" She was suddenly sure that she couldn't go another day without someone—without him—to lean on.

"You'll be fine," he said softly.

Something about the way he'd said it made all the heat of her hurt—hurt she hadn't known she was feeling—gather in her throat, behind her eyes. She turned, not wanting him to see it, and busied herself folding two sweaters while he silently looked on.

He had to be sent away, she told herself; she was a married woman alone, and his showing up at nightfall was a form of degradation. What was more, the hurt he was causing her by presenting himself here was more unbearable than the hurt of her having no one, because it reminded her how impossibly and inevitably alone she was.

"Khin," she heard him say, just as softly, and she set the sweaters down, turned out the lamp, and crossed to the hallway that led to the kitchen, where her sleeping mat lay under the mosquito net.

There, the only thing to waver was the firelight. He came to her, and she submitted to the thing inside her—the force—that knew exactly what she wanted, that waged a revolution against her strength.

And he was a force to be reckoned with, she discovered. In the firelight, without a word, he possessed her comprehensively, almost dutifully, as though her need was his cause, and he was there to serve it, to very thoroughly serve it. And that service was like a trapdoor through which, all at once, she fell, blessedly ceasing to exist.

Or blessedly coming into a new existence—one where she was unleashed from her chronic will to cease, to escape the deadening strength that had been her burden since she'd held her choking father's intestines in her hands and survived. This new version of herself was anything but unscathed. And it hurt, it hurt terribly, when Lynton—his service suddenly completed—threw on his fatigues and left her alone under the mosquito net.

She found him smoking on the stoop under the stars. "I have soup inside," she said, embarrassed, clutching her already bound sarong to her waist.

"Sunny will be waiting," he told her, not coldly. "We're heading off early."

"To the front?"

"When we're back, I'll look in on you and the children."

He put out his cigarette and stood, turning to her so frankly, she felt more naked than she'd just been. "Is there anything you need?"

The tender way he'd asked the question told her she hadn't been a disappointment—at least not entirely. "When will you be back?" she ventured.

He didn't reel from her, but something about the way his jaw tensed, the way his head slightly shifted even as his eyes still burned with something like desire, conveyed everything she needed to know about his need for freedom. And suddenly—because of his stiffness, because of what she'd just been through at the hospital—she pictured him dead, lying stiffly in the reeds with no one but Sunny to acknowledge his passing.

A few days later, she arrived in Kyowaing to find the children dressed in tatters and hesitant to meet her eye, hesitant even to acknowledge the gifts she'd brought on the back of an elephant—tins of condensed milk and meat and biscuits, silk sarongs and sweaters and embroidered dresses. As though to seek out the Forest Governor's wife's permission to enjoy, the children peered guiltily at the woman rather than face Khin—until Louisa snatched up a dress, vanished with it into the back room, and emerged minutes later resplendent yet somehow as though in costume, or armor.

The dress—pale blue and dainty—had been made for a little girl; but *this* girl was clearly no longer the child who in Tharrawaddy had delighted in the frock cut from Khin's eyelet petticoat—not even the child who'd pranced around her sixth birthday party showing off her flaring skirt while trying to swing dance with Saw Lay. No, this person, this eight-year-old, stood poised in the Forest Governor's kitchen, staring back at Khin with wounded pride, as if to prove something—that she was still Khin's daughter? Still intact? And she *was* intact, wasn't she? She was more beautiful, even, though the dress was all wrong on her—too childish, and hanging from her lengthened frame in a way that made her seem overdeveloped. And she was more beautiful as only a full-grown woman usually could be; it wasn't just that she'd shed much of her appearance of innocence (and Khin hoped that shedding had nothing to do with the weight Hta Hta was worrisomely gaining around her waist); it was that a self-possession more radiant than any innocence now shone from her, and this self-possession had been steeled by experience, Khin saw—by disappointment, heartache, and something that appeared to be a sense of her own power of body and mind.

"Take it off," Khin found herself instructing Louisa. "Now's not the time for that kind of thing." Khin gave the wife an embarrassed, commiserating shrug, as though she were more in league with the woman than with her own daughter.

Could it be, she wondered later, as she led the children away from the place, that she'd been responding not only to the other woman's envy, but also to something like envy rumbling in her own unruly center?

Back in Bilin, they were all soon safely installed in the house that was almost their own, where Khin's seamstresses were skillful and kind, and where Lynton shortly reappeared to press his smiling eyes on them as though he were an old family friend.

Lynton—mysterious, ardent, given to flashes of hilarity and somber distraction . . . Over the following months, he was no stranger to Khin's bed. True, he could sometimes disappear to the front lines for weeks; but he seemed to exist apart from the war when he was with them. And, with him, Khin seemed to discover a life as true as the one that had come before.

Every morning, Louisa, Johnny, and Grace would scamper off to school in shoes made from bits of blown tires, while Hta Hta watched Molly, and Khin put in her hours at her tailoring shop or the cheroot factory that she soon started (located in a rented house, where her hires seasoned dried palm sheets rolled into the mild cigars). The afternoons were for the hospital, where she continued to volunteer, just as she continued to write letters of inquiry about Benny during breaks. Then, around five, Lynton would show up at the house if they were lucky, a cigarette between his lips, a bottle of something in his fist, a pocketful of candy or marbles or bottle caps for the children, who, save for Louisa, would race out into the dusty yard to greet him, as he pretended not to know what they were after.

They rarely spoke Benny's name—out of respect for him, it seemed to Khin, but also to shelter this new life from his memory—just as they chose to talk around what Lynton had become to her. They were so desperate for laughter, for the respite of carefree hours, and it was easier to find their own smiles by sequestering unpleasant subjects to the realm of private thought. The topic of the war at large—and the truth that this provisional happiness was at that war's mercy—was also kept to a minimum. Certainly, they saw soldiers sauntering through the streets, heard references to fighting in conversations between Lynton and his friends, witnessed war's horrors in every wound that Khin nursed at the hospital, where the children were sometimes brought along because, Khin told them, "We must not pretend suffering doesn't exist." But those reminders of trouble also instructed them to enjoy what and while they could.

Now and then, Khin would be laughing with a seamstress about something one of the children had said, or taking her evening air and refreshment with Lynton, and the thought of Benny—of what he might be suffering, of the possibility that he was already dead— would strike her so startlingly she would struggle to get her bearings, as though after a vertiginous nightmare. And, gazing around at the pieces of her new life—the holier-than-thou neighbor scowling at them from a window, the children squabbling over a chicken in the yard, the cigarette drooping from Lynton's lips, Hta Hta's undeniably swelling belly (what had happened to the poor girl while she'd been in the care of the Forest Governor?)—Khin would seem to see through to the hopeless transience of it all. She would flush with shame, recognizing how far they had fallen, until certain words she'd heard years before would come back to her, words spoken by the rabbi of Rangoon that struck her now like an answer to a long-awaited question, like a pardon: *We must find a way to rejoice in our circumstances. We must find a way to do more than endure.*

Lynton rejoiced and endured by drinking and joking and making music—if possible with his soldiers—and often after dark, when the air was cooler, the house transformed into a dance hall of sorts. Lynton would play his harmonica or the ukulele he'd found in a trash heap, while his men took turns spinning Hta Hta and the seamstresses and Khin around, until Khin's limbs were so drowsy with release she almost fell down in joy. If the mood became too earnest, Lynton would break out with one of his absurd stories. ("I tell you what happened to Sunny the other day? Soldier from another brigade says to him, 'This is a very good herb, a delicious herb—put some in Lynton's food and he'll never replace you.' And Sunny, loyal bodyguard that he is, though a bit daft—I hate to break it to you, Sunny—oh, look how he's blushing! Well, Sunny has a voracious appetite—goes without saying—and wanting to protect me, he decides to taste the curry he's made with the herb before giving me any, and it's so good he has another mouthful, and another, and soon I find him beside an empty pot, dozing in the rain, right there in the mud, with a smile plastered on his face, and the soldier who gave him the herb is laughing his head off over him. I missed out on something good, didn't I, Sunny?") And as if unable to stop partaking in the merriment—for fear of stumbling upon its permanent absence—Lynton would sometimes leave the house arm in arm with the soldiers, singing and joking as they staggered out of sight. "You're not staying?" Khin didn't dare ask him. Something told her that to lay claim to him in any way would only taint the joy they'd found together, a joy whose essential feature was freedom—from their pasts, from responsibility to anything but the pleasure they took in each other's company.

Even on the nights when he stayed, only to quit her bed abruptly in the predawn hours—even then, when the lightness of his mood and step could strike her as disrespectful both to her and to the gravity of their times (the stench of fire could be burning in the air, and he would still leave her with a kind of heedless twinkle in his eyes, as if to say, *You'll be all right, old girl*; or: *After all, you're not my wife, my responsibility*; or: *And if we die? Well, then we die. To do our part, that should be our wish, and to do so with as much merriment as possible*)—even on those mornings when he left her wanting more and fearing indefinably for her life, she held her tongue. Did he have other women? And was she—if Benny were indeed alive—cashing in on something owed to her with this adulterous affair, or creating a debt that would be impossible to repay?

She couldn't think of any of it for long, because it all seemed beside the point. The point being that Lynton had restored her—to happiness, to life. And to turn her back on him would have been, in a sense, to choose death over life. She knew, from what she'd heard at the hospital, that he was the most fearless of soldiers and the most brilliant of military tacticians. And there was something about his *body*, something exceeding breath and blood and flesh, as though he carried in his cells and sweat the life force of all humanity. Watching him disappear down the desolate street on the mornings after he had been hers for a time, she stood stunned in the light of his mortality, and their secret knowledge of each other, and her certainty that she was but part of his passing enjoyment—less wanted than wanting, yet undeniably happy and still alive.

And yet she wasn't immune to darker feelings around him—feelings not dissimilar to those that had blighted her reunion with Louisa at the Forest Governor's house. Sometimes, when she was in both Louisa's and Lynton's presence, she would see him catching on the vision of the girl, who might be sitting solitarily with a book, or kneeling by the sewing machine while turning the hand crank for a seamstress. Khin would know then, or almost know, that Lynton's interest in the girl wasn't anything to be alarmed by. And she would tell herself she couldn't blame him for noticing what anyone with sensitive eyes might; Khin, too, was often arrested by the girl's composure and also by Louisa's unawareness of being noticed: there was nothing desperate about her beauty, which gleamed with serenity, seeming almost to have been ordained. No, Khin couldn't blame Lynton; but she smarted at the way he began calling the girl "Little Grandmother," as though the teasing, reverential slight could shake the poise out of her, and at the way he sometimes attempted to make the girl laugh by dancing a jig to the tune of her hand-cranking, or by pretending to pass out from boredom when Khin scolded the children. Then there was the afternoon when he and Sunny returned from some mission with a pair of boxing gloves for Johnny (could the boy have mentioned Benny's promise to teach him to box when he turned six?) and a rusted bicycle for the girls, which Lynton encouraged Louisa to use in order to escape her chores. The bicycle, along with the implicit suggestion that Louisa challenge Khin's authority, brought a smile to Louisa's face, one quickly swallowed up by a pinched look of regret (the girl was apparently bent on resisting anything to do with the man, no doubt out of allegiance to her father). And Khin was left feeling as frustrated by Lynton's misdirected attentions as she was exasperated by Louisa's reasonable ingratitude toward him.

But all those feelings came to an end one early morning in October, when she was sleeping beside him and he reached out to take her hand. Something about the tenderness of the gesture—the lingering way he clung to her fingers—frightened her, yet he sprang from the bed as though nothing had changed.

"Shall I make you something?" she said.

"Sunny will have breakfast for me."

"Then some tea?" There was no coffee to be found anywhere.

"Don't trouble yourself."

He pulled on his trousers and a shirt, and hesitated over the washbowl, pouring some water over a rag and then roughly cleaning his neck and face.

"Has something happened?" she said. She realized he could have learned something about Benny—or about Saw Lay, whom they'd lightly spoken of, and under whose command Lynton had apparently fought against the Japanese.

Now he checked the bullets in his pistol. "Let me tell you something. If you hear gossip about the war, me, anyone . . . don't be quick to believe it. Trust only your instincts . . . And remember to be on guard. Assuming we determine to hold to our vision, this war could go on indefinitely." He put the gun in its holster and turned to face her. "You have to be smart. You can't just trust any nice person who comes along."

She had no idea what he was getting at, only a sense from his tone that disaster was imminent and that she must soldier on without him. And to keep him here in the room with her a moment longer, she rose from bed, all at once ashamed of her naked and well-used breasts, which never failed to remind her that Lynton, at twenty-four, was four years her junior. She wrapped a sarong under her arms to hide from his unflinching gaze.

"I've received a message," he went on. "Nothing you should worry yourself about, but we're being moved to a place where we're more necessary."

And there it was. The end. And how absurd—after all that she'd survived, much of it without a man to bear her up—that she should feel utterly incapable of enduring any of this without him. Allowing a young man such as Lynton into her life, a man who lived for freedom . . . It had only ever thrown into relief how burdened she was, how hopelessly weak and dependent.

"Don't be angry," he said, giving her one of his quiet, attentive smiles.

"Why should I be angry?"

That was enough to make him break out into one of his merciless laughs. He took her into his arms, and she—bathed again in his vibrancy, in the heat and light that emanated from his skin—allowed herself to pretend that she had been wrong, that everything would continue between them in a way she hadn't yet guessed.

"You'll take care, won't you?" he said, the smile in his voice slackening. "You'll take care of the children?"

"What a question!" She'd meant to scold him, but her words caught in her throat, and she felt as though she were scolding herself instead.

She had never felt at home in Bilin, occupying another family's abandoned house. The air was stagnant, the Christian school was pickling the children's brains, and the neighbors were a pack of pious gossips. But now, in the aftermath of her happiness with Lynton, she saw how savagely those neighbors and even her customers peered at Hta Hta's expanding belly and hissed about Khin's affair with Lynton, suggesting that—according to her seamstresses and cheroot rollers—he had been one of her many adulterous lovers, and that his absence now opened the way for her to more freely pursue their husbands.

And she was startled to find that she had become rather careless with her businesses during her recent carefree days, not always registering which wages she had distributed or which debts she had paid in her logbook, but scribbling notes she'd massed in piles around the house if she'd kept them at all. (Could it be she owed such an exorbitant sum to the shepherd, whose wool was so fine, and whom she'd thought she'd long since remunerated? She was sure she'd recently paid him, but in which pile in which part of the house lay his dashed-off receipt?) Part of her success as a business owner had arisen from her willingness to defer payment for her own goods for sale; and now she found that she had been just as careless, during her liaison with Lynton, with records of debts owed to her. Had the holier-than-thou neighbor always avoiding her eye ever paid for that case of cheroots? The thought of confronting the woman, with her reproving looks, was just as stomach-turning as the thought of facing the disorder of the piles—a disorder reflecting, more than anything else, how undone Khin had been by Lynton, by the miserable joy she'd taken in him.

One particularly oppressive night, after the children and Hta Hta were in bed, she scoured the house for piles of her papers and receipts, and then, her head pounding, spread everything out over the kitchen table. For hours, she struggled to cross-check her memories—some vague, some quite clear—with the numbers that had been recorded, and in the end all she was certain of was that she owed hundreds more rupees than she could reasonably claim to be owed, and that soon she would have no way to pay her employees' wages or the cheroot factory's rent, and no way to purchase basic staples to feed her children.

Near her face powder and the mirror reflecting her sobered, candle-haunted features, she kept a secret lockbox, and when she opened it now she found—instead of a roll of bills—only a single, rumpled ten-rupee note. Of course she had borrowed from her store of bills from time to time to pay this person or that, but she had reminded herself to replenish the box whenever she could, hadn't she? What had been important was to keep going, from day to day . . .

In the kitchen, Lynton had left a half-drained bottle of whiskey, which she grasped by the neck before stumbling out of the house into the light of the full moon. The air outside was still and drenched in the heavy scent of something sickly. For a moment, she stood taking swigs of whiskey, feeling disconcerted by the cloying smell and the immense quiet of the sleeping street, which seemed to mute the roaring in her mind. *The bitches,* she thought, remembering the evil words the neighbors were said to have spoken against her. The haughty bitches who obediently sat in church all Sunday, listening to lessons about tolerance and the golden rule, only to be quick to cast stones. They couldn't wait to prove their superiority, and only showed their own smallness of heart and mind instead.

"You think I'm having affairs?" she screamed into the silence. "Can't you see I'm full of juices? I'm so fertile, if a man touches me, babies pop out! You could go to bed with an elephant and nothing would happen!"

For the next three days, storms blew in unremittingly from across the mountains, like a cosmic injunction that Khin should shut herself in with her thoughts. But she shrank from those thoughts, as though unworthy of them. *Never again,* they commanded her. Never ever again should she allow herself to lose her way in the inebriation of a man's company. Never again should she so recklessly put herself in a position of inviting others' censure.

The sky cleared on the fourth day, and, with the new sunshine filtering in through the trees, her mood began to lift. She asked Hta Hta and the children to follow her outside to a damp tangle of grass under the tree in the yard, where she set up a lunch made from breakfast leftovers. And as she glanced up at the shimmering road and the opening doors of her neighbors, it occurred to her that if she were to move the cheroot factory into this house and sell off the sewing equipment, the money saved and made would be enough to gradually pay off her debts. And couldn't she, with very little labor, make something that these neighbors would enjoy far more than sweaters or tailored sarongs? Take a leaf, steam it, throw in some chopped betel nut and a dash of lime, a little anisette, maybe some tobacco if there was any leftover from the cheroots . . . Her mother had long ago taught her how to make betel so pungent and intoxicating, no one would be able to get enough of it. Which of her neighbors didn't have a mouth reddened and teeth blackened from betel?

Now she watched Johnny run out to the gate to escape the mosquitoes hovering over their meal, and she had the sense of having nearly evaded disaster. With her first separation from the children, she had allowed herself to forget that they alone were the true center of her world. Yet here they were, by some gift of grace, within her line of sight: Gracie dashing out to meet her brother, Louisa calmly following after, while Molly grabbed at a handful of wet grass. Here they were, all four of them, resilient and curious, alive.

And soon they would be joined by another.

"You're pregnant, Hta Hta," Khin dared say to the nanny, who had started pulling blades of grass from Molly's wet mouth. "Was it the Forest Governor? One of his sons? Did he injure you? You can tell me."

For a moment, the poor girl only looked at her in a kind of dazed grief. Then she said, obviously ashamed, "I don't know what you mean."

Khin reached out and touched the side of her plump, soft cheek. "I'll help you raise it."

Never had she spoken so openly and affectionately to Hta Hta, in whose eyes there was now a gleam of hurt and also of relief, as though the source of the terrible ache festering in her had finally been identified. With time she would accustom herself to that ache, Khin told herself.

"Is it a troupe of dancers, Mama?" Johnny called from the gate. He was pointing to a line of bullock carts trundling down the road. "Can we go see? Can we, Mama?"

"Yes, Mama!" Gracie joined in. "Please!"

Khin stood and drifted to the gate to stand by Louisa, while Johnny and Grace galloped up the muddy road.

"Is it a funeral, Mama?" Louisa asked, so calmly it put a chill on Khin's spine.

Only then did Khin glimpse what the girl had seen: piled onto the bed of every approaching cart were three or four coffins.

Bubonic plague had broken out, the infected carried away swiftly and with excruciating pain. By twilight, it was agreed that Hta Hta would take the children to live with the family of one of the seamstresses, who came from a remote village on the plains of the tigers, about eight hours away, while Khin would stock the family with supplies by selling whatever goods she could on the road.

And just like that, they were saying their good-byes again, the children collected in the rear of a horse cart that Khin had hired with her ten rupees, and Khin kissing each of them—not as Benny might have, with a chaste peck on the brow, but as a Karen, by placing the side of her nose against each of their cheeks and inhaling deeply.

"Who will deliver my baby?" Hta Hta asked, as if the parting had finally awakened her to the child who would soon be wrenched from her body.

"You'll find that if you look there will be people to help you," Khin told her.

A violent wind picked up, the driver hit the horse with his switch, and the cart began to roll away.

Khin stared at the departing children, trying to sear the picture of them into her memory: Johnny looking back at her with eyes reflecting the deepening night; Gracie avoiding her gaze by nestling into Hta Hta's swollen side; Molly, fed up with the seamstress's feeble attempts to console her, whining and reaching her chubby arms back toward Khin; and Louisa, now taking the baby into her own small lap. But a wild, frightened expression suddenly broke over Louisa's face.

"Promise we'll be all right?" she called to Khin over the wind. And, following after the cart, Khin cried, "Never lose faith!"

11

The Faithful

It had been Ducksworth's smile, false and scared, that had spoken of disgrace to Benny seven months earlier, in April 1949, when his old friend had come for him in Thaton. And it had been the way the man's fingers had instantly recoiled from the envelope he'd dropped in Benny's hand, the one containing the letter from Nu. And then it had been—as Ducksworth and Benny had sat on the plane bound for Moulmein, confined to a physical proximity they hadn't shared since their days around the same desk at B. Meyer—the way the man's skin had given off the damp odor of anxiousness and avoidance. No, Ducksworth wasn't settled, Benny saw; he wasn't settled at all. But whether his disgrace was *merely* that of having joined the Burma Army's ranks after his long habit of colonial apologism, Benny couldn't be sure.

"You going to tell me how you ended up a lieutenant in their army?" Benny attempted on the plane, putting on his own (unintentionally) false smile. He could feel the heat of that falseness burning his pinched, trembling cheeks.

"*Their* army?" Ducksworth said stiffly.

"You know what I mean." If Benny could just turn his old friend's disgrace into something to laugh about (however mordantly), if he could just reel back eleven years and remind Ducksworth of their once easy, rancorous banter, he might stand a chance. "What happened?"

"What happened is that you've lost your manners." The rebuff ought to have reassured Benny, but it was delivered coldly, as if confirming something suspected.

Ducksworth stared, tight-lipped, toward the cockpit, almost at ease—until the plane rapidly descended, causing him to grip the armrest between them. He nearly bolted out of his seat when the plane touched ground; then, on the dusty, desolate tarmac, he cast his eyes around like a bewildered child waiting for some adult to claim him after an arduous excursion. "Now there should be—there should be—someone here to meet us," he sputtered.

That someone was a swarm of armed guards, who surrounded them in the modest airport and demanded—amid curses and insults and jabs with their guns—that Benny get back out to the darkening runway. Benny's last look at Ducksworth was of him covering his head with his hands—in shame, or self-defense. And then Benny was herded out, bracing himself for the fatal shot, and having the odd instinct to look back and cry out to his old friend. As though in Ducksworth's face he might find one last vision of faithfulness, one last glimpse of affection or regret.

But he was not killed. Not yet. In Rangoon's notorious Barr Street lockup, a temporary holding place for the most hardened criminals, Benny was thrust into a cell without explanation and without an opportunity to speak to anyone in charge. Yet he was not left entirely alone in the eight-by-twelve-foot cell, whose clanging steel door closed his world off completely from the prison, and whose only amenity—save for a thin, sordid blanket—was a bucket hanging from a rope in a narrow hole in the floor. It was out of this hole that his company crawled. The moment the trap in the bottom of the steel door grated open twice a day, an army of rats invaded, watching with rapacious red eyes and twitching whiskers as Benny's food—thin rice soup for breakfast, or a gelatinous mixture of rice and bits of meat for dinner—was pushed on a tray into the cell. But to call these creatures rats was to do them an injustice. Big as cats, with sinuous, almost hairless bodies and scaly pink tails, they hurled themselves at the dish with piercing shrieks, and Benny had to beat them back with kicks while they snarled and snapped, trying to sink their long teeth into his ankles. They begrudged him every mouthful, and he was forced to defend himself each second that he stuffed the food into his mouth. Cheated of their meal, his cellmates wrestled with one another, snarling and biting, or slavering and uttering hoarse cries at Benny, their fierce eyes greedily watching his every move.

That would have been enough; but as night fell, and the sickly light emitted by a small aperture near the ceiling died away, the creatures were hideously emboldened and scampered freely about the cell, scuttling into corners, chasing each other around the walls, squeaking and chattering until Benny passed out and they scurried over his inert form, tearing at his face and throat and testicles before he beat them off and, in the blackness, murdered as many of them as he could with his bare hands.

Because he was given only a mug of water every third or fourth day, his tongue grew swollen and his mouth and skin, already covered with scabs from his fights with the rats, cracked. He was so chronically exhausted and in pain that he might have been lured by the solution of the rope from which his toilet hung. But the ravaging hunger of his companions fed his own animal instinct to keep fighting, to survive.

Though *he* wasn't the one who survived precisely. No, the creature who survived as the rats' contender and companion was more villain than prizefighter, more vermin than man. *Bloody sons of bitches,* he taunted the rats, and he scratched a strike into the wall for every one of them that he killed, beside his tally of the days that passed. *Bastards. Devil fucks. Earth scum.* He counted the rats and recounted them, and their numbers only seemed to multiply, and he often lost track and had to count and recount them again. *You belong here. Dirty Jews. Born in the dark. The sewer. Go to hell—no one wants you. Think they care what happens—the humans? Your mama knew what would become of you. Better off dying.*

Someone outside his cell went on providing him—or whatever he was—with just enough to exist on, and for those few precious seconds twice a day when that *someone* shoved his tray through the trap, Benny seized on the sight of a nervous, spotted, obviously masculine, immediately withdrawing *human* hand. And then, when the trap grated shut again, he clutched at the hope that this someone, this male human beyond his door, would linger long enough to hear, to comprehend, everything he spontaneously shouted at him—his most constant plea being for water, and then for relief from the rats, and then for an indication of how long this torment, this hell, would go on.

The answers, all the answers, came on what he thought might be his ninetieth day, when, for the first time since he'd been shunted into the cell, the door creaked open, and Benny, blinking in the blinding light of the corridor, saw the shape of a soldier. Or rather, of a general. Of the commander in chief of the Burma Army. Of Ne Win himself.

Was it a hallucination? The features of the man stepping into the shadows of the cell seemed to blur into one another as he stared down at Benny and began to speak, almost to soliloquize. "You are repulsive," the man said quietly. "Strange, that you managed to produce such beautiful children. Your eldest—*Louisa*, is it? She's quite the temptation to the spies we have in Bilin . . . Does that upset you? It shouldn't. Because we can keep her safe if we choose. We can keep your wife safe. Not that she thinks of you as her husband anymore . . . I've caused you pain. I am very sorry. But you can understand her position, no? . . . Is she a widow? Is she still married? She has no idea. And her appetite for men who aren't Jews is quite extraordinary . . . Don't be angry! It's amusing! Men of all ages passing in and out of the house she squats in, passing in and out like shadows with erections. Imagine her squatting over all *those*! Why aren't you laughing?"

Now, at last, the man, Ne Win—there was no mistaking his foaming voice—moved, reached into his pocket, and threw something at

Benny, who instantly, almost ferociously snatched it out of the air. But it was only a cigar.

"You *are* repulsive," said the man, laughing. "And your repulsive wife thinks she's very clever trading in sweaters and cigars. Look at the one in your hand . . . Strange how much a man's hand resembles a claw when he is starved . . . See how she's put a band of her own design around the thing? Clever, your wife, isn't she? Started up a little factory modeled on the ones built by her husband—excuse me, by the man to whom she is false . . . Doesn't realize she's being *allowed* to live, to feed her little beasts, her hungry vagina."

"What do you want?" Benny growled. He could snap; he could *allow* himself to snap, to snap this man's neck in a few seconds.

Ne Win put his hand on the pistol at his hip and stepped back a foot, into the corridor, so that the light fell harshly across his own feral features. "Only to tell you a story," he simpered, "a story of something that just happened. You see, some of your Karen leaders thought they were going to be very smart and meet with an American in Thailand—a CIA man, no doubt. Can you imagine? Here it is, almost August, with the rains so heavy—but they were adamant about getting over the Salween River. And when they reached the village on the edge of the river, the headman put them up in a tiny bamboo hut in the middle of an isolated field. Only stupid Karens would have agreed, don't you think? Only stupid Karens would have waited for the rains and the swollen river to subside. But you already know what happened, don't you? Go on . . . tell me."

It was of Louisa that Benny thought then, and Khin. And only after, of Saw Lay. "Murdered."

"You aren't stupid at all like them. You remind me of a particular lieutenant of mine. We like to call him the Butcher. And he was the one, very early in the morning, before dawn, to lead the ambush. Those poor, stupid men. Every one of them done for . . . except your friend. Yes, him. You know exactly to whom I'm referring. Don't look at me like that. Enough to make me nervous, that look. He lived, your friend! Just as your dirty children will live, and your dirty wife, *if* . . ." He paused to stare down at Benny with a smile so fixed it seemed panicked. "We're going to catch your friend. And when we do, you'll be the one to talk to him. To get intelligence from him. About your insurgent operations, of course. And also about the Americans. About what exactly their spies are doing on our turf."

Benny couldn't process Ne Win's words; the physical presence and threat of the man were too insistent. But he kept his eyes watchfully on the general, who in the gleam of the corridor returned Benny's animal stare, and then breathlessly, almost disconcertedly, murmured, "Have you understood a word I've said?"

The next evening, Benny was transferred to Insein Prison, where he was made the only class A prisoner among at least two hundred mostly Karen class B and class C political prisoners. Assigned a servant to cook his meals and to maintain his clothes, and, just as uniquely, allowed to roam the men's barrack nearly at his leisure, he ought to have experienced the change as an enormous leap toward liberation. But if he found comfort in the plentiful food, and in the freedom of space, and in the inexhaustible supply of water—the gallons and gallons that he daily gulped and doused himself clean with in the drab communal shower—he could not escape the feeling that he was even more constricted here, in the company of other men. More constricted because he'd come to believe, inescapably, that the extraordinary thing—the truly extraordinary thing—was when others treated you well, not badly. He expected every other man to betray him; and he expected disloyalty of himself.

He was put up in a room with two narrow beds, the other ominously empty—waiting, he knew, for his "friend," on the loose somewhere beyond the prison walls. In the hours after Ne Win's visit, he had vaguely pieced together what the general had suggested with his mention of the Americans—that not all the Allies had left

Burma to its own devices, that the Americans were somehow still involved in the country's, and perhaps even in the Karens', affairs. But this, all of this, was overshadowed by the more surprising realization that he, Benny, would be willing to betray Saw Lay in order to keep himself and his family alive. And to hide his diminished face from the specter of Saw Lay in these new, almost lavish quarters, he turned his back on the empty bed, turned his back on the other prisoners, who were hungry to hear his counsel about the revolution, about their cause, about the state of a Karen future that Benny felt he'd also already betrayed. Sometimes, stretched out on his hard mattress, he felt so annihilated by infidelity to his past that he imagined his body crumbling into dust that floated up in the stagnant air, all the way to the window through which, if he lifted his eyes, he could see over the top of the facing women's prison to the bruised sky. What a negligent husband he'd been; what a sense of entitlement he'd had to the gifts of Khin's body, to the gifts of her grace. And how pathetic he'd turned out to be as a man, ready to betray his highest ideals, to bow before the power of the ignoble for survival's sake. He drank the cup of humiliation to the dregs, praying to God not to be spared.

But perhaps a month or two after his transfer, he happened to be standing on his bed, looking for a hook or a nail embedded in the beam above, when he was startled by the face of a woman in the window opposite his. She stood eight or ten feet away, separated from him by two walls and two sets of bars (his window's and hers), yet her eyes seemed to speak directly to his. (*Are you on your bed?* those eyes said. *Yes, I am on a bed, too, and, like you, seeking to understand my options. You won't kill yourself yet—that would be rash; but it's important to know what your escape route will be if one becomes required.*) She could have been twenty, thirty, this woman, with a delicate-featured face enlivened by excitable dark eyebrows that rose up a half inch before falling toward the gracious smile she flashed him. And then she was gone.

Her name was Rita, and she had been a medical student at the University of Rangoon until her arrest five months before, when she'd dared to question why, at the hospital, Karen doctors were allowed to work while Karen patients were barred from treatment. Benny learned these details the following day, when, around noontime, she held up a pillowcase on which she'd written the compressed story of her recent past in bold English letters. So that he could read every one of these letters between the bars, she moved the pillowcase slowly from side to side, before replacing it with her worried face. (*Have I embarrassed myself by reaching out to you?* she might have been asking. *Please write something back!*) But then she ducked down once again, holding up the backside of the pillowcase, on which she'd written: "SAW BENSION?"

Of course, it was possible—entirely possible—that this woman was a trap laid to ensnare him. Yet her eyes . . . the gracious smile . . . He felt powerless not to throw caution to the wind. When he asked for something to write with, he was granted a pen and a journal of fifty-odd sheets. Given how huge he would have to make his letters in order for Rita to read them, he would be able to write little more than a sprinkling of words on each page. For hours, he was paralyzed by the necessary economies of phrasing: each time he went to write something to her, it seemed stale, clichéd, lacking the agitated understanding Rita's eyes had instantly made him feel. "Do you need anything?" he thought to write. But that was foolish, because he would never be able to provide her with what she wanted. Or: "Is there someone looking for you?" But again, what could he do to ease her loved ones' worry?

"Soon I will betray my friend to keep my children alive," he finally wrote—not on the journal's impossibly small pages, but on his own pillowcase.

As soon as he held the case up to his window, though, he regretted the self-revelation. If she *were* there to entice him into making disclosures, could he have more expediently assisted her in that task?

But it was a different sort of regret that afflicted him when she replied, on a section of her bedsheet: "Lack of courage keeps us from understanding others' perspectives." Was she chastising him? Calling him cowardly for giving in to betrayal? Or, on the contrary, was she telling him in her abbreviated terms that it was cowardly not to empathize with men like him? Before he'd come up with a reply, she went on, as if in explanation: "And what makes us great can limit our greatness."

The *immediacy* of her depth. The absolute *absence* of stock introductory phrases. Never before had he encountered anything like it, and his every last defense was broken down. Her words reminded him of his children: how he'd come to feel that they were nearly the only meaning he'd achieved in life, yet meaning that had the power to cause him to commit betrayal, to snuff out the meaningful. He wanted to explain as much to her, but to narrow his thoughts to such an extent that they could be clearly communicated in just a sprinkling of words—nothing had prepared him for that particular difficulty.

"We shouldn't blame anyone for lacking courage or greatness," she wrote a few hours later on her sheet in response to his continued silence and, he thought, his utter cowardice.

"But you don't lack it," he wrote, finally, on his own bedsheet.

"How do you know?" she responded.

What he knew now—just about the only thing he knew now—was that here in prison he'd suddenly discovered the freedom to face himself.

"How does man forgive himself for the lives he's taken even in the name of saving lives?" he wrote on a piece of paper that he tore from the journal and persuaded the crooked-backed servant who cooked his meals to pass to Rita.

"He doesn't," she responded on the paper the servant tersely returned. "Only those who have reduced their humanity to almost nothing put their virtue and ethics and faith in an unbreakable safe."

Him: "Is the man who seeks the limelight the one we should be suspicious of?"

Her: "Perhaps he is the one we should pity."

Him: "I wish you didn't know who I am, or that you hadn't seen my face."

Him again: "Then you wouldn't know my race. I don't want to know yours."

Her: "Nor do I want you to know it."

Her again: "Because I don't believe in it."

Him: "The most perilous symptom of suffering is self-pity."

Her: "When we think we hold exclusive rights to suffering."

Her again: "And we have the instinct to deprive others of theirs."

Him: "Tell me of your suffering."

They never spoke directly of their growing love, but that love was the subject of their every exchange. And he was unspeakably grateful for it. Unspeakably.

And then there was Saw Lay, suddenly sitting on the bed opposite his. "It's nice here," his dear friend said coolly. It was evening, sometime toward the end of 1949, and they leaned against their respective walls in the semi-shadows, too disconcerted by their contrived coming together to face each other in the remaining light. "We can almost pretend the war doesn't exist," he went on. "That it never existed in the first place."

Was Benny being sensitive, hearing a measure of reproach in Saw Lay's tone? Surely his friend suspected that they had been quartered together for a reason, that there would be a price to be paid for their mutual survival, perhaps even that Benny had been put up to informing on him. Yet Saw Lay also seemed to resent the change that had come over Benny, his new freedom in the safe harbor of this cell.

"Tell me about it—the war—the suffering," Benny said to him. "Tell me what has happened. I know nothing, my friend."

Hearing Benny utter this term of endearment with such old familiarity and tenderness seemed to surprise Saw Lay, and he lifted his eyes so that the light hit them, and he looked at Benny with an expression of amazed pain. But then he turned and cast his glance around the shadows of the room, as though to seek out a wiretap in them. And he said derisively, as though also addressing the enemy, "The Burma Army would be heartened to know that we've been reduced to digging up whatever ammunition—whatever buried Japanese or British three-pounders and artillery shells—we can find. And, of course, making arms that misfire—.303s whose brass shells have to be repeatedly used—that is, after they've been filed down to the scale of our rifles' chambers, filed so thin they sometimes blow up in our fingers."

"But there's hope," Benny hazarded, hearing the premonitory quiver of guilt in his voice.

"*Hope*," Saw Lay returned ruminatively, sarcastically. "We have more fighters than ever before—twenty-four thousand at minimum. And still we're slowly being pushed east, into the hills . . . It's not just a matter of our lack of arms. Not any continuing disorganization of our forces. In fact, we've become much more disciplined, skilled . . ."

Down the corridor, someone—another prisoner—cried out in physical or spiritual agony, and Saw Lay became very alert, his ear turning toward the door as the corridor filled with the shouts of guards. But it was only the commotion of a group of men being escorted to the showers. Soon the pipes in the wall began to clang, and then came the sound of running water and the sudden rise in pitch of a few prisoners' voices, the temporary escalation of mood that so often accompanied the prisoners' escapes into the shower room.

The moonlight beginning to filter in through the bars of the window had washed Saw Lay clean of some of his scorn, and when he directed his eyes at Benny again, it was with a question in them. "It all comes down to trust," he said quietly. "If we could trust them, we could actually talk." His melancholic voice seemed to stretch compassionately toward Benny, suggesting subjects of which they would never speak. "But without trust, we become divided, we who were so unified in our desire for a dignified life."

"Must we be divided?" Benny threw out. There it was again, the tremor of guilt in his voice—but also a loosening knot of anguish. His question, he knew, was wrong, even immoral, given what he would soon do to betray Saw Lay and their joint cause. But he felt like a child about to cry over a petty crime he'd perpetrated because a bully had made him do it.

"You cannot make me reveal what they want revealed," Saw Lay said. He spoke very calmly, very firmly, and also with a punishing parent's depths of love. "And they cannot prevent me from revealing to you what they don't want you to know."

Benny was so stunned by the reversal in the conversation—from an obscurity in which all was mere suggestion to utter forthrightness—that his heart began to race. He felt caught, found out, and also frightened of what would soon be disclosed. And, like a child, he wanted to hide from it all and to deny the truth that was suddenly exerting its pressure on him. "I don't know," he stammered, "what you are referring to—"

"The British have been funding the Burma Army's liquidation of our revolution," his friend quickly returned. "I don't mean the British aid program to Nu's government that has been in place since independence. This is an arms program specifically designed to stamp out our uprising."

When Benny didn't respond—he couldn't, so much did his system refuse to believe in the extent of the British betrayal—Saw Lay went on: "It was one of them, wasn't it, a British lord who said that 'absolute power corrupts absolutely.' Nu and his satraps—Ne Win—*those* are London's allies now, and London will stop at nothing to keep them in power, so that the West keeps a foothold in the increasingly communist East. Apparently, they've convinced themselves of the legitimacy of Nu's parliamentary democracy . . . So you cannot blame us for beginning to splinter over the question of trust itself, some of us even looking to the Communists in Burma, who as you know have been waging their own revolution against the government, and who are eager for us to join their cause, which none of us really believes in—"

"The *Communists*?"

"I don't want such an alliance—but tell that to others as we're being betrayed by the arbiters of democracy themselves . . . You see what I mean when I speak of hope now. Where is the *hope* in the face of duplicitousness, in the face of such colossal betrayal, in the face of our likely internal schism over the question of whom to trust?"

And the Americans? Benny wanted to ask. Where did they fit into this broader, terrible global picture? But then he realized that to ask such a question would only betray the faithfulness Saw Lay was showing him—his refusal to betray Benny by divulging anything with which Benny might betray the cause and their friendship.

For a while, they each retreated into the remote corners of their unspoken questions and doubts. Then Saw Lay looked back at Benny, as though to push past the mental argument that had just been occupying his silence. "Should someone from the outside make an overture to you . . ." he said very carefully.

Benny's first thought was of someone outside this cell, outside the men's prison—of Rita, who, indeed, had made an overture to him all those months ago. And then of Ne Win, *the* someone responsible for his continuing to be imprisoned. But on the heels of this came his awareness that Saw Lay—who was staring at him persistently and darkly—was referring to someone outside *Burma*. And all at once he recalled, with excruciating clearness, Ne Win's words about the ambush on the banks of the Salween, about the Karen leaders who had *"thought they were going to be very smart and meet with an American in Thailand."*

Saw Lay continued, very quietly now: "Should someone who goes by the name of Hatchet reach out to you—"

"*Hatchet?*"

"If he does make contact, remember to consider the question of trust, Benny."

The question of trust was just what seemed to throw them into a renewed silence that only rang with still more questions . . . questions about everything that Saw Lay's disclosure yet kept concealed. And when the wind beyond the window began to whistle plaintively, Benny watched with relief as it carried Saw Lay's attention away from him, away from the cell, to the night and the revolution spreading out under the stars.

"I remember, during the war," Saw Lay said at last—"I mean the Second World War, when we were fighting the Japs and the Burma Independence Army—I remember coming upon a village that had just been scorched. There was a young woman who was picking through the remains of what must have been her hut. I still can't bear to imagine what exactly she was looking for. But what struck me was her calm, the way she seemed almost practiced at this, as if it had been written into her fate, a fate that she already knew—and, even more astonishingly, a fate she had accepted."

Saw Lay inhaled sharply, as if to keep hold of nothing less than his life, in spite of his own doomed fate. "You know, I have never had a need to be seen, to be recognized for doing anything. In fact, I prefer to be invisible. Nothing seems more appropriate than to pass out of this world as invisibly as I passed into it, remarked by only one or two who truly cared for me. Perhaps that is a Karen trait, that inclination toward self-effacement, toward standing in the shadows. Our modesty that runs so deep it is almost self-annihilating. But now . . . now, suddenly, my invisibility—our relative invisibility—strikes me as very sad. Very sad, indeed . . . If you stand for a moment behind *their* eyes—behind the eyes of anyone for whom modesty is not an ultimate virtue—we appear to value our lives less than they do. It is a kind of permission, in their eyes, to ignore us. Or, even more ominously, to stamp us out like a weak strain of bacteria . . . I never thought of the British as being racist, but they must know Nu has declared he wants all Karens wiped out. How can they, then, with this arms program targeting us, not also be accomplices to genocide?"

Past the window, the wind beckoned to them again, and Saw Lay seemed to ponder the possibility of following it. "Sometimes it seems to me that I am nothing but a thirty-five-year-old boy," he finally went on, "brokenhearted because his daddy, who he thought saw him as precious, as unique, as loyal, as good and worthy, never really loved him at all—because his daddy loved him only as a convenience. Suddenly everything is altered—one's sense of right and wrong, one's old affection for the smell of the streets. No one to lean on anymore, nothing to believe in . . . You must know I'll never get out of here, Benny. Not alive."

"But there's hope," Benny said again, without any kind of belief.

Saw Lay seemed to hear the defeat in his voice. With a half-smile that was almost comforting, he said, "Ne Win and his men—the soldiers who've been hunting me—they certainly don't have any hope that I'll come around to their side. You know where they finally found me? Back in my brother's house in Tharrawaddy. I couldn't even bring myself to hide."

For a time neither of them spoke, and in the silence and the darkness there was nowhere to take shelter from their powerlessness over what would be. It seemed to Benny that there was nothing he could do to catch hold of his friend, to keep him there. That Saw Lay's disenchantment was too profound.

Saw Lay suddenly pushed himself off his bed and crossed to the window, where he stood looking up over the women's prison at the far-off moon. Benny didn't get up to stand with him, but he had the distinct inward impression of following his friend, carried by the whimsy of the wind, over sleeping Rita, past the tainted prison grounds, to a sparkling river, where they stood before the open branches of the forest, with the fields unfolding behind them. So this was the place where their paths would diverge.

"I can't," Saw Lay said gently. "You mustn't be hard on me, Benny. I know my faith requires forgiveness and steadfastness. But I can't. Try to remember that in the face of duplicitousness betrayal is forgivable."

PART THREE

Ascensions
1951–1962

12

The Burma Problem

A stonishing, how one could go from absolute intimacy to utter estrangement, Benny thought over a year later, as he sat for the first time across from Khin in the visiting area of Insein Prison. It was January 1951, midafternoon, an hour when he would normally have been napping; but a few minutes earlier his favorite guard, Zay, had popped his head into the cell, a strange half-hysterical smile suppressed on his lips, and said, "You have a visitor, old man"; and then Benny—still groggy and feeling he was in a dream—was led out into the glare of the yard, past some commotion between two class C prisoners, to a large shed in which he immediately recognized, sitting alone among a shadowy cluster of otherwise desolate card tables and chairs, his wife blinking back at him.

For a few moments, after he had seated himself across from her as Zay hung back by the door, all Benny could do was mutely take her in while he palpated the peculiar texture of their apartness. A clamped hardness had taken hold of Khin. She held her now-ringless fingers tightly together on the table, so that her knuckles appeared blanched, and her mouth—once so supple, so tentative with words and yielding to his advances—was fixed in a line that seemed merely to express her staunch refusal to betray anything but her determination *not* to break into an outpouring of joy or relief or despair at seeing him again. Even her blouse—plain, opaque, in an unobtrusive black that might have been designed to deflect the eye's attention (whereas Khin had preferred to dress in light colors before, and to feature her voluptuousness with delicate fabrics and formfitting cuts)—spoke to him of hiding, of ethnic concealment and feminine woundedness. What had life done to her?

"Are they alive?" he heard his strangled voice come out with.

Her eyes had been distantly but steadily watching him (taking in, no doubt, the dimensions of his own altered body and being), but now her gaze fell to the table, to a fly resting on one of his fingers, poised inertly between them. He saw her flick something away from her cheek, and then she brushed the fly from his hand, which she took and pressed as she finally began to nod with unmistakable suffering, so that he understood that, yes, the children yet lived, but that they—and she—had barely come through with their lives.

"Saw Lay?" she said finally, in a small voice, as she lifted her gaze to meet his. "Have you heard anything?"

Now he was unable to hold her gaze, instead grasping her hands with his, as though to restore the flow of warm blood in them. "They caught him," he said, the partial confession catching in his throat. "He was brought here. We were together. But . . . he was disenchanted."

He felt her peering watchfully at him.

"He—?" she said when he finally glanced up to meet her assessing gaze.

He nodded. "I found him."

Her eyes narrowed, but only slightly. And he seemed to see in them the distant look not quite of suffering or incomprehension, but of resignation—or was it envy?

Another moment passed and, as if from a distance, he looked back at their hands, still clasped uncomfortably. Those hands appeared to be trying to hold on to the difficulty that he and Khin had encountered while apart, and trying to loosen themselves of culpability for having clawed their way through everything.

"Where are the children now?" he managed.

After a pause, she said, "Home with me. In Insein." The continued smallness of her voice, its constricted quality, told him that in fact she had been shaken by the news of Saw Lay's suicide and that she was struggling to contain her sorrow. "I wanted to come back—to Insein—alone when I heard you were here," she continued. "I didn't know if it would be safe. But . . . we'll talk about that later. I found the children—that's what matters."

"They weren't with you?"

Emotion flared in her gaze, pleading with him, he thought, to rush with her past wherever they had been. But it was only a moment. "I almost brought them today," she said, "but I thought . . . too much of a shock for them, and you. They're very eager to see you, Benny. When they learned you were alive . . ."

She pulled her hands from his, regaining her composure, her flinty coolness, and she took something from her lap—an envelope, from which she removed a clutch of photographs that she spread before him on the table.

"That is Molly." She pointed to a dark, sturdy little girl with a dimple in her chin and a gleam so fierce she seemed to be considering pouncing on the camera as though to capture and eat it.

"She's two?" Only now did he realize he'd begun to laugh through tears.

"Almost three. She never takes no for an answer, never stops fighting. Knows just what she wants and how to say just about everything." The pictures had given her a way into familiarity; he heard, in the far reaches of her voice now, the distant lilt of anguish and release. "And this . . ."

She pointed to a second portrait of two children lengthening toward the imperfections of adolescence. Johnny and Grace. "We had these taken in Rangoon last week. They spent all morning telling Hta Hta how to groom their hair."

"Tell me about them."

He heard the tightening of her breath as she stared down at the pictures of their children between them.

"Johnny is grateful to be back, to have clean pressed clothes, to be studying 'seriously' again, as he says." The tentativeness, the precision

175

of her phrasing, made him acutely aware of the Burmese they were speaking, of its formality. They had always mostly spoken Burmese together by necessity, but he'd become much more proficient in the relaxed, unadorned grammar of Karen these past years, quartered as he'd been with so many political prisoners; more than ever, the convolutions of her Burmese struck his ears as a wall between them. "And Johnny takes *himself* very seriously. He's nearly nine, with such a mind. Gracie worships him, and he wants nothing to do with her. She daydreams, climbing trees with a book and then forgetting the book and napping on the branches . . . And here's Hta Hta and her little girl, Effie."

"Hta Hta's a mother now?"

"Another product of the war . . . We were at the Forest Governor of Kyowaing's house. One of his sons, I think. Poor Hta Hta—she'll hardly speak of it." She touched the image of Effie, as though to caress Hta Hta's child. "Feisty little girl," she said with a laugh. "Gives Molly a 'run for her money,' as you used to say." She blushed, having used the anglicism, perhaps because she was trying on English for the first time in years. Then, as though to move his attention away from her again, she pushed forward a portrait of a child who had been made to look like a doll.

"What is this?" he sputtered, more repelled than intrigued by the image, and yet, somehow, spellbound by it.

She began to tell him of how she'd recently made inroads with the wife of the local district commissioner, under whose jurisdiction this prison lay. The wife organized child beauty pageants, one of which had been held in Insein a few days after their return. "She's very 'keen on' Louisa," she said, using his English again, as though to somehow implicate him in what had been made of Louisa.

And it *was* Louisa, the creature in the photograph, dressed in Burmese court clothes, her curls coiled perfectly, her lips and eyes and skin exaggerated with lipstick and charcoal and powder, her gaze fixed, and her smile guilelessly directed over a shoulder. Yes, it was

Louisa (could it be that she was *ten?*), but he could see at once that under the surface of her cosmetic transformation, something different had come to the front of her beauty. On the one hand, she seemed to have aged significantly, to have come past her innocence. But there was also in her face a marked absence of discontent and gravity, which had pulled at the corners of even her happiest expressions. She seemed instead now to be too composed, to have been conquered by acceptance—of the condition of her life, of its being an endless battle with loss, never to be won.

"You see, she doesn't wear a sash," Khin was saying. "She didn't win. But it was a success, her participation in the pageant. Yesterday, she visited the woman and her husband at their home. She was invited in for tea, and she told the district commissioner of your innocence—"

"Innocence?" He could hear the irritation in his voice, though in fact he was deeply affected by what his daughter had done for him. By her courage.

"How hard life has been without you."

"Any day I could be hanged for treachery, Khin. It won't be so easy maneuvering my release, convincing the district commissioner." He wasn't sure just what he was defending himself against, but it seemed he was being held accountable for something and he wanted nothing to do with it. "To call any attention to me could—"

"He said he would see what he could do about your case."

She stared at him from behind a mask of—of censure? Or was it only anxiety? Then all at once that mask gave way, and he saw a deep welling of fear in her eyes, as she said, with such defenselessness he felt utterly ashamed, "Don't you want to come back to us, Benny?"

Three weeks later, he found himself standing in the cavity of his old living room, a tinny trio playing some welcoming tune in the flat light of the opposite window, while his children—looking more delightful in person, but more heartbreakingly unfamiliar—strained to sing along to the tune and simultaneously to smile at him. On the other side of the room an assortment of old friends stood arrayed beside a table laid with dressed-up provisions—rice and curries no less thin, from the looks of it, than what he'd received every day in prison. And there was Hta Hta, smiling shyly at him behind the guests, her peering little girl on her hip.

"We still have a lot to do," Khin said at his side, drawing him by the elbow into the room. "Put your things down."

His "things" were little more than his journals, and he was loath to part with them, but he did as she said, stooping to put his sack by the crumbling doorway.

"The property's not what it was," Khin went on. "I'm still trying to get the gas station out of a neighbor's hands. But your old employees have helped me to fix things up. They're working on credit now, so you have to get going as soon as possible. I've already visited the ice factories—one's been stolen from under us, but your manager handled the other as he could. The trucks are gone. The government's taken over the trucking company. And the bottling plant—a lost cause . . ."

He took in the splashes of darkness (old blood?) under a coat of paint on the walls; the bullet holes—they were everywhere and shabbily patched; the boards of plywood in the otherwise teak floor; the empty display case shoved up against one wall; the ebony piano with a missing leg, propped up by a table stacked with books; and the complication of odors—the overtone of spoiled curry, the under- tone of wood rot, of death. The first shots of the civil war had broken out across this house, he well knew, but he hadn't guessed that the house itself had sheltered battles. My God, how many men had been slaughtered in this very room?

"Come greet your father!" Khin called to the children.

They had been watchfully taking their father in, their faces trem- bling between looks of excitement and despair. But now Louisa began to pull her reluctant younger sisters across the room toward him, while Johnny hung back, fists tightening at his sides.

"That's not my father!" Molly hollered. "Don't let that Indian touch me!"

"What a terrible thing to say!" Khin scolded her, as the guests broke into peals of laughter.

Now poor Johnny began to bawl noiselessly behind his sisters.

"Of course he's your father!" Louisa cried, her serious, gleaming eyes on Benny's—but there was doubt in them. And when she ran to Benny and fiercely embraced him, she called out as though to the heavens, "He *is* our father! He is! He is! He *is*!"

After Saw Lay's suicide, he had lost all but the most superficial interest in the revolution and politics. Ne Win and his satraps had promptly seemed to forget him, and Benny had been happy enough to return the favor and disregard them. Of course, his fellow inmates often spoke about the ongoing war, and he'd been generally kept abreast of the state of affairs for the Karens (that much of the delta had been lost, including Insein; that the revolution was slowly being pushed up into the hills, and that U Nu had designated a corner of the already-lost backwater "Karen State"). But these dispatches had only confirmed Benny's growing sense that to be overly taken in by news of the moment was a grave mistake (the story that the Karens now had a state to lightly administer was just a story, wasn't it?—only 20 percent of Karens lived in that remote area, where there wasn't one urban center). And, bit by bit, Benny had recovered in prison, which had become his bulwark against the world. Recovered from the shock of losing Saw Lay, recovered from the tyranny of the moment—in large part through the fragments of writing which he'd continued to exchange with Rita, and by which he'd learned to tend to his inner landscape. Not that he'd been merely acquainting himself with *himself*. Rather, by means of his correspondence with Rita and the time he took just to think, he'd seemed to be clearing a view from which he could peer out at the broader human predicament. The sense of timelessness

CHARMAINE CRAIG

he'd experienced then, of expansiveness, of losing his insignificant self to the sweep of humanity, had been undeniable. It had felt akin to looking out at an ancient moonlit valley and then up at the unfathomable stars. He'd thought ceaselessly of his family then; he'd dreamed of them, worried over them so intensely he'd sometimes feared he would go mad. And sometimes, by means of the inner view he was cultivating, he'd felt as though he were mysteriously looking down over Khin and the children. But it was also a view that reminded him to be grateful for what he had in separation from them. Rita's far-off, infinitely patient, tender smile had been part of that.

And now the separation was a thing of the past. Now he was apparently a free man, yet he felt strangely sentenced to solitude all over again. For one, all the pleasure he'd taken in socializing was gone. Khin prodded him to arrange dinner parties to reestablish old business contacts. The British Rowing Club had been replaced back in '48 by the Union Club, which was frequented by government officials. "But there are other clubs," Khin said. "Go. Go!" It was as though she couldn't stand the stink of who he had become, the man who grew nauseated at the thought of meaningless talk, at the thought of strained smiles, exchanges that skipped over the shallows of halting drivel, only to alight—for a tense moment—on the possibility of depths beneath, of actual intimate exchange . . . No. No. It wasn't for him, not anymore. He had become far too sensitive for all that.

Many mornings after waking beside Khin—who didn't touch him, and whom he couldn't muster the confidence (or, he feared, the interest) to touch—he would sit in his old chair before the view of the hillside he'd so loved, the view that looked out over the Karen village of Thamaing, which Khin said was slowly being rebuilt after having been burned to the ground. He couldn't imagine why he had ever thought he had the right to interfere with Karen affairs. And anyway, the place itself seemed foreign to him—not Insein, per se, not even Burma, but the planet. The feeling of the rain when he

180

reached through the window to touch its wetness, the open expanse of the bunching clouds, and then the lush hillside along which the drive he'd had constructed snaked its way with such . . . *certainty*. It all seemed to be made for someone far surer of his place—or *any-one's* place—here. The sound of his children would drift through the house—the sound of his daughters singing or pretending ("Pretend you're a princess, Louisa, and your parents died, and an evil witch took over and made you do all the chores"), or of stout Molly gallop-ing down the hill with Johnny tumbling after ("That's *my* net, Molly! *I* get to catch the shrimp! *Mama!*")—and he would be overcome by feelings of sorrow for the inevitable pain they would feel, and then for the inevitable loss of that capacity to feel. God only knew what pain they'd *already* endured while he had been locked up—another source of his feelings of displacement; he had been told only, and in the vaguest terms, that the children had been moved to Kyowaing, where the Forest Governor lived, and then to Bilin, and finally to a remote Karen village, while Khin spent most of her months away from them, trading on the road and vainly seeking news of him.

Increasingly, he shut himself into his old study, retreating from Khin's beseeching looks and the younger children's noise with the excuse that he was coming up with a business plan. ("For . . . ?" "Phar-maceuticals. An import business. I have a Swiss contact. Perhaps you've heard of La Roche?")

"Have you finished the plan?" Khin would ask after nervously popping in on him.

"Still working the figures," he'd say. How he pitied her! She still held out hope that the man in front of her could be restored to the man she'd thought significant.

In the widening space between them, he seemed to see shadows of the men she had known during their days apart. (*"Passing in and out like shadows with erections"*—wasn't that what Ne Win had said?) What did Khin need *him* for? She had survived and supported the family without him.

"I'll turn in, then," Khin would say at last, looking weary and defeated.

And in her absence, the silence of the house would become excruciating.

And standing to follow her, he would confront his reflection in the oval mirror by the door. And before he could turn off the kerosene lamp, he would see his face staring back at him, fallen, with puffy drooping eyelids and a twisted glistening mouth—haunted—but still somehow gasping for air.

He had been afraid that, up close, Rita's soul would be less recognizable to him, or that, on the contrary, their recognition of each other might be so complete that he would have no choice but to call an end to his marriage. But as soon as he was led into the visiting shed, nine months after his release—as soon as he saw Rita sitting in the failing light—he knew he had no reason to fear. There was a kind of silent declaration of being emanating from her skin. It filled him to bursting with compassion. It made him want to shout with regret, with rage over her aloneness and constriction. But not with passion.

For a while they just observed the unexpected awkwardness of sitting together. He sank into the rickety chair across from her and allowed her to take him in: middle-aged (could it be he was really only thirty-two?), wrecked of body, somehow surfacing from a grief as profound as any he'd succumbed to in his life. And he confronted the realness of her face, her extraordinary thinness, which seemed to have something to do with the faint lines over her thickly lashed amber eyes, with the knot of her wiry hair, and with the dryness of her fine fingers resting on the lip of the table. He didn't want to notice her dissimilarity to what he'd imagined, her slight and innocuous imperfections, but, yes, the animal in him confirmed what it had sensed the moment he'd walked in: that he was safe from chemical interest in her, and just as helpless not to give off cues that would tell her as much. Would she be disappointed?

As if to prove to him that she was beyond either baseness or judgment, she broke into that familiar expression of generous kindness—her smile!—and he had to look back at the door for a moment in order to conceal his sudden rush of emotion.

"I don't see Zay," he muttered stupidly.

"Who?"

Her voice! Even with this simple, banal question, it resonated with gentleness, centeredness.

He turned back to the vision of her still smiling searchingly at him. "I tried to come before," he stumbled. "Several times. But they were intent to have me wait only to turn me away. Once I brought a cake—a pineapple cake Khin made—"

Was he imagining that a subtle change came over her face at the mention of Khin's name (which he hadn't *meant* to mention), a diminishment of her smile's generousness, a closing of her eyes' vast reach? Or was it only that he was seeing her through the lens of his own intensified embarrassment—about being sorry for recklessly mentioning his wife, about having lied to that wife by repeatedly claiming to be visiting an old business colleague, about knowing—*knowing*, now—that he did belong to Khin.

"One of the guards," he persisted, "had a fine time turning the cake into a pulp with a rod, looking for razors or some such thing. And then today, they waved me in with no trouble at all. Makes no sense."

Whatever hesitation he thought he'd seen narrowing her features was gone, and it sent him into a faltering silence, through which her smile (of empathy? of remorse?) only deepened.

"Your voice," she said after a moment. "It's much lower than I'd expected."

"I'm surprised you didn't hear it in your cell. Have a devil of a time keeping it down."

He'd often seen her laugh, but to hear laughter falling from her lips in such loose, forgiving waves filled him with warmth, with worry for her, with guilty awareness that though he loved her, their romance had ended the moment he'd left prison.

"I wish I'd heard your voice when you were here," she said. "It would have been something . . ." But she couldn't finish, and he had to glance back at the door again.

"I thought," she said after a pause, in that gentle, steadying voice of hers, "that maybe you wouldn't visit."

The vulnerability of the confession, like a hook under the ribs, drew his gaze back to hers. How nakedly, how honestly, she faced him.

"What I mean is that I miss what we had, Benny . . . The writing . . . But I would give up all communication, keeping in touch, if it hurts you. If it keeps you from your life and the world. I wouldn't want you to hold back on my account."

Was that what he'd been doing?

He was too moved by her humanity to answer, to do anything but reach across the table and take her thin, cold hand in his. Silenced, she stared with choked relief into his eyes, and he clung painfully to her hand, aware that he was being rescued by her again, though not in the way she would have wished.

Time took on its old sprinting character after that day, when he determined to claim as much time as he could—with his children, in service of emancipating Rita, and for Khin, the woman from whom his time had been stolen.

The truth was they hardly saw each other anymore, he and Khin. Of late she had begun moving some of her personal items into one of the guest rooms, as if to decamp from him, and she often headed to the Karen village across the highway to tend to the sick or deliver a child (or make love to a better, kinder, bolder man, Benny had to wonder). When they did pass each other in the hall or kitchen, he felt her looking at him with respectful, frightened anticipation, as though she were waiting for him to speak the words that would restore them to the closeness they had once almost perfectly shared. But he somehow couldn't come up with those words, couldn't manufacture passionate gestures. And anyway, there were other kinds of loving gestures to be made, he assured himself—ones just as expressive of his investment in their marriage and her happiness.

The government was swiftly nationalizing companies, and their family had been limping by on sales of ice, which he no longer had the rights to distribute, and by selling off pieces of their property. At last, he earnestly tried to put together an import deal with La Roche. He had developed ties with some of its executives at the height of his prosperity, and they were intrigued now to learn what Rita had disclosed to him in prison: that Rangoon General Hospital had long been perilously short on medications. (It didn't hurt that pursuing this particular line put him in regular touch with the hospital chief and officials in the health ministry—any one of whom, Benny was convinced, could maneuver Rita's release in return for certain favors.)

Under the cover of this La Roche business, in the shadow of the broad black (government?) car always trailing his own decrepit one, he was also putting together a dizzying picture of what time had done to the country. Just as Aung San had, U Nu was beating the unity drum, claiming to want to overcome discord among the ethnic groups ("to convert their clanism into patriotic nationalism so that any insult or threat to the Union becomes as unbearable as an insult or threat to one's family" were the prime minister's words); yet the programs Nu had recently put in place promoted what Benny thought of as a Burmanization of the country. There was Nu's mandate that only Burmese could be used in governmental affairs and in schools, and that history be taught from a perspective of Burman nationalism; then there were his Ministry of Religious Affairs' loud efforts to spread Buddhism. Lately Benny had heard rumors, from vendors sporadically floating up his drive, of other more hushed-up discriminatory policies—including the government's stripping of land from "foreigners" (even those whose families had lived in Burma for centuries) and the widespread denial of applications submitted by minorities for licenses, loans, and citizenship. He wouldn't have been surprised should the prime minister decide to scrap the country's anglicized name along with the foreigners, and rechristen the place Myanmar in honor of the Burmans' more erudite word for their own ethnic group. At least then it would be obvious to the rest of the world—*wouldn't* it?—that this government had an agenda to monopolize power for the Myanmar people.

The rest of the world. More and more, as his days of freedom sped by—as he played with the children, and plotted Rita's release, and worked to restore for Khin a semblance of their old life—it became clear to Benny that there was something else he must do with his time, something directly pertaining to his wife and her people's freedom. And that something had to do with beaming a message out from Burma to the other side of the world. But how? And precisely what message would he send?

One sweltering night he paced his study in nothing more than his underpants, mumbling to himself. "The problem . . ." he said. "The problem . . ." The clock on his desk ticked with extra force, as though to comment on the slowness with which he was trying to arrive at his inchoate point. He put out a cigarette and passed by the faltering light of the floor lamp. The problem was that there would always be problems among men, and neither Nu's "unity" nor communism accounted for that, or allowed men to negotiate their problems through government. Only democracy did that. "But even if *I* believe that we are all brothers and sisters—in spite of our differences—deserving of the same respect . . ." he said to himself. "Even if *I* believe it with all my heart, if *you* don't believe it—if you abuse my brothers because you feel they are not yours, that they are inferior—then I am forced to protect the brotherhood you abuse."

He lit another cigarette and smoked it broodingly for a minute, peering out his small open window at the moon. A breeze drifted in carrying the heavy scent of Khin's flowering trees and of the rain dripping warmly from the rooftop. He might have still been in prison.

"Yes . . . yes," he went on. He seemed to be picking up the trail of some truism. A man who lived in a state that, through Burmanization or the like, had *vanished* that man's culture no longer had the right—the freedom—to choose to live as a member of that culture. He was in a kind of prison . . . So . . . He took another languorous puff. "What if we divide the country into ethnic states within a larger federal democracy? Each of those states could enjoy a degree of self-determination."

Even as he said this, though, he felt defeated by hopelessness, by the humidity of the night, and by a host of problems that his solution would give rise to. "Bah!" he spat, putting out the cigarette with disdain. "In any case, the Burmans will never give up territory!"

"Daddy?"

When he turned with a start, his heart leaping, he saw Louisa standing in the doorway, her long braids stretching mournfully halfway down her nightdress. They seemed, those braids, to be a strange gesture to a childhood the girl had already left behind. She was tall for her age and undeniably beginning to develop, taking on the lines of a woman with all the attendant complications and sensitivities. Yet in her eyes he saw a young child's need for reassurance. Lately, she'd been popping in on Benny when he least expected it, peering at him as if trying to ascertain how much of him had survived—how much of the father she'd once known remained in this house, indeed in this life that they were all trying to remake.

"Can't you sleep, darling?"

"What are you doing?"

There was nothing insincere about the question, nothing snide or accusatory. Yet something about her eyes, about their impenetrable stare, made him feel cornered, small, utterly effete. They seemed to shine with worry, with her latent fear that he was now impotent. That what he was doing was *nothing*, merely a waste of time.

Through the window another saving breeze drifted in, and he had the sudden instinct to escape. But he found himself turning to her, as if she were the solution he had all along been seeking, and he stammered, "If you aren't prepared to fight against injustice—if you aren't prepared to risk *everything* to defend the liberty of all human beings—"

"Yes?" she said quietly, and he saw how pale and alertly frightened she'd become, fixed in the doorway.

"Go to sleep," he said, more shortly than he'd meant to. And then, to soften her stricken face: "It's very late."

He met the two Americans at the Orient Club in April 1954.

He'd first seen them loitering at the bar, thumbing their drinks as they watched the couples on the dance floor floating by. Soon he was buying them another round and describing, as quietly as possible under the shrieking music, the editorials he'd recently submitted to American and British venues without response—"all in English, of course, and meant for a Western audience, but about Burma. You don't have any contacts or know how a chap could go about getting something like that published? I thought perhaps the *Times*, or *Newsweek*—"

The younger, more amiable one of the pair seemed to appreciate his deference to their perspective, and put on a thoughtful face even as he continued to leer at the ladies, while the older one scrutinized Benny over the rim of his perpetually raised, seemingly untapped drink (or at least he looked older, with his uniformly graying thicket of well-combed hair, the paunch ill concealed by his wilted button-down, and the cumbersomely oversize glasses behind which he hid his assessing eyes).

"It's got to be topical," the younger one said. "I dabbled in journalism for a while, and I can tell you that you have to find a way to *frame* your story—link it to something people are *talking* about. Nuclear power. Or something friendly. Take Miss America—they're putting the pageant on television later this year. Now, that's a feel-good story. Also links into people's dreams. Maybe you frame your story with the Miss Burma pageant—*is* there a Miss Burma pageant?"

"Communism," the older one put in carefully. All along, he'd been observing the conversation, and now, pushing his glasses up over the slick bridge of his nose, he continued, just as cautiously. "Vietnam. The Domino Theory."

"The *Domino Theory*?" asked Benny. He hadn't heard of it.

"Yeah, well, those are obvious," the first spat. "I'm giving him an angle that'll be *unique*."

The older one didn't cringe exactly, but his gaze seemed to retreat, to move inward, as though in shame, or in buried anger. What an awkward chap, Benny thought. He had the sense that the fellow's unbecoming appearance—the wide rings of perspiration under his arms, the way the few pink pustules on his skin glistened—was caused less by the room's stifling air than by a chronic hesitation and uneasiness within him. It was terribly clear he had little respect for the younger chap. So what was he doing with him here?

"I'm sorry," the awkward one said now, setting down his drink and mopping his brow with his sleeve. "I have—I have a train to catch." And without offering his hand to either of them, he lumbered away into the crowd, like an outcast.

For a while, Benny and the guy's friend just stood remarking his clumsy retreat.

"What did you say brings you here?" Benny said finally.

The other, appearing even more relaxed, leaned back into the bar and began to eye the girls again. "Oh, we're Bangkok based," he said lightly. "Work for a corporation you wouldn't know—building airstrips, that kind of thing."

"May I ask the name?"

"Sure you can." He flashed Benny a twitchy smile. And then he said, too brightly, "It's called Sea Supply."

The "falling domino" principle, Benny learned, was a term used by Eisenhower in a speech made earlier that month. "You have a row of dominoes set up," Eisenhower had said, speaking of communism in Indochina, "you knock over the first one, and what will happen to the last one is the certainty that it will go over very quickly." In other words: if one country in Southeast Asia aligned itself with the Communist Bloc, all of Southeast Asia would soon do the same—followed by the Middle East, if not Japan and Europe.

There was no reason to assume that Eisenhower's theory justified the strange American duo's presence in the country. Yet something unsettled about each of the fellows had left Benny to wonder if their feats of engineering with Sea Supply were really as modest as "building airstrips" and "that kind of thing."

It turned out Benny didn't have long to wait for his answer. In July, the broad black car that had been increasingly tracking his excursions from the compound through the rain followed him as far as the American embassy, to which he'd been invited for a casual reception as the guest of one of his La Roche contacts. Soon enough, he found himself standing shoulder to shoulder at the buffet with the American ambassador himself—a scrubbed-pink, arrogant sort called Sebald, who looked like just the type to live in terror of catching some vile disease, and to whom Benny wasted no time emphasizing the country's need of more access to good medicine.

Yet Sebald couldn't be bothered to dignify Benny's attempts at conversation with even the briefest look of interest. Instead, the ambassador scooped himself dollop after dollop of gelatin salad, and then stared unhappily at the glistening green mound on his plate.

"I'll tell you what I find interesting," the man suddenly announced, straightening himself up and smiling with satisfaction into Benny's face, which appeared to look keenly foreign to the foreigner's eyes. "The natural resources in this country. Can you *imagine* the benefits through trade? It all depends on reinforcing internal security . . ."

But Benny, having drawn back from the liquored haze of the man's breath, was already noticing something else—*someone* else— scrutinizing him from across the crowded banquet hall. It was one of the Americans from the Orient Club, the older, awkward one, with the oversize glasses and the cautious gaze. He was standing, clutching his drink, and staring at Benny with a kind of focused alarm, as though to say that he'd seen everything, and knew all about Ambassador Sebald and all about Benny.

As though to say that in this nest of vipers, he alone was an ally.

That same day, after Benny contrived to cross the banquet hall to the American, who offered him a drooping hand and a covertly extended damp card that read "William Young, South East Asia Supplies Corporation"—that very night, as planned during a brisk telephone conversation, Benny showed up at a dingy guesthouse with no evidence of having been followed, and there he was, William Young, opening the door, with his paunch and his rumpled shirt and his carefully combed nest of hair and his glasses, which he pushed up his nose before uneasily beckoning Benny inside.

"You want to sit there?" he said to Benny, gesturing to two chairs at the foot of a hastily made bed, beside a window whose sealed shutters seemed intent on closing in the room's heat, its sourness. But there was no odor of insidiousness that Benny could detect as he sat and took in the meager quarters: a table with a clock and a typewriter and an untidy pile of papers, a lamp without a shade, a door open to a view of a primitive lavatory. No personal effects, no suitcase or book or evidence of liquid drunk or food eaten. Save for the decrepit toilet and the bed with its bunched mosquito net, the room was stripped of every sign of human need and weakness. A temporary holding place, without question; but also a sort of description of the American's provisional character. What did he do to satiate himself? Benny wondered. And for love? Perhaps he consumed what he required as expeditiously as possible, taking care of his human urges shyly out of view of the rest of his life.

"I'm afraid I don't have anything to offer you," the American said, so redundantly it almost caused Benny to laugh, until he saw the nervous, disheveled way the fellow seated himself across from him.

"Mind if I smoke?" Benny said. "I've become enslaved to the habit in recent months."

The American raised himself from his seat and lumbered to the lavatory, returning moments later with an unwieldy glass ashtray that he must have kept alongside his toothbrush. "I guess you'll have to hold it in your lap," he said, thrusting the ashtray at Benny.

"That's fine," Benny offered with forced joviality. He was trying to dispel the tension in the room, and indeed it was almost agreeable, lighting up and filling the sour air with the bittersweet scent of his tobacco. Rather than face each other, they sat listening to Young's loudly ticking clock and to the sounds of the night—the spattering of rain and a volley of honks outside the shut window. They seemed to be observing their shared atmosphere of smoke, as though it might unveil some possibilities between them.

"You do have me wondering why I'm here," Benny said finally, noticing that the American's face was now beaded with sweat. "Perhaps you could tell me what exactly you do at Sea Supply—or South East Asia Supplies Corporation. Do I have that right?"

Young appeared to retreat further behind his glasses, even as his eyes darted to the cigarette at Benny's lips (in disapproval?). With a certain rebellious impetuousness, Benny found himself leaning forward and offering him the cigarette, which the man considered with astonishment before accepting. He put it awkwardly to his distressed lips. "Maybe you've heard," he said, shoving the cigarette back at Benny, "about a group of Chinese who've based themselves inside Burma's borders. For the past few years, they've been trying to stage attacks on the Chinese Communists from Burma. It's sort of a secret war that's mostly come to an end and that we were secretly assisting."

"*We* . . ." Benny ventured.

"My job was to coordinate the transfer of American arms—arms and ammunition—from Okinawa to these people's airstrip in Shan State. Under the radar of the Burmese government, of course. U Nu doesn't want to give China the impression that he's in any way supportive—he has to toe the neutralist line between the West and the Communist Bloc . . . And also under the radar of most of our own people. Ambassador Sebald. The State Department."

"But why under the radar of *your* people?"

The American turned his head slightly, so that the lenses of his glasses caught the lamplight.

Benny took a different line. "I can only assume that Sea Supply is some sort of Central Intelligence Agency front. And that if this secret war is mostly over, it has mostly ended unsuccessfully . . . What are you and your Sea Supply associates still doing here, Mr. Young?"

The American turned to Benny now with a kind of sorrowful frankness. But just as quickly, he bent over and pulled the ashtray away, silently urging Benny to put out his cigarette; and then he stood and made for the lavatory, no doubt to dispose of the evidence of the intimacy and transgressions they had just shared. Watching him, Benny seemed to see a picture of the man's entire life—the waking each morning in a sweat, the standing under a cold shower, the nights of stifled sleep, and, beneath it all, that private sorrow, that aloneness. Perilous, the instinct Benny had to identify with the stranger.

When Young returned to his chair, he took refuge in his habit of adjusting his glasses, yet there was something defended, something determined, presently animating his gaze. "You need to watch what you say around Sebald," he told Benny. "Ambassador Sebald has a certain perspective. It makes him suspicious of people like you."

"Like *me*?"

"What you described to me that night when we met—your editorials, your vision of a Burma with different ethnic states, one of them being Burman, a federal system—that's the last thing someone like Sebald wants to see happening to this country."

"You do realize that my interest has always been in what *Burma's* peoples want to see happening to this country—"

"Don't be naive."

"Excuse me?" Benny was surprised by the emotion in his own voice—by the high, hollow inflection of hurt.

"Sebald's perspective," the American went on, "the State Department's perspective, is that the Burmese government is inherently anticommunist. That it enjoys broad popular support among its citizens and therefore deserves our support and understanding."

"I see." What had Benny expected of the United States? What, really, had he expected? After all the hopeful, stupid editorials he'd dispatched to their papers with no response . . . His opinion didn't matter, because Burma's peoples didn't matter. Burma mattered only so far as it posed a problem for the countries that *did* matter: America, China, Russia.

But Young wasn't finished. "And because Sebald equates the local opposition groups with a threat of communism—"

"That's insanity—"

"Because he believes groups like the Karens are uniformly left-leaning, he argues strongly that the United States should be working to strengthen the Burmese central government and its army in order to assist in the opposition's liquidation."

"That's the term he uses—'liquidation'?"

"It's a common term to use in these kinds of cases."

"And does Sebald have Eisenhower's ear?"

"Certainly. To an extent."

"And yet here you are."

"We're not all State Department."

The rain had fallen off. When Benny, all at once desperate for air, stood and went to the window and cracked open one of the shutters, he could smell oil coming off the clean-washed tar road.

"It's important to keep that window closed," the American said quietly.

A distant figure walked briskly along the road, and something about the sight of that solitary human seemed an outward expression of the incredible sense of abandonment that Benny had been carrying around for nearly all his life. Yet at this very moment he was just as keenly aware of the proximity of, if not a possible friendship with Young, a balm to his isolation. He drew the shutter closed and turned back around.

"You still haven't told me what you want with me, Mr. Young."

"It's Hatchet."

"Say again?"

"My code name. If I contact you going forward, that's how you'll know me."

It was as if Benny had finally fallen off the ledge on which he'd been trembling—not of his freedom, precisely, but of time. He could have been back in his old cell. He could have been back with Saw Lay, hearing afresh his old friend's admissions and forewarnings. *"Should someone who goes by the name of Hatchet reach out to you . . . remember to consider the question of trust, Benny."*

"Hatchet?" he heard himself utter breathlessly to the man, who seemed to be nothing less than an intruder on what had been. "Doesn't exactly ring of *trust*. One could easily imagine it implies an agenda on your part to *cleave* the unwelcome elements from the body of Burma . . . And is that what you're trying to do with me, 'Hatchet'? Acquaint yourself with another Karen all the better to eradicate the opposition? Saw Lay warned me about you."

The American pulled his glasses away from his face, as though to hide from Benny's recognition of him.

"It was *you*, wasn't it?" Benny said to him, remembering *"the American"* whom Ne Win had described to him in the Barr Street lockup, the *"CIA man, no doubt,"* whom Karen leaders had been trying to meet in Thailand before they'd been butchered on the banks of the Salween. "The American our leaders trusted," Benny sputtered now, "the one they were attempting to get to when they were ambushed and Saw Lay escaped. And were you the one who gave Ne Win's 'Butcher' the tip about their location?"

For a minute, the man's unfocused eyes seemed to cringe from some terrible vision beyond Benny. Then he put his glasses on. "I can't say if you should trust me, Mr. Bension," he said, a quaver of emotion in his voice. "I can't say I trust myself with any of this. But I *was* trying to assist Saw Lay and the Karens. Not all of us forget what you people did for us. And I'm as upset as any of you about Ne Win's brutality . . . I can't do this alone."

"Do *what*? What is it that you are trying to *do* exactly?"

The man swallowed deeply, as though to keep down some unpleasantness destined to come out between them. "After the revolution broke out," he tentatively began, "Saw Lay introduced me to someone. A battalion commander in the Karen army—someone named Lynton."

Lynton. Benny had a vaguely disconcerting memory of having met a fellow by that name back in Khuli, when so many strong Karen soldiers had trudged through the village on their way to the front lines.

"He and Saw Lay served together in special operations under the British. I only met the guy once—but it was enough."

"Enough?"

Something like exuberance crept to the edges of the American's eyes—and of his voice. "You see, I'm just like you, Mr. Bension. I'm trying to find a solution to the Burma problem. And I believe Lynton can play a key role in that. In a pan-ethnic, anticommunist opposition coalition—one that could eventually influence the center. The problem has been making *contact*. Lynton's notoriously quick, impossible to catch, to intercept. Last time I talked to Saw Lay, a couple of weeks before they got him, I asked about the guy, what he was up to, and Saw Lay said . . ." A blush rose to the fellow's cheek, so that Benny felt almost sorry for him. "He said if I wanted to know about Lynton, I should ask your wife."

13

An Indistinct Figure

Sometimes when Khin thought of the period after Lynton had quit her bed—when she thought of how in desperation to provide for the children she'd started trading in peanut oil and cheroots and betel leaf, becoming part of an imprecise network of traders hawking their wares at open markets across the hot, wet, forested hills of eastern Mon State—what she remembered was the hours and hours, the weeks and months of walking. Walking without the burden of anyone or anything but what she had to trade.

What she remembered was the fog, the damp, the rain that came slanting across the sky like relief, the watchful trees, the hungry mothers at the markets, the muddy paths that ruined her feet, the vastness of the peaceful sky, and the fields and fields of rice. Certain days, she would head out into the depth of those fields—unsure of whether she was crossing into enemy territory—and the lush green stalks seemed to regard her, in turn, an indistinct figure walking in an indistinct place.

What she remembered was the burned-down villages and gouged, fallen bodies crawling with mosquitoes. And the sweat. Her sweat. Her smell. And the coldness of the Salween River's tributaries. Sometimes she would be squatting by a river, building a fire for the night or cooking herself a bit of rice, and she would have the instinct to tell one of the children to take care not to fall into the current. Or she would be caught in a heaving crowd at a market, and someone would all at once *see* her, and she would be seized by the desire to divulge her suffering—to speak of her four children, of the husband who might be dead or alive. It seemed to her then that the roof of the sky had been ripped off, and that they all had been left to wander aimlessly in an unending night.

Sometimes during that period, to banish the lightness of her solitude, she spoke to Benny, heard his voice in the wind's sighs. *This unknown is unendurable,* she told him. And once she heard him reply, *Someday, after we are gone, the unknown will come to light.* She had no idea what he meant, didn't care to muddle this moment of communion with misunderstandings. *How will I find you in the meantime?* she asked. *Keep looking,* she heard him say. And she shivered with the thought that he'd been referring to the afterlife, and she saw herself shrouded and bent over, doomed to wander and wander in search of him and safe territory, like all the Karens, for all eternity.

Some days, the walking consoled her, as did the weariness of her limbs, the heaviness of the physical load strapped on her back. It diminished the burden of her heart, of her memory, of her powerlessness over what would be. More than once or twice, when she met with the eager advances of men whose paths she crossed—traders or soldiers or displaced villagers, just as unhinged from what had been—she was arrested by an old instinct to cease. To give them what they wanted would be to die unto the agony of missing her family, and also to be born anew in relation to others—others untainted by her private past and memory. She was so terribly lonely! But the mandate to move on—to walk and walk and survive as some version of herself for the sake of the children to whom she dispatched supplies—spared her the indignity. There had been Lynton, yes, and before him there had been Saw Lay, and each had made his impression. But there were no others.

Until that night when she was on the threshold of reunion with Benny. Nearly a year had passed since she had closed her sewing shop and sent the children away—away from the ruthlessness of not just the plague, but also the pious, gossiping women of Bilin. But in early

November of 1950, she found an abandoned room in a quiet corner of the city, and she wrote to Hta Hta, asking the girl to bring the children back to her. News in Bilin, then still under Karen control, was that a man was standing trial for treachery, a Karen soldier whose own father had accused him of spying across the region for the enemy. Evidence was gathered, the man freely confessed to the crime, and a date was set for his hanging, the morning of which—before the children had yet returned to her—Khin appealed to the court to be allowed to question the prisoner to determine if he knew anything about Benny. The man was brought out to the visiting area with his hands cuffed together, his eyes already making an argument against reverence for his last moments of life. "I know everything," he boasted to Khin after she had presented him with her case. "The man you speak of is in Insein Prison. Has been for years. A traitor to the state, they say. If you can get to Insein, if you can get through Burman-occupied territory, you'll find Insein hospitable to Karens at this time."

Her subsequent reunion with the children was painful and hasty. Within days of greeting them, she was kissing them good-bye. Disguised as a Chinese woman, she set out to cross through Burman territory. Benny was alive! But in what relation to his former being? It seemed to her that all of them—and not just the Karen traitor—were guilty of making an alarming mistake, that they had been meant to disperse, to get along, to live together, and even to lose themselves in one another rather than destroying themselves in the mutual effort to survive. And one evening, in a state of distracted worry, she stopped in the gloom to build a fire under the shelter of a stand of mangroves by a stream when she noticed some shrapnel on the bank and lifted her eyes to find a man under the trees. That he was a Burman soldier was immediately obvious to her: he was armed with a rifle and a sword, and wore the star of the Japanese infantry on his cap. Their eyes locked. Then she was turning to flee, and falling onto the bank, falling under his weight, a beetle skittering past her face as the soldier shouted out words that were a slur on Chinese.

Five evenings later, an old trader found her in a hut where she'd stitched herself up in the middle of a rice field. He recognized her from the road, brought her medicine from a clinic, and promised to look in on her children in Bilin. Shouldn't she head straight to the comfort of those children? his anxious glances asked her. Yet she couldn't bear the thought of bending into their embraces only to feel their awareness of something profound in her body and soul having changed, couldn't bear to see the reflection of her horrified face in their eyes.

So it was that as soon as her swelling began to subside, she proceeded toward Insein, crossing nearly a hundred miles of swampy coastal thickets and clearings under the cover of several nights, understanding viscerally that at any moment she could be stopped, shot, done in. But before she arrived, a rumor reached her that Louisa had been slain during an invasion of Bilin. Wild now with terror, with the desperate wish to prove the rumor false, she reeled around, bursting back along the tracks of tangled land she'd just crossed. The earth itself seemed to have gone mad; though it was the dry season, rain came reproachfully, implacably, in unceasing torrents bent on impeding her progress. The surging tides, too, were a nemesis, as were the daylight, the roar of army trucks on the road, the questioning faces of the cared-for children in each village that she passed. Wanting to evade them, she plunged into forests lining the shore, into regions where bamboos and vines closed over her head, and where she cut tracks through the mud, through the vines, swearing to the fates that if she found the children, if she found them *all* alive, nothing would have the power to desolate her again.

Would she be able to enter Burman-occupied Bilin without being killed? It was a question that caused her to pause on the final morning, about twenty miles northwest of her destination, in a town called Kyaikto, the home of the old trader who had helped her, she remembered. And it was with the memory of his kindness and promise to her—his promise to look in on her children—that she stumbled along a row of shanties fronting a muddy stream, blindly hoping to catch sight of the elderly man and to receive, if not the miracle of good news from him, some wisdom.

Then, the vision: hundreds of feet down the muddy bank, in the haze of the weak morning, two small figures appeared, ambled to a launched boat, and climbed up onto it. Her profound sense of unreality, coupled with the impossible coincidence of the moment, didn't allow her to believe that she was looking at Louisa and Johnny. Even when some force of nature compelled the figures to turn their searching faces toward her, she couldn't trust the feeling rushing in—the feeling that they had all evaded the foreordained, or else intersected with the mysterious providence of grace. Maybe the children also doubted their eyes, because, as though equally unable to bridge the final distance between them, they merely watched her across it for a minute.

That minute was enough to return Khin to her body, to her awareness of its having changed in a way Louisa and Johnny might recognize. And when they soon broke from the boat, broke from their place on the bank, running and shouting, she opened her arms to receive them, yet she couldn't go on to press them to her chest with complete abandon.

Even after the trader soon made arrangements for all of them, including Hta Hta and her Effie, to be transported to Insein while hidden in the rear of a lorry—even after they were *home*, confronted by the shock of limbs floating in their well and blood spattered across their walls and bullets falling from their trees when it rained—she couldn't shake her sense of self-consciousness. Over the following weeks, she inadvertently kept her physical distance from her children, drawing away from their needy touches as if the toll she must pay for the staggering gift of their mutual survival was her isolation in her now-defiled body. A toll, she knew, that they also paid.

And when she finally faced Benny again in the visiting shed of Insein Prison, she couldn't help exacting a similar toll from him. She took his weak hand, but she could not embrace him.

Now and then, during the several years that had passed since that time, she had the instinct to confess to him what had happened to her during the final days of their separation, how a soldier had fallen on her off the Gulf of Martaban and raped her until she had lost consciousness, and then roused her by slicing off one of her nipples and slamming her ribs with the butt of his gun. But to confess would have been to let Benny in again, to let out the cry that might never stop coming. It was easier, it seemed, to be distant. To be quietly hurt by his inability or unwillingness to notice how much she had changed. It was easier to escape to the Karen village across the highway, where the sick and needy whom she served had nothing to begrudge her and only surprised thanks to provide.

Easier, that was, until 1954, when everything about *Benny* changed.

By now, Louisa was going on fourteen, too composed and concerned about others—about her father—to dare remark on the frenzied interest Benny had begun to take in the world again, the way he would often rise from his chair in the middle of supper and mumble something about needing to meet so-and-so for a drink. Johnny, at nearly twelve, was openly defensive on Benny's behalf ("It's too boring here—with too many girls!"). And Molly, not yet six, still treated her father with little more than wary curiosity. Only Gracie, at nine, seemed to be extinguished by Benny's increasing absences. When he happened to be out late, the girl refused to be put to bed, begging Khin to be allowed to light a lamp and wait up by the window for him. If Gracie was still awake when the lights of his car flashed up the drive, her eyes shone with a renewed happiness that Khin tried not to be unsettled by (why did the girl love Benny so much more than anyone else—only because he'd been missing for so much of her life?), just as she tried not to concern herself with the thought of what Benny was actually doing during these excursions: whatever that was, she told herself, it must be keeping him going.

But one July night, as she sat on the sofa with Gracie sleeping beside her, she heard the car stop out by the portico, and then there was a long pause before the creak and slam of its door. The delay told her that Benny was reluctant to return, and she had the sudden, old impulse to hide, to evade a collision with the future that would cause them pain. The sight of Gracie's precious and defenseless sleeping face on the worn seat of the sofa—the face of Saw Lay in softened form—held her there. Then the front door was opening and Benny was standing in the entryway. He must have expected to find her there—the lamp was lit, as whenever she and Gracie waited for him. With his hat in his hand, he looked at them across the glowing living room, and she saw something powerful and aroused in his eyes. He could have just emerged from a bracing mountain lake, or from a bed in which he'd plunged into an unexpected passion. And there was something ferocious in his stare, something never before directed at her: the scorn of a man seeing his wife, whom he'd thought noble and beautiful, with fresh disappointment.

"Are you in love with her?" she found herself saying, not with spite, but with genuine hurt and a need to understand.

He seemed confused, then irritated. Then that awful, killing disappointment washed over his face. "It's not what you think," he said.

She thought that he was finished—he turned and proceeded to the staircase.

But he stopped and looked around, almost with resignation. "Someday," he said, "not now—I really couldn't stand to hear anything else now . . . you'll have to tell me about Lynton. If you know where he is. If that's why you leave the house so often."

Someday. The closest they came to it—to coming right out and addressing the subject of Khin's former affair and present blamelessness—was about a week later, on an early morning just past dawn, when she was sitting in the kitchen with Hta Hta, drinking coffee before the commotion of the school day.

Unexpectedly Benny appeared in the kitchen doorway, fresh from the shower and dressed with care, and bringing with him the scent of cleanness and something like estrangement. He stood surveying the women at the table and the contours of the small room, where so much life happened in his absence. Then he turned his defended eyes to Khin and said, very matter-of-factly, "It strikes me that it was unfair not to tell you how I learned of Lynton." He'd swallowed down Lynton's name, and maybe to recover his nerve he went on very swiftly: "The point is I'm not at liberty to say. Though I can tell you that my source had his information from Saw Lay, who must have had it from one of his men. And I shudder to think what the news did to our old friend."

She couldn't react for a moment. Something twisted in her chest, and she was so immediately breathless that she heard herself beginning to pant. That Saw Lay had suffered because of her—that the embarrassment she'd suffered in Bilin should have reached him, should have caused him hurt—that Benny should want to inflict this on her—that *he* should be so hurt . . . As though to prove that her own sudden suffering didn't exist, she said, with a calmness and viciousness that astonished her, "I wish I did know where Lynton was, because I'd run to him."

The expression that this put on Benny's face was pinched with injury, with dismay. But gradually a smile of satisfaction spread across his face. It seemed to tell her, that smile, that he suspected as much of her. He closed his eyes, though, and then he said, with genuine feeling, "One's treachery is such a difficult thing to admit."

What she wanted was to come clean about it all, to tell Benny everything, to say something about their time being short: now all of that was over—what had happened with Lynton, the various breaches that had hurt their marriage over the years—now they were together and there was no excuse for them not giving each other all of their forgiveness and all of their affection. Lynton had been a means of survival, she wanted to say, whereas Benny was her sense of significance—and wasn't she his?

Fifteen years had passed since they'd met on the Akyab jetty, nearly half their lives, and she still vividly recalled the surprise of Benny's hungry eyes, the smell of the dense salt air, the sound of the waves smacking against the floats of a seaplane, the way he'd smiled tenderly at her and the boy who was her charge. Now when she saw Benny across a room and noticed how rigid he'd become—as though his back were hurting, or as though he hadn't been softened by a loving touch in years (whereas, until recently, she'd supposed he'd resumed his love affairs)—now when she remembered her first startling impressions of him in Akyab, she thought he'd grown more dignified because he carried more evidence of having lived and suffered. And she was flooded with remorse for having kept her physical distance from him since his release from prison. Shame had held her apart, fear of how he would look at her once he saw what had become of her body, of her breast. It struck her that to care about him, to continue to ask for his care, would be to accept the damage that the future would bring them. And she understood that she loved his damaged body, loved it with her own damaged one. She wanted to take off her clothes and lie in bed with him, to press herself close to his skin, to give him everything she had to offer.

But other times, when he shouldered past her up the stairs, or returned to the house without bothering to greet her, she found his coldness to be desolating. It was as though he'd forgotten she was the same person who had shown him so many years of warmth. She tried very hard to proceed without expectations, to remind herself that what she thought of as the normal attentions owed to a wife by her husband were meaningless, that as long as she fixated on her disappointment she was doomed to live an unhappy life. She tried very hard to take the gifts as they came—when Benny gave her a strained smile, say, or took a few minutes to laugh with the children. But as many times as she set out on any given day to shower him with gifts of her own—to make a loving remark, or even, perhaps, to take his hand—that terrible twist of resentment and humiliation would stop her, and in spite of herself she would remain aloof with him, and in her thoughts she would cough up recriminating words. *How dare you hold Lynton against me after all of your cheating years? You're the one who took those women to bed right under my nose, whereas I didn't know if you were alive or dead when I was with Lynton. You can't imagine what that man made me feel—the pleasure he took in the wife you spurn!*

Lynton. Increasingly, she was overpowered by a physical desire to be overcome by that beautiful man again, to be overcome by the sheer, strong *certainty* of him. The thought of never again being vanquished by such satisfactions staggered her. And she started shouting at the children because she couldn't take her frustration out on anyone else. "He's gotten fat and lazy, your father," she told the younger girls as she tugged at their unruly hair. "He sits around, expecting to be served, as if it were the old days when he was making money. His lordly ways. Doesn't even see what the rest of us do for him. How I have to sew the shirts he sweats in. Hta Hta doing the work of ten servants while he refuses to pitch in. It must be wonderful to pretend that chores and bills don't exist."

Under the influence of her roughness, the younger girls grew peevish. "You're hurting me!" Molly cried, while Gracie dashed out of the house to climb the trees.

"Stop it!" Khin screamed when Johnny slugged Molly, who swung wildly back at him with her fat little fists. "You're twelve, for God's sake, Johnny! What's *wrong* with you?"

"How do you expect any of them to behave when you're so mean to Daddy?" Louisa challenged Khin one evening.

Khin had been trying to get the younger children ready for bed, having told Hta Hta to take a break with her own little Effie, and having just bathed Molly with extraordinary difficulty. Louisa, it seemed, had come to the nursery to tell them good night—she was heading out to a party—and Khin was stunned to see how serene and striking the fourteen-year-old appeared, standing at a sort of regal remove from the rest of them and wearing her best sarong, with her hair done up and a scarf draped elegantly around her shoulders. Khin was reminded of that moment during their reunion at the Forest Governor's house, when Louisa had emerged in the dress that Khin had brought her, looking transformed by newly discovered self-possession. And hadn't Khin, too, been transformed then? Transformed by a subtle envy toward Louisa that would later blight her days with Lynton.

Now, in the girl's wide-set eyes, there was the spark of upset and accusation, as if she stood in judgment of her mother—of Khin's pathetic diminishment in the face of ordinary motherhood and her own superior dignity. Never before had she dared look at Khin that way.

"You *are* your father's daughter, aren't you?" Khin snapped at her.

And it was true. Louisa had always adored Benny, as he had her. The injustice of that exclusionary love—the injustice of all three of Khin's eldest children preferring Benny after everything she'd done for them—struck her so forcibly, she had the momentary thought that she hated Louisa, hated all of them.

In October of that same year, a terrible thing happened. They woke to a loud banging coming from down the hill, and soon discovered half a dozen Burma Army soldiers assembling a hut at the bottom of their driveway. Benny had been sentenced to an indefinite term of house arrest, one of the soldiers informed them. "Without charge or trial?" Benny asked the soldier, but the ignorant thug had no idea what he meant.

Khin had all but forgotten the larger world of politics, of the war, since returning home to Insein. Of course, she knew from Benny that the Burma Army had been focusing its offensives on the hills rather than the delta region, and she'd thought with concern of Lynton out on the front lines. But the threats he faced—the threats they all continued to face with the war unresolved—menaced her as if for the first time.

And all that first day of his house arrest, Benny sat as if menaced in his study, amid the forest of his papers and books, staring at the shadows on his wall to glean some truth they obscurely reflected. He could have been a child both fascinated and frightened by his unknowable surroundings.

To rescue him, Khin finally charged into the room with a shot of brandy. "Does this sentence have something to do with what you weren't at liberty to tell me?" she ventured to ask. She meant what he wasn't at liberty to tell her about the source who'd informed him of her affair with Lynton.

The face Benny turned to her twitched with confusion. "If it does," he finally responded, "either I've been discovered, or I've been an idiot."

That was all he would say. But it was enough. Khin later reasoned that he had either been turned on by someone he trusted or discovered by the enemy—that enemy being U Nu's government or Ne Win's army. Ne Win, whose children attended the same school as Louisa, Johnny, and Grace, she thought with a shudder. How carelessly Khin had brushed shoulders with that despotic general's wife, Katie, whose tight little mouth always seemed to be suppressing a smile of disdain when she passed Khin on the school grounds. How stupid Khin had been not to find a way into the woman's good graces. How self-absorbed and naive. It would be impossible now for Benny to conduct business—and, as it was, the diminished returns from his ice plant were barely keeping the children schooled and fed!

Still, there was something reassuring about the thought of Benny being hidden from others' scrutiny, hidden from others on whom he might turn his own scrutinizing eye. Surely his view of Khin would be altered now that she was the only woman within his sight.

The Miss Burma idea came about several months later, when they were hosting a dinner for a small gathering of friends, one of whom asked what Benny proposed to keep himself busy with, to which Khin spontaneously answered, "With his thoughts, of course."

She hadn't meant to be derisive, but all she'd seen Benny do since his house arrest was sit and scratch out the occasional line in one of his notebooks (notebooks she'd peeped at to find an impenetrable morass of tangled English script). Anyway, her mocking tone with Benny and his with her had become something of a habit, so she wasn't surprised when he, seemingly unable to restrain himself from deriding her in turn, surveyed the dining table with a sort of glee and said, "Khin would no doubt rather I spend my time drumming up business from within my new prison. Or, if I really must engage my higher faculties, she'd probably be happier if I were to join the government's scribes and report for the *Nation*"—the *Rangoon Nation* being one of the country's sanctioned newspapers. "You would prefer that, wouldn't you, darling?" he said, turning to her. "Just think of what I'd write. Perhaps a little ditty about the Miss Burma pageant later this year—if I could somehow contrive a way to go and watch it."

His outburst—which she'd heard over a pounding in her ears—seemed to have taken him aback more than it did her; yet on the heels of it came a suggestion that deeply injured her: "Or, even better," he pressed on, while his friends hid their embarrassed faces over their soup bowls, "I could do much as you once did, my dear, and get to work on a campaign making our Louisa over and entering her into the beauty pageant."

"She'd have to win Miss Karen State first," one of his friends helplessly put in.

"Why not use her loveliness to our advantage?" Benny said, ignoring him.

It was a new low for him, these depths of cruelty to which he sank; not quite submerged within their murkiness herself, Khin made out obscurely the resentment he must have felt toward her since she'd sacrificed some of Louisa's innocence for the possibility of his release—a release he hadn't actually wanted, she suddenly glimpsed. And now he was stuck in this house with her.

"Now that I think of it," Benny said to the table, "Louisa becoming Miss Burma *would* give me something useful to write about, wouldn't it?"

"Come now, Benny," his friend said, sweating over his soup. "Hang this beauty pageant business—"

But Benny was too far into an argument that, once made, he'd never be able to take back, she feared. "It would certainly give Louisa— and us as a family—a platform in the international sphere, wouldn't it?" he sputtered. "Yes, that would be 'an angle' as the Americans put it. Might even get us back in the government's good graces. And the money! It's no secret that I'm an utter failure as a businessman, that Khin has had to make terrible sacrifices—"

"Stop," she heard herself say weakly from her end of the table.

Her face was trembling, and it made her all too aware of how pathetic she must have appeared, like a debased servant who'd been made by her master to impersonate the mistress of the house.

"I can't deny that the idea of Louisa being crowned appeals to my vanity," Benny kept on. From his tone it wasn't at all clear that he was still speaking facetiously. "To think of my daughter's picture looming on *their* billboards . . ."

To think of exactly that, for Khin, was suddenly to imagine herself becoming even less distinct. The more prominent her daughter became, the greater the shadow she would cast. And hadn't Khin been at risk of standing in that shadow as far back as her freest days with Lynton? She could already see it . . . Lynton alongside Sunny in some army truck on some highway, coming across just such a billboard featuring Louisa's outsize beauty.

But a thought occurred to her, one as frightening as it was rich with possibility. Well, and what if Lynton did confront such a glaring reminder of them?

Might not the memory of *Khin* outshine Miss Burma's face?

14

The Miss Burma Problem

Who was the ally and who was the enemy?

It was a question that preoccupied Benny soon after he was thrown into house arrest. It was a question that preoccupied him partly because the indefinite sentence was entirely benign given his sporadic meetings with the American (to whom he'd repeatedly insisted that Khin was ignorant of Lynton's present whereabouts), and partly because all communications with Hatchet had abruptly come to an end. Of course, William Young might have given the tip that had done Benny in. If that had been the case, well, Young could have been placed in the field precisely to assess the Karens' threat to America's and Burma's interests and relations. Or perhaps it was as simple as Hatchet having wanted to finish off their association the moment he'd accepted that Benny was never going to lead him to Lynton.

And it was a question that preoccupied him whenever he dared to consider the question of Lynton and Khin. Had she passionately loved that Karen warrior, who had managed to care for her and the children in Benny's absence?

Benny had made the preposterous suggestion about Louisa running for Miss Burma with Lynton in mind. After all, Khin had been fresh from the man's bed when she'd entered Louisa into the child pageant with the supposed aim of securing Benny's release from Insein Prison. Her every act of loyalty since their separation—including her persistence now by his side, in this house-cum-prison—struck him as compensation for the greater happiness she must have known with that other man. And in the presence of their dinner-time guests, without really wanting to hurt her (but perhaps wanting to goad her into an outburst that might relieve them of everything that had gone unspoken between them), he had pushed so hard for Miss Burma as his new solution that she'd visibly cowered at her end of the table before saying, "If you're so convinced, Benny, I'll see what I can do about it."

And, God Almighty, did she ever proceed to do just that!

Of course, he could have spoken up instead of mutely standing by (beside equally mute Louisa) while Khin went on to pore over fashion magazines and cut patterns for gowns and bathing suits, to be stitched together from her own dismantled petticoats and sarongs. Of course, when she later that year announced that she'd registered Louisa for the 1956 Miss Karen State pageant, he could have put his foot down and cried defeat, demanding this must not go on. But Louisa showed no sign of being negatively touched by her mother's carrying on. Rather, the perpetually serene looks the now fifteen-year-old girl increasingly cast Benny seemed intended to reassure him that he shouldn't trouble himself with concern about this pettiness. And he knew that to say *anything* to Khin would mean claiming responsibility for what he privately came to refer to as the Miss Burma *problem*. ("But I thought this is what you *wanted*," he could imagine her arguing. "A subject for your writing—what did you call it? An angle? A platform?")

The truth was Khin seemed to have become *invested* in Louisa's winning the ultimate title—as if, in addition to the potential financial and political rewards, her own self-worth might be salvaged by means of it. There was something personal and desperate about the way she began to harass the girl, constantly detailing how Louisa could improve upon herself ("Don't tug at your bathing suit—it's supposed to be tight—and pull your stomach in whenever you think of it." "You could do some toning exercises." "Are you washing your forehead up to the hairline? You don't want pimples all over your face!" "You see the women in the magazines, how each of them stands without slouching, as though she's wearing a beautiful necklace she wants everyone to see . . ." "Your calves are too big—that's unavoidable—but if you stand just so it will be less evident." "You're not going out without makeup, I hope!" "Pinch the tip of your nose for ten minutes a day—your father's is so big." "One scoop of rice, no more." "Did you forget to apply your face paste? Your skin will be ruined." "If you see Mrs. Ne Win, address her politely. She greeted me this morning. We're making an impression!").

Something unsuitable was happening to Khin. She seemed to be alternately harassed and exalted by the visions she was intent on conjuring out of the substance—certainly not the soul—of their eldest daughter (as though what she were conjuring were a perfected version of *herself*). At any given minute, she might instruct the girl to put on some dress she'd sewn and call for the family members to come admire it (Benny was quite dazzled by the sight of Louisa, whose figure had worrisomely taken on the dimensions of various Hollywood starlets', in a gleaming mandarin gown and gold lamé heels, the latter of which Khin had "borrowed from a friend," or more likely purchased on credit). Then she would just as suddenly decide that her creation was inadequate, that the outfit in question had to be altered; and, after commanding Louisa to take the thing off, she would station herself at the dining table to rip out seams and reposition hooks, while inconvenienced Johnny would invariably skulk off, and the rest of the household would be thrown into disarray—the younger, neglected children grabbing for attention that Louisa and Hta Hta could only semisuccessfully supply. If Khin was determined to remake her own world, she was just as effectively unraveling their shared one.

Yet one day—about a week before the Miss Karen State pageant—Khin seemed to remember her stake in him. All afternoon, light had poured in through the window in his study, enlivening the dust motes that rose from his desk while he wrote a long letter to Rita (with whom, since his latest incarceration, his correspondence had again become of urgent significance to him). The night was already deep, though, the last light having left him alone—relentlessly alone with his thoughts of Hatchet and Lynton, of whom he dared write only in his private journals—when suddenly Khin appeared in his doorway.

She was wearing a kimono, something silken and festooned with flushing pink orchids (something new, he anxiously observed), and she had just bathed. He seemed to feel heat coming off her skin in feverish waves, and when he turned to more fully take her in, he noticed she'd applied makeup to her eyes in the style she'd some-times worn when they were young, with little black wings darting out from the far corners of her lash line. That gesture—toward her youth and away from their aging—touched him, as did the gleam of girlish embarrassment in those made-up eyes. He was reminded of the first time they'd stood alone together, when she'd bared herself to him with such complete submission to her new role as his wife, to the requirement of their spontaneous intimacy. And it came to him that all of her maddened activities of late might have been directed toward just this—toward a rekindling of something almost extin-guished within her and between the two of them.

"Am I interrupting you?" she said softly.

"Not at all," he told her.

"Would you make love to me, then?"

"Excuse me?"

What an idiot he was, asking her to explain what he all at once utterly wanted. She was still a young woman, not yet thirty-five, still lu-minous, still hungering for a contact he could provide. But as though to convince him of all of this, and as though to persuade him to give her what she needed (just as she had on their wedding night), she took the comb from her hair (the same sandalwood comb he'd given her then!), reenacting her initial gesture of seduction—the unraveling of her incomparable hair, which he'd always been powerless to defend himself against.

For a moment, he stood observing her, now cloaked by the hair that reached to her feet and seemed almost to want to protect her. Then he went and took her warm face in his hands, and kissed her, and found alcohol on her breath. And (shoving away the thought that perhaps she'd been less loosened than *misdirected* by that alcohol's influence) he drew the kimono off her shoulder.

"Don't stop," she said, clutching the kimono and closing it again over her chest.

"Khin—"

"Don't speak."

"All right."

He buried his nose in her hair, in the crook of her neck. It was like entering a deep and endless flower, his senses primordially awakened.

"Tell me you want me," she said.

"I want you."

Firmly again, he drew her closer and pulled the kimono aside (and then pushed away his confusion about why she was fighting to keep herself clad, drawing the kimono up over her shoulder again).

"I want to see you," he said.

"Please don't talk."

"But you're beautiful."

"No."

He reached within the kimono to try to take her ample breasts in his hands, but she jerked away, staggered back, wrapping up her fountain of mussed hair with one hand, clasping the kimono over her chest with the other.

"What is it?" he said.

With a desolate, panicked glance she took in the surface of his room—of his desk—where he spent so many of his hours away from her. She seemed to be looking for an outward cause of a festering inner condition.

"Were you writing a love letter?" she said. And there it was: the old accusation, a habit she couldn't quit.

"Maybe," he lied, because he couldn't seem to quit the habit of their distrust, either.

"Who is she?"

"Someone I got to know in prison. Someone very dignified."

Immediately, he was sorry. But it was too late. In her stricken face, he saw so much hurt he couldn't speak.

Not even when she said, before rushing out of the room, "Why is it so hard for you to love me?"

Over the next few days, before the dreaded Miss Karen State pageant, Khin retreated behind the fog of their thickening estrangement. When they were in the same room, her glance would not penetrate as far as him, and he had the sensation of vanishing, of *being* vanished. He no longer existed for her. All that existed was Louisa's beauty—or Khin's refashioning of it. That was the lighthouse that promised to deliver her from the life she'd built with him.

She woke before dawn on the day of the contest—Benny heard her scurrying up and down the stairs—and by the time he came down for breakfast, she was dressed and almost calm, having her morning conversation in the kitchen with Hta Hta, while Louisa sat in her bathrobe at the dining room table, her own hair and makeup already done. There was nothing garish about that makeup, he saw as soon as he sat across from his daughter. On the contrary, the artistry typical of so much of Khin's sewing and gardening—the delicacy, the naturalness—had been brought to bear on the girl's lovely face, so that his next impression, when Louisa smiled sympathetically at him over the light morning meal of coffee and fruit she'd been permitted, was that somehow Khin had managed to clarify rather than muddy what was already there: the imprint of authenticity, of decency, and also of . . . of what? As Louisa continued to take him in, he became aware of being read by her intelligence, of being *assessed* . . . And there was something smoldering beneath the surface of her astute gaze, something that told him that she, too, was acquainted with inner demons. What she had survived (whatever she had survived, for Benny still didn't really know what had happened to his children during their years apart)—what she had suffered and overcome—had made its mark and dignified her beauty, made it extraordinary.

All of this, Khin, too, must have seen. And it unsettled Benny. It unsettled him all that morning and afternoon, as he sat waiting, stupidly, for his family to return to him.

"I made the mistake of suggesting this stupid business to your mother," he said to Louisa later that day, after she and her entourage had returned from the pageant, and Khin and Hta Hta with the little ones had disappeared upstairs. Louisa lay stretched out on the sofa across from him, smiling vaguely up at the ceiling, as though she were actually glad to have been named Miss Karen State.

"It doesn't matter," she said, the blush of exertion—or excitement—on her cheek.

"How did you get through it?"

Now she turned her amused eyes to him, as if to say that there was nothing about the subject she had to avoid. "I pretended to be somebody else," she said simply. "As somebody else, I could actually sort of enjoy it . . . Of course, the *real* me saw how funny it was—to be standing in a bathing suit with a bunch of other girls, in front of an auditorium of people who were fully dressed. Funny and embarrassing. To act the way the other girls seemed to want to act, silly and flirty, like you've never read a serious book, and you're desperate to be looked at—like you think your body's so interesting. '*Just look at me!* Don't you *love* my big behind?'"

She laughed, and without a false note, he observed. And how reassuring that she'd found a way to cope, to lessen the pageant's seriousness and power to demean her by casting herself as a player in a parody.

"Not so big," he said with a chuckle.

"Yes, it is!"

It was marvelous, the way she could laugh at herself, laugh the whole thing off, not to shield an inherent vanity, but because too much vanity was repellent to her. He loved to watch her laugh, something she did more freely, he'd noticed, when they were alone together, and when she seemed to leave her body and her beauty—to leave it on a shelf—in order to more fully become herself.

"You can picture Mama," she said, as Johnny ambled into the darkening room, a tormented look on his brow. "*'Tighten your buttocks! It jiggles too much when you walk! Tighten it!'* I was so worried about what she would think as I jiggled across the stage, I could hardly think."

"You're giving Daddy the wrong idea," Johnny interrupted, sinking into a chair near Louisa. "You belonged to the audience. You *were* Miss Karen State."

Louisa's laughter had dropped off, and now she looked at her brother with a sort of distressed solemnity. "That's sweet," she said.

"It's not sweet," Johnny told her. "It's undeniable."

She seemed to be waiting—and hoping—for the compliment to take the usual turn, to veer into a brotherly bout of teasing, but Johnny just allowed his statement to breathe in the air. And Benny was left to contemplate the silence within his other child, his son, who suddenly looked older and sadder to him, and so unlike the little boy who had scrambled around this room before the revolution. They had never really recovered from their separation, he and Johnny. Somehow, the chasm that had been opened between them was already, even at the time of their reunion, too wide to be bridged. Benny hadn't been there to protect him from other men's influence during the important years. And that, too, must have been part of what was inexorably separating them, that influence of other fatherly figures—or of one in particular—something the boy himself seemed forever to be arguing against. He was thirteen now, Johnny, and so smart with figures—determined, or so he said, to become a "businessman" like Benny, though the fact of Benny's present business failure obviously troubled the boy. He often complained about the injustice of their poverty, and had recently taken to reading books on economics and finance, as though in them he might find his own solution to the problem of their oppression. But the books, or what he discovered in them, seemed only to oppress him further; sometimes he sauntered around the house with the look of someone reckoning with the terrible limitedness of his own future prospects, the terrible narrowing of his view, a view that gave way only to obscurity. And Benny wanted to urge him to shake off his hopelessness, to remember the greatness that no amount of money could buy: the greatness that could be achieved only through a more forgiving reckoning—with life, with its painful truths, and with its beauty. But how could you force someone to see beauty before which injustice finally paled in significance? How, when Benny himself so often was blind to it?

Now, sitting in the darkening room with his children, in the presence of their unsounded thoughts, Benny was possessed by awareness of the moment's perfection. In another moment, this one would be gone—he couldn't hold on to it. And he seemed to see that this moment—*exactly* this—was what he'd been endeavoring to reach all along. This moment of sitting with his children, on furniture that was so familiar it seemed to be extensions of them, pieces of their existence. This shared, comfortable silence, while outside the night encroached, with its secret sounds, a siren on the highway, the threats they didn't have to mention to comprehend . . .

In the darkness, he heard Louisa sigh, and then she sat up with a reluctant smile, and turned on the lamp by her side, and said,

"Time for bed." And she stood and crossed to him and caught his hands in her delicate ones and kissed him on the head—something her mother would have hated because even to touch an elder on the head was to show him disrespect. "Good night, Daddy."

Then it was just Johnny facing him—Johnny, with those sad, large eyes, with that simmering intelligence and intensity that put him at risk. Looking at him in the glow of the lamp, watching how he began to nervously fidget—pulling at the knees of his trousers, and then drumming his fingers on the arm of his chair—Benny had the terrible thought that the boy was beyond saving.

But he said, "How have you been doing, Johnny?"

The boy's glance flitted up to meet his. It was clear from that glance that Johnny had come into the room with something to say. Benny could feel it now, the pressure of whatever it was on Johnny's mind exerting itself on the air between them.

"All right," he said. "School is hard sometimes. Not the work— that's too easy. I mean other people."

"I'm sorry to hear that."

"Just the usual meanness."

"That's disappointing."

"I guess so."

"Is there something on your mind?"

He sighed, as though to leak out some of that pressure building up in him. "Not especially," he said. But he turned his eyes more fully to meet Benny's, so that Benny was taken by their dignity, by their handsomeness and gravity. "I was talking to a kid at school," he said. "A government official's son. He was bragging about how they got money out of the Americans. I guess the Americans have too much wheat. Hundreds of millions of bushels more than they need. Their government wants to keep their wheat prices high, so they have to subsidize it, offload the wheat, sell it abroad, or even dump it at a 'special' price. And I guess that's what they did here. Sell it at a loss—of something like five million dollars. But they got something else for it, for the five million. They made our government put all of it in a bank here on deposit."

Listening to his son's story, Benny felt an old tug—their want of money, and his instinct to meet that want, to fight. Recently, one of his prison mates had spent the evening with him, prodding Benny to gamble, and Benny had been so thrown by the losses that he'd felt driven to raise the game's stakes, until finally Khin had burst in on them with a wad of cash with which she'd all but chased the friend away.

"Why would the Americans do a thing like that?" he said to Johnny now, trying to keep the curiosity out of his voice.

"I'm getting to that," the boy said with impatience. "See, the money's supposed to be used for *Americans*—to lend to them if they start doing business here. And the point is the money's just *sitting* there. It's been a year at least, and no one's touched it, no one's come forward, because no one *knows* about it. Our government's not going to say anything. And I thought . . ."

No doubt the boy was onto something, but pursuing that something could lead him only deeper into the void. America, the Burmese government: he was no match for them. Johnny's sights were fixed on the darkness, and Benny wanted to tell him to turn to the light.

"I thought," Johnny continued, "with your American—"

"*My* American?"

Johnny blushed, a kind of fury rising to his dark eyes.

"Have you been reading my journals, Johnny?" Lately in those journals, Benny had begun to address Hatchet directly—to address the American with the outrage of a person abandoned by someone trusted, by someone almost cherished—and the thought of the boy seeing that was deeply upsetting.

"The money's just sitting there," Johnny said again. "If he knew about it—if he knew how *much* there was—"

"What?"

"You could go into business with him. Show him how it works here—"

"And you think the Burmese government would dutifully hand the money over to him—that he'd dutifully hand me my cut? Listen to me, son—listen to me clearly—you're going about this all wrong. You can't work with them and expect any personal gain. They'll listen, they'll suck up your intelligence, but then they'll leave you to rot with your recriminations."

He wanted to go on—to speak of the beauty that had mostly evaded his own notice, the beauty that Rita had helped him to see. But the thought of all that made him feel foolish suddenly.

And Johnny said, with a contempt that further shamed him, "The money's just *sitting* there. *You're* just sitting there. *I'm* not going to sit here with you and suffocate!"

It began before it had begun, Louisa's reign as the nation's beauty queen. With still two months before the big pageant, the papers began to feature her "special" status as the "image of unity and integration," vaguely referring to her mixed heritage, all but denying her affiliation with the Karens (or the Jews) particularly.

"They've got us," Benny several times found himself muttering guiltily to himself during these days. He'd wanted, with this Miss Burma business, to have something to write about—or so he'd claimed; but it turned out he'd only given the *Burmans* an angle. Or, no, a *weapon*. A weapon of Burmanization. A weapon against revolution. For if Louisa, as the racially indistinct product of assimilation, was already a symbol of a "higher form of unity," as Aung San had once put it (one that might serve "national tasks and objectives"), then her *winning* the pageant would be an argument that racism in the country didn't exist, that there was no discrimination to fight against.

Just as appalling was Khin's seemingly willful blindness to the discrimination behind the media's fixation on Louisa. By all appearances, Khin was hoping that the media would soon similarly fixate on *her*! In the weeks running up to the pageant, she began to take tremendous care with her dress (adorning herself in some of the flashier shawls and sarongs she'd professed to be assembling for Louisa), and emerged from her bedroom every morning with increasingly youthful styles of hair and makeup. She was basking in a reflected light, experiencing the thrill of being an object of interest by proxy—all while the actual object (at least at home in Benny's sight) appeared determined to pretend that she herself was not being thrust perilously into celebrity.

It's nothing, Louisa's easygoing manner and laughter seemed intended to reassure him, as he hid from mental pictures of her posing on some garish stage, in some garish bathing costume, hands on her hips. Only once during this period did he see a twinge of similar horror pass over the girl's face—when Khin found the two of them at the dining table and thrust forth a magazine featuring the upcoming pageant's "front-runners," including a giddy-looking Louisa being crowned Miss Karen State.

Their family had been granted two special tickets to the Miss Burma pageant, and Khin had somehow contrived for him to have permission to attend (though she'd insisted on telling everyone—including Louisa—that *he'd* made the arrangements, so shamed was she, he thought, by his ineffectualness). So it was that on the day of the event, hours after Louisa and Khin had left, he found himself abruptly free. Or at least *rather* free, his "escort" being one of the Burma Army soldiers who manned the guard hut at the bottom of his drive. How very strange it was—strange and somehow ominously touching—when, at the bottom of that drive, the escort slowed his truck so that his fellow guards could sincerely applaud for the father of their nation's prospective beauty queen.

Evening was falling by the time they approached the Central Railway Station. Already a crowd was coming over the road leading to the stadium that had been named for Burma's liberator and protector of the populace, Aung San. Looking out his window at the commotion, Benny had the strange impression of taking in alternately a collection of individuals—a mother tugging at the hand of a young child, a delicate man hawking snacks, a police officer sectioning off a side street, a legless girl being wheeled along by a dog—and a collective force. The urgency and excitement in the air were undeniable, and in spite of his own cynicism (and in spite of the armed soldiers patrolling the road up ahead), Benny felt the tug of elation. It was breathtaking, the vision of this panoply of peoples, young and old, able-bodied and destitute, blameless and criminal—all taking possession of the streets. It was also irrational and oddly undemocratic, this impulse of thousands to catch a glimpse of whoever was crowned; the poorest among them wouldn't possibly be able to pay for even the cheapest tickets. But there was nothing rational or democratic about beauty itself, Benny told himself. And still, beauty was not classist or racist. From the looks of it, these people were prepared to adore whichever girl, of whichever origins, became their queen. Perhaps beauty alone had the power to transfigure people so. And yet, Benny reminded himself with a shudder, there was something insidious about beautifying the country's image by means of a girl, whatever her background, for somewhere in the darkness beyond the delta, innocent people continued to be shot and killed.

Half a block from the stadium, the truck came to a stop beside a jeep where two soldiers were waiting to escort Benny through the overspill of would-be spectators surging from the station. The narrowing evening was giving way to a deeper darkness, heightening the assault of sights and sounds and smells on Benny's desensitized soul. Soon, he was marshaled past a throng of beggars being rebuffed by a guard, through a stadium gate, into a tunnel, and out into an arena, where—in the shadows of an enormous stage that had been erected—he discovered Khin seated in a lower section of the packed stands. She claimed him with a look of relief as he stumbled toward her along the narrow aisle, and he was overcome by a feeling of belonging, of being bound to her by years of experience. How easily he'd forgotten the powerful pleasure she'd so willingly given him, the sensual offering of loyalty and children. Intoxicating, not just their early years, but *all* the years until his imprisonment—years when they had given themselves over to the lives they'd remade in order to be together. Now, approaching her, he seemed to see every one of their children's faces in her own still-lovely one. And when he sat on the hard bench between her and a heavyset man, and she leaned in to say something in his ear ("Did you see Katie Ne Win? She's sitting with *him*"), he was immediately comforted by the familiar sound of her voice and by the clean scent she was wearing, undercut by her own, almost undetectable deeper fragrance.

That feeling—of renewed appreciation for his wife, of closeness with her—only grew when at last the stadium lights went dim, and a hush came over the assembled thousands, and sweet music began to sound over the loudspeaker. It wasn't long before yellow floodlights shot up from the stage, and then a procession of bathing-costumed girls appeared before them. Many of these girls, he saw with a pang of sympathy, were too heavily made up; most wore smiles that were too theatrical; some tottered and swung their hips, as though to impersonate feminine confidence and magnetism; others cast defeated glances at the audience or blinked out at the darkness as if to find reassurance there. Then Louisa emerged in a simple white suit, and it was as if a switch were thrown . . . And *was* some amplification of lighting responsible for her skin appearing so luminous? Her smile seemed to reach out past him and across the stadium, to reach out as if to fling the gates open and let everyone in.

Who was this creature? he was still asking himself a quarter hour later, when Louisa was invited to present herself uniquely to the judges. Who had taught her to move on those gold heels—not cheaply or brashly; not frantically—no, there wasn't a tense or unnatural note in the way she fell into a smile, cast her eyes over the stands, turned, looked with another unabashed glance back at the audience. Here, rather, was a young woman radiant with self-possession. Yes, this was precisely what distinguished her from the rest. Not the mechanics of her beauty (the way her eyes were set above the sculpture of her cheek-bones, or the voluptuousness that Benny preferred not to notice)—all of these girls were knockouts, mechanically speaking. Rather, what distinguished her was what she *did* with her looks: disregarded them, so that the outer luminosity gave way to a more resplendent inner one. Wasn't it a truism that a virtue was a virtue only by dint of its keeper's unconsciousness of it? And didn't she seem to be unself-consciousness made manifest, a sort of heavenly body obediently prepared to shine on for the others spinning and circling around her composure, until the light of that composure must finally perish? I give you my light, she seemed to communicate, that you might have a measure of grace. I give you my naturalness, that you might see a simpler, more natural life, one unspotted by the shadows of divisive-ness. Yes, I have the blood of various peoples coursing through my veins, but what of it? We are all various. Don't despair. Stop these arguments. Content yourself with enchantment.

Benny reached for Khin's hand, and, by the grace of the moment, she took his fingers in hers.

Then Louisa was drawn into the shadows upstage, to be replaced by another contestant whose strained smile and panicked glances cried, *Look at me! Like me! Admire me!*

And Benny, casting around for some sort of respite from the agony of his feeling for the poor girl, turned from the stage and saw him. Saw Hatchet. One row up and across the narrow aisle—but could it be? There was the same nest of hair, the same perspiring pink skin, the same glasses, hiding the same intent, guardedly embarrassed gaze—a gaze now directed, it seemed in profile, past the poor girl in question, toward the shadows in which Louisa stood futilely trying to hide her light.

15

The Great Pretender

From the moment Louisa first posed as Miss Burma, with the crown on her head and the sash around her shoulder and the red roses in her fists—already, even then, as the cameras began to flash, it had begun: her long engagement with pretense.

Pretending not to be hurt by Mama's pinched look of defeat in the stands. Not to be troubled by Daddy's haunted smile of reassurance. Not to be desperate to apologize in the face of the losing contestants' shamed, strained felicitations. Not to be appalled by the clichés soon spewing from her own lips ("I'm so surprised! So honored!").

Pretending to want this.

And then pretending, as she took her victory walk, not to wonder who or what (other than her own compliance) was really to blame for her participation in the pageant (she had been told by her mother only that it, like the preceding Miss Karen State, was "important to the Karens"). And also pretending not to wonder who or what was really to blame for her "success." ("Image of unity" aside, how could a *Karen* prevail in a contest presided over by a panel of mostly Burman judges? How, really, could a *Jewish* Karen win, whose "foreign" father was an enemy of the state and under house arrest? How during this time of continued civil war, in a country bent on weakening "the influence of outsiders" and denying anyone's difference? How, unless Daddy *had* managed to fix the results, or unless her success had actually been part of some official plan to prove that if the minorities played by the rules, they, too, could be championed?)

And then, after the pageant, pretending not to notice how her change in status seemed to change everything else—how the fights that sometimes exploded between Mama and Daddy became more frequent, more violent, with plates (and even knives!) clattering against walls that harbored an even more stifling silence; how Johnny wouldn't meet her eye and cowered in his room studying for the Cambridge exams because he had to place first in order to secure the scholarship that would get him "the bloody hell out"; how Molly cried with more abandon and Gracie hid in the trees for longer stretches and Hta Hta and Effie made themselves scarce and even Louisa's best school friends had a need now to tease her, batting their eyes and flashing her coy smiles ("You went just like this!") and clipping her pictures from the papers and pinning them to the bulletin board (in playful support or jeering indignation?).

Pretending to smile through it all, and pretending to herself that she accepted her new life, her new lot. And then making light of that lot, of the press soon penetrating the most private corners of her existence—a press that seemed to collude with her pretense: not one of the reporters interviewing her acknowledged the hurtfulness of the labels they slung around her ("minority," "product of assimila-tion"), labels that narrowed her personhood; not one of them raised the subject of her father's former incarceration, or of his involvement in the ongoing revolution, or of the indefinite term of his current house arrest. And, in response to *their* avoidance, she smiled and posed for the photographers (in Burman dress, of course), and she calmly spoke about everything other than what most concerned her: the reality that at any moment Daddy could be taken away, thrown back into Insein Prison or hanged, and for no better reason than that she, Louisa, had not succeeded in pretending convincingly enough that all was harmonious, that *Burma* was harmonious, free of injus-tice and ethnic discord.

And when the falsely bright reports about her began to appear (about her "picture-perfect life," and her "dreams of stardom," and her position as a "top student at Methodist English, the same elite school that Ne Win's children attend"), she hid her embarrassment, which was almost as intense as if the reports had abased her. And she became accustomed to the garish colors with which her likeness was painted on billboards and reproduced in advertisements. Wasn't she to blame, in part, for their tasteless lack of shadow or depth, a lack that her own pretense had mirrored? But what choice did she have? she argued with herself in rare moments of self-confession.

She could feel it, at those moments, the small flame of her older self, the self she had become acquainted with in the absence of her parents during the early years of the revolution, after Mama had left her and the other children in Kyowaing, and the Forest Governor's wife had begun to beat them. Their crime was their existence, Louisa had obliquely understood, and she had heeded Mama's plea that they must not make a noise, taking each blow soundlessly, keeping her tears on the inside, until the lake of her grief had become so wide it had seemed almost inviting, a thing into which she could escape. Johnny and Gracie, too, had kept their anguish stopped up behind their features, which had grown composed and vacant as the beatings persisted. Only Hta Hta had wept unabashedly with baby Molly, saying privately to Louisa that the elder son was a scoundrel and that she couldn't endure another day. But gradually Louisa had begun to find strength in the nature that surrounded them. Sometimes she would catch a glimpse of a far-off mountain between the mists, and it would speak to her of forces beyond their control. Then, just as suddenly, something about the mountain's power and permanence would strike her like a bolt of insight, and she would know—in a flash—that the physical world was a kind of curtain before another world in which none of them were separated. The Forest Governor kept a herd of elephants to haul felled logs, and often after the completion of her morning chores, Louisa would crouch behind the house and watch the great lumbering beings traverse the fields along the valley floor, towing their burdens with their expressive trunks. Now and again, one of the elephant riders would prod a creature with a glinting metal hook driven into its head or the secret folds behind its ears. What sadness the elephants' heavy, assuaging steps spoke of; what modest willingness to submit, as though they had forgotten the fact of their great physical power. Louisa had hurt over the elephants' suffering, over what she knew was their silent yearning, and in her thoughts she had addressed them, just as she addressed Mama and Daddy. Those conversations had transported her from her private corner of anguish, giving her the feeling of being part of a great process of conferring silent and invisible love.

Until one night she had comprehended, suddenly, that there was no more need to keep silent, to cringe. A storm had been coming, wind thrashing against the Forest Governor's house as though to attack or possess it, and Gracie had been so frightened she'd dropped a soup bowl, prompting the wife to lock her outside. Soon Gracie's small cries had begun to flay against the front door. "My sister is scared," Louisa had found herself saying to the wife, who was disciplining the startled fire in the hearth with a poker. "Get back to work," the woman had told her, yet something like worry blighted her voice. That worry was enough to allow Louisa to start for the door, and soon her hand was on the latch, and another blast of wind was knocking against the door, which opened almost of its own accord. Then she had Gracie in her arms, and she was leading her back inside, all but daring the woman to try to strike them with the poker.

She shuddered now, remembering what had become her routine boldness there in Kyowaing and then later, on the plains of the tigers, after the plague had blown through Bilin and they'd been separated from Mama for most of a year. The agonizing waiting. The wondering if they would ever see Mama or Daddy again. The looking to nature day after day for lessons and comfort. The sheer, animal, honest grace of finding a dignified way to endure and to protect themselves and even to grow while parentless. Then the invasion of Bilin, only a few weeks after Mama had left them there and gone in search of Daddy.

They had been sitting in a circle around Gracie, who was shaking with fever, when two soldiers with bloody knives had burst in on the house they were squatting in. "What's this?" one said. "Saw Bension's children?" "My sister is sick," Louisa told them. "She needs medicine." The men seemed almost surprised by themselves as they led her down the road to their medic.

Would Gracie have lived—would any of them have lived—if Louisa had stayed silent? Would they be *here*, tucked into the same ruined house as Daddy, if Mama hadn't gone on to enter Louisa into that child pageant in Insein, and if Louisa hadn't subsequently had the gall to head to the pageant organizer's house and very sincerely describe to the woman and her district commissioner husband how much they missed Daddy, how they loved him, how they needed him, how they yearned to kiss and hug him and talk to him. How they missed his face, his voice, his eyes, his afflicted smile, his funny ears, and his breath. Daddy. Daddy. She wanted her daddy. Could she have her daddy again? The tears she spilled had been an offering of truth; the tears elicited a cup of trembling from which she drank.

It taunted her now—that older, braver self—telling her that Miss Burma was an empty coward.

"A father knows things," Daddy said to her one evening, when they were alone in the dining room together. His eyes took her in, as though not wanting to see the change that had come over her, and yet compelling him to confront the hell she was in. "Are you—" he tried. "Should I be doing something to help?"

But to stop herself from dropping the pretense—a pretense she was suddenly desperate to confess—she broke into a mocking laugh, kissed him apologetically on the cheek, and left.

And to stop her own inner voice from tormenting her further, she began to take a little sip of her mother's palm wine, her "tonic," every so often before bed. And then occasionally before public appearances. It was easier that way to laugh with her friends, and to bend over in her bathing suit and touch her toes when she was asked to demonstrate exercises at bodybuilding conventions. It was easier to relax when she was told to sing on the radio. And she really did love the Penguins and the Platters and Johnny Mathis, though sometimes, as she sang one of their tunes (*"Oh, yes, I'm the great pretender . . . pretending that I'm doing well . . . My need is such I pretend too much . . . I'm lonely but no one can tell . . ."*), it occurred to her that perhaps those American singers were famous, not *in spite* of their minority status in their country, but because there was something acceptable and even reassuring about a minority playing the part of a happy clown (*"Yes, I'm the great pretender . . . just laughin' and gay like a clown . . . I seem to be what I'm not, you see . . ."*).

And to suppress this thought, she began to look at the articles about her that she'd thought she was above reading (and to convince herself that their occasional depictions of her bearing as "dignified" and "artless" proved her greatest concerns wrong). And when that didn't help, she took a bit more tonic, just enough to smile more loosely at the ribbon cuttings, to speak more unself-consciously at galas. Just enough not to fret whenever Ne Win's wife, Katie, stopped her in the schoolyard ("I'm having a little party this Sunday at the old Government House—there'll be tennis and swimming and cards . . . Come!"). It became almost easy to pretend to be unflustered—to pretend that this woman's husband, who led the army that some said had become "a state within the state," wasn't her father's jailor. Almost easy to find the words and lightness to graciously, gaily (clowningly) turn down Katie Ne Win again and again.

But in 1957, Johnny placed second in the nationwide exams and practically fell apart ("Tell me it's really true that a state official's son won first!"), and the movie offers coming in became impossible for her to refuse ("Think of how just one of these films would help—Johnny so desperately wants to attend university abroad"). And soon she was pretending not to hear the hissing protestations of her most religious friends, who wouldn't even attend a movie, or any other kind of "entertainment" ("When you do God's work you do it with your whole heart, and when you do the devil's work you do it with your whole heart, too"). And she was conceding to her brightest friends that, yes, in the past, "nice girls," "educated girls," didn't make movies, but *now?*

And, to her surprise, she found that acting—the pretense of it—relieved her of the pretense of not pretending. Or more simply: it allowed her deeper hidden self to seep out through the cracks between her pretend self and whatever part that pretend self was playing in a film (a governess who fell in love with a member of parliament and died before that love could be discovered; a Burman soldier's wife who searched for him only to discover him dead). Mama came with her to every shoot ("to be sure there is no funny business"), and even in the face of Mama's quiet, startled scrutiny, she felt freer to let go—to weep and laugh openly under the cover of the roles she assumed.

But there were consequences. As the movies began to play around the country, her fame swelled, as did the crowds increasingly surging in her path when she left the house. She pretended at normalcy, graduating from Methodist English and enrolling in an English honors program at Rangoon University ("Pursuing English wouldn't be a bad idea, Louisa," Daddy told her. "I'm gratified to have learned it so well in India, and you already speak beautifully"). But as though to sabotage that attempt, she agreed, in 1958, to make a bid at Miss Burma all over again. Now, though everyone from her fans to the pageant's coordinators had pressed her to run, she couldn't pretend to blame her participation on anyone or anything but her own weakness and self-deception. Oh, yes, the thought of going through it all sickened her, but it seemed easier to submit—especially given her family's chronic need of more money—and she convinced herself that she couldn't *possibly* win again. Oddly, the relief she felt upon winning was as acute as her sense of doom. Somewhere along the line, she had become more afraid of public failure than of false success.

With her attainment of still greater fame, Katie Ne Win's invitations came by telephone with cheerful menace ("So you don't want to associate with us?"), and were met by Mama's panicky admonitions ("You're giving her a reason to turn against us!") and by Daddy's remorseful opportunism ("Tell Mrs. Ne Win there's a Burman medical student named Rita Mya, a dear family friend, who's been held for over a decade in Insein Prison for no other reason . . ."). Then U Nu—who was being blamed for the ongoing insurgent problem and for running the economy into the ground—stepped aside so that Ne Win could helm a "caretaker government." To refuse Katie now was to refuse the interim prime minister's wife, and though something in Louisa understood that to accept Katie was to agree to a sentence whose terms she couldn't fathom, she focused on how flattered (rather than frightened) she was by the woman's invitations, and allowed Katie to send a car to pick her up.

Of course, it wasn't sustainable. Every story of ascent has its reversal. But at that first party on Katie's rooftop—where tables were laid with such lavishness that they suggested a poverty of refinement, and where no one seemed to know when to laugh or when to fall serious—she discovered a refuge from her mounting dread. For all of Katie's pushiness (and bad-girl, fame-entranced, youth-worshipping, quick-talking, thick layer of pretense), she was kind. And she had a trace of the startled foal about her. The excitements that spread out over her expanding world were not atrocities, her flashing glance seemed to say; they were flirtations. And if the man who kept her was of a threatening sort, what had she to do with it?

Soon a car was coming for Louisa every other Sunday, whisking her to Katie's garden on Ady Road, where college lecturers and wives from the British embassy assembled; or to the old Government House, where brashly made-up stars strained to act like children, splashing one another in the pool, gorging themselves on waffles, and pretending at helplessness on the tennis court; or to the Ne Wins' rooftop, where ambassadors and international types hobnobbed with Katie's teenage "friends." And sometimes Katie would tell her, "Go dance with the English fellow!" or "Keep the party going!"

That Louisa was still a child with respect to certain adult matters (that she had only an abstract knowledge of how two bodies managed to become one), that she was actually still largely innocent didn't seem to matter. It didn't matter because, in fact, Katie's parties were only ever *about* pretense. No one tried to go to bed with anyone within Louisa's line of sight. She was never even introduced to the ruler himself (who, as "caretaker" of Burma, had moved his troops into government posts, arrested politicians, and deported refugees from the capital to establish "law and order," while his Defence Services Institute assumed control of banks and transportation and various business interests). No, if Ne Win was present at the parties, it was aloofly, only to putt on the Government House golf course; and if he sometimes ascended to his rooftop on Ady Road, or descended to his living room when guests were there, it was only to coldly converse with one of his generals.

And against this eerie tableau of diversion, in the home of the warden to Burma's woes, Louisa seemed to arrive at her own temporary solution—to the problem of not knowing anymore when she was pretending rather than simply *pretending* to pretend, or where her old self ended and her new self began, or if there even was an authentic self to sully with self-deception. As far as she was concerned her previous self—which had sought to cultivate inner beauty and alleviate outer suffering—was dead.

Then one night in 1960, she was sitting alone in her bedroom at the old dressing table that was also her desk, when she looked up to find her previous self staring back at her in the mirror.

A few months earlier, Ne Win had returned the country to the civilian government and called general elections, which U Nu had won again. But there was something doomed about that victory. And as if to compensate for his inherent weakness, U Nu had soon decided to bring a delegation of more than four hundred "luminaries"— including Louisa—to the People's Republic of China to meet Zhou

Enlai. There, endless banquets—held to sweeten negotiations final-
izing a border long in dispute between the two countries—had cured
Louisa of every last illusion about communism (there was no stronger
medicine than to be subjected to ten-course meals under the super-
vision of the starving, and everywhere on the streets of China there
were so *many* starving). And after her return, she had been sick to her
stomach for days, unable to purge herself of the pressure of her growing sense of culpability. Hadn't she stuffed herself in China because
she'd been expected to? And didn't that describe many a cowardly
and evil act? She was no better than any government administrator
if she complied with the government's unjust requirements, never
standing up to them.

On this night, she saw in the mirror how pale her face had
become, its irises covered over by dark disks, its cheeks hollowed
and skin waxen. Yet tears of feeling suddenly filled its eyes, and, as
if in response, or in compassion, her hand surprised her by finding
the penknife she had been using to open letters and tenderly lifting
it to her throat. Through the point of the knife, she seemed to feel
her heart begin to pound, and she forced the knife down. But again,
her hand lovingly lifted it, now to the fragile, purplish skin beneath
one of her eyes. *Just one quick, deep slice,* an inner voice prodded her.

"Don't be foolish," another voice cut in.

It was Mama. Through the mirror, Louisa saw her standing in
the doorway, looking remotely back at her reflection.

"Mama—" she started, turning, but her mother drew away, left
the room, left her alone with the knife and the tears that suddenly
wouldn't cease falling.

In the desolate hours that followed, Louisa had every ugly thought
about herself and her parents. It seemed to her that they were all slaves of
their circumstances, living in a kind of permanent estrangement within
these walls they shared. Even Daddy . . . There had been a time, after his
release from prison, when she had gone nearly nightly to find him in
his study, even though she'd come to believe that nothing could rival his

affection for the old peeling desk where he seemed to do battle with his political convictions and his commitment to Mama and the family. From the shadows beyond the doorway, she'd listened as he paced back and forth in the half-light of the kerosene lamp, or as he raved and dashed to the desk to write a line, or moaned and cursed without ever noticing her. "What I believe—what I actually believe—dare I confess it?" he might say to himself on one of these nights. "What I actually believe is that in some ways Nu is right to despise clanism. Don't I despise it—that veneration of *my* virtues, *my* laws, *my* faith, *my* heritage, *my* songs." Or: "Who are my people? Who, other than the dead?"

Back then, she had told herself that she trusted—and, in fact, did mostly trust—in Daddy's trustworthiness, in his sanity and courage. But she had also been unable to avoid viewing him through the lens of the courageous man who had temporarily replaced him: Lynton. And though she'd felt like a criminal, she had sometimes longed for Lynton, for his quick wide grin, his decisive laugh, and his steady convictions. "For every day we are given, we owe that day our courage and vigor," Lynton had once told her, before teasing her for having a piece of rice on her cheek. He was the first person who'd made her feel that he, too, could be unburdened of that thing that seemed to oppress all humans: the desperation to persist, a desperation that could alternately take the form of cowardice and brutishness. And perhaps because she had understood the dimensions of Lynton's freedom from fear, she had been transfixed by fear of losing him. And when he had finally left them in Bilin, she had secretly wept and made a vow to herself to forgive him—and to forgive herself for caring about him—should he live through the war.

Years had passed since she'd permitted herself such thoughts, or dared to intrude on Daddy in his study. But now, near midnight, with the penknife still beckoning to her, she fled from her room and crept down the dark staircase.

Daddy was there, past the partly opened door of his moonlit study, seated in a chair before the small window that looked out to

the wild backside of their property. And he was talking to himself—
or talking to God, she understood—as he used to. "Whom to trust?"
she heard him say.

She almost called to him, but he said it again: "Whom to trust?"

It wasn't until her third year at university, in October 1961, that she
was finally granted a reprieve from her own isolation and distrust.

One minute she was moving down a corridor to class, en-
shrouded in the solitude she kept when not in front of the cameras
or her fans, and the next she heard someone whistling something
melodramatic that could have been composed by Henry Mancini.
Then there he was—a boy striding to keep pace with her, whistling
in time with his step (or walking and whistling in time with *hers*?).

And what an attitude, what a swagger he had, this undeniably
good-looking, tall young man—if you could call him a man (when
she glanced at him, she saw that, appealing as he was in *that* way, he
hardly had a hair of stubble on his chin). He smiled, as if in return
for a smile she hadn't offered, and then kept on with his exuberantly
whistled song, which he occasionally interrupted with a tuba-like blast
from his lips. Was he making fun of her, suggesting that she had the
plodding walk of a—of a farting, fumbling creature from the Black
Lagoon? She felt herself flush with shame and immediately feigned
irritated indifference. But he cast her another unabashed grin and
loped off, whistling his way into one of the lecture halls.

Only then, with him out of view (but hardly out of her mind's
eye), did she recall where she'd seen him—with one of Gracie's closest friends, called Myee, a kid whose father was a Shan leader and an
important political figure. Myee had even introduced her to this boy
at one of Gracie's parties—but what was his name?

That afternoon—after she boarded the bus, stopped in the aisle
to sign several autographs, tucked herself into an empty bench, and
hid her face in a book—he abruptly reappeared, plopping himself

down beside her and causing her to yelp, which caused him, in turn, to laugh.

"You don't recognize me?" he said with a huge grin.

She meant to tell him that she *did*, but was so aware of the inquisitive eyes staring at them from up and down the now lurching bus that she said, "We're being watched."

"I know," he whispered in response. "Should I speak more loudly so they don't have to strain to hear?"

Involuntarily, she smiled—though she was sure he was teasing her, and she generally despised sarcasm (she had too much of it everywhere!).

"Yes," she found herself replying, as sincerely as she could. "That would be considerate."

His look of astonishment told her he hadn't been prepared for that. But a moment later, he dusted off his lap and stood, turning on unsteady legs to face their onlookers.

"My name is Kenneth!" he announced to the old ladies and the toothless men, to the mothers and kids and university students now watching him with smiling interest. "I'm sure you know Naw Louisa—"

"*Don't—*" she whispered, pulling on his trousers, and feeling a jolt of excitement at the intimacy of the gesture.

But he was already having too much fun. Motioning down to her, he continued: "She and I are actually old friends, though she doesn't seem to remember we've met *several* times. You see, her sister"—and he said this with a punishing glance down at her—"happens to be pals with a kid who's like my brother."

From the bus, there came comically sober exclamations of "I see" and "Aha," then all fell silent, waiting, it seemed, for him to go on. But he appeared to have grown self-conscious. He faced the stony stares, flashing the riders a gracious, flustered smile before concluding, "Just wanted you to know, because Naw Louisa was very worried about you feeling left out of our conversation."

He gave a nervous bow, and when he sank back down, it was to look bashfully at her. "Did I go a little too far?" There was a blush on his cheeks and also something like familiarity in his stare.

What was it with this boy—this Kenneth—who made her unwillingly smile even though he seemed only to elicit and take pleasure in her embarrassment? "A little," she said. "We'll probably read about it tomorrow in the papers."

"You read what they write about you?"

Now she felt herself color with humiliation. "I try not to."

Her honesty surprised her, and she was suddenly so disconcerted she found herself opening her book again and pretending to read a line, though she knew she was obviously failing to be convincing at that. And even as she tried to assume a look of concentration, the heat of her blush intensifying, she felt him watching her—as if to see how long she could endure pretending not to notice that her play-acting was pathetically unpersuasive. From the corner of her eye, she saw him finally reach into the sack at his feet and pull out a heavy textbook, which, when she glanced over (she couldn't help it), she saw had the words "*Probability Theory*" in its title, and which he flipped open, finally landing on a page of equations that she (also unwillingly) stole peeks at.

This was ridiculous.

She closed her book, looking squarely at him, but now he was mocking her pretense of indifference, alternately scowling at his page of problems and gazing up at the flaking ceiling of the bus, squinting and nodding.

At last, looking pleased with himself, he turned to her and said, "You have something to write with?"

"What?"

"A pencil. A pen. Something to write down an answer."

"There's no need to show off. If you want to have a conversation, we can."

But just then the bus passed into shadow, throwing them into a darkness that made her feel exposed, and she looked away to the reflective window at her side—and caught him glancing at himself and (vainly, adorably) running a hand through his longish hair. Their eyes met in the window, and then they were thrust into the light again.

"Why are you so miserable?" he said, almost shyly, as if avowing his own miserable crush on her.

"Excuse me?"

"You go around, your eyes downcast, like the saddest girl in the world. It's very romantic, but—"

"There's a difference between being miserable and . . ."

"And what?"

"Wanting a bit of seclusion."

"Is there?"

"In fact, I'm very happy."

But her words made him look at her with sadness. He didn't believe them, and suddenly neither did she.

She felt an inward surge of grief overtaking her—and another of anger. And, dizzied by the vacillating tides of her emotions—and of his cockiness and self-abasement, joshing and sincerity, put-downs and praise—she steadied herself with the view of her book, mentally reciting a litany of complaints against him.

"Do you eat?" he interrupted her.

"Don't I look like I eat?" she said to the book.

"I wasn't sure. You seem—"

"What?" This was said with coldness and directly at his earnest eyes.

"Never mind—let's get off."

"I have another six stops—"

"I know, but there's a Chinese café on the next corner. You look like you could use some noodles."

Over noodles, then, and Chinese tea—both remarkably delicious—in the humid café and the presence of still more pressing onlookers, they sat sweating and slurping and falling into increasingly relaxed conversation, only occasionally lapsing into silences more intimate than awkward, in which she seemed to feel him assuring her that imperfection was what he yearned for: the imperfection of her wit, the imperfection of her composure, the imperfection of her beauty, and even the imperfection of their uncannily easy and evolving rapport.

They spoke sparingly and tenderly of their families. His father, a Chinese prince, had passed away when Kenneth was a child; like Myee's elders, his were based in Shan State, and had been pressured two years before by Ne Win to abdicate their sovereign rights to their people in favor of an elected administration (despite their having no confidence that such an "elected" government would represent those people's interests). Yes, it seemed that Ne Win had cooperatively handed the reins back to U Nu, and even that U Nu was beginning to consider eventually sharing governmental power with ethnic states in some sort of genuine federalist system. But Ne Win and his army loomed in the shadows, and there was no need to discuss that continued threat.

As Kenneth talked, she saw—beyond his own beauty and intelligence and playfulness—an innocent soul that longed for truthfulness. And it asked her, in many ways and again and again, to come out of the box in which she had been keeping her own inmost, honest self. It welcomed embarrassment, because embarrassment was the entry point to candor. And it basked in the light of self-revelation.

"What was that tune you were whistling in the hall today?" she asked him. "Or should I say whistling while making fun of me?"

"Something inspired by you! Not to suggest anything inappropriate, but it came to me the other day in the shower."

Now she freely laughed. "You think I'm ridiculous."

"A little bit."

And again he began to whistle and wiggle around, as though in impersonation of someone's lumbering walk.

"I do walk like that, don't I?"

"You do!"

"How embarrassing."

"You should be proud of it! Exaggerate it a little. Like this . . ."

He jumped up by the table and, to the astonishment of everyone but her now, began to strut in time to the tune. And, relishing her humiliation, she waited a minute before beckoning him back to the table, something *he* thoroughly seemed to relish.

For a while, they sat perspiring again over their soup, and then she said, suddenly seeing there was really no reason not to, "I like you, Kenneth."

That November, hours in advance of a party, Katie Ne Win sent a car to bring Louisa to the Government House. Because of Kenneth—and because of the honesty he inspired in her—Louisa had determined finally to raise the subject of Daddy's friend, Rita Mya. But as soon as she and Katie were alone in the drawing room of the Victorian mansion, Katie—in lavish jewels, and with a gleam in her eye—drew back, peering at her with a smile.

"You're keeping a secret," she said to Louisa. "Yes, I see it. The shining eyes. The confidence. The clearness of complexion, the charming reddened cheeks. I'm not wrong, am I? Ah! This is something to savor! Louisa has a secret! And tell me, what is his name? Someone you've met here?"

Feeling the heat of her feelings for Kenneth rise to her lips, Louisa nearly divulged everything. But she saw a flash of pain in Katie's eyes, of something more personal than jealousy. And instantly she understood that it would have been an unforgivable mistake to confide in Katie, who relied on her to mirror her own need for diversion from truth and its ugliness. And yet, blinking at the woman, Louisa found herself uttering, "What is it?"

The question was, if not unwelcome, clearly too much for Katie. She rushed away to the table, where she found a box of cigarettes and then searched around for a light.

Trying to make up for her blunder, Louisa took some matches from her own handbag and said, "Let me," and went and lit the quivering cigarette at Katie's mouth, before the woman turned to a window and the far-off view of her husband bending over his golf club on the lawn.

"He's been in a foul mood," Katie said after a minute, and then she gave a little stifled laugh. "Ever since his last trip to China he's wanted everyone to call him 'Chairman.' Will you be shocked if I tell you that he asks me to refer to him like that when we're—" She turned and gave Louisa a wicked wink. But seeing Louisa's timidity, she added, "You're still very naive, aren't you? That's why I like you. Stay just like that."

As always, her every word seemed to have a second meaning, and a third, leaving Louisa to wonder if Katie wasn't faulting her for an innocence she envied, and also warning Louisa against persisting in that innocence for long.

"Sometimes I think his men love him more than I do," she continued saying now to the window. "Aung Gyi. Maung Maung. They love to call him 'Chairman.' . . . Chairman Ne Win. Disgusting, don't you think?" She took a suck from her cigarette, while beyond her, on the grounds, Ne Win peered out at a distant target. "Aung Gyi would do anything to wrest the throne from U Nu and seat my husband on it. But, like a lover who never has enough attention, he'd also do anything to hurt him . . . Now you know love's torments, don't you, darling?" She turned to Louisa, as though remembering her all at once. "Just wait until your new flame sees you around other men. Do you know what Aung Gyi said about me to Win? That—ha!—he saw me flirting with someone else. So what?"

She smiled at Louisa again, yet her eyes shone with mortal fear. And Louisa, frightened for the woman—for *them*—stepped forward, reaching out to touch her arm.

Katie thrust the smoldering cigarette at her. "Take it," she said. "It makes me sick."

And as though to sweep her revelations further out of sight, she called abruptly to the servants, and then broke into a series of complaints about all she had to do to direct them in preparation for the afternoon's party.

Louisa moved to take the cigarette, still extended toward her, though the falseness that had reclaimed her hostess and this room seemed suddenly unbearable, suffocating. And as she took the damp cigarette between her fingers, grasping for something else—for some speck of goodness and truth—she sputtered, "There's a woman being held in Insein Prison—a Burman medical student by the name of Rita Mya. We've never spoken of my father, but he—"

"What nonsense are you saying?"

The servants had appeared, and before Louisa could answer Katie rushed at them, throwing her gold shawl over her shoulder.

"I expect you to play doubles with me in lawn tennis this afternoon," she said to Louisa in passing. "We must prevail!"

But at the door she stopped, adding without looking back, "I *will* see about the medical student, Louisa. I know it's hard, but chin up."

Several nights later, Gracie appeared in Louisa's bedroom, looking pallid and afraid and filled with tender affection. She was carrying something, a little amber-colored medicine bottle, which she half concealed in her slight hand.

"Is something wrong?" Louisa said to her.

Gracie seated herself on the edge of the bed, where Louisa was studying for her midyear examinations. Earlier that evening, the two of them had gone to see a Burmese movie with Kenneth and Myee, and on the bus ride home Louisa had been mildly diverted by Gracie's own preoccupied state, so at odds with her usual smiling lightness.

"Tell me to stop talking," Gracie said now, still hiding the medicine bottle in her hand.

"Why would I do that?"

"Because—because I don't know if I have the right to say what I'm about to."

Louisa felt a chill of apprehension as she smiled and grasped Gracie's free hand. "You have every right to say anything you want to me, little sister."

Gracie gave her hand a quick squeeze, then instantly dropped it. "I can tell how happy Kenneth makes you," she said. "And how obviously happy you make him. But are you sure about what you're doing?"

"What is it that you think I'm doing?"

Louisa had tried to speak without accusation, yet a look of defensive anger coursed through Gracie's usually placid face, and she jumped up from the bed and covered her eyes even as she continued to clasp the bottle. "It's Mama!" she moaned. "She put me up to it! She doesn't want you to marry him. And she gave me one of her stupid potions to make you fall out of love."

Mama. Yes, the woman had been unusually cold with Louisa of late, never forbidding her to entertain Kenneth or his friends at the house or to go along with a group to the city, but distantly on the lookout for a sign of—what was it? Misbehavior? Disloyalty to the family? A joy so complete it might lift Louisa forever up out of her mother's longstanding misery?

"Give it to me," Louisa said, reaching for the bottle.

With a look of almost comical remorse, Gracie relinquished the innocuous thing, which Louisa quickly uncapped, and whose bitter contents she downed in several choked gulps. "There," she said, wiping her lips. "Now you've done your job. And I hope you'll be glad to know that so far it hasn't taken effect."

"Of course I'm glad," Gracie said after a moment, but with such doubt and sorrow Louisa was instantly seized with regret.

There was very little she didn't regret after that:

The party at the Government House to which she brought Kenneth (almost in defiance of Katie, Mama, and Gracie) and at which

Kenneth noticed Ne Win's generals leering at her behind. Their subsequent fight, instigated because she was unable to ignore Kenneth's sullen irritation ("Just tell me what's wrong." "You really want to know? I can't accept the foolish way you're living. These *ridiculous* parties—" "Then you don't accept *me*—don't *understand* me. If you understood me, you'd know a person can be many things, some truer than others—" "And if you understood *yourself*, you'd see what you're doing to arouse men's lust—" "That's not fair!"). Then the way she'd been unable to accept his copious expressions of contrition (he'd kicked the helmet of his motorcycle, swung around, fallen on his knees, and buried his head in her lap, saying, "I don't know what's wrong with me. I'm senselessly jealous. Forgive me. Forgive me," and she'd stroked his beautiful hair, but with fingers that had felt suddenly deadened).

If she'd been better at assuring him that night and in the aftermath of the fights that followed, if she hadn't begun to build a wall around her innermost, secret self, would he have believed in her innocence when the tabloids—as if tired of the established newspapers' championing of her as a symbol of harmony—issued reports all but naming her as Ne Win's mistress ("Naw Louisa Bension Seen Leaving Ne Win's Private Apartment at the Capitol," "Naw Louisa Bension Accompanies Ne Win in State Vehicle")? Of course it was ludicrous; she'd never in her life been alone with the man, let alone introduced to him. But instead of simply defending herself to Kenneth, she hid behind a wall of offended outrage and cool reason. ("Katie says Aung Gyi started the rumors—that he wants to hurt Ne Win." "I thought you said Aung Gyi was devoted to Ne Win like a lover. It makes no sense." "You've been with me *every minute*." "Not *every* minute.") She didn't want to conceal her hurt from Kenneth, couldn't help blaming him for the hurt she felt, yet unhappily found herself retaliating with hurtful aloofness, which only further provoked his suspicion—particularly when Katie stopped inviting her around and rumors began to swell that she, Louisa, was pregnant with Ne Win's baby.

Of course she comprehended that it was possible to know that one's beloved was innocent and simultaneously be lured by the temptation to believe her faithless—just as she comprehended that beneath the storm of Kenneth's suspicion lay a wellspring of conviction about her strength of character and devotion to him. But she was so disappointed by his vulnerability to the rumors that she refused to admit the extent to which they were also tormenting her ("We hear you have very powerful friends," her dentist said when she was in his chair; *"Ne Win, Ne Win, Ne Win,"* a group of boys at the university taunted her in the hall). If only she could have confessed that her family members' cool refusal to address the subject of those rumors left her wondering if they, too, doubted her. If only she could have been patient with Kenneth instead of extinguishing every chance of tenderness with frosty rebukes. ("Can't you see it's better to clear the air and confess?" "If you think I'm guilty, *leave*.")

A kind of wickedness had thwarted his love of honesty and turned her honest protestations into something as wounding as gunfire. And one morning, on the second of March, after they had fought until nearly midnight beyond the sentry's hut in front of her compound, and he had sped off on his bike, and a passing car had slowed and delivered her a volley of slurs, and she had walked up and down the highway in search of him only to return alone to the house to find Mama anxiously waiting up and peering at her with such frightened, accusatory eyes that she'd erupted into an unprecedented tantrum of returned accusation, shouting, "Why do you *hate* me?"—after all that, she woke with a headache to discover that they had all crossed beyond the portents of disaster. For the past week, U Nu had been quietly meeting with ethnic leaders to discuss the question of a federalist Burma, and in the middle of the night tanks had spread out around the capital and Ne Win's troops had seized control of the government. U Nu, many of his chief ministers, and their minority counterparts had been taken into custody, and now the Burma Army was guarding the city.

"I have to inform you, citizens of the Union," Ne Win announced in a radio broadcast at 8:50 that morning, "owing to the greatly deteriorating conditions of the Union, the armed forces have taken over the responsibility and task of maintaining the country's safety."

"Bloodless," a subsequent report called the coup—but it wasn't bloodless. The father of Gracie's friend Myee had been one of the minority leaders meeting with Nu, and at two in the morning, when Ne Win's soldiers had stormed into the father's compound, Myee—darling, blameless sixteen-year-old Myee—had been shot and killed.

"I'm so sorry," Louisa told Kenneth on the phone that evening. She had stretched the cord from the table in the hallway to her closet, where she crouched in hiding without understanding why.

For a long time, Kenneth was silent—so silent she could hardly hear him breathe.

Then he said, "I'm sorry, too, Louisa. Sorry that the life we all almost had is gone."

The real end came four months later, in July 1962, after Ne Win had abolished the supreme court, the constitution, the legality of all but his ruling party—after he had staffed his Union Revolutionary Council with Aung Gyi and other army commanders and veterans of Aung San's Burma Independence Army—after he had established his platform, the "Burmese Way to Socialism," by which every sector of the society was nationalized or ruled by the regime.

Right away, government officials descended on the family property, measuring it; counting rooms, beds, vehicles; tapping phones. Right away everything was rationed, everyone made to line up for scanty provisions at army-run stores. No one knew quite what was going on. Was it true the soldiers were allowing up to eight potatoes per family, while guarding mountains of them that were going to rot? Was it true the soldiers were mixing bad oil in with the good, making thousands of people sick?

Don't complain! The soldiers are quick to shoot.

Quiet! Remember the phone goes click click click.

No one knew what to expect, what to believe.

Was it true, what they were saying about Louisa—that she had gone to Hong Kong with Ne Win and married him in secret there? As confused as the Karen villagers who came inquiring about all of this, Mama alternately defended Louisa, snapped at her, and hid upstairs. And Louisa—overwhelmed by the truth and lies, by the justifications and the doubts, by the evident and the incomprehensible—choked on her food, couldn't sleep, couldn't go out in crowds, became pale and anemic, hyperventilated. The doctor came and administered tranquilizers, and she crawled into bed, sure she was dying.

But one afternoon, Gracie appeared at her bedside. Since Myee's death, Gracie had seemed almost absent from her body. Now her eyes shone with warmth, with life, and she bent over Louisa and kissed her cheek. "The students have called a meeting at the university," she said, and she went on to explain that a nine o'clock campus curfew had been put in place, along with other university regulations, prompting students to assemble in protest in the student union building. All of Myee's friends would be there and, yes, probably Kenneth, whom Louisa hadn't seen in months. "But forget him, Louisa," she said, pressing Louisa's hand to her eyes as if to stanch something. "He's worthless if he doesn't know who you are."

Together then, without saying a word to Mama, and never speaking of Louisa's new dread of mass gatherings, they took Daddy's unused car and drove into the city. Already at the university, hundreds of protesting students were pouring out of the student union, which was positioned behind the main gate. "They've arrested our leaders!" one student called to them, and immediately Grace fell into step with the rally, beckoning to Louisa to join in.

Much as the students were undeniably on the side of freedom, their fist-pumping unanimity and the deafening pitch of their cries frightened Louisa. It was here that Aung San had held his "Burma for the Burmans" campaigns, here that Nu had risen with shouts and fist-pumps by his side. She stumbled, trying to keep up with Grace.

And then she saw him—saw Kenneth—standing near the gate, under a tree in the slanted light. When their eyes met, he smiled spontaneously, as if avowing his honest, abiding, difficult love for her. And just like that, all the difficulty between them seemed to subside. And catching her breath, and feeling a smile brighten her own face, she stood watching him on the edge of the glowing quadrangle.

"The army!" someone cried.

In the blur of what followed—the roaring of trucks, the swarms of soldiers surrounding the campus's leafy gates, the bursts of smoke, of tear gas obscuring the quadrangle and making everyone instantly retch and burn and go half blind—in the heat of the students' hurled insults and the soldiers' frenzied efforts to shut the entrance and Louisa's impulsive decision to drag Gracie out before it was too late— she lost sight of Kenneth. But out on the street, past the gate, quaking with Gracie like two slim, spared trees standing alone on a plain, she had enough time to take in the view of what was happening up ahead: the soldiers padlocking the entrance to the campus and drawing their guns up to their eyes. She had enough time to find Kenneth, standing in a group a few feet from where he had been.

Then the chaos broke open with an explosion of shots. And, as she grabbed Gracie's hand and the two of them began to run away, she glanced back and found him one last time—still standing—but covered in the blood of the fallen.

At least a hundred had been killed, said the friends who escaped to their house later that night. Sitting under blankets in the living room, holding teacups with trembling fingers, these friends described to the family how the soldiers had shot into the crowd on and off for minutes at a time before finally opening the main entrance and dragging out bodies, some still squirming, and throwing them in stacks into the lorries to be scorched, dead or alive. The friends had managed to get out then, though many other survivors had fled to the dormitories, to the student union. "What about Kenneth? Did you see him?" "Yes, he was there. I saw him running into the student union." "Thank God." "Yes, thank God."

The shakes and the guilt that had begun when Louisa and Gracie had escaped from the campus only intensified, and soon Mama was pulling them away from the group, drawing them a bath, and stripping them like children. "Your resistance is down," she kept saying, her voice catching. "You will succumb to fever if you don't release this from your bodies." While they crouched in the bath, each half hiding from the visions behind the other's eyes, Mama sang an ancient song and poured water over their backs.

"He will come," Louisa said aloud, thinking of Kenneth, but neither Grace nor Mama replied.

Long into the night, after the friends had gone to sleep on mats spread out across the darkness, Louisa sat on the sofa, peering into the night, sure she heard Kenneth's motorcycle on the highway. Instead the first light came, and she quietly crept from the house and released the car's clutch and break, so that the car rolled noiselessly down the drive, and not even the soldiers sleeping in the guard hut bothered to wake.

It was a few minutes before six when she parked several blocks up from the campus. There were tanks on the hazy street corners and soldiers ranged along the gate, whose main entrance was opened slightly. Beyond it, she could make out the unassuming student union, its windows darkened, its lights turned off inside (had the soldiers shut down the electricity?). Something about the building's solidity, its wider-than-tall design, assured her that the students within were likewise hunkered down, prepared to protect their right to outrage, along with their lives. Perhaps they had managed, those students, to catch a few hours of sleep within their bunker. And was *he* dreaming inside, she wondered, as he had been on the night they'd mistakenly fallen asleep together under the sky?

A month or so after their first encounter on the bus, they had sneaked out to the yard behind his brother's flat in the city and lain down in the darkness under the trees, pressed up against each other's heat. "You are so beautiful," he'd told her. "So much more now that I know you." Later, holding hands and looking up at the stars that had been watching them all their lives, they had talked jokingly of how many children they would be having. She'd surprised herself by saying she wanted four or five, and he'd laughed and said they had better get going. And then—without ever realizing they had fallen asleep—she was waking at daybreak to discover his sleeping face, still turned expectantly toward the sky. How peaceful he had seemed, how free of suffering and restlessness, his breath coming without a trace of discernible effort, his mouth almost smiling. She'd had the sense that if she touched him, roused him, a piece of his life—contained by sleep—would be released like a bird, and that she wouldn't be able to catch it. And for a few minutes, in spite of the risk of being discovered by his brother, she had allowed herself to watch him continuing to sleep, at once far from and close to her.

Now, in view of the sturdy building reliably safeguarding his life, she was comforted again by the thought of him being contained, perhaps captured by sleep. And as if she were pressed up against his heat again, in spite of the street and the gate and the walls between them, she felt her longing for him spreading over the surface of her body. And it seemed to her that all her life she had been yearning for the closeness he had given her freely, much as she had imposed upon herself a sort of estrangement from others, born out of some inhuman service to strength. Wasn't it this very distance—which she had been maintaining from her loved ones, from him, from her own weakness—that was to blame for his incapacity to trust her fully? Her impermeability to his fever—the unsteadying, infectious fever of his feeling—had left him cold, but *she* wasn't cold; she was only afraid.

Across the misty distance, she saw several soldiers appear around one side of the building sheltering him. They were making hand motions, scurrying agitatedly toward the path leading to the street. Suddenly, a few dozen more rounded the other side of the building, and in a throng they all began to charge back toward the gate.

She had only a few seconds to comprehend her molten, rising instinct to run—to scream—to rescue or warn him and the others inside the building. Then the blast came, so deafeningly she cringed and covered her ears in the jolted car, as another reflex compelled her to look up, to look for him in the pluming yellow cloud of debris, ascending with all the souls, and all the plaster and wood of the student union, into the vast breaking day.

PART FOUR

Suspicions
1963–1965

16

An Unexpected Proposal

O n the eve of his thirty-eighth birthday, in March 1963, General
Lynton of the Karen Revolutionary Council directed his driver
to take him from the capital to Saw Bension's compound in Insein.

He had come to Rangoon having recently broken off from the
main branch of the Karens. The year before, Ne Win had seized state
power in order to protect Burma from "disintegration" (to protect it,
in other words, from U Nu, who had become increasingly responsive
to the calls, from the Karens and other resistance groups, for a form
of government that would have made the domain of the Burmans
just one of many constituent ethnic states within the country). Under
military rule, even Burmans had no right to dissent—hence the dy-
namiting of the student union building at Rangoon University by Ne
Win's troops and the subsequent arrest en masse of top politicians.
Yet here Lynton was, along with various other resistance leaders, on
the verge of peace talks with Ne Win.

Here he was, in the rear of a state-issued car, pulling up to the
guarded gate of a political prisoner. Were the guards merely keeping Saw Bension in? Might they not also, because of Saw Bension's
famous daughter, be keeping the likes of Lynton out?

Not that Lynton was anything like one of Louisa Bension's crazed
fans. True, he'd managed to sit still long enough to suffer through
the imbecilic plot of her latest film (no more romances or war stories for Ne Win's public; it was workers' struggles and the toiling of
peasants for those ordered to march the Burmese Way to Socialism).

True, he'd been maddened while watching this latest film not only by her beauty (an unsettling beauty, because it seemed to vibrate, to defy categorization or knowability) but also by her almost artless aspect of innocence. That innocence was something she had seemed to wander toward and away from even in her youth, when he'd felt guilty about depriving her of whatever innocence remained to her (she'd never witnessed anything specifically intimate between Khin and him, but he'd *been* there, in her father's place). And to see her now on the screen (and in the newspapers, and in the magazines, and on so many billboards) was to see someone he might have unintentionally hurt and someone he couldn't *have*—on account of his past with Khin, of course, and also on account of Ne Win, Louisa Bension's purported lover, whom Lynton really shouldn't risk offending given their agreement to a temporary cease-fire.

No, he wasn't here to take Ne Win's mistress, he reminded himself as his driver muttered curses at the guards, sluggishly fumbling with the gate, nor was he here to *save* her. His car at last passed into the compound, and he caught a glimpse of Bension's hillside mansion, whose bombed-out wings gave it the appearance of a giant bird shot out of the sky and breathing its last gasps of air. He was here, he supposed, to purge Louisa Bension from his system. What better way to prove to himself that she was off-limits than to confront her alongside her parents, both of whom he felt he'd also wronged all those years before?

It was Khin, some minutes later, who came to the door of the crumbling house. Before either she or Lynton had said a word, he understood she would do it all again if given a window of opportunity. There was the way her eyes clung to his, in disorientation and then in relief; there was the way her nostrils subtly flared, as if she would laugh, or shed tears. She was still Khin, after all. He saw it in the faint lines around her eyes: all the old grace, all the old vanity and disappointment and vulnerability, and also the traces of selflessness that seemed to explain the streaks of gray now in her hair, the dusting of liver spots on her cheeks—spots that told him she was, or would soon be, past her childbearing years. And there was the residue of sweetness emanating from her like a scent. Strange how the mouth, the lips, hadn't changed at all. And the irises—they were the same deep red brown, with the same frightened, gathering heat of desire.

"You found us," she said breathlessly, her voice a notch lower than it had been before. Just as quickly, she seemed to grow embarrassed, and silently, awkwardly, she beckoned him in.

A moment passed before his eyes adjusted to the room's darkness, but then a moment was all it took for him to comprehensively take in the room's features. The first shots of the civil war had broken out across this house, he knew—but it wasn't the damaged floorboards or torn cane sofa or crudely patched walls that spoke principally to him of the effects of war; rather, it was the silence, the stagnant quality of light and air, a sort of stifling absence of oxygen that suggested a lack of full-bodied, hopeful respiration. If this house was a monument to lives lost, it was also a testament to lives being lived in constriction.

He tried to return Khin's desperate smile. She had closed the door behind him and now stood to his side, smoothing down her wrinkled sarong as her peering eyes echoed with unspoken questions. What had she just said—that he had *found* them? Suddenly, he sensed another presence enter the room.

"You've been impossible," he said, forcing himself to remain focused for a moment more on Khin's alert stare, "to avoid."

"Have I?" Khin said, her voice trembling.

"I'm sure the general is referring to the reports in the papers," came the other's voice—unmistakably *her* voice, yet sparkling with a sarcasm unknown to her film personae.

He turned and found Louisa in the doorway giving onto the dining room. She was less substantial than she seemed on the screen, more haunted looking. Voluptuous, to be sure, but delicate, thinner in the face—more spirit than flesh. Yet her eyes caught his with a physical force. Like her voice, those eyes seemed to mock him, to mock the "reports" to which she referred—reports, Lynton knew, which had in turn mocked her by detailing the minutiae of her alleged affair, including not only a supposed abortion, but also a recent (and nonsensical!) stabbing by the ruler's jealous wife. Each of the sensational stories had been accompanied by a damaging, though obviously manipulated, photograph of Louisa's head affixed to another woman's provocatively posed naked figure. One would have thought the pictures' evident phoniness would act to exonerate her, but no. No, when the herd wanted to take refuge in an idea, it preferred to be blind to that idea's opposite. Just the other day, Lynton's car had idled on the street corner near a boy hawking tabloids whose cover image was matched in vulgarity (and inanity) only by the kid's slogan, promising that Louisa herself could be purchased for the price of a coin—*"Louisa Bension—one kyat!"* And Lynton, who'd long propped himself up with the thought that he didn't care a whit what the herd thought, had nearly emptied his pockets of kyats in order to buy up (and burn) every last paper the boy had to sell.

"What I like about our papers, the high and the low," he now found himself saying to Louisa with an unintentional gruffness, "is that they don't even pretend to be truthful or objective. I've been reported dead at least a dozen times—or so I hear. And by their count I have something like sixty-nine wives."

He saw this bring a smile to Louisa's eyes, if not to her mouth— and the light from that smile seemed to counter the room's darkness and all the darkness of his memories of her as a girl. During the early days of the revolution, he'd carried a harmonica in his pocket, and though Louisa had always found a reason to dawdle in the room when he was playing it, though her eyes had often lingered on the thing if he left it out on the table, she wouldn't openly acknowledge the interest she took in it, as her siblings did. "My father's harmonica is much nicer," she'd surprised him once by saying. "He bought me an accordion, but I had to leave it in Thaton . . . Will you be going to Thaton?"

"How many wives *have* you had, General?" Khin now broke in, straining to laugh.

He was unable to check his embarrassed grin—he felt it break hotly from ear to ear. "Lost count," he muttered.

The response—and his awkwardness—clearly pleased Louisa, whereas Khin, thrown into a panic, began to ramble on about how welcome he was in their home, how lucky they were to have gotten their hands on tea today, how sorry she was that her younger daughters, Grace and Molly, were visiting friends, and how proud she was of Johnny, who was earning an advanced degree in finance in America, and who had prematurely wed. "He was only fifteen when he went abroad," she said, gesturing for Lynton to sit in the chair across from her. "A mistake letting him go off to college so young, but he'd placed second in the national competition. Actually, he'd placed first, but the prize went to a government official's son—do you know him?" She smiled nervously at Lynton, as if she'd committed a civil offense. Could it be she thought that he was actually in bed with Ne Win, and that the peace talks were a cover for something more tacit and sinister between them? "First prize would've taken him to Cambridge," she quietly explained. And then: "Cambridge was what my husband wanted for him."

Somewhere during the beginning of this speech, Louisa had disappeared, and now, with its apparent conclusion, Lynton allowed himself to peer into the dining room after her. "Is he here, Saw Bension?" he asked, trying to divert himself and Khin from the direction of his interest. He *had* come here to make amends with Bension, after all.

When he looked back, Khin was wearing an inscrutable expression—of her own swollen interest, of dashed expectations. "Always. Indefinitely," she said. "He sits in his study from dawn to dusk, writing letters to America. Letters he can't send. He thinks they'll actually do something, the Americans."

"About his case—his house arrest?"

She scoffed. "His house arrest? That's a comfort to him! It gives him permission to lock himself up—with his writing, which he somehow believes will help the Karens."

"And why shouldn't it?" came Louisa's voice. She'd reentered the room carrying a tea tray, which she proceeded to plunk down on the table between her mother and Lynton, as though she wanted to be sure of making it known that she resented everything he took that was rightfully theirs—tea, or her mother, or—

"Allow me," he said, leaning forward to pick up the pot.

"Don't be silly," Louisa shot back, and got down onto her knees, into a position of false supplication, and poured tea for them. "Milk?" she said, dousing his tea with cream. "There's nothing left in the sugar bowl."

"I prefer mine unsweetened," he said.

"You never much liked sweets," Khin added.

"You're above such human impulses?" Louisa asked him.

The question prompted his very human impulse to laugh— loudly and with relish—because years had passed since anyone had dared speak to him in this manner, and because the question's insinuation of rage meant that something in Louisa was already fixed on him. But even as he laughed, he became aware that there was something physically wrong with the young woman. Her brow, lightly perspiring, looked wan in the soft light of the room, the shadows under her eyes more ancient than her (twenty-two? twenty-three?) years.

"Khin," he found himself venturing, "would you mind if I spoke to your daughter alone?" The question seemed to surprise Khin less than it did him. How many times had he gone over his anticipated and alternative courses of action en route here? *This* decisive move hadn't figured in any of them; yet the sudden surrender in Khin's eyes told him she was well practiced at being passed over by her daughter's fans. No sense having delayed the decisive blow if it had to come, he counseled himself, though he knew Khin's suffering would be prolonged because of what they had shared. "There's something official that I need to communicate to her," he added.

Khin blinked at him for a moment and then stood, making a visible effort to hold up her head as she said, mouth quivering, "Of course. Of course." A haze might have cleared, revealing to her with naked clarity her failure to recapture whatever it was he'd glimpsed in her all those years before. And she paled, as if in comprehension of that failure, just at the moment that he felt an unpleasant, uncustomary stab of guilt for having failed her—now and then.

What a reckless, cocky fool he'd been in his younger years, taking and discarding whatever he pleased with little regard for the fallout. But he had left Khin *not only* because he'd failed to be more devoted to her than to the war. He'd left also because of the child. Because of Louisa. Because of his concern about what the affair was doing to her.

"I'll see to dinner," Khin muttered, and crossed out of the room, as if to obey the trajectory of his thoughts.

For a while, neither he nor Louisa made a move. She was still kneeling and wouldn't look at him, wouldn't follow her mother's exit with her gaze; she appeared instead to be looking inward, at some invisible record of trouble past and future.

"Sit," he told her.

It was very difficult for him, in times of stress, to temper his instinct to give orders; the instinct still sometimes flustered him, yet it didn't obviously unnerve Louisa now. She pushed herself up from the floor and sat across from him, while he fumbled for his cigarettes and held the package out to her. Without a beat, she leaned forward, took one of the cigarettes, and allowed him to light it for her. She was more in her element in her mother's absence, he thought, and she was finally able to breathe a bit with the cigarette held to her lips.

"Mama doesn't allow smoking in the house," she murmured between draws. "And I don't approve of it, either."

"Forgive me," he said, lighting up.

"Impossible," she said with a smile, but it was a smile full of the sadness of her childhood—a childhood, he told himself again, in which his presence had been understandably resented by her. He had only wanted to help her then, to reanimate whatever spark of innocence and joy remained buried within her. But somehow his present interest in her (of an entirely different sort!) made him ashamed of the interest he'd formerly taken, as though that older interest had prefigured this one.

"I'd almost forgotten you were an unforgiving child."

She looked squarely at him, curiosity—or was it pain?—settling down around that perfect mouth.

"You disapproved of everyone and everything, especially me," he continued.

"Did I?"

"I called you 'Little Grandmother.'"

This seemed to please her. She drew deeply again from the cigarette. "I don't remember."

"What happened to you after I left? I heard a plague broke out."

Now the lights in her features dimmed. She stubbed out her cigarette on a saucer. "What happened," she echoed, gazing down at the butt, or back at the time when they'd parted. Abruptly, her eyes lifted to his. "What happened," she said, "was that we were sent away, and for nearly a year none of us much saw my mother. I still don't understand why, when the plague had run its course, we weren't swiftly brought back to her." She paused, as though he might be able to explain what she couldn't understand. "Do you remember Hta Hta?" she went on. "The servant who was pregnant? She's still with us." She gestured vaguely toward the kitchen. "She'd been raped after Mama left us in Kyowaing. And she was the one to accompany us to the village on the plains of the tigers when we left Bilin . . . Every other week, I had malaria. I would shake with chills and want Mama, but . . ." Her eyes darted back to the package of cigarettes on the table in front of him. "May I have another?"

Again, he held out the package to her, and she took a cigarette and put it between her lips as he lit it.

"I loved that little village," she said, audibly aiming for a lighter note. "A tiger came to prowl around our hut at night, because Hta Hta's baby had been born in sin—or so the villagers said . . . I was baptized there, in a pool so deep it was said to have no bottom. The minister thought he had convinced me to be baptized to atone for Hta Hta's and my mother's sins . . . I felt very old, as though my childhood were far behind me."

"See? Little Grandmother."

Now she smiled openly, laughing along with him for a while. But as if to subdue herself, she all at once put out her cigarette.

"You have a right to personal happiness," he said.

Instantly, he saw that she was affronted by the sheer presumptuousness of his words. And what the hell *had* he meant? That she could do better than Ne Win? Better than self-imposed house arrest? That he, of all men, could liberate her from the constraints of a sadness that reached back to her earliest childhood?

"Is that some sort of Americanism?" she said. "The *right* to personal happiness—"

"Americanism?"

"Do you always think in such facile, all-or-nothing terms?"

Up to this point, he had felt fairly sure of himself, if not of his swiftly altering tactics of engagement with this woman. "Yes," he tried. "Absolutely. I'm all for 'all or nothing.'" When she didn't laugh, he gestured toward the reaches of the oppressive room. "Locking yourself up in here, that *is* submitting to unhappiness—isn't it?" He smiled—he couldn't help it. "And it calls for revolution."

"Interesting, coming from a man presently in peace negotiations."

"Marry me."

CHARMAINE CRAIG

For a few seconds, she merely studied him, as though gaug-
ing the sincerity of his expression, of his request. Then she broke
into a laugh that rang with all the fanaticism of hatred—for him, it
seemed, for herself, for the ugliness of the world they shared. "So I
am to be a *seventieth* wife, General?" Still, she laughed with frightening condemnation. "Have you forgotten I'm the dictator's mistress?
That I aborted his child and survived a stabbing by his wife? Do you
not read the papers?"

His heart was racing wildly, and he had the instinct both to
defend himself and to attack. She, too, was panting, staring at him
in what looked like open, defensive preparation for combat. Yet beneath this, or within it, he recognized the alarm of a warrior who had
glimpsed a respite from long battle, but was ill prepared to trust, to
rest. Could it be that she wanted him—that she, too, had divined the
relief they might discover in each other?

All at once he lunged forward and seized her wrist—not as gently as he would have liked, but with palpable affection, with palpable
respect.

"Even if the papers are telling the truth," he told her, "it doesn't
matter."

17

A Revolutionary Decision

When Louisa had seen Lynton standing with his pistol on his hip in the darkened entrance to the house, she had been afraid that she might leave with him.

But after he asked her to marry him, after he lurched forward to take her wrist, she noticed the lump (a buried bullet?) lodged in the bone by his ear, and all her resistance gave way to raw relief.

"Take me away with you," she found herself instructing him.

She had done her time as the submissive daughter, as the symbol of integration, assimilation, subjugation: as "Miss Burma," as "Ne Win's whore." She had done her time as the victim of ethnic woundedness, of slander, of the regime's ruthlessness. Oh, she loved her parents. And she would be very sorry to leave her sisters. But her time in exile was over, and she was ready to stand up actively for those who were oppressed. One could achieve nothing of greatness without risk. What she wanted now was to be linked to the rebel par excellence, to the warrior-womanizer who couldn't care less about dishonor. Could it be that he thought she might have really slept in Ne Win's bed—the same bed she had recently imagined murdering the monster in? What she wanted was Lynton's capacities of heart, a heart that was even willing to wager that there were circumstances in which a woman could be towed into a liaison that was morally repellant to her. What she wanted was a man so enamored with justice, he hadn't the time to worry about morality or his own death. What she wanted was the pistol on his hip and the blood on his hands and the bullet in his skull and a life stripped of pretense.

"Now?" he stammered, his face pale and expectant. "Take you away *now*? But your mother—your parents—"

"Now," she said. "Now. Yes."

That Lynton was ostensibly in Rangoon in order to pursue peace negotiations with the monster would have been a problem had she believed Ne Win capable of negotiating anything: no doubt, their new dictator would make various promises that might suit both his own and the ethnic leaders' ends; but if Ne Win's predecessor, U Nu—a man far less nefarious and far more open to considering the ethnic question—had invited leaders like Daddy to talks in order to throw them into prison, then surely Ne Win was capable of shooting *his* peace-pursuing guests across the diplomatic table. Surely Lynton was savvy about this. And surely these talks were a pretext for him, too . . .

No, the problem, she confessed to herself after instructing Lynton to wait for her in his car (she needed to break the news to her parents in her own voice and on her own terms)—the problem, she comprehended with a twist of nausea, as she heaved clothing into the suitcase thrown open across her bed, was that in escaping with Lynton she might be permanently rupturing her already tenuous peace with Mama. The problem was Mama's *claim* to Lynton in light of what had been.

Downstairs, she left her suitcase by the front door and set out with trepidation toward the kitchen. These days, Gracie and Molly spent most of their time with friends or at their respective schools (Gracie was finishing her first degree at the now government-controlled Rangoon University, where instruction in English had been abolished, while Molly continued on as a scholarship student at Methodist English, where Ne Win had incongruously kept the younger members of his brood enrolled). With Hta Hta's daughter, Effie, having entered what looked to be an unmanageable tract of teenage years, Mama and the nanny had drawn more tightly into their private sphere, and could nearly always be found in quiet company together in the kitchen.

They were there when Louisa entered, Mama sitting silently over her tea and Hta Hta moving stoically around her, singing a hymn and preparing their dinner.

"Hta Hta," Louisa broke in, as Mama took a long sip of tea, resolved, it seemed, not to acknowledge her daughter, "would you mind telling my father that I need to speak to him? If he'll come to the living room, I'll be there in a minute."

Hta Hta glanced uneasily at Mama, then wiped her hands on a dish towel and set it on the counter, as if in begrudging surrender.

Only when the woman was gone did Mama look up from her cup and set her fierce eyes on Louisa, still standing opposite the table from her. And for a few moments, across their persistent silence, it seemed to Louisa that anything could happen between them: that they had never been closer to perfect understanding, now that they were poised to part.

What she wanted was to fall down on her knees and tell Mama that she loved her.

But a question rose in Mama's eyes, and then those eyes all at once went dim, and she said, "He acts quickly, doesn't he? No time to think. 'You in or you out?' That's Lynton . . . What was it—a proposal of marriage? Or just an invitation to be his mistress?"

"Please don't—"

"*You* don't—don't pull out your acting tricks! Pretending to be contrite when it's obvious you've been wanting to get away from us for a long time."

The accusation that she was *acting*—that the worry and remorse Louisa had come into the room with were contrived—was there any crueler form of depriving another of her right to be? It occurred to Louisa dimly that her years of pretense had been encouraged by a mother who was frightened of her daughter's feelings. And for a moment, all she could do was stand there, fighting off the tremors of old hurt and rage, as Mama threw her hands over her own face, as though to hide what it had to say, or as though to hide from what its eyes might perceive.

"Sixty-nine wives," she heard Mama mutter from behind her hands. "Aren't you *ashamed*?"

"Of course I am."

This brought Mama's peering eyes out from behind her fingertips. It seemed she was uncertain whose victory Louisa had just declared.

But it wasn't a victory.

"For a long time," Louisa confessed, "that's all I've been— *ashamed*. Disgraced." She was referring not only to the rumors, she realized, but to her whole run on the catwalks and at the parties and before the cameras. "I've gone along with it," she pushed on, remembering how she'd felt at her first Miss Burma pageant, "because we're *all* degraded here."

The truth was never in her life had she felt more naked than now, baring herself to this woman, whom she loved beyond any other, and to whom her nakedness and truthfulness were so obviously threatening. But something in Mama's questioning eyes told her to keep trying to explain.

"But I can't go on indefinitely *enduring*. I want to *serve*, Mama. And service is Lynton's life."

"Is it? Maybe service to whatever he happens to want."

The explicit reminder of the service that Lynton had rendered Mama, and that she had rendered him, appeared to raise the cup to the woman's repelled lips. She pretended to drink and then set the cup down in feigned indifference.

"You've been overly influenced by your father," Mama finally continued with lowering eyes. "Two of a kind. Sentenced to your own self-importance."

"I hope that's not true."

"You have a low opinion of me. You see nothing but an ordinary woman content to sit here at her kitchen table, day after day."

What Louisa saw was a woman who couldn't help suddenly throwing a beseeching glance up at her.

"I've never met anyone stronger," Louisa said, and she found that she wasn't lying. And there was only quavering honesty in her voice when she went on: "The way you help people—the way you've *always* helped people, everywhere we've gone. You've never thought twice about it. The sick. The children who needed to be delivered. The dying. All of us. You never stopped serving. I'm also *your* daughter. And you need to give me the freedom to do the same."

She hadn't meant to refer to what Mama had done with Lynton, but she saw—by the dark blush that consumed Mama's face—that her final words had thrown that dimension of their past straight back into her mother's sight line. And too shamed or bewildered to reply, the woman simply sat in the echoing implications of all that had been said.

Then finally she announced, with defeat, "Go then. Make every mistake I made." *You might as well hold me accountable while you're at it,* she could have added. Instead, she said, "A mistaken marriage is also a life sentence."

This last assault took Louisa's breath away.

"Is it so impossible with Daddy?" she managed.

"Your father is *my* burden to bear. You think, so long as he's locked up here, I can just do as I please? Your father gave up everything for us. His freedom. He could've escaped to India when the Japanese came. That's what all the other Anglos were doing. But he stayed. He became a Karen. He gave his life to my people. He *belongs* to me . . . And whenever I see him, ugly as he's grown, with his foul breath in the morning and his disgusting belly and his bad manners, the way he wears his torn underwear in his study and talks with a full mouth . . . Whenever I see him, with his other woman on the side in that hallowed prison—"

"Other woman?"

"Yes, I know—who am I to talk?" Now she peered back into the recesses of her cup. "Whenever I see him, I see a man who nearly sacrificed himself to the Japanese so that we wouldn't be slaughtered—you and Johnny, my children . . . my children, who are my life . . ."

She seemed to have lost her way. With tremendous sadness, she lifted the cup to her lips again, and this time she drank. She drank deeply. And Louisa wanted to say something, to say everything, to convey the depth of gratitude and pain that was her inheritance.

But the fear of seeming false held her silent.

And then Mama said, "Go. Have your freedom with him. He'll assert his freedom from you soon enough."

She didn't find Daddy in the living room. Instead, she discovered Hta Hta standing by the suitcase she'd placed by the front door—open to a view of Lynton's imposing black car and the general seated beside her father in the rear.

"He must have seen them driving up," Hta Hta whispered guiltily. "I couldn't stop him from going out there."

"It's better this way," Louisa said, though dismay kept her pinned in the doorway a moment more.

Alongside the car, a man in uniform—no doubt Lynton's driver—paced through Mama's beds of roses. He raised his glance bashfully to meet hers when she emerged and then watched as she proceeded out from under the portico, finally stopping a few feet from the car. Evening was coming along with a breeze that drew her anxious gaze down the hillside. Was Mama right? Was her desperation to leave this prison so intense she had to flee with the first man foolhardy enough to offer her a means of escape? She hardly knew him!

A noise drew her attention back to the car—one of the doors was opening. Soon Lynton emerged, and everything about him confirmed the soundness of her rash choice: his straight stance as he faced her, his aura of respectful calm, the reassuring smile he cast her (a smile that was, well—yes, *dashing*). And the pistol. That ultimate form of resistance that partly expressed his ultimate strength and that she sensed he would resort to using only in the direst of circumstances. *Don't you see?* his searching glance seemed to tell her. *All of that—that suffering you put yourself through—it came out of a need not to offend. And as long as you concern yourself with upsetting others, you're in prison.* And: *As I see it, you are your father's daughter. He was a warrior, too, in his way. Trust him to endure this.*

Another gust of fresh wind seemed to impel him to approach. Yet his eyes were tainted with worry when he came and took her firmly by the elbows and said, "Wouldn't have been right not to ask for his blessing. Just to steal you away—not when he doesn't have the freedom to steal you back." There was a note of laughter in his voice, the laughter that came from their need to make light of the harm they were doing.

"If it makes you more comfortable to believe you're *stealing* me," she tried, "I'll go along with the story."

"Go to him," he said very tenderly. "He wants to speak with you." And he strode out to the edge of the flower beds and took out his package of cigarettes.

It was strange, sliding onto the backseat beside Daddy, sliding into the strange car—which belonged to a stranger to whom she would soon belong—in order to talk to a person who all at once appeared strange. They seemed somehow to be very far away from each other, she and Daddy, as far as they'd ever been, and yet also physically closer than in such a long time.

He didn't immediately turn to face her, so she had a moment to take in the disorientation everywhere on his pale and bloated face. He appeared to have just woken, all of his alertness sopped up by sleep. In one of his hands, he held a flask—it must have been Lynton's flask—and something about the way he grasped the delicate silver thing, almost as though he didn't quite know how it had landed between his oversize fingers, deeply affected her. She'd always loved his strong hands; while the rest of him had shriveled and withdrawn, those hands seemed still to be waiting to be made full use of. How had they landed with the rest of him here, in this position?

For another moment, she and Daddy sat in silence, and she seemed to hear the ticking of the car, but maybe it was only Daddy's old watch.

"I'm sorry," she said finally.

He turned to her and said, with an indistinct smile, "One of these days it was bound to happen." And he raised the little flask, as if to toast her. But his face fell flat. "Your mother will take it personally, of course. You've told her, I imagine?" He didn't wait for her to respond. Instead he turned his large, knowing gaze to the window—to Lynton, who had strolled out under the mango trees beyond the rose garden. "I've never been able to keep you safe," he said very quietly. "And now you're walking right into the storm."

"That's where I've been for a long time," she found herself replying. When he turned his eyes back to hers, she went on. "Years now."

In Daddy's look she saw curiosity, comprehension—and, finally, empathy. But that look narrowed suddenly, and with a rawness that chilled her he said, "Have you considered the possibility that you are being used by him?"

Unwittingly, she turned her glance back to the man who was to be her husband. He was standing stiffly away from them with a cigarette held to his lips. How perfectly groomed he looked out there in the blustery evening, the branches of the mango trees whipping over him.

"Anyone who thinks the rumors happen to be valid . . ." Daddy was continuing. "Anyone who happens to think that you have special *inroads* in the capital . . ."

Could it be more than mutual and visceral attraction that had compelled Lynton to command her to be his wife? And what if he *were* using her to—to get to Ne Win? Wasn't she also using him, if only to begin to draw on her own untapped reserves of strength?

"Lynton must have his own inroads," she insisted blindly. "He wouldn't engage in this so-called peace process without them."

"I wouldn't say that's quite the same thing."

Daddy's words could have been an insult, but she heard the countervailing assurance in the way he'd spoken them—assurance that at least *he* believed her innocent.

"There are forces bigger than any you might have imagined," he said now, gesturing past Lynton and the mango trees. "Forces at work on all of us."

Whenever he spoke that way—suspiciously, obscurely—she was plagued by pity for him. He appeared something of the raving fool, discontent with his small place in the world, and determined to enlarge it by imagining swelling powers that pressed down on his own diminishing ones. He'd never permitted her to read his editorials and essays (his "writings"), but she'd long ago formed the impression that the tottering, circular, effete nature of his verbal rants formed the character of whatever arguments he happened to be making on the page—that he never got anywhere past supposition, accusation. And yet, glancing back at the man waiting for her in the windy twilight—a man presently peering out over the hillside and the distant village of Thamaing as if to glean the scope of forces that not even he could fathom—she wondered if *she* hadn't been the fool to reject Daddy's rants so entirely.

"You're correct that a man like Lynton isn't naive," Daddy went on. "He has his plan. His strategic plan. His broader connections. His allies and enemies." He glanced, as if suspicious, around the car. But it was only embarrassment, she realized, that kept his eyes averted from hers now. "A man like that doesn't just allow himself to be conquered by impulse and infatuation. It would be *different* if you two had previously been acquainted."

Or *have* you been? his nervous glance seemed to imply. Am *I* the one who's been kept in the dark about certain alliances?

"Are you asking me not to marry him?" Louisa interjected, partly to evade the subject of those alliances, of her own past with Lynton, of

Mama's past, of which she urgently wanted to keep Daddy ignorant. But she had the sense that she was also trying to keep herself in the dark about Daddy's latent suspicions.

"I'm asking you to understand that if you go ahead with this, you become his ally," he said. "You ally yourself with a man who has been rumored not just to have died repeatedly on the battlefield and to have been repeatedly resurrected, but to have led a raid on a Thai police station because he thought he'd been cheated on an arms deal. A man who supposedly derailed a train en route to Moulmein. A man who, according to your mother's acquaintances, has never had a taste for monogamy. A man who, according to my own friends, may be pursuing this 'so-called peace process,' as you put it, only in order to secure an elevated place within Ne Win's regime."

So repelled was she by this last bit of speculation that a surge of fury rose up within her now-battering chest, and she said, trying to contain the fright in her voice, "No doubt in order to *undermine* that regime—that is, if your 'friends' have it right . . . Aren't we beyond rumors, Daddy? Don't we know better than to give them credence? I'm past caring what others think."

"Past caring what other Karens think?"

"What are you saying? He has our people's support."

"And rumor would have it that he's tended to go his own way in order to achieve it."

"There you go again with rumors!"

"Not all Karens are thrilled about what he's doing, Louisa. One of his rivals in the Karen army, a man who goes by the name of Bo Moo—a hotheaded, trigger-quick son of a bitch, they say, and also the only one who can scare Lynton half out of his wits. Apparently, he is adamantly against trusting the regime, against talks of any kind—even talks with the West, by whom we've also been burned repeatedly—while Lynton seems to be courting conversation with the CIA."

"Is this just conjecture, Daddy?"

She might have said: How can what you are saying be anything but conjecture when you're locked in your study, with your only source of information being the ex-convicts who visit you out of pity?

"It sounds like nonsense," she persisted, "Lynton wanting in with the tyrant, on the one hand, and in with the powers of democracy, on the other—"

"They're more linked than you might believe—"

She couldn't help waving a hand over her face, as if to sweep away so much rubbish. And it hurt him. She instantly saw injury pinch at Daddy's afflicted face.

"What I mean to say," he tried more feebly, "is how will you feel if you end up allied to a man responsible for the Karen Union's undoing?"

The man in question was by now halfway down their property; when she looked, she saw Lynton descending the brushy hillside at a quick clip, as if he meant to burn up his own inner torment.

"If that happens," she found herself replying when she looked back into Daddy's troubled eyes, "if Lynton is responsible for the Karen Union dissolving, I will believe it is the best thing."

She'd never dared pursue such a radical thought—how could she, given Daddy's part in the Karen Union's *solidification?* But hadn't the university massacre taught her that if ethnic hatred had fashioned the nation's history, its new dictator was making the country over with an even broader, blinder, indiscriminate hate? *Burman* students had also died in the massacre. And if the nation was to heal, if the nation was to do away with both the hater and the hatred, the nation's peoples must do so together. Undeniably, ethnic minorities had suffered and were still suffering more than any Burmans: rape, beheadings, dismemberments, slavery, not to mention chronic humiliation, chronic displacement, a chronic sense of inferiority—non-Burmans had suffered for ages just because of Burman supremacy. But Burmans were also victims of Ne Win's military dictatorship; they, too, had grown up—perhaps enough to recognize that they were no more deserving of protection and justice.

"What *I* mean to say," she ventured, "is that I trust Lynton to determine if the time has come for us Karens to give up the dream of our own nation—or even the dream of a state within a federal democracy—so that we might pursue something better for a nation that already exists."

For a long time, Daddy merely considered her, as if in distant suspicion of the person she seemed to have become overnight. Then he said, "You're more of a revolutionary than I am." And after a pause: "You really think the Burmans can get past their racism?" And when she didn't straightaway answer: "You have faith in Lynton . . . But you still haven't told me *why*. Why, when you don't even *know* the man?"

She was still desperate not to provide her only justification—that a long time ago she had indeed known Lynton. Yet whom had she really known but a strapping boy-man who'd brought her a rusted old bike and danced a jig in order to make her laugh while she worked at a sewing machine's hand crank? Who had he been to her but the embodiment of hope and lightness during a desolate time? A fantasy. Just like her fantasy of a cohesive nation untainted by centuries of prejudice. And who was *she*, anyway, to argue for that nation when it had been the sight of Lynton's *pistol* that had detonated her own will to strength?

The most striking feature in Daddy's face was his eyes: large, bulging, seemingly unblinking—a witness to his decades of enchantment and disputation and suffering. When he studied her now with those eyes, she had the impression that he was reading her thoughts, so that it would have been redundant to answer his question aloud. And after a moment, he appeared to acknowledge this.

"If it's really *trust* Lynton's after," he said, and she wanted to stop him, to confess that she couldn't claim to know anything about the man or his intentions, "if he really means to build trust between peoples, then I hope to God he succeeds. The fortitude it takes to trust when they've robbed you of your dignities, when they've tried to turn you into the vermin they believe you to be . . . It's beyond most people—beyond me, I'm afraid. Maybe Lynton can find a way to touch evil without being sullied. Whatever Ne Win is up to, maybe Lynton can escape it alive *and* morally strengthened. Maybe . . ."

But just as she was preparing to divulge all her doubt, he turned directly to her and put his great strong hand on the top of her head and cupped it with his palm and said, "I commend you to God and to the world of his grace." The press of that hand told her that he was trying to be brave in giving her away, even though he couldn't summon adequate faith to believe she would come through unscathed.

And she was suddenly afraid that they would never sit this way again, side by side. Reaching to embrace him, she knocked the flask out of his hand, and then they were knocking their heads together as they bent to extricate the thing from the crevice into which it had fallen, the smell of burbling whiskey expanding in the air between them.

"One last drop," Daddy said with a smile after he'd retrieved the thing and was sitting straight again. He tipped the flask back to his lips, and she sat watching him, until finally he seemed to give up, and he set the flask down on the seat between them. "I just can't see why . . ." he muttered to himself, almost inaudibly.

"Why what?" she asked gently.

From the way he turned to her now, she had the impression that he thought she'd already left him behind.

"Why Lynton should agree to Ne Win's terms for the peace talks," he said matter-of-factly. "When I told him I wasn't sure I wanted a man for a son-in-law who proposed marriage with a gun on his belt, he said if that was all, I shouldn't worry—that he'd decided to surrender his arms, to surrender his entire brigade's weaponry."

18

Allies

How could she expect to be trusted if she couldn't manage to trust? During the first few weeks of their marriage, as Lynton prepared to enter the peace negotiations that would apparently also be his surrender, she allowed her doubts about him to go unspoken. What he really wanted to achieve by means of those negotiations, what he really wanted to achieve by means of *her*, what *she* really wanted to achieve by means of their new alliance—these questions, too, she submerged beneath her pressing desire to draw closer to this man, to whom every day she grew more attached.

There was a flower that she had seen long ago through the window of her room at the Forest Governor's house: white, broad as a plate, protruding from the end of a long green stalk. It had opened only at midnight, and only two or three times before it had withered. And now she—who had bloomed as a girl in Kyowaing, and then again in an equally difficult incarnation as Miss Burma—felt she was blooming anew in the clandestine, dark light of Lynton's love.

And as if, before his surrender, he also wanted to flower once more beside her, Lynton ordered some of his men to construct a floating hut on a nearby lake to which they periodically escaped. Fed by a waterfall, the lake was surrounded by an orchard of papaya and banana trees whose branches were reflected on the surface of the clear water. Each morning that they rose in the hut, they would leap out into the cold lake and float on their backs, her stomach facing the sky like some promise of their future together. And in the dimness of the

hut, whose small space threw them into greater warmth and closeness, she would look lengthily at him. Revolution, justice . . . what
were those compared with the resolute earnestness of his beautiful
face, or with the privilege of residing in this provisional home on
this magnificent lake? To be here, to feel *this*! They could have been
the first humans, momentarily making contact with the shared inheritance of their descendants. He spoke of the clean air, of the taste
of the water, of the texture of her skin, and he clasped her face, held
her breasts, laughed, shook his head, kissed her. It was impossible
for her to doubt the sincerity of his affection.

True, whenever they returned to Rangoon, where they were stationed in his government-owned cottage, they were greeted with tabloid
reports that pegged their marriage as one he'd orchestrated in order
to get close to Ne Win, or as one she'd agreed to in order to evade the
glare of gossip about her affair with the strongman, or as one through
which she'd lured him into Ne Win's trap. True, these same papers
delighted in the tawdry details of their significant age difference and his
just as significant (yet evidently untallied) number of "marriages" and
illegitimate children. (Though about the subject of his former ties to
her mother—which ought to have rendered their union unthinkable by
any typical standards of decency—the papers were thankfully ignorant.)
But part of the heroism that she was increasingly attracted to was the
ability to liberate oneself not just from others' disparaging opinions,
but also from a common and narrow view of such things as decency.

Oh, she still hurt for Mama and mourned their severed tie,
blamed herself for the embarrassment she'd caused her; yet that hurt
and self-reproach existed separately from her courage to feel the full
force of her relief to be with Lynton. They would have been fools not
to hold fast to each other. They would have been allowing others'
condemnation to desecrate their attachment. They would have been
cowards, and neither of them was, by nature, cowardly.

And what a blessing Lynton's conviction could be! At the various
dinners and official parties they began to attend in Rangoon, Lynton

stood by her side not as Kenneth once had—anxiously, innocently—but as he stood up to life. In everything he did, he risked himself to the extent that he worshipped at life's feet. And he plunged into it all unapologetically and without fuss. The reckless way he danced, spent money, and drank—that was Lynton. No Karen self-effacement. He was a sovereign of his own kind: a man so seemingly beyond the law that he took what he wanted and forced open a zone through which she could peaceably, if dishonorably, pass. *What does it matter that there's more gossip about us than ever before?* he tacitly reassured her. *We mustn't disgrace ourselves with consideration of such things.* And: *Let them think what they like. It only makes clearer our mandate not to bother with pleasing the mob.* And: *Let them damn us, but let's not damn ourselves for them. Let them disgrace themselves with their scorn—don't let's justify their scorn by retreating back into hiding. Go boldly! Greatly! And, by all means, with much exuberance!* What a relief to leave the fakery behind.

Of course, the entertainments and hobnobbing would have been insufferable were she not also reassuring herself that she was preparing to serve some higher purpose alongside Lynton.

"Teach me to shoot," she blurted out to him one late morning. They were at the lake again, and the previous night, around one or two in the morning, she had woken and turned on her spirit lamp to find Lynton staring up into the folds of their mosquito netting. She hadn't dared question him—to do so, she sensed, would be to tread on some inviolable private territory whose boundaries he counted on her to respect. And it had been easy, given the intimacies of their quarters on the lake, given *their* intimacy, to ignore the vast reaches of uncharted terrain between them. But the question of what had been keeping him awake exerted itself on her half-roused mind, even if she hadn't entirely been conscious of it until this morning, until this moment. And it seemed to her that the answer to that question might be triggered by his response to this demand—that he teach her how to shoot, how to use that pistol on his hip, which he would so soon be relinquishing.

His soldier and sometimes cook, Sunny, a sweet man six or seven years Lynton's junior and someone she vaguely remembered from their days together in Bilin, had made them a picnic of fried pancakes and milky coffee, which he'd set out on the shore for them. The sky had been swelling up with vapors all night, and had finally burst and drained itself of every last drop earlier this morning, so that now they could sit and drink up the air coming off the refreshed lake while leisurely enjoying Sunny's meal. But her request made Lynton put down his cup and look with interest into her eyes.

"Teach *you* to shoot?" he said, his emphasis, interestingly, shifting the focus of her words from her violent impulse to her apparent inability to receive instruction.

His glance darted to the edges of the orchard fronting the lake, where, about a hundred feet off, a furry monkey the size of a small dog sat grooming itself near the top of a banana tree.

"If you hit that," he said, pointing to the poor creature, "I'll give you all of my money."

"You're already obliged to do that by law," she said. "And besides, it'll all be worthless if Ne Win goes ahead with his plan." In the past week, rumors had started that Ne Win intended to divest their currency of its value in order to combat black marketeering, or more likely to control the distribution of whatever currency he would go on to print.

"Then I'll give you something else you like," he said with a gleam in his eyes.

"That's more of a mutual favor than a gift, I'd say."

"In other words, you don't think you can hit it?"

"I'm not going to *kill* it just to prove a point."

"I thought so," he said smugly.

And to prove a point, indeed, she commanded him, "Give me your pistol."

With a certain swaggering and absorbed delight, he leaned over and took his pistol out of its holster and said, handing it to her, "Be my guest. It's uncocked as it is. Just don't shoot me." And then, in a way that made her want to do nothing *but* shoot him, he leaned back on his elbows and sighed as if to express his ultimate ease.

"If I hit the bunch of bananas in the tree to the right—" she said, getting to her feet and squinting across the orchard and trying to avoid the trigger on the volatile object between her hands.

"Yes?"

"You owe me your loyalty to the end of your days."

"I already owe you that by law," he said with a self-satisfied smile.

"Since when did the law mean anything to you?"

"Exactly *my* point."

She grunted in exasperation and, turning to the banana tree in question, focused on the bright green tiers of fruit emanating from a flowering stalk half hidden beneath a fan of feathery leaves. Or rather, she focused her *frustration* on the innocent bananas, and then on the stalk holding them up. Her frustration about her diminutive position as a woman who was expected to fail at this. Her frustration about being no less in the dark regarding Lynton's dealings than she had been on the day he'd charged back into her life.

She didn't even have to take aim twice. As she reeled back from the muzzle blast, she saw she'd hit the stalk, causing the entire bunch of bananas to drop, a flock of birds to spring up for cover, and the poor monkey to jump off into the shadows.

"Goddamn," she heard Lynton say over the ringing in her ears. And then, using one of the anglicisms he liked to sprinkle his stories with: "I suppose now you think you're a 'big shot.'"

She sank back down beside him, trying not to shake. "I think I'm a '*crack* shot.'"

Gingerly, her heart still banging away in her chest, she passed the pistol back to him. It occurred to her that she would have been justified in marrying him just because he had the strength of spirit to lay down his arms and try peace talks for a time. But for some reason she went on: "Is it really true—that you're surrendering your arms in order to negotiate? Tell me it's a formality, that you have stashes of weapons hidden all over the place."

He couldn't have guessed how exposed she felt, divulging what she knew he'd kept concealed from her. He couldn't have guessed that she was asking for a place by his side politically. Nor could he have imagined that she would take any refusal to grant her entry into that covert world as a declaration of, if not war between them, a stalemate of a kind.

Or perhaps, by some ineffable sense of the soul that had already begun to pass into him long before, he glimpsed all that lay behind her question. But a darkness spread over his usually shining face. And he said, "Trust me," and put the pistol back in its holster, and looked off toward the banana tree. Did he see something there, too, or was she just imagining that, in blasting its one stalk full of fruit, she'd wrecked something precarious in the universe, tipped an invisible scale the balance of which she and he, and maybe all the Karens, were dependent on?

Trust me. She wanted to trust him, but how to trust when she wasn't entrusted with his confidence? How to trust when she was troubled by certain things he was doing in the name of trust?

On the night before the inaugural session of talks, when she was newly pregnant, she accompanied Lynton to the Government House, where, only fifteen months before, when their world had been a different place, she had last seen Katie. She had very nearly bowed out of going along with Lynton (the headache she'd been battling all day was less a convenient excuse not to attend the statehouse party than a manifestation of her dread of doing so), but Lynton's firm look of gratitude when she donned the brilliant blue silk sarong he'd given her spoke of nothing but his trust that she would come through for him tonight. And, well, hadn't she had her own reasons for regularly entering the viper's pit in her previous life? And weren't Lynton's reasons far nobler than the self-protective and cowardly ones that had once been hers?

The headache, it turned out, was an early symptom of the sickness that swept over her as soon as she was back in the Ne Wins' atmosphere. The smell of too much disinfecting fluid mixed with the perfume of cultivated flowers, the sour taste of fear on the air, the hysteric whine of false laughter—it all activated in her an old nausea that she'd thought she would never have to feel again. While Lynton charged through the Government House's crowd toward some official-looking pair, she stood bracing herself in a corner, no more able to plunge into one of the overwrought conversations unfolding before her than she was willing to feign interest in the loud painting of Katie on one of the walls. Instead, she looked frankly at the real version of her hostess, theatrically holding forth across the glittering hall. From the way Katie evasively threw her eyes in Louisa's direction now and again, it was obvious that the woman had noticed her and also that she wanted to pretend not to be interested in what she'd noticed. Was it only Louisa's own coming-of-age that imparted a weary bitterness to Katie's expressions, which appeared, instead of willfully playful as they'd once been, somehow obedient to her present circumstances as the wife of the country's new dictator (who was nowhere to be found at his own party)? How hard, how *final* Katie's face had become during this past year.

Abruptly, the woman spun around toward her with an unattractive smirk almost worthy of pathos. It seemed, that smirk, to admit to Katie's fear that the rumors might be at least partially true.

"My dear," she said when she had traversed the parting crowd and stood before Louisa. "What are you doing, gaping away at me as if we've never been introduced before? You're very changed." She eyed Louisa from head to toe with the bluntly appraising eyes of someone who had no reason to conceal her spite for others.

"I suppose I am," Louisa told her.

"You've certainly lost your manners," the woman said. "No doubt being married to a boor doesn't help."

Rarely had Louisa encountered such rudeness. Yet she seemed to hear something personal in Katie's words—as though what the woman begrudged her was not so much her new boldness as the fact of her marriage to Lynton.

"I'm afraid I lost my manners even before marrying," Louisa told her. "You remember my last boyfriend . . ." The woman had never paid much attention to anything she didn't care to notice, and now she looked at Louisa with glazed perplexity. "I brought him here with me—before the rumors."

The smile that pressed itself into the corners of Katie's mouth was almost moving—it so visibly attempted to erect a defense against the memory of what those rumors had reported. And all at once Louisa felt a pang of contrition.

But the woman said, "That simpleton? He must have been devastated to learn you ran off with our most famous womanizer." She gestured toward Lynton, and the speed with which her waving hand located him in the thick of the crowd told Louisa that her interest also lay with him.

"He's dead," Louisa said, to redirect that interest. "He was in the student union building." *The student union building that was dynamited by your husband's henchmen,* she didn't have to add.

The way the woman's eyes blinked: it was as if her body were more compassionate than she was, or as if she were trying, with all her might, to stop that body from submitting to its innate capacity to feel for another soul encased in flesh. She was shocked—and appalled—that much was evident. But she couldn't break out of the meanness that must have become her way of surviving.

"You've been invited here to *enjoy,* Louisa," she said finally, "not to trouble others with your complaints. Take a lesson from your husband. He knows how to play nicely with the toys he's given."

That husband had clearly seen the storm about to break. Suddenly, he appeared at Louisa's side and put his arm around her waist, peering at her so reassuringly that she was powerless not to want to trust him in his pursuits all over again.

"I see you two have started up where you left off," he said with a laugh that was disarmingly sincere.

"I've always found your wife amusing," Katie told him. "But *you* know what I find amusing, don't you, Lynton?" And without giving him a moment to respond: "What was the name of that woman, Louisa? That doctor you wanted me to try to help—the one in prison?"

It was enough to take Louisa's breath away, to make her wonder if she'd somehow misjudged everything about Katie tonight. "Rita Mya," she stumbled. "From what I understand, she's still being detained."

There was a flash of something vulnerable and sad in Katie's eyes. "What a shame," she said quietly, before she turned her gaze to some cluster of guests across the room and made a show of urgently needing to speak to them.

As they watched her slip away, Lynton leaned in and whispered, "Don't believe a word she says."

Louisa watched the woman join the group of spontaneously laughing guests. Then she said, "It makes me sick to think of you talking to her husband."

She couldn't doubt Lynton, though. There was something almost spiritual about the way he proceeded to disarm himself. Even the way he stared up at the ceiling before turning out the lamp at night told her, over the next few difficult months, that his surrender was exactly the measure of his rebellion, that under the cover of this strained peace an action greater than any on the battlefield was taking place.

Still, she was surprised to find that one of his allies was American.

It was October, she was several months into her pregnancy, and she and Lynton were having cocktails at the Orient Club with a British embassy man named Tom Erwin and his handsome German wife, Hannah-Lara—two in a long line of Lynton's "friends" to whom Louisa had recently been introduced.

Settling into the club had meant navigating the hullaballoo that still followed Louisa in public: one or two people—this time a soldier with a rifle near the entrance—would recognize her and from there the attention would swell like a wave that she tried to crest or dive under with as much good humor as possible. Now, with that first great swell past them, and only ripples of persistent interest pulling at them, she concentrated her attention on Tom and Hannah-Lara and the shamelessly optimistic band playing on the other side of the dance floor by which Lynton had stationed them.

"But listen—" Lynton was saying to the table as he flagged down a waitress and gestured that he wanted another round. "Listen to what my refined wife did last night with a mosquito net."

"No, no—first you have to tell them what you did," Louisa insisted. "There we were, about to go to sleep, and it was hot, and our tempers were high—" It was almost as if they were a normal married couple, out to banter and intoxicate themselves with another lightly frustrated couple.

"And let me point out that this woman can shoot a banana out of a tree from a hundred and fifty feet off, " Lynton interrupted her. "Enough to threaten my masculinity."

"—and suddenly," Louisa persisted, "he yanks down the mosquito net and throws it at the door and barks at me, 'This one's torn! Get me another!'"

"What a pig!" said Hannah-Lara. As if to reassure Louisa of the authenticity of their friendship, she'd been shining smiles across the lamplit table all night—graceful, unguarded, generous smiles that

Louisa couldn't help interpreting as reminders of Lynton's isolation. They seemed to say, each one of those smiles, how regrettable it was that the West was indifferent to the Karens' plight.

"I'm staying unaligned on this one," Tom muttered, fingering his empty tumbler. "Never comment on marital spats. That's my motto."

"But you haven't heard the best part," Lynton returned. "Louisa bounds from the bed, pounces like a deranged cat onto the mosquito net, and lights the bloody thing on fire."

Now Tom and Hannah-Lara began laughing (in confused dismay, it seemed) while Lynton's eyes, Louisa noticed, darted across the congested dance floor. He couldn't have been surprised that the swaying couples kept casting them glances, she thought. Yet she saw a strain of apprehension in his gaze when it fell on her.

"You must adore me to have been so incensed," he said to her.

"I've never been so ashamed."

"One of these days, you'll learn that shame is useless."

"Isn't that *Will?*" Tom cut in.

When Louisa turned, she spotted a Westerner entering in a stiff suit and overcoat. He'd come in from the rain, still wiping his glasses. That she'd never laid eyes on him, never even heard of him, was inconsequential; just the way he froze when he put on the glasses and caught sight of Lynton told her that he was significant to them.

And Lynton—if only for an instant—looked all at once disarmed by the man's appearance in the club. When the stranger approached their table, Lynton jumped up and threw an overeager arm around his shoulders. "You know Hannah-Lara," he said. "And this is Louisa."

Like Lynton, the man could have been somewhere in his late thirties or early forties; his hair was all gray yet he smiled the bashful half-smile of a boy—a smile in which his peculiar combination of deference and remoteness seemed to melt and become embarrassment. His eyes landed on Louisa's slightly distended abdomen, and, in the low light of the bar, she could see him color. He stepped back—to reel away from what he'd noticed, perhaps. "The general speaks highly of you," he said to her, in the monotone accent she instantly recognized as being American.

She took the hand that he thrust out at her and was struck by the cautiousness of its clasp.

"Sit!" Lynton commanded him, as the waitress appeared. Lynton grabbed a Scotch from her tray and handed it to the American, while the astonished girl proceeded to set down the rest of their drinks. "My friend Will here," Lynton told the table, "he never ceases to be fascinated by the question of whether or not the end justifies the means. I keep arguing my point that amusement with friends justifies the abundant consumption of liquor."

"That better be all it justifies," Louisa said.

Lynton gave her a playful wink, which seemed to scandalize the American, though he tried to laugh along with Hannah-Lara and Tom.

"I'm determined," Lynton pressed on, "to use whatever substance I can to keep Tom away from the subject of Vietnam."

"You can't keep me from discussing the Burmese economy with him," Tom jumped in. "You're a businessman, Will—what do you make of the mass exodus from the country of all the foreigners who were holding the economy up? With the export-import businesses nationalized, with Ne Win's demonetization of the currency—I daresay the situation's hopeless."

Only a Westerner could speak with such openness, Louisa thought, an openness that presumed to exist in a protected sphere.

"Sometimes it strikes me," the American ventured after a tentative sip of Scotch, "that the hard times—the way everyone's savings have vanished with the demonetization—it's all had the effect of fueling the various insurgencies. Everyone is angry, disenfranchised, and that must have a relationship to the new movements springing up—like the Muslim National Liberation Party." His eyes moved to Louisa's. "Of course, it's true that the economy is a shambles, which is why certain people are exiting, as you say. But others are fighting harder for a Burma whose face could look very different. I see hope in that—"

"And I see a wife who needs to dance," Lynton interrupted him. He'd been drinking at a fever pitch, and now he wiped his own brow with his sleeve and gestured toward the band's crooner, who had launched into an endearing interpretation of one of Presley's hits, "It's Now or Never."

The American looked humiliated. He stared down at his knees, waiting, it seemed, for Lynton to do Louisa the honor, while Tom took a cue and drew Hannah-Lara out onto the dance floor. Then Lynton spotted someone he recognized across the room and sprang up after him.

A minute passed as they, who had been left, adjusted to being closed in together around the diminished cocktail table. "Are you an embassy man?" Louisa asked, at the very moment that the American blurted out, "Did I hear you met Zhou Enlai in China?"

She laughed as he fell visibly into his embarrassment again, and in their questions' reverberations she heard all the tension of two people trying to make sense of a system of alliances in which little was knowable. His question, like hers, had been uttered offhandedly, yet the swiftness with which it had fallen from his lips betrayed that he had come to the table with it. It also revealed what Louisa took to be the American's desperation to position her within his world-view, divided as it surely was between the Reds and all the rest. And something in her wanted to rebel against him (as she hadn't been able to against U Nu, when he'd insisted through Katie that she join his delegation of celebrities to China, and as she hadn't entirely been able to yet against Lynton, with all his secret alliances); something in her wanted to refuse this American, with his wish, no doubt, to declare her exclusively one of *his* or one of *theirs*.

"Not an embassy man, then?" she said to his increasingly worried expression.

"I'm sure I saw a photograph of you with the premier," he said, flashing her a strained, false grin.

"I wouldn't be surprised if you've seen many incriminating photos of me, Mr.—"

But Lynton came bounding back, more agitated than even before. "You haven't gotten her to dance yet?" he reprimanded the American. "The song's almost over!"

Lynton was up to something, she knew—something that might have been as simple as his wanting the American to shut up and pretend he had nothing to hide in this very unprotected sphere. And all at once the American did seem as though he had nothing to conceal or fear. He smiled that awkward boyish smile again, looking bashfully at her—almost as though *he*, and not Lynton or the crooner, were pleading with her for the last time to come hold him tight, to be his tonight. And suddenly she felt apologetic about her pregnant figure, her rebelliousness, all the indelicacy she'd just shown him.

"Come on," she said, sliding out of the booth. "We have our orders."

"I can't—"

"It's now or never," she threw out with a laugh.

Only when they were fumbling into each other's embrace did she notice the identical, cheap, government-issued sarongs and suits on almost everybody scampering across the dance floor. She and Lynton had been followed by spies before, though never by this many—at least thirty, forty . . . Of course, Lynton must have seen immediately that they were spies and trotted her out—to deflect their attention from *him*.

"Lynton?" she said instinctively.

She found him standing in the light of their table. But he wouldn't meet her gaze. Wouldn't dodge her fear and accusation with one of his frustratingly gallant smiles. Wouldn't look at her at all. He was staring, searchingly, at the man locked in her arms.

19

Conspiracy Theory

I t wasn't so unusual for Lynton to show up alone at the door with a few cartons of cigarettes or bags of rice (as if in guilty compensation for what he'd robbed Benny and Khin of—and what he'd robbed them of appeared to have too much pride to tag along during these visits). But right away when the man appeared in late December, a few days before Christmas, Benny knew—from the steeled look in Lynton's eyes—that something had happened.

"Is it Louisa?" he asked the general when Hta Hta had left them alone in the living room (Khin was still too proud or ashamed to show her face to the man who'd chosen Louisa this time, and she'd scurried upstairs as soon as Lynton's car had appeared on the drive). "She's—" Benny sputtered, meaning to mention something about Louisa's delicate state. He'd heard from Grace that Louisa was well into a pregnancy.

"She's all right," Lynton said, and held up the bottle of whiskey he'd brought with him. "May I?"

Benny sank breathlessly into his chair while Lynton poured them out generous doubles.

"A little nausea, that's all," Lynton went on, in a way that made Benny doubt him. He came and pressed a glass on Benny, along with a forced smile.

"Isn't it late for nausea?"

Lynton shrugged as he sat, as if to indicate that such things— women's things—were neither of interest nor comprehensible to him. Then, for a minute, he drank and stared at the wind-ruffled trees

296

beyond the window. How out of place he seemed, poised tensely on the chair in this dilapidated old house where no action had occurred for years, other than that which was hidden, internal.

"Have I ever told you," Benny uttered, surprising himself and trying, he realized, to put off whatever blow Lynton had come to deliver (and also trying to reclaim something *else* that Lynton had stolen from him?), "have I ever mentioned how it was I came to marry Khin? I was a preventive officer in His Majesty's—the King of England's—armed forces. It was my job to inspect the ships and seaplanes coming in and out of the port." He could have been boasting, but he found himself gazing down into his glass as if not comprehending the clear liquid it contained. "One afternoon, after I'd searched a plane, I was crossing back to my office when I saw the most astonishing woman at the end of the jetty, dressed all in red, and accompanied by a child. Khin was a nanny, then—did you know?"

But Lynton only peered remotely at him, as though transfixed by his own inexorable confusion.

"She was pointing to something," Benny continued. "She mouthed a few words to the child, and they looked out to the sea. At what? I wondered. I knew every vessel and man that came within five hundred feet of that shore."

"I'm going to have to take your daughter underground," Lynton said.

Benny was conscious of the blow having come, of what Lynton meant: that Louisa was in jeopardy. He was conscious that Lynton was speaking of nothing less than their lives being imminently threatened; yet everything about the man's presence defied this easy interpretation: the steadiness of Lynton's voice, the clarity of his gaze, the frank way he faced Benny, his perfectly groomed head, how he filled out his uniform, even his hands, which had set down his glass and were composed on his knees yet enlivened with something—a readiness to fight, to win. Yes, everything about Lynton insisted on his being absolutely resplendent with life, absolutely inextinguishable.

"Should we have another round?" Benny finally said.

With genuine respectfulness and a gleam of remorse in his eyes, Lynton stood and filled their tumblers to the top again.

"I always thought the most unbearable thing, the very most unbearable," Benny said when Lynton had sat back down, "would be to have to leave Rangoon. I was born here, you know. My grandfather was this city's rabbi once. I'll never forget the day the Japs started bombing. My fellow officers, most of them, had left. I could have sought refuge in India. Khin wanted me to go. But she wouldn't leave Burma with me. Louisa was—she must have been one, or two. We still thought of her as a baby."

But he couldn't speak another word. All at once, he burst out in convulsive sobs.

"Her mother will be devastated," he found himself blubbering. And then, over Lynton's silence: "She pretends to be outraged, but she loves Louisa, painfully!"

He felt Lynton watching him as he collected himself and blew his nose, until, finally raising his sheepish glance to him, he took in Lynton's firm, frank face again.

"The talks aren't over," Lynton said. "But the Burmans are cornering us. It may not be possible to stay in Rangoon until the birth."

"And William Young?"

Benny was as startled by the turn he'd taken as Lynton appeared to be. There was a moment of hesitation, almost of interest in the man's disoriented gaze, which soon narrowed, telling Benny that he'd violated something—if not Lynton's privacy, then his personal code of conduct, in which he alone held the power to determine what he would and wouldn't disclose.

But Benny, powerless to stop himself anymore from pursuing the course of his rushing boldness, leaped up from his seat and dashed out of the room—all the way down the hall to his study, where, from his peeling old desk, he snatched up the latest volume of his writings.

"Read it!" he said, when he'd returned with the inflammatory thing, which he immediately began to wave wildly at Lynton. "Prove all of my suppositions wrong! And, by all means, pass it along to *him* if he's someone you're working with! It's all I have to give!"

Lynton gave no sign of being staggered by Benny's outburst. Rather, he watched him with renewed fortitude and even reverence. Yet suddenly he stood and formally seized the volume from Benny's hand—to claim or confiscate it—and, just as abruptly, he bowed and said, "She will be protected."

And because a single act of courage can incite similar acts, Benny shouted to the retreating man, "Do what you can before it's too late for Rita Mya! She's been held by the monsters for fifteen years in Insein Prison!"

A few days later, by some universal principle by which misfortunes strike more often in aggregate than in isolation, they received a letter from Johnny's young American wife. It had been tampered with, the letter—its seal broken, its carefully inked script pooling in fingerprint-sized spots, as if the government meddler had just washed his hands before sifting through the thin pages, or as if that meddler had wiped away his own spontaneously elicited tears. It was enough, these heart-aches in aggregate, to make one wonder what it was all for. You strive, you strive to do right, to make something of your life, to find a way to make peace with others, with yourself, and then you drop dead. Or else the ones you are trying to make peace with vanish or are felled.

After reading the letter through several times, Benny took it upstairs and knocked on Khin's door. She called for him to enter—or, rather, she called to the person who she must have thought would be Hta Hta to come in. When he hesitantly opened the door and leaned his head inside the yellowing room, its curtains only partially drawn, she appeared to be as surprised to see him as he was shocked by the state in which he found her—laid out stiffly on the bed, her hands positioned over her startlingly narrow chest, her color off in the afternoon light filtering through the window.

"Has something happened?" she said, spotting the letter in his hand.

She seemed to struggle to sit up and flinched with some pain—in her abdomen, he observed.

"Are you sick?" he ventured.

"Tell me what it says."

She set herself against the headboard with worried expectancy, and he sat in the chair opposite the bed, guilt passing over his heart. Since the first Miss Burma pageant—when from his seat in those stands he'd glimpsed what Louisa might radiantly have stood for—his anger toward Khin had raged as never before. Raged because of Khin's part in what had been made of their daughter. At some level, he'd even blamed her for the disappearing act that Louisa had felt compelled to stage with Lynton, though he took no satisfaction in the particular suffering that act must have caused Khin. And he'd come—perhaps solipsistically, he realized—to view what Khin had done to launch Louisa into celebrity, and what she'd done much earlier with Saw Lay and Lynton, as part of her personal (if ultimately unsuccessful) revolution against him, against her unhappiness with him. But seeing her now, seemingly trapped in the bed, trapped in her body, he glimpsed how terribly partial that view of her had been. The truth was she'd never *been* trapped. *He* was the prisoner. All along, she could have moved on with her life, walked out on him. Yet she had chosen to stay. And he was so suddenly moved by her loyalty that for a moment he couldn't speak. What was astonishing, he thought, wasn't that their union had been meant to be; very possibly they could have built equally meaningful lives with others. What was astonishing, rather, was that this loyalty existed in spite of their not having been meant to be together. What was astonishing was that *leap*, unique to every less-than-perfect marriage.

"Whatever it says, Benny, please tell me," she urged him, and he saw that she was bracing herself against the headboard.

He coughed into his fist and opened the letter. "It's from Nancy"—Nancy being Johnny's plain, bespectacled twenty-year-old wife, whose blurry photograph they had received soon after the young couple's precipitate marriage nearly two years earlier. "She is very reassuring," he added—a lie. "She promises that nothing has changed as far as her devotion to Johnny goes." Another lie—this one told by Nancy, who no doubt had been struggling to believe the lie herself. Again his eyes took in the smudged contours of the girl's careful handwriting, pressed into the thin pages between his fingers. "It seems our boy has suffered a nervous episode. He was studying for oral examinations, and at the same time managing the money of friends and several faculty members. How his *instructors* could have allowed themselves to put a student in such a position is unimaginable—"

"But he is alive?"

When he glanced up, Khin was staring at him with desperation. He couldn't do it: he couldn't subject her to one more heartache. What he wanted was to shelter her from heartbreak for the rest of her life.

"Yes, my darling," he assured her, rather than telling her of Johnny's rise and fall while playing the stock market, rather than describing how one night Johnny hadn't come home, and Nancy had driven around the cold Michigan campus, finally locating him near midnight, crouched in the snow, without clothes, and defecating. "He is alive." Alive in a mental institution, he did not elaborate.

Now she exhaled, her body seeming to release itself of something more than breath, so that suddenly he felt frightened of losing that breath's ongoingness. And he was filled with tender pity for her. It must have been very difficult for her, he admitted to himself, that their daughter had found freedom with a man who had once freed Khin herself—from heartache, from aloneness, from captivity by loyalty to him.

Not a week passed before Hta Hta woke him at midnight, a lamp in her hand, saying a white man was waiting for him downstairs.

In the bafflement of his half-wakefulness, Benny fumbled with his trousers and pressed down his hair. Yet he was somehow unsurprised to find Hatchet in the semidarkness of the living room, peering at a photograph of Louisa pretending at serenity under the weight of her Miss Burma crown.

"I imagine you bribed the thugs at the bottom of my driveway," Benny said to him.

Hatchet turned—not in surprise, exactly, but with obvious anxiousness. And with dismay. Yes, from the way he took Benny in, it was evident that time—ten years of time since they'd last met!—hadn't been any kinder to Benny than it had been to the poor chap. The slope of Hatchet's enlarged belly, the cant of his neck (even with his head thrown back just so)—each feature of his appearance spoke of his having been defeated by gravity, by the work Burma had made of him, or the work he'd made of Burma. Only the absence of his old pustules now dignified him. So he was finally past his adolescence. Finally past it, and already an old man.

"One of them," the American said now, though Benny had forgotten his own question by then. "The rest were sleeping on the job."

"Will you have something?" Benny said, heading for the bar, where one of the bottles from a stash Lynton had previously brought stood nearly emptied. Benny had gone to bed having had too much, and he had told himself he would be more moderate come morning, and here it was, around midnight, and he could hardly steady his hands enough to divide the dregs of the bottle into the tumblers he hadn't bothered to wash.

Hatchet gripped the glass that Benny thrust at him, staring at its amber contents with a hangdog look. He seemed to be gathering up his courage finally to reveal his own human dependency on something—on liquor, on intimacy.

He touched the glass to his lips, but a moment later drew the glass back down.

"For God's sake," Benny said, "what is it?"

"I guess I don't drink," the man said, blushing to the jawline. "I've never really developed the taste." The way he confessed it: it was as if the deficiency of that taste betrayed some greater deficiency of spirit.

"So why accept the glass?" Benny hadn't meant to be cruel, but even as he regretted his tone he snatched the glass from Hatchet and defended himself with a few swift gulps of its contents.

"It seems to make others more comfortable," Hatchet said, looking rather shocked.

"You're wrong. It makes people far more uncomfortable when a man isn't easy in his skin. So you don't like liquor. So what? Say you don't drink. That's a respectable position. For heaven's sake, don't take a glass and fondle it and dab its rim around your lips."

"Okay."

"I didn't mean to hurt your feelings," Benny told him.

"You haven't hurt them."

"For God's sake," Benny said.

Another bloom of embarrassment rose to Hatchet's cheeks, and Benny had the sudden, unreasonable instinct to protect the devil—and then, just as swiftly, to punish him for needing protection. What he wanted was to take him by the collar and give him a good shake.

"Why did you name yourself 'Hatchet' of all things?" he demanded instead. "Leaves a terrible tingle on the back of a man's neck."

"I don't know. Just came to me."

"That's a cop-out if I ever heard one. It must've come to you for a reason."

"Maybe it's related to a story my father used to tell me."

"Your father?" Why was Benny astounded by the entirely ordinary revelation that Hatchet was someone's son?

"I grew up in New England, Boston—that's—"

"I know where it is."

"My mother was raised there. But Dad was Southern, the son of a Presbyterian minister from a place called Prattville, Alabama.

That probably doesn't mean anything to you. Back home, the difference between the South and the North—it meant even more when Mother and Dad married in the early twenties. He came to Boston to go to MIT, a university—"

"Of course."

There he was, Benny, wanting to pummel the fellow again.

"I guess he converted to Mother's perspectives—Republican, Congregationalist. And she apologized for his old ones. She liked to say his ancestors had been 'nice to their slaves.'" Hatchet laughed as he said this, with a spite Benny had never seen even in the shadows of his most stifled expressions of interest or pain. "Whenever I used to get dreamy, or sleepy, or talk about some scheme I had when I was a kid, my father would tell me the story of what he did to the Negro working under him when he was a boy. I guess they were ten or eleven, and one day my father was left in charge, and the other boy—a sweeper—fell asleep on a cracker barrel, and my father told the boy to wake up, to get back to work, but the boy kept sleeping. So my father picked up a hatchet and threw it at the cracker barrel, where it stuck, while he shouted, 'When I say wake up, I mean wake up!'" The American was laughing more fiercely now, laughing with that awful spite in his eyes.

But all at once the laughter stopped, and he said, "Maybe I will have something to drink, if it's not too much trouble," and he sank onto the sofa, beside his balled-up overcoat.

When Benny returned with a couple of bottles of beer from one of Lynton's stashes, Hatchet took his warm bottle by the neck and drank absently. And it was suddenly pleasant, drinking in the shadows with him. They seemed to have found a way to be together.

But when Benny's bottle was empty, it occurred to him that a man's personal vulnerability could blind one to his cold cruelties.

"Did Lynton send you?" he said, startling Hatchet out of his daze. Benny hadn't spoken sharply, yet the accusation in his tone must have been audible.

A sort of sourness pinched at the man's mouth now, and he put down his own half-drained bottle, as if unable to manage the taste after all.

"I was a little hurt by what you wrote," he said. "But I guess I deserved some of it."

Almost sadly, he sifted through the mess of his overcoat and brought out Benny's volume. "You should have it," he said, holding it out.

Benny took the thing between his fingers, wanting to protect it from extinguishment. "Has Lynton had the chance to read it?" he said, his heart thumping in his throat.

Hatchet didn't seem to catch on to the significance of his question. "I imagine so," he said quietly. "He's very well-read."

"You haven't told me what you think. I have thick skin. Tell me where I've erred."

Hatchet seemed to consider this a moment. "I can't speak to everything about the past. And I guess I don't understand the value of all the time you spend on it. But your conjectures about recent events and what's going on now—"

"Hold on a minute," Benny interrupted him. "Don't you see— don't you see that one of the values of examining the past is that it allows you to escape the tyranny of the present? I mean the tyranny of the self in the present. A self that is terrified of diminishment in the face of the past, in which it played no part."

The fellow looked at him in pity and confusion. He couldn't follow where Benny's thoughts had taken him—beyond history, beyond circumstance, to the realm of the spirit. He couldn't follow it, and he mistook his confusion for Benny's.

"I'm sorry for not finding a way to make contact before," he said. "The pressure has been intense. I mean the pressure not to interact with insurgents or anyone involved in insurrectionary activities."

"Yet you've kept in touch with Lynton."

Now the man couldn't hold his gaze.

"Am I correct, Hatchet? Correct in what I describe about America playing a role—if not in overthrowing U Nu and installing Ne Win on the throne, then in keeping Ne Win on that throne . . . U Nu came too close to bowing to the demands of the 'ethnics,' didn't he? Too close to giving in to federalism. And your government doesn't want that kind of fragmentation, as you told me. That might open the region to communist influence. Whereas the Union is safe in the dictatorial fist of Ne Win—provided, of course, he maintains his so-called posture of neutrality regarding China. Never mind his Marxist rhetoric, that he's staffed his ranks with old communist sympathizers, that his party controls everything . . . And his army's program to 'liquidate' minorities, as you people like to call it—the executions, the way he's relocating villagers en masse to camps, forcing them to serve in the Burma Army . . . Am I right that America wants Ne Win to succeed—to kill off the minority problem? . . . And Lynton—are you behind his 'surrender'? Have you promised him support as long as he works with Ne Win? Hatchet?"

"Will. Please call me by my name."

"For God's sake. Answer me."

There was a pause, during which Hatchet—Will—seemed to be trying to decide his next course of action. Then he looked at Benny very plainly, and he said, "I have it from a reliable source that Ne Win will be seeking substantial military equipment from the United States any day. I'm not talking about the aid program already in place, what you write about in your diary. I'm talking about substantial amounts of advanced stuff: Trainer, transport, and tactical aircraft—fighter-bombers of the Mach 2 class. Patrol ships, minesweepers, torpedo boats, auxiliaries, amphibious craft. Washington is going to say yes to him because it'll be seen as an overture. And because, bottom line, yes, our government thinks the ethnics are the problem. As far as Washington is concerned, the United States hasn't been involved in aiding the opposition since the embarrassment with the Chinese anticommunists."

For a long moment, Benny was too winded to speak. "What have you been doing here, then," he finally stammered, "as far as your people are concerned?"

"Doing our part," the American said softly. "Buffering Thailand from Peking by winning over rebel armies."

"Winning them over . . . while facilitating their destruction."

"I imagine so. Yes, that's right."

Hatchet picked up his beer and took a forced swallow. And now Benny was the one to laugh—to laugh at him. The little man, the little son of the bigot, who, not knowing he yearned to cleave to his father, to America, had struck out to cleave himself away from them. He'd made his plans with Lynton, striking out in the name of loyalty and courage; but he would follow America's policies to the last line.

"And is Lynton aware?"

"I've tried to warn him."

"There's no excuse anymore for keeping your cards to your chest, Hatchet!"

"It's not a question of that . . . He's determined to expect the best of us."

In the light of the man's admission—in the darkness of Hatchet's evident shame before it—they sat, lost and speechless. Then the American stood and went to the table where Benny had found him—to the photo of Louisa, as if to a saving grace.

"It's true I was there," Hatchet said softly.

A moment passed before Benny understood that he was referring to his presence at Louisa's first Miss Burma pageant, something to which Benny had referred in the volume.

"I only wanted to see the girls . . . But there's something about her." He reddened as he confessed this, yet it was with more pain than embarrassment that he went on. "You're wrong about me proposing her to Lynton, about me putting into his head the idea of his marrying Ne Win's mistress . . . I'd never have sacrificed her to a scheme."

"I realize that. I was out of line."

"But do you think *he* married her to get to Ne Win?"

"She was never the man's lover."

"*Lynton* might have believed the rumors . . . I danced with her, you know. A few weeks back at the Orient Club. She's an awfully good dancer."

How intolerably isolated William Young was. It took someone equally isolated to recognize that.

"Are you suggesting that he married my daughter the better to execute an assassination plot?"

"The thought occurred to me."

"Could you blame him?" Benny asked.

Now Hatchet turned back to him with a haunted, hunted gaze.

"Let me tell you something," Benny pressed on dangerously. "One of the things I've been trying to find out all these years in my journals is whether or not we—in defending our rights with this revolution—have the right to kill. I'll admit to you that I am nowhere near finding my solution. It seems clear enough that violence, murder even of the murderous, is a surrender of a kind, as doomed to end in bitterness as a life of slavery. But have we the right to stand by and watch people be made slaves—to watch them murdered, as through Ne Win's policies, in the most disgusting and undignified ways?"

Hatchet watched him vigilantly.

"Of course I realize that our fight," Benny persisted, "our fight which has justice and freedom as its aims, is now at the point of facilitating their opposites. We have Lynton, and then we have his foil, Bo Moo"—Bo Moo who had reignited the Karen revolution in the jungle, while Lynton had been doggedly trying to "talk," or whatever it was he'd been up to—"and each seems prepared to kill the other for the sake of his particular vision of justice and freedom. Sometimes this contradiction is enough to make one—to make me—want to shrivel up and die. If we can't trust one another, why should we expect anyone to trust *us*? Of course, it could be argued that *your* people's treachery led us down this path of distrust. I don't mean to play the continual victim, Hatchet. Part of inhabiting the role of the rebel is to find the courage to tell the truth about unpleasant things. And it can't be denied that there's something brilliant about Lynton and Moo. Without them, flawed and frighteningly precipitate as they are, the light of our hope would be extinguished entirely."

Through all this, Hatchet had continued to watch him steadily, as if in expectation of a final revelation that would put to rest all his remaining questions about Lynton. And now, with Benny's speech having subsided, he looked washed over by disappointment. Benny was filled with a rush of pity for him.

"I have no idea, no idea at all, what Lynton is up to," Benny told him. "I can guarantee you that anyone who claims to know is a liar or a fool. He's too savvy to confide fully in anyone. Even you. Even my daughter, I imagine."

The reminder of Louisa—of her marriage to the other, unknowable man—seemed to force Hatchet's eyes back to her picture and then away, to the photograph beside it, one of Khin as a hesitant young bride.

"She's beautiful, your wife," he said gently, and not without a trace of envy, so that Benny's pity gave way to his old frustration with the man, and he was seized by the rebellious desire to disabuse Hatchet of all his juvenile fantasies.

"If my wife stood accused of going to bed with Ne Win, I should be apt to believe it," he said.

Hatchet turned to him with a start. "That's a terrible thing to say."

"Is it?" But of course the fellow was right. "I'm not too proud to admit that I've been a philanderer in my time," Benny continued. "Or to admit I have no right to begrudge my wife her own disloyalty to our matrimony. I have no idea what the extent of that disloyalty has been. For a long time I believed it to be a kind of rebellion against me. Retribution for my philandering. If she were to leave me—now that would be a revolution! But she stays, and she endures a loveless, trapped life, and she hates herself and life all the more."

Benny had disclosed far more than he'd meant to, far more—it was evident from the fellow's disapproving stare—than Hatchet had ever wanted him to come out with. And before retreating to a safer subject, he hastened to add, "What I should do is *liberate* her by leaving the country myself . . . For so long, I've been waiting for something—for my prison friend's release, for *my* release, for Khin's release from disappointment in me, for Burma's release from captivity—when all along I might have tried to free myself . . . You don't suppose you could help me, Hatchet? Help me secure the necessary immigration papers. Living in America wouldn't be half bad."

A moment passed while Hatchet gazed at him in bald bewilderment. "I guess I could look into it," he said finally.

And to press him a bit by taking a more sympathetic line, Benny said, "To answer your initial question, I doubt very much that Lynton, shrewd as he is, married my daughter to get to Ne Win. I imagine he fell in love with her, plain and simple. I imagine he felt he had the right to love, absent all political aims. And I imagine he felt *she* did . . . I don't know, Hatchet." He couldn't help it—honesty compelled him to divulge his secret self again. "I've loved rarely in my life, and when I have, love has been mysterious. It's only sometimes had the quality of soul speak. I find it difficult to explain. We are bewildered most of the time and doomed to be lost to history. And yet we find that there are others who are unlike us in every conceivable way, yet to whom we are bound."

Whatever condemnation and shock had lit up the man's eyes before had dwindled again to disappointment. And it came to Benny that they were more alike than dissimilar. "I'll tell you something," he went on to the fellow: "since my house arrest, there's always a question in people's eyes when they come to visit me. A sort of guilty, dirty, secret question: Why go on living, old chap? Where is the meaning? Just to shovel food into your mouth? To live, to choose to live, Hatchet—it's no less an act of solidarity for the prisoner than it is for the free. I mean solidarity with the rest of humanity. With the dead, with the living, and with those future beings who will never be able to know precisely what we did or didn't do for them. I am still, after all, a fighter, though my fight is now limited to the page." He chuckled in self-mockery. "The pages that will never see the light of day."

"Don't say that."

"You're a decent fellow."

It seemed there was nothing more to add.

But Benny, all at once afraid of letting the man go, of reaching the end of something that wasn't yet complete, uttered, "Say!"

And Hatchet looked up at him in blind desperation.

"I've been reading one of your people these past evenings. A fellow called Ralph Waldo Emerson. No idea how I came by his collection of essays. Have you read his writing?"

"In school, I think."

"Do you mind if I read you one or two lines? Sit. Sit down and finish your beer while I read."

Tired and obedient, his eyes red-rimmed with feeling, Hatchet went and sat back on the sofa and picked up his bottle and put it to his mouth, while Benny took the lamp from the side table and fumbled toward the cabinet that he'd made into a bookcase.

When he had returned to his seat with the book and put on his spectacles, he cleared his throat and, calling on his old St. James' education in elocution, read: "'If you would serve your brother, because it is fit for you to serve him, do not take back your words when you find that prudent people do not commend you. Be true to your own act, and congratulate yourself if you have done something strange and extravagant, and broken the monotony of a decorous age.'"

Hatchet made no sound or sign when Benny closed the book, removed his spectacles, and looked up into his simple and absorbed face, in which it was impossible now to read meaning.

"Don't give up on Lynton," Benny said. "You must be very strong, Hatchet. Very strong. You must continue what you have begun. You must never waver from your innermost sense of what is right."

20

A Retreat and a Return

Eight weeks before the baby was due, Louisa woke around midnight to hear voices through the wall. Since their confrontation with the spies at the Orient Club, she and Lynton had been sleeping in a different location near Rangoon each night. Now they were staying with Sunny's ailing mother, in the Karen village across the highway from Louisa's family property, and the first thing she thought—after hearing the voices, after registering that Lynton had left the bed—was that the old woman needed to be protected. But the voices—two of them, one being Lynton's—were speaking a hushed and innocuous-sounding English, over the rise and fall of which she began to hear the woman's contented snores drifting down the hall from the recesses of the small house.

Almost unconsciously, she pushed herself up to hear the conversation more distinctly.

"What about the shipment from Taipei?" Lynton was saying.

"Apparently, the Americans are pressuring the Thais to prevent traffic," the other answered. She recognized the voice, the jaunty, open-throated pressure on the English vowels. "State Department," the man continued. "I'm afraid the shipment's stuck in Mae Sot." It was Tom Erwin, Hannah-Lara's husband.

"Exactly why Will's old plan makes sense," Lynton said. "We need a base in the Tavoy—somewhere arms can be delivered by sea."

"And Will's invitation? Have you thought it over?"

For a moment, Lynton seemed to rebuff the question with silence. All was quiet save for the ailing woman's escalating and agitated snores, which almost begged to be smothered. Then Lynton said, with a measured laugh, "Are you trying to cut me out of the picture, old man? You think I need to go and train under the Americans? Can you imagine me behaving myself at their base in the Philippines?"

That was all—or all she could clearly catch. When Lynton returned to their cell-like room, she was pretending to sleep, her heart banging away in her chest, the baby kicking against her ribs as if to compel her to act—to question Lynton about what it all meant. But she needed a moment to make sense of what she'd heard before determining her own tactics. *So Lynton hadn't surrendered—at least not entirely . . . So he was trying to receive shipments of arms . . . So Will was working with him to assemble a base, and had invited him to train in the Philippines . . .* She should have been relieved, but she had the nagging impression that Lynton didn't entirely trust his British and American friends.

She was half dreaming, her mind untangling a thread in a complicated design, when she woke in the early morning with the nausea that had been worrisomely plaguing her advanced pregnancy and that was now accompanied by intense cramps. By the time they reached Rangoon General, her water had broken. And then they were told that there was nothing to be done: she was going to deliver their child two months early.

The labor was quick but arduous. How tiny the child was, a boy, their son. They knew he couldn't long survive. It was his undeveloped lungs. Minutes after the delivery, he was sleeping and struggling to breathe in her arms, with Lynton beside her, and then his eyelids fluttered open and he seemed to peer past her, as though at something both haunting and extraordinary beyond her shoulder. His head shifted slightly and he looked directly into her eyes. His own eyes became frighteningly wide—big unblinking orbs, fighting against some unseen force to remain open. He stared at her, into her—to communicate something, or to absorb part of her, or simply to register for as long as possible a human face. Did he know, in his way, that he was dying? That they were fundamentally failing him? Did he feel pain when his heartbeat ceased?

The frantic doctor injected Louisa with something, and when she regained consciousness the next day, Lynton was sitting next to her with bloodshot eyes and empty hands.

"Where is he?" she demanded.

"Returned to where he came from," he said. She thought he would smile—his eyes gleamed the way they did before he tried to make light of something that pained or concerned him—but instead, while she began to weep, he looked off toward the window, as if at some indescribable inner picture of wherever it was their son had gone.

"Now," he said, "we have to earn our place by his side."

Louisa hadn't known that Lynton's underground operations had long been headquartered in Kyowaing, where she had once lived in the Forest Governor's house. A week after the delivery, he informed her that they had to relocate to the village, deep in the heart of the territory he now controlled. "Pressure's too intense here," he said. "The time has come to move back in-country."

How absurd that at the very moment she was ready to give up, to give in, he was ready to trust her more completely—and even to count on her.

Who are we to say the death wasn't fated? he seemed to want to say as they were secretly preparing to head out, ten nights after the birth. She was still losing blood, her breasts still senselessly knotted with residual milk, and Lynton kept flashing her blazing glances, as if to enflame her old will to fight. *Who are we to say,* he seemed to go on, *that the loss wasn't in some way necessary for you to be born to new strength?*

Enraged by her own fleeting thought that their child might never have been meant to be, she inwardly accused him (or, rather, herself) of convenient and weak-minded thinking, and made the point (again, to herself) that many argued there was no more meaning to life than suffering. *By that count,* she silently contended, *Ne Win's atrocities could also be justified! And Kenneth's death! No! No!* Yet she didn't *really* believe that suffering—if causeless—was also utterly meaningless. In her heart, she felt that only those who had suffered could discover grace. So wasn't it possible that grace made way for suffering in a mysterious way? And she was washed over with tenderness for Lynton, the brave man packing his few belongings before her; surely his past losses and sufferings had been great.

After a hasty and dissatisfying parting from her parents and sisters—whose startled looks and silence, as she said her good-byes, she attributed to her recent loss as much as to her sudden appearance in the house after her long estrangement from it—she and Lynton headed out. En route to Kyowaing, a journey they made largely on foot, Lynton spoke to her more openly of what he was facing. His revelations—muffled by the spurts of rain, and the running of the streams, and the wet steps of the elephants humbly transporting their belongings—did not overwhelm her; rather, they were modulated, moderated by her persistent thoughts of the child they would never know. And even as she was transfixed by painful memories of the boy's life and death, even as Lynton described to her the most dismaying things, she was aware of being strangely comforted by their surroundings, these familiar hills and ample moist thickets where everything appeared in its place, where they seemed to be plodding past the happenstance of human history into a more lasting order of things. The birds sang, as though in counterpoint, the passing clouds putting the entire human element in its shadowy place in the landscape, yet also recalling to her the shadows of her own past in these hills, in Thaton and Bilin and Kyowaing.

"Ne Win is only escalating his military program against the people, the ordinary villagers," Lynton said as they climbed. "Particularly in the delta, the plains. Resist in any way, make contact with one of us, with a rebel soldier, and you risk execution. They're conscripting everyone at gunpoint—children, women . . . no one is spared. And they're making it impossible for our soldiers to move as we once could. A virtual web of human threads spreading from side to side, across the whole delta and beyond."

Did this—Ne Win's barbaric stepped-up military program, coupled with Lynton's mounting fear for their lives—mean that Lynton had given up on the peace negotiations? There had been a time when Louisa would have seized on his openness as an opportunity to probe him; but she still didn't have the heart for discussions of his conflict, or the will to engage with anything but the richness of mind their loss had bequeathed her.

They stopped, in the space of her silence, to rest under an ancient pine from which they could look down over the river that bent back toward Bilin, and she was overcome still more powerfully by the sensation of evading history—personal and human—in this lush terrain, even as she made contact with the past in it. Hadn't she once stopped in just this place with her mother and siblings en route to Kyowaing? It seemed she could recall Gracie asking where Daddy was, and Johnny giving Grace a nasty look before a flock of parrots broke through the haze of their grief, allowing them to trek on in pursuit of what their future would bring.

The memory took her back—as everything did now—to that nearer memory of the baby's passing, that horrifying fact that lay at the new center of her life. And, again, Lynton drew her insistently toward the immediate. "The Burma Army isn't our only problem," he said, nudging her toward the crest of a ridge, past which all she could see was the great canyon of the sky, riven with massing thunderclouds.

"You remember I worked under Saw Lay when we were fighting the Japanese? Force 136, special operations. Someone named Bo Moo also worked with us. We worshipped Saw Lay. Utterly full of ourselves, the two of us kids. And Saw Lay disciplined our difficult alliance. Our allies and enemies were clearer then . . . But Moo, he couldn't forgive the British afterward. Still can't forgive the betrayal. If it were up to him, the Karens would be pursuing a program of hard-nosed insularity. Trust no one. Not the West. Not the East. Not the Burmans. Not other 'minorities.'"

He stopped to face the view of the wide, lush valley below. "His territory abuts mine. Just out there, on the Dawna Range," he said, pointing out across the valley. "And if I fail—"

"In what?" Her question surprised her. Perhaps he was managing to revive her after all.

"In building trust, of course."

"I thought you wanted to build up arms, build a base in the Tavoy."

He looked at her in confusion. But a twinkle of relief also danced in his eyes. And it was with a nod that he persisted: "Yes, we need all that for leverage. But there are many on the inside who are just as disgusted as we are by what's going on. And there are ethnic leaders all over the country ready to work with us. With enough trust, we shouldn't have to use force—at least not for long . . . Military action can force a point. But with or without our own states, Louisa, we're going to have to find a way to get along. That takes compromise, letting go of the past . . ."

He passed her his canteen, and she took the cold river water into her mouth instead of giving in to the lump of relief rising in her throat—instead of voicing her questions about what *would* happen if he were to fail in this, whether Bo Moo wouldn't attack his territory in order to unify the Karens.

"We are a peaceful, conciliatory people," he said, taking the canteen back. "It's true we've been betrayed, that we had reason to rise up. But does that mean we should give in to endless war?"

"I don't believe in peoples or nations," she found herself abruptly, emotionally answering. He turned to her with surprise, and, in fact, she had surprised herself with the radical thought. Something about the death of their child had led her here, to this feeling that it was wrong for anyone to claim exclusive rights to a corner of the earth—wrong for no other reason than that everyone was passing. And the inner child in her—the mixed-breed, raceless, rootless little girl who had been homeless in just this place—knew what it was to be rebuffed by some who temporarily had more and taken in by others who had long had less. The paradox was that she was suddenly sure that Burma's most beautiful feature was its multiplicity of peoples.

"We have to find a way to reconcile," Lynton said gently, in tacit understanding of, if not agreement with, her dangerous assertion. "We must find a way to get over the past."

The British-built brick-and-wood houses of her childhood had vanished, and with them the teak plantation that had spread out across the valley under the gaze of the far-off pagoda. But upon first reentering Kyowaing she recognized the rocks, the stream that cut the same path through the land. And she knew every detail of the hill on the top of which Lynton's men had built her a house in the shadow of the Forest Governor's disappeared one.

"What happened to the old teak plantation?" she asked Lynton on their first evening in the village, when they were sitting in the lone, large house on the hill. They had just finished a surprisingly beautiful meal made by Sunny, and now a slew of boys—who'd run away from their homes to join the revolution, and whom Lynton had taken on as his charges—were cleaning their dishes, singing and bantering while Lynton and Louisa talked over tea at the table.

"Burned by the Burmans in the early years of the revolution," he told her.

"And the Forest Governor and his family—do you know what became of them?"

"Escaped or captured, no doubt."

"It's haunted, you know," one of the boys said, peering defiantly at her with a dripping plate in his hands.

"What's haunted? The *village*?" she asked him.

"The hill!" the boy said. Sunny whipped the boy's backside with a towel and told him to keep on task, but the boy pressed on: "Everyone who lives on this hill perishes!"

"Precisely why I choose to live on it," Lynton said, and then let out one of his dismissive, disquieting cackles. "The past is the past—all over now."

But it was and it wasn't over.

During the following weeks, Lynton came and went on missions she didn't press him to explain—she was too desperately afraid for his life. And her memories of what had been in the old house on this haunted hill mingled with her memories of her boy, and she experienced the shock of his death with a clarity made sharper by the village's lost luminance. She looked out from the open veranda of the house, looked out over the vaporous valley where the old teak plantation had been, and she seemed to see Mama walking away from her, disappearing into the vanished trees. And superimposed over this, she saw their boy's eyes staring into hers before he drew his last breath. And even as she saw this, she also saw the long-ago lumbering elephants that the Forest Governor had kept to haul his felled logs of teak. Beautiful creatures, those intensely private beings, whose lives had seemed a lesson to her in the value of modesty—gone! Gone with all the rest!

Had the universe—or God, if the universe had a soul—been indifferent to those elephants' suffering? To the decimation of the teak fields? To the decimation of Kyowaing? To her boy? Here, now, with her perspective on the past, she seemed to see that, from the perspective of eternity, our tragedies might not look so very bleak. And she remembered how every afternoon she and Johnny and Grace had been released from this house onto the hillside to catch fish and collect vegetables and firewood. Their appetite for freedom had intensified with the breaking cataclysms of afternoon rain, rain that cleansed them of their heartache and tried to wash the earth of its sins. How the parched earth had revived in that rain, bodying forth waves of leafy mossy fragrance. How they, too, had revived, earthen creatures that they were. They had leaned against aromatic tree trunks, listening to what those protective silent beings had to say—that the tallest among them were preparing to die, that death itself was part of the way of things, that the Forest Governor's wife and sons were also passing by, that the shades of Mama and Daddy were carried in the same light that struck the trees' generous leaves. *I am right here with you*, those leaves had told Louisa. *See as we do.*

And what a mercy it had been to see that way:

When a mother bird lays eggs, she sits in her nest for a long time. The eggs hatch, and she feeds her babies and remains near the nest. Then she backs away, until one day she abandons the nest, and the babies cry. If she were to keep feeding them, they would never learn to fly; eventually, they would fall out of the nest and perish. Sometimes a baby bird falls from the nest. Then the mother is sad and leaves the other babies to die. Or a baby bird starts to fly and is eaten by a snake. Then the sibling still in the nest is too frightened to fly, to cry. Ignored by its mother, it freezes into fear's hard shape.

Deep in the forest, you can pick fiddle-leaf fern and sweet oranges. After the rain starts to fall and the river water is muddy, the fish can't see your line. In the morning, the monks who live in a monastery at the base of the pagoda beyond the forest receive food in their bowls as alms, but they abstain from eating after noontime. If you visit them in the afternoon, you might be offered leftover rice and curry; as you eat, you will also receive the blessing of the monks' approving gaze.

To make shampoo: find a pod that looks like tamarind; boil the pod in water; then peel the bark off a certain tree, rub the bark between your palms, and mix the slippery sap with the pod liquid. To bathe: descend to the stream, but don't copy the little children who go naked; instead, emulate the big girls, the women, who wrap their sarong under their arms and wash their torso through the sarong. To feel relief: clamber up the rocks, and stand without moving under the waterfall until something throbbing is pounded out of your shoulders. To soften the eyes of the Forest Governor's wife: collect the red seeds of a certain tree with which she can make strands of beads.

"What will you do with your time here?" Lynton asked Louisa one evening—not with accusation, but with a certain disquiet in his eyes.

He had recently returned from a clandestine mission, and was already preparing to head out again. But all evening he'd been playing a noisy card game with Sunny and the boys in the kitchen, and he'd come into the bedroom to find her lying awake on their bed.

"I should send you out with Sunny to shoot some birds for my dinner," he said, sitting on the bed beside her and taking her hand. "I'm sick of vegetables. Or I should charge you with the task of teaching the boys how to shoot. We need more sharpshooters."

She looked at him, half wanting to laugh, half wanting to defend herself against his insinuation that her reflections and grieving did not constitute a meaningful life.

"I'll teach your boys," she found herself replying. "But it's literature and math they need."

And, in fact, there was no nearby school for the boys or the village children to attend. "Don't refine all the ruffian out of them," he said gratefully.

She soon organized the construction of a simple schoolhouse, into which she went on to pour all of her longing and energies. Lynton's boys couldn't easily be taught much of anything, but they and the other children adored her, basked in her tenderness and reprimands and high expectations, much as she complainingly reveled in being the butt of their pranks.

And, by means of this unexpected mutual fondness, her grief diminished, and the past, which had been so initially present for her in the village, began to recede. To give to these children—who were exiled from the country that was supposedly their birthright, who were of a provisional people in a provisional place—to be the object of their secret yearnings and ceaseless teasing, to be the witness to their minuscule achievements: it was a very small and almost invisible kind of service. She found that while she sometimes missed acting in films (the sheer escape of self that came with that), she never longed for the imposed sense of significance she'd felt in her older life (when she had so glaringly stood for something, if only the nation's ideal of beauty). And she understood that it was up to her to give her new humbler vocation and existence all of her largeness, without restraint.

The boys and Lynton were her nation now. Kyowaing was her nation. And she began to live in it as never before. Not just to live as if she were at home in her body—to savor the contact her skin made with the dense air as she trudged down the perspiring hill on her way to the schoolhouse, or to relish Sunny's delicious curries, his succulent, perfectly pickled eggs—but to live as if she were finally at home here among the boys and all the officers and soldiers and villagers, here among the unchanging rocks and the stream and the haunted hill that, along with her, remained.

How cherished she felt, even when Lynton was away! How cocooned in safety—not the false safety a child yearns for when she seeks reassurance that evil will never touch her, that no one she loves will ever die—but the safety of acceptance, a safety that accompanies the feeling of being free to laugh with an open mouth, and to nap and snore loudly, and even to shed tears of grief. A safety that came, for her, now, with a relinquishment of the place she'd held in Burma's consciousness and of the greater place she'd held in her own experience of the world. These people clearly knew of her fame and silly titles; but they were all too happy to oblige her wish that all of that be left behind. They loved her in the most ordinary of ways, for being the most ordinary, inconspicuous of women; and, out of the public eye, she was free to love them—to love life—indiscriminately.

"You've never looked so beautiful," Lynton told her one sleepy morning when they were still in bed. She knew, from things she'd heard him mutter to his men, that his hours away from her were fraught with tension—nothing was certain—yet he, too, had never looked so unburdened, so free to inhale his fill of air, to rest, to enjoy.

To rest, to enjoy, and to do so while in love . . . To be understood, and to understand, by means of two frank, flawed bodies. To be touched by, and to touch with, the hands of conviction—conviction that one is enough, more than enough: necessary. To be assured, and to assure, with a kiss, with a look that says one is incapable of disappointing. To be accepted and wanted in spite of one's imperfections. To be the recipient of the pleasure the other has to give, and the provider of small courtesies ("Let me pull the blanket up over you"). Yes, fiery arguments still sometimes exploded between Lynton and her, and at times they surprised each other with displays of aggression or outrageousness or momentary cruelty, and beneath this, too, shone nothing less than absolute trust, an intimacy that staggered her. No more need to hide, to pose, to feign strength—what was already within either of them, all the greatness and all the humanity, was everything the other saw.

If their hour was at hand, so, too, was the fulfillment of their longing. With Sunny's gentle assistance, they parented the boys. Lynton bought her two elephants on whose expansive beings the lot of them lavished their affections, and at night they humans would sit up in the house on the haunted hill, sit around the glowing fire, and laugh about the goings-on of the day, or else sing some ancient

CHARMAINE CRAIG

Karen ballad and enjoy Sunny's cooking, never speaking directly about where they were headed.

One evening, after Sunny and the boys had cleared out of the house, Lynton came to her and told her to close her eyes, and then he led her out to the stoop under the veranda, where he asked her to sit, and he put something between her hands—something cumbersome and stiff, yet yielding—a small accordion.

"Found it in one of the boy's huts," he said, when she couldn't speak. "Don't want to know where he got it. Probably pillaged it from some poor Burman's hut."

"They're too young to fight," she said—one of her refrains when they were speaking of the boys. Not that Lynton's cease-fire with Ne Win's army had been broken yet, but they were subtly preparing for that inevitability, and the topic of the boys' fitness for soldiering had been part of those preparations.

"Go on," he said. "Play it for me."

The rain had fallen off a few hours earlier, and now the evening sun shone clearly over the valley. From where she sat, she could see past the gleaming river snaking into the mountains to where she knew Thailand lay.

"I thought you knew how to play," he chided her, as though to tease away her silence. "You told me your father gave you an accordion that you left in Thaton."

Had she told him that?

"Go on. Play the song your father hums—'God Will Take Care of Me.'"

She scoffed, yet there was something chesty in her voice, something about to give. "That's absurd," she managed. "You can't expect me to sing you promises of divine protection when I don't *believe* . . ." But she trailed off, and he looked at her with anticipation. They had never spoken of the limits of their faith, never even identified

324

themselves to each other as *being* of any particular faith, or of being of faith particularly.

Don't you, his quiet gaze asked her, *in some unfathomable way?*

He closed his eyes, as if trying to see her more clearly, and she shivered at the sight of him so still and undefended. A bird in a nearby bush began to sing of solitude, of yearning.

"The talks aren't going well," he said, regarding her again with grave eyes. "It may be soon that you hear I'm dead." He spoke very tenderly, very sincerely. "Don't believe it. I'll come back for you. But in the meantime"—he pointed across the valley, to the dark green slopes of the Dawna Range beyond the pagoda—"go to those mountains if the Burmans come."

The Karens from whom he'd split off were headquartered in those mountains; she remembered this, and was bewildered by his suggestion that she would be safe with the very people with whom he'd been in conflict—with Bo Moo, whose ruthlessness Lynton's men referred to only in whispers.

"We're not alone in this," Lynton said, putting his arm around her waist. "There are others who want the same things, as I've said . . . If we look past our petty proclivities, past our troubled history; if we see the broader common goal—we Karens, and also the Kachin, the Mon, the Shans, the Muslims, the *Burmans*—everyone with an eye to democracy . . . If we find a way to come together, they won't be able to stand in our way. And our friends will be there to help us."

"Friends?" Tom's and Hannah-Lara's amiable faces flashed before her eyes, and the American's embarrassed, hesitant one.

"Yes, friends." There was impatience in his tone now.

"You're speaking in riddles, Lynton. Be plain with me. Why would Bo Moo protect me if you're still working with them—with Tom and—and the American? What's happened?"

But to banish the strain rising in him, to banish talk of every alliance but their own private one, he nudged her lightheartedly with his knee, and said, "You can't deny me some little ditty on the accordion now—now that you know they may soon be peppering their papers with my obituary."

He gave her a silly, pleading smile that made her smile in turn, that made her want to cry, and she stared down desperately into the creases of the accordion, saying, "I hate this," which only provoked his laughter.

But he leaned in toward her and touched his nose to her cheek, so that she smelled his clean river scent, and he said, as though to apologize, "We mustn't despair. We have so much to do—this is only a stopping ground. To despair is to forget what we owe others . . . Promise me you won't despair."

He was right there beside her, with his beautiful shining face and worried eyes, and soon she might not be able to catch a glimpse of the light that remained of him.

Again, her memory reached back, back to those days in Thaton before Ducksworth had come for Daddy, and she found the fingering, the words of the hymn—yes, one of Daddy's old standbys.

"Be not dismayed," the hymn began.

But she was—as dismayed as she'd ever been.

21

Come Back

Two months after Benny had left with Molly and Grace for America, Khin stood at the window of her bedroom, staring down at the view he had so prized: the mango trees now lashing against the wind along their darkening drive; the highway outside the gate, with its single passing car throwing beams of light into the evening; and, beyond the highway, the old Karen village of Thamaing. That village breathed, it slept and strived, yet it hadn't really overcome the beginnings of the civil war, when it had been fired on, torched, and reduced to ashes. No, it had lost its fundamental beauty, its hope, Khin thought, aware of a nearer view: the sharpening image of her face reflected in the window, and the hopelessness in her eyes. And now the feeling came again—the ache that had been increasingly radiating through her bones and pelvis since Louisa had gone underground with Lynton. *They're gone,* she said to herself, as though to soothe the pain, or to explain it. *They're gone, and soon I will die.*

"Mama, do you know that when a spirit leaves the body, you have to call it back?" Louisa had asked her, so long ago, when they were newly reunited in Bilin—after Khin had walked away from the children in Kyowaing, only to fall into Lynton's youthful arms for a time. "If a spirit gets frightened, it flies away and you get sick or go crazy. And when a woman has a baby and cries too much, her spirit leaves and she can die. And when a baby thinks it's falling, its arms fly up and its spirit leaves. And when a child is dying, the spirits guarding the trees can be convinced to save the child's life. You have to make an offering of rice wrapped in banana leaf and leave it on the riverbank. Or kill a chicken with the right hole in the right part of the spine. You have to *invite* the spirits back to the bodies. Say, 'Come back from the fields, come back from the forests, come back, come back, come back, come back.'" Louisa had been standing by one of Khin's sewing machines, all her tangled curls haloing her mournful open face as she enacted the ancient Karen ritual, and Khin had shuddered, knowing that in some obscure sense the child was asking her to call back their own disembodied spirits, lost to them somewhere along the line.

And now even her children's bodies—still in the realm of breath, she prayed—were far away.

In fact, there had been three farewells. Three farewells that seemed like aftershocks of that earlier rupture at the start of the civil war, when Benny had been led away, and Khin had lost herself and her senses in the haze of Lynton's body.

Now, she turned from her glassy reflection in the window to the bed that had become only Benny's at a point. She could almost see it, the impression of his shape on the blanket, how he perched his spectacles on his nose when he read in bed every night, and then the way his plump fingers released their grasp of the book as he fell asleep. Some nights, before he had left for America, before she had moved back into this room, she would ask if she could keep him company, and then she would sit in the chair by the window, pretending to knit and watching him read, watching him peacefully slip away.

She lowered herself onto the bed and took from the nightstand the clutch of photographs he had left for her, or merely decided not to take. The first photograph was of the two of them in the flush of their early intimacy, his arm around her waist, her hands clasped in front of her groin, as if it might give her away. They hadn't yet been able to imagine the faces their closeness would bear. Almost to explain that mystery, the second photograph, which she held up to her eyes, showed the six of them sitting under the damaged portico after

Benny's prison release. How much they'd recently come through, yet the children's eyes were lively and forgiving—forgiving first and foremost, it seemed now, of Benny and Khin's original choice to be man and wife. Yes, the children's faces cast that choice in the afterglow of inevitability, along with everything that had given rise to it: her own inability to save her father's life, Benny's parentlessness and desperation for belonging. If only she could touch them again, her children. If only she could fall before them and draw them to her chest and kiss them and beg for the forgiveness they so easily gave.

The first two farewells had come one on the heels of the other. One afternoon, Hta Hta—her faithful remaining servant—had appeared in the kitchen doorway, where Khin was drinking tea, to say that Benny was napping and that Lynton had arrived.

"Should I wake Saw Bension?" Hta Hta had asked sheepishly. Of course, the servant knew that since Louisa's elopement, Khin had refused to speak to the same man who'd once spun them around their sewing shop with his men in Bilin.

"No, no," Khin had told her. "It's nothing."

Maybe it was instinct that compelled Khin not to snub Lynton this time. She had known of Louisa's pregnancy and wasn't quite surprised to find the general in the living room with a swaddled bundle, held neither clutched to his chest nor out at a distance. Instantly, she understood that something had ended. And she listened, with all her stifled senses, for what blessing or blow he had come to deliver. She listened to his bloodshot eyes, charged with expectancy and ruin, with shock and exhaustion.

"And Louisa?" she found herself saying when those eyes reluctantly met hers.

He didn't recoil from the question, but simply stood with the bundle, taking her in.

"Alive," he said finally. "But the child was too young."

Before she could respond, he escaped from the house, and all her hearing seemed to rush back to life with the slam of the door and then with the startled report of gunfire outside. When she looked out the window, she saw him beneath the mango trees, holding the bundle in one arm as he shot bullets into the sky.

But she hadn't been spared Louisa after all. One night, about a week later, her eldest appeared at the house, thin and perspiring, her stomach still swollen from pregnancy. It was the first time they had faced each other since Lynton had come back into their lives, and, as if to give them the space they needed to reckon with their estrangement, Benny and the girls—who had been standing with them in the living room—excused themselves and fled to their rooms.

"You aren't eating enough," Khin said to Louisa finally, and immediately regretted her words.

Louisa flinched and knelt a few feet from Khin's feet. "We have to go . . ." she said softly. She lifted her shining eyes to meet Khin's. "But I can't—not without your blessing." And she leaned forward and pressed her head to the floorboards, prostrating herself as Burmans did before monks and elders. "Do I have your blessing, Mama?" Her voice broke with longing, her need to be embraced becoming a palpable thing. "May I, Mama? May I have your blessing? Do you forgive me?"

Khin hadn't been able to speak. And when Louisa raised her face to meet hers again, Khin could do no more than mutely signal her assent.

Then Louisa was gone, and the terror that came with her being underground, the knowledge of what would be done to her if she were discovered by the Burma Army . . .

As if possessed now by the need to escape her mind, Khin put down the photographs and pushed herself up from the bed, feeling the pain in her pelvis again. She crossed to the window and, almost hoping to find her missing family through the glass, braced herself on the casement in order to peer out. Seeing nothing but her own translucent, haunted face, she pushed open the window and leaned into the sweaty body and breath of the night, thick with coming rain.

This is what it is to be a ghost, she thought. This is what it is for the world to disappear before your eyes, even as you are doomed to go on existing as a shadow. Hadn't Benny the right to want to leave this endless imprisonment? Why had she been so afraid of leaving with him, of missing the Burma she had been missing all her life—a Burma that thousands of years ago her ancestors had found in this place they called "Green Land," and that had vanished to the point of invisibility? For a chilling moment, she thought she truly might be dead. This was not her house, but a sarcophagus from which she would never make her escape.

But the rain began to lash down from the cracked-open sky, and she closed her eyes and seemed to break from the confines of the house, of her body, to a place from which she could perceive the rise and fall of the oceans, and the crumbling of the cities, and the cries and strivings and silencing of all humanity. What a merciful, if brutal, view.

Then she opened her eyes and the view washed away with the rain. What stayed was the feeling of missing something—of missing everything profoundly.

One evening several months earlier, Benny had called her to his room—this room—and asked her to sit, and then he had paced before her and explained that a certain American, whom he would not name, had managed to arrange for the family's exit to his country. They'd be able to visit Johnny (who, she understood, had suffered some sort of nervous breakdown), and jobs had been secured for Benny and the girls: he would sell sewing machines at a place called Sears Roebuck, Gracie would steward Pan Am flights, and dear Molly would teach Burmese to marines. "I'm going," he said decisively, yet with a question in his voice. When she didn't answer—didn't tell him that there was no question she would join them—he went ahead and asked as a formality: "And will you come with me?"

He didn't argue when she told him that she would not and then cheaply justified her decision by saying she'd spent enough of her life as a minority (to be Karen in Burma was bad enough, she said; she'd heard what Americans did to those who weren't white). His willingness to go without her, of course, was as much a confession as her unwillingness to leave: a confession that, if they had once been entwined enough to stay together during the Japanese invasion, they were no longer. There was no need for promises of fidelity. There was nothing left between them to be faithful to. Nothing but memories of what had been and this faltering friendship, this limited understanding.

"Do you imagine it's true?" she'd said, still in her chair, and looking up at him, fixed before her in the golden glow of the oil lamp. "Do you really think that God loves each of us, as if there were only one of us?"

He seemed taken aback by the question, and for a moment he blinked at her in surprise, or sudden faithlessness. Finally he said, "I couldn't presume to know."

"But do *you* love that way—each of us, as if there were only one of us?"

She was referring also to the other woman, of course. The other woman, with whom, she knew, he had continued to correspond sporadically—during these ten years of his house arrest—by means of their ex-convict friends who alternately visited the prison and this house.

Understanding had dawned on Benny's face then, but he didn't—perhaps he couldn't—speak.

"You're leaving her, too?" she said.

"For God's sake, Khin. Don't make me regret my decision. At least she's encouraged me to leave. And it's not—it's not what you think, my affection for her."

"You must be filled with regrets. You must regret calling me from the jetty that day."

This made him look at her in fear, as though he were all at once perched on a splintered series of planks that might at any moment give way to the restless waters beneath them.

"Don't speak," she said. "Don't immediately deny it. Just listen to me, and let me read your eyes."

But he threw those eyes down, away from her stare.

"Yes, I thought so," she said.

And as if to rebel against her verdict, he threw those eyes back at her—with defiance, she saw, and also with heartbreak. He looked very fierce, and suddenly she felt like a girl, someone seeing him for the first time: he was strange, and beautiful, and hard-lined. And aging. How tired he looked.

"Who did you think I was?" she said. "A girl on the end of a jetty, holding the hand of a small boy . . . Why *me*, of all women? I'm not especially pretty—"

"I won't stay silent when you're desecrating the past!" he erupted. "It's all very well to demystify that—that thunderbolt—to say it was only passing *lust*. Just hair. Just posture. Just the way your hand seemed to clutch that little boy's, as though you were holding on to him to stay safe and not the other way around. As though *he* were keeping *you* on that jetty. It's all very well to say that the roundness of your arms, the roundness of your cheeks, their luminescence, the way your lips parted without words—it's all very well to write it all off as superficial. To write off my burning interest in you as *physiological*. Just a man wanting to procreate with a member of the species whom he found especially fit. But I *saw* you on that day, Khin. I don't know how else to explain it."

The way he'd uttered her name—it caught her, and she couldn't speak, couldn't defend herself against her feeling for him.

"And I felt you seeing me," he said quietly, and then lapsed into silence for a time. "You asked about my faith," he went on at last, "if I believe we are so precious after all to God—if God *is* . . . I know you loved Saw Lay—don't deny it. There's no need . . . You know, sometimes I hear him talking to me? I hear that modest, moved voice, rending the night . . . Is it a fantasy? Maybe. But sometimes I believe it's his immortal voice. I'm not speaking metaphorically. I mean when others enter us—their words, their wisdom, their counsel—all of it lives inside us and will not be extinguished. No, the voice I hear, the words that echo in my ears—they seem to *live*, in memory, yes, but also in—in what I only know to call eternity."

When he and the girls were gone—when all that life was sucked out of the house with their quick, irreversible departure—everything had gone mute for a time. Even her mind. And as if to shock that mind awake now, she leaned farther out the window, out into the thrashing rain. Her rosebushes, twenty feet below, flailed in the wind, describing her anguish. But if she wanted to escape her thoughts and her pain, she no longer had the instinct to escape the world. Could it be that, after everything—after all her yearning to vanish, to slip into the waves of oblivion—all she wanted was to *persist*? Could it be that, now that she was finally free to die, all she wanted was to inhale the fragrance of the earth, of the rain, and for all of it—for all of them—to come back to her?

"Auntie?" came Hta Hta's voice.

Khin turned and saw her faithful servant, whose own daughter, Effie—only fifteen—had recently left them to join the revolution. The girl had linked up with a boy—a Burman—who out of disgust with Ne Win had decided to join the Karen cause, and who credited his revulsion also to the rampant racism of even the monks, and the closing down of all but the government's newspapers, and the restrictions on literature even of a religious kind, and the persistent "Burma for the Burmans" rallying cry of Ne Win's party. Hta Hta, too, had been a teenager when she'd fled this house with Benny and the family after the outbreak of civil war. And here she was, past thirty: leaning against the door frame, hardly able to support her own weight.

"Would you like to eat rice?" she asked Khin in her mild, fond manner.

And when Khin crossed to her, Hta Hta took her by the hand and led her down toward the kitchen, where they could nourish their bodies and their memories of what had been.

* * *

But that night she fell into a fever, and apprehension began seeping from her pores like a premonition of ruin. Hta Hta's cold compresses soothed the apprehension away; still the fever escalated, and soon Khin was watching herself rave and repel Hta Hta and pull at her bed linens as if they were offensive to her spirit.

"Khin," a woman said to her, and she realized it was Rita. Rita wrapped in grace, who, as if the butt of a cruel cosmic joke, had been freed only six weeks ago—after the three farewells were complete. Why was it that the dry woman came and pestered her with visits every few days? Pestered her with reminders of Benny and Lynton, the latter of whom had maneuvered Rita's release as part of his ongoing negotiations, or so the woman said.

"She won't eat, no longer knows me," Hta Hta lamented.

"Khin," said Rita again, "this is only a passing thing, this fever. You will pull through this. Tell yourself you will."

"Did I fail?" Khin stunned herself by crying.

But Rita seemed anything but astounded. She sat at Khin's side and took her hand in her own thin cool one.

"Tell me," Khin pressed on. "Did I fail? *Did I fail?*"

In the dim room, illuminated by the lamp and the generous moonlight, Rita's eyes looked very deep, even bottomless. "Why think in such terms?" she responded finally. "The only question is whether or not you've done your best in the face of your circumstances."

"So it's the end for me?"

Again, Rita hesitated. "There's no reason you shouldn't pull through this."

"But is *this* all?" Khin pursued madly.

A new suppleness suffused Rita's face. She peered down at Khin while seeming also to peer inward, at the limits of her own being. "Does it matter?" she said uncertainly. And then, almost as though to apologize: "We're here together now. This turn of ours isn't up."

"I tried to take turns," Khin confessed, blinking up into the depths of her eyes. "With *you*."

This turn didn't strike Rita, by appearances, as anything so benign. She made a visible effort to keep her gaze affixed to Khin's. "It is true," she said cautiously, "that I have affection for your husband, and that has put you in the position of having to share him . . . Would you—would you like me to explain my feelings?"

The acknowledgment of what Khin had endured—and of what Rita continued to share exclusively with Benny—sucked the wind right out of Khin's chest, and she thought that she would gasp, or cry. It occurred to her that Rita had also just lost him to America, to another life. That Rita had lost him without ever having had him, really.

"I imagine," Rita said, "that for a long time I have been moved by his brokenness. He can't help reaching for what he knows will evade his grasp. But the failing doesn't stop him from continuing to care, from trying again."

The way Rita said it—not in grief, but in joy—made the happenstance of her having known and lost Benny seem a blessing. And how fortunate they all had been, Khin realized, to intersect when they might have missed one another entirely.

And all at once she seemed to see Benny standing with his hands in his coat pockets and gazing down the wrong direction of a foreign boulevard. Time had already transformed him in this image she held now in her mind: he was whiter, puffier, with the bewildered despair of the aged. But his exile was not only from youth. His despair was also that of emigration. The greatest shock was seeing him out in the open air—an open air that in its indifference seemed to obliterate him. For so long, he'd been in prison or under house arrest—his significance continuously underscored, albeit negatively. "Benny!" she called to him, and she seemed to see him reel around toward her with something vacant, something foolish—a touch of stupidity—in his eyes. It took a minute for his gaze to settle on hers and another minute for anything but confusion to register on his features. "Where are the children?" she asked. But he didn't answer. He leaned toward her, and she knew—from the stiff fragility of his torso enclosed in her arms, from his disorientation—that he wouldn't long survive the displacement.

"Khin!" Rita called her to the room again. "I need you to be strong. There is something very tragic I must say."

Hta Hta was singing a Karen ballad. "Yea, though I walk through the valley of the shadow of death, I will fear no evil . . ."

"Khin!" Rita repeated, and the shadow of Benny rose up between them, annihilating the ache of envy, of apartness. "They say Lynton's dead. There was a parade in the streets celebrating his capture. Do you hear me?" Rita peered into her eyes, pinning Khin deliberately to this life. "You're all Louisa has here. You're all she has."

22

Miss Burma

On the evening the reports about Lynton began to come in over the wireless, Louisa bolted herself inside their bedroom in the house on the hill. She had the sense that she needed to gather her thoughts, to keep out the confusion of the reports in order to determine how to go on. *He's alive. He's alive,* she kept telling herself, remembering what Lynton had said—to expect the news of his death, which wouldn't be true. *He'll come back. He's only hiding out.* But even as she thought these things, the collective force of the reports made her crouch down on the bed. And then she put out the lamp, the better not to see—not to confront the horrible likelihood of the reports in aggregate being fact.

Five hours earlier, Sunny had come for her at the school, where she had been giving a literature lesson to the boys and the village children. Without a word, he had led her to the wireless operator's hut, and there she learned that the session of talks Lynton had been attending in Thaton—a cease-fire zone—had derailed. What they knew was that Lynton and his senior officers had ventured inside the walled ancient city to meet with the Burmans, and then all entrances had been barricaded. Neither Lynton nor any of the officers had been seen coming out, and nearly half their soldiers who had been waiting for them were already beginning to desert, believing all was lost. What was more, the Burmans had obviously stolen their codebooks, and it was now impossible to tell which of the messages coming in a flurry over the wireless were to be trusted—messages that told crucially different versions of what had befallen Lynton. In all versions, he had been having dinner when the Burmans broke in and began to shoot; but whereas roughly half the accounts reported that he had made an escape and was hiding out wounded, the others reported that he had been killed. And the difference seemed to hinge on the question of culpability: in the versions in which he lived, only the Burmans were at fault for violating the terms of the cease-fire; in the rest, an unnamed member of his inner circle had drugged and set him up.

He is alive, Louisa told herself again, and in the intensifying darkness she seemed to feel the heat of him in the bed beside her. The heat of his brain. Of his will to go on. Of his relentless interest in her. Had she committed the error of so many of his devoted men and made him some sort of false god? The brilliance of his frequent laughter, his neglect of caution of the usual sorts, his resurrections after the previous reports of his death, his guarantee to her that he wouldn't die, that he would never really be dead—all of it had seemed capable of rescuing her, rescuing them all, from menace. She'd always intuitively understood that part of the cult of the war hero was necessarily his veneer not only of faultless decisiveness, of immortality, but also of immunity from torment. And like everyone else who believed in him, she had come nearly to worship at the altar of his invulnerability. She, too, needed something to believe in. Life was too oppressive without a measure of faith.

Shivering on the bed, she seemed to be perched on the precipice of a terrible chasm whose darkness appalled her. Could Lynton have been prepared for betrayal by one of his own friends? To obscure the memory of his face, she sprang up and fumbled with the matches on the table beside the bed, struggling to light the spirit lamp and hold herself on this side of the chasm—the chasm of the unknown. But the frailty of the lamplight only reminded her of how she had eavesdropped from another dark bedroom on Lynton talking with Tom in Sunny's mother's kitchen. If not every member of Lynton's inner circle could be trusted, neither could Tom nor the American, whose "invitation" Tom had seemed to urge upon Lynton. And what had that invitation been? For Lynton to engage with American military personnel, or to be disappeared by them?

There was a knock at the door, and she yelped, jumping around, but it was only Sunny. His voice came quietly through the door. "I have soup," he said.

The sight of his face behind the door—soft and vulnerable and frightened—gave her the strange, almost passionate urge to kiss him, to take his warm face in her own blood-warmed one and console him.

Out in the kitchen, he watched while she sat and took the soup into her mouth, submerging her fear spoonful by spoonful. She was an animal, just an animal. It was the mind, not the body, which was alien, the cause of torment. She had only to dwell—and keep dwelling every moment—in this animal self in order to go on.

"There are more messages," Sunny said when she was done, speaking in a voice that was at once embarrassed and reverential. "The Burmans say you are forgiven. They invite you back to Rangoon to be with your mother."

She did not raise her eyes to meet his.

He went on: "Another message says that you must never return. That their army has plans for you."

The silence he followed this with was immense, and when she finally turned her eyes to him, she saw that he had begun to perspire profusely, as though he could no longer contain the anxiety behind his pores.

"And that they have already hurt your mother," he continued.

"My mother?"

"Broken into her house and kicked her around. But maybe," he quietly added, "they want to frighten you into surrender." His eyes, peering down at her, shone with intention. "We believe our senior officers have all been arrested and transported to Rangoon. Our men will need a leader. You must establish a grid line."

She was possessed by a strange, familiar feeling of dissociation, as though she were being called, again, to play a part she didn't want, for which she was ill prepared. She had been born into war, and war had never let her go, but she hadn't *made* war. She had never *really* wanted to make it. And yet she said, "What is a grid line, Sunny?"

"A boundary of villages the Burmans can't cross without us opening fire."

"And if the Burmans cross our grid line and we have to open fire . . . will we have enough men and munitions to deter them?"

"Maybe. Not for long."

"And where will we go if we need to retreat?"

But she remembered that Lynton had already given her the answer: on the night he had spoken of his impending "death," he had pointed across the dimming valley, toward the lush slopes of the Dawna Range, and he had said, *"Go to those mountains if the Burmans come."*

She had determined nothing, established nothing, seemed only to be caught in a net of continued disbelief, when, several hours later, she learned that one of the boys, the youngest, had developed a high fever and was at risk of death.

She found him on his bed in a hostile delirium. "I told you the hill is haunted!" he shouted at her when she approached, but he didn't balk when she soon stripped away the bedding covering him and pressed him to her body to absorb some of his heat.

He was an orphan, as were most of Lynton's boys. "Every year, three or four people in every Karen village are shot like his parents," Lynton had told her, "made to die by the hands of the Burma Army so that the people know to be frightened and to submit." Now, as she held this child, she had the visceral sense that he was a replacement for her own little lost one, or rather that she could hold this boy so closely because her own boy wasn't here to fill her hands, her life. And she was overcome by the fervent wish that he not die.

"Everything is all right," she found herself murmuring to him, and she laid him back and doused him with the cool water Sunny brought to her. *Everything is all right*—an absurdity because nothing was as it should be and perhaps nothing ever would be right again for them. Yet she was consoled by her own words, half believed them. If she could just save this one boy's life—if she could just keep saving it and saving it—disaster would be kept at bay. Hush now. Sleep. I'll stay with you. Don't cry. Yes, yes, I'll stroke your back. You need sleep. Everything will be all right.

For several hours, they fought to hold on to the boy's life. He had two frightening seizures before he fell unconscious. And as her hope began to recede, she perceived another meaning in the assurance she'd given him: one way or another, they would all come to an end; but they were *meant* to come to an end. Everything would be all right—and nothing would be all right—because he would die as they all assuredly would. And, perceiving this almost trivial truth, she told herself that she must go to Mama and surrender herself to the Burmans.

But around midnight the boy took an inexplicable turn for the better. He awakened, his raging fever broke, and, after changing him and helping him back into the freshly made bed, she sat watching over him in a state of rapture. She hadn't forgotten Lynton, nor did she discount the possibility that Lynton was dead and the Burma Army was poised to invade Kyowaing. But she seemed to see the entire mysterious panorama of their predicament through the keyhole of this boy's narrow escape from death. Was it a trick of her present circumstance that, from this perspective, she perceived that her own life, which had never been worth much to her personally, was worth saving because it was meant to serve and save others? She felt filled with an aching, profound love—not for herself, which seemed to have grown thin and dissipated—but for the boy and for her mother, for Lynton's men and for all of Burma's persecuted. None of them was worthier than any child born to the planet, but they were worth defending, worth loving especially, for the very reason that their worth was in question. Indeed, the fulfillment she had been anticipating—her fulfillment with Lynton—had finally arrived: now, at last, she was free to give herself utterly.

And what did that mean, to give herself? The question seemed to bear on nothing less than the Karen problem—a problem of trust, of whom to trust, of the difference between trust and suicide. She saw the scope of their immediate problem: that the Burmans were bound to invade, to cross the grid line which she must right away make known; that the remaining men in Lynton's brigade would be too few to repel them; that the only place to flee would be hostile Karen territory; that this territory itself would be jeopardized if Kyowaing was overrun; and that Bo Moo would have no choice but to surrender or combine forces with others—with her own soldiers, if she could persuade the man to reconcile with them. But, of course, Bo Moo was the door she must throw open, as Lynton had said. There was no other choice.

After she arranged for a village woman to watch over the sleeping boy, she ascended the hill in the predawn light, entered her empty house, and went to the bedroom, where she found shears and sat before a mirror. Years before, she had sat down in just this way—that time with a penknife in hand, yet with no understanding of where her instincts were leading her. Now she saw that there was no need to mar herself in order to take possession of her inner strength: she only had to remove the last shred of her pretense, the pretense that would prevent Bo Moo from trusting her and prevent her from becoming the fullest expression of herself.

She'd never been in the habit of seeing Miss Burma's beauty, had hardly been able or wished to see it, so it was with some surprise that she now registered her still unblemished skin, her clear, deep gaze. Her hair was up, and as she began to unpin it, and as pieces fell darkly around her pale face, she was strangely taken by the vivid picture the contrast made. For an instant, she thought she hadn't the courage to cut it away, to deprive herself of this unearned advantage—or disadvantage, for hadn't she been shackled to pretense by means of this "advantage"? How easy it would be to break the shackles; she had only to want to break them. With a flush of embarrassment, she remembered Lynton's refrain about the necessity of living free from shame. And, as she stared at her face, she saw in it the presence of Mama's and Daddy's longing and valiance and rage. There, beneath the surface of the skin tightening around her eyes, was the same startled stamina she'd witnessed when Mama had tripped after the horse cart carrying her and the other children away from the Bilin plague. *"Promise we'll be all right?"* *"Never lose faith!"* There, behind her searching gaze, was the same bewildered conviction she'd discovered night after night in Daddy's study, when he would stub out his cigarette or throw a glance out the window, as if to throw so many punches at an obscure fate. *"If you aren't prepared to fight against injustice—if you aren't prepared to risk everything to defend the liberty of all human beings—"* She was the completion of each of her parents, as much as she was now the completion of Lynton—dead or alive.

Lynton. The picture of him riddled with bullets all at once exploded across her consciousness, across her reflected, horrified face. And without wasting another minute she picked up the shears, grabbed a fistful of hair, and began to cut.

Neither Sunny nor the wireless operator said a thing later that morning down by the operator's hut, where she appeared shorn and wearing Lynton's fatigues. Neither of them looked at her when the three of them sat down across the operator's narrow table to determine the grid line, or when, that grid line having been established and communicated over the wireless, she faced them frankly and said, "I see no choice but to approach Bo Moo about reconciliation."

"He will kill us," Sunny responded, finally staring into her face with agony. He seemed to have ceased breathing.

"Do you think I am mistaken?" she said to them. "Do you think we can fend off the Burmans on our own?"

Sunny continued to stare at her in silence while the operator fiddled with his instruments.

"Tell me," she said, "is there someone else—some other group—to whom Bo Moo can turn if our territory is overrun?"

"There are the Communists," the operator quietly put in, raising his eyes to her at last. He was a small man, timid by nature, and for a few moments, she struggled to reconcile his aspect of hesitancy with the force of his revelation.

"Which communists?" she said. "Isn't Bo Moo opposed to communism?"

"I mean the Karen Communists," he said. "The ones based in the Tavoy. They are few, but well funded by Peking. I've been listening in, and they are trying to pay Bo Moo a visit."

It was hours past dawn and the sun shone strongly in the window like a grace, yet she had the sense again of standing over a chasm whose depths she could hardly fathom. Again she remembered the overheard conversation between Lynton and Tom. "*Exactly why Will's old plan makes sense. We need a base in the Tavoy—somewhere arms can be delivered by sea.*" Had the American wanted to position Lynton in the Tavoy as a defense against communism and further communist incursions? And had Lynton knowingly gone along with being *used* to such an end? She was seized by the impulse to back away from the depths of her incomprehension, to run toward Bo Moo, who had doggedly trusted no one: not the Burmans, not the West, not Lynton himself, and not Peking—as yet.

"We will go to him regardless," she said.

"His men will ambush us if we enter his territory without permission," Sunny cried. She saw him shiver, as though he were caught in a wind from which there was no escape.

"With the corrupted airwaves," the operator added, "communication is impossible."

"We'll communicate by hand and runners, if necessary," she said.

And then she forced herself to look past their frightened faces to the window, to the sunshine, still pacifying the day.

That night, under the cover of the mist and the darkness, with a gun that still felt unnatural on her hip and a rifle in her hands, she left the village with Sunny, the operator, a medic, and a platoon of eight other men. They had sent a runner ahead to make contact with a farmer whose property straddled the opposing brigades' territories—and whose soldier sons were no less divided—with the hope that the farmer would be willing to approach Bo Moo as a neutral party and communicate their desire for safe passage to his headquarters. Sometime in the next few hours, they trusted, they would intersect with the runner and learn their next step.

She had not slept in over a day, but as she proceeded into the forest she was drawn deeper into her acutely alert state of mind. She followed her ruined body over paths that plunged, that slipped, that climbed, that vanished into streams whose currents came up to her knees, that propelled her and the others all at once onto brief clearings from which she could see, through the parting mists, the moonlit ridges of the Dawna Range. Then back, back they burrowed, freezing, into the forest's comprehensive darkness, leaving time, or rather entering another kind of time—the time of the dead. The mire into which they sank was that of the decomposed. The nocturnal beings peering at them from the trees were the dead's descendants. And the rustle of a snake in the underbrush was the angel of death calling them home. A cemetery, old as the earth, with traps laid to bury them. And yet she seemed to sense an invisible hand drawing her forth with every pace. Sunny's tense shape ahead of her, the silhouette of his rifle and grenade launcher in the shadows beyond the shadows—those might have been Lynton's.

Dawn was breaking when the mists gave way to white fields of paddy, and the men recognized the farmer's hut on the edge of the far forest. The rest hid in the brush while she and Sunny proceeded through the sodden field as far as the hut, where they gently called out to make themselves known, and soon discovered the tousled head of the runner emerging from the doorway. He had made contact, he told them, and the willing farmer had left sometime in the middle of the night. There was rice and tea for them inside. They must eat, and then hide in a hut farther on in the forest until the man's return. No cooking during the day, no smoke the Burmans might see, no movement at all until the farmer returned with Bo Moo's answer, and that could take four or five days.

An enforced pause. A *maddening* pause, during which they could only listen in over the wireless, mutely watching the terrible action from afar. They knew the Burmans were on the move, knew—from the escalating warnings that their own men in Kyowaing were sending out—that Taung Kwin, on the grid line, was under threat. Any moment gunfire would erupt, while they were left to reckon with the paltriness of their plans.

Or rather, *her* plans, because there was no question anymore that she had become the leader of Lynton's men, that she alone was responsible for arranging and conducting this entire, if halted, movement toward Bo Moo's camp, which would either save or destroy them. And yet she knew so little of the menacing figure on whom her aspirations were now pinned.

"Tell me more about him," she said to the men each night, when they felt freer to breathe, to speak. And slowly a picture began to crystallize in her mind—a picture of revolution made manifest. Bristling hair, eyes shocked with contempt, furious and thick-fingered fists . . . Bo Moo had staged an attack on Lynton's camp before the peace talks had begun, the men told her, and he was known to impose the harshest sentences on soldiers who committed crimes, sentences he himself executed with his bayonet . . . From a peace-seeking perspective, he would appear to be a demon. *And will I become like that?* she wondered in this sanctuary of the indefinite.

Because not only could she not comprehend Bo Moo, but she hardly knew what she meant to do with the man should he not kill her on the spot. She would endeavor to convince him that he should accept reunification—but beyond that? Her first thought was to persuade him to trust in Lynton's plan of building trust, of looking West while working toward democracy; but of course she no more knew if she trusted Lynton's allies—his senior officers, Tom, the American, those Burman government insiders who had been willing to lend Lynton an ear—than she knew if she trusted in the possibility of democracy and trust itself. Consider, on the one hand, survival by means of a rejection of the ideals one used to hold dear; consider, on the other, victory by means of the risk of holding fast to them. One instant she had the evil fantasy of surprising the Burmans who had shot at Lynton, surprising them in their beds with a volley of shots from her own rifle; another appalled instant she thought she would prefer to call her men to her and pray for divine inspiration. Who will we *be* from now on? she seemed to be asking herself. Shall we be described as the crystallization of revolution, too? Shall we be defined by hatred and suspicion and contempt, absolved by righteousness and a bloody thirst for revenge?

On the fifth morning, the farmer finally wandered out of a tangle of trees in the forest accompanied by one of Bo Moo's colonels. "I was a friend of your father and Saw Lay," the colonel told her immediately, surely to put her at ease. But as they sat down together for tea in the farmer's hut, the embarrassment with which he stole glances at her made her all at once conscious of her shorn head. "There is a long journey ahead of you to headquarters," he said to her. "I'm afraid you won't be permitted to bring more than one of your men along."

With Sunny—of course it was Sunny she chose—they left the farmer's field that evening, pressing forward into the mountains in a truncated column. The colonel was so soft and almost feminine that she could hardly believe him a warrior. He held his hands folded together as gently as he strode over the steep terrain, as lightly as he seemed to wear his boots and cap. She sensed he was predisposed to taking her into his confidence, yet he kept his silence as the fogs fell over them, and she kept Sunny between them—Sunny who, every hundredth pace, looked back worriedly at her, his eyes gleaming like stars in the deepening night.

As her bones began to throb and she trudged into the shadows that grew increasingly sinister, she felt alternately seized by a desperate desire to survive, to save her men and people, and lured by a call to rest, to surrender, even to die. Was this how Mama had felt, after they had parted in Bilin, when she had walked with her wares on her back, bearing the burden of her children's survival? Even as Louisa wondered this, her thoughts slipped back to the children she'd left in Kyowaing, to the sick boy. Without the wireless operator accompanying her, she had no way of being reassured that he was still safe; she was submerged in her individual experience, as Mama had been during those months and months of their apartness.

An early blue light broke as they were making a strenuous, desolating climb up a gorge, and through the rising mists she glimpsed a tiny village clinging to the mountainside. The sight took her back to the initial trek she'd made to Kyowaing, after Daddy had disappeared and the Burmans had broken the Thaton cease-fire. Her dawning awareness of the repetitions—the disappearances in Thaton, the broken cease-fires there—filled her with the bewildering sensation that she was reading the future in the past, or reading the future of the past in the present. Again, she seemed to be a girl passing a mystical mountain village, and again Mama seemed to be telling her that its inhabitants had never seen a car, that the rice and vegetables they ate came from their fields or the bounty of the forest. *"They know of no artifice."* *"What is artifice?"* *"The way one tricks oneself into forgetting that death is nearby."* Then she and the colonel and Sunny reached the crest of the gorge, and she was past the village, past her memory of what had been—born to and wrenched from her impressions so swiftly they seemed to have been dreamed.

Only when they drew up to a mountain station overlooking a wide russet-colored valley, whose waking beauty all at once blindsided her, did the colonel break his long silence. "You must be very smart about this," he said, and he nodded to the valley, as if to humble himself before it. "There are things the general believes you have done."

"Things?"

She understood he was referring to the rumors and that he was too shy to elaborate.

What he did instead was to complicate the picture she had been forming of Bo Moo, a man whose fanaticism for the Karen cause had apparently been intensified by his conversion to Christianity. Moo had grown up, the colonel said, an animist in the local Papun hills, where he had first confronted the barbarism of Aung San's Burma Independence Army, whose units had been composed of so many bloodthirsty convicts. One of the early massacres had occurred in Papun, with seventeen elders machine-gunned, and the stray survivor bayonetted into his grave. The incident had been the first of a flurry of increasingly unimaginable atrocities, one of which the colonel himself had survived. "You see," the colonel told her, dabbing the now lightly falling rain from his eyes, "Aung San's men liked to say the Japanese sanctioned their extermination of Christians. Whether this was the case, I cannot say. But there is no doubt they had Christian blood on their minds when they arrived at the Roman Catholic mission where I was then boarding, in Myaungmya, as an orphan."

Sunny retreated to the rear of the open station, as if to hide from the colonel's description of how one of the priests, in his sickbed at the Roman Catholic mission, had been burned alive, and another shot through the stomach before the soldiers had burst into the orphanage. The children and sisters had fled upstairs while the men shot after them, shot up through the ceiling. And it was only by hiding beneath a mattress that the colonel had escaped the axes and machetes that took the lives of those around him. "Over a hundred and fifty. Even a six-month-old baby . . . So you see," he went on quietly, not a note of self-pity or righteousness in his voice, "though the general was an animist then, the targeting of Christians couldn't fail to make an indelible impression on him. I think it very nearly *prepared* him for conversion—and when you speak to him you must keep this in mind, his devoutness."

Before she could form the question taking shape in her mind, he continued, less ambiguously: "He was a teenager at the time, and he did something interesting. Rather than joining the British army, as so many of our people did, rather than fighting against the Burma Independence Army or its allies, the Japanese, in the name of loyalty to the British—or rather than immediately joining British intelligence, as your husband did, pretending to spy for the Japanese and sabotaging their communications"—she made an effort, listening to these revelations, not to betray her ignorance of Lynton's past, or her interest in it—"rather than doing anything like that, General Bo Moo joined the Japanese police. You know from your father, no doubt, that it was the Japanese, unbelievably, along with Aung San, who eventually put an end to the particular viciousness of the Independence Army's miscreants. What General Bo Moo did was a very clever way of openly protecting our people at a time when we had no real protector at all. And it seems to me that he must have *learned* something from the Japanese then."

The colonel gave her a knowing, ominous look just as the wind picked up at their backs. "Of course, he joined up with the British eventually," he went on. "And he was not spared that special disillusionment felt by all of us—including your father and Saw Lay—when they left us to our own devices. It explains his reluctance to have confidence in the CIA, in *anyone*, the way your husband"—he looked worriedly out onto the valley again—"the way General Lynton was intent on doing."

Night was falling again by the time they arrived on the banks of the Salween River, where Burma came to an end. Bo Moo's headquarters were on the other side, in the relative refuge of Thailand, and through the gloaming she could see—beyond the far steep sandy bank—a thicket of teak from which several paths emerged, some leading down to the river, others following the shoreline before reentering the forest farther downstream where the trees surged forward to meet the cliff. There was a raft tied to those trees, but no vessel that she could see on the near bank.

The colonel showed them to a simple hut without walls near the water, where he said they could rest and nourish themselves while he conveyed the message of their arrival to headquarters. Then he disappeared into the forest down the shore, and she and Sunny, entering the open structure, seemed to be plunged into an aloneness and an exposure so comprehensive, all they could do for several moments was to stand with their guns pointed out at the expanding evening. Every odd call of a bird, every splash from the river, was a threat, reminding her of their utter vulnerability.

Sunny seemed to force himself to set down his rifle and reckon with the provisions left for them, and she turned her eyes to the calmly glistening river. How narrow it was, and how easy it would be for the Burmans to traverse it and overrun the last remnants of the Karen stronghold. She understood—at last, and viscerally—why Lynton had been so intent on seeking outside allies: in this isolation they could defend themselves for only so long. She felt a pang of sympathy for the man across the river, whom fate had also made her enemy; there he was, somewhere beyond the dark water, somewhere behind the slim forest of teak trees, full of pride, no longer able to cope alone with the evil he faced.

She glanced back at Sunny, who was pouring grains of rice into an empty pot. His movements were mechanical, his fingers almost imperceptibly trembling, as if he were trying to fulfill an obligation to persist. With an alert glance at her, he stood with the pot and left the hut, bound for the river—for the water, she saw. She watched him walk out to the very edge and stoop down and wash the rice. Then he stood erect, a kind of defeat in his shoulders, before he crossed to a nearby thicket of trees. A few moments later, he was back, beside the hut with the waterlogged pot and a few forked branches that he had plucked and presently used to construct a stand for cooking. Normally, he would have darted back out to the forest for vegetables or birds—he'd done as much every night when they had been waiting at the farmer's field—but this meal was not about their nourishment, she knew; these preparations were about his terror of discontinuing. And, watching him struggle to light a fire under the stand, she tried to halt the stream of her own sunken thoughts, rushing dangerously toward a mental picture of Lynton's last supper and the stunned expression that had snatched the smile away from his face.

But he's alive! she argued with herself inwardly, forcing her mind away from the images that were such a disgrace to the living man she loved.

She turned back to the river, trying to conjure Lynton's voice, as she had done with those of her parents when she had been separated from them in childhood—and instantly he was speaking to her, repeating what he'd said on the stoop of their Kyowaing house: *"If we look past our petty proclivities, past our troubled history; if we see the broader common goal, everyone with an eye to democracy . . . If we find a way to come together, they won't be able to stand in our way. And our friends will be there to help us . . ."*

How easily she had let herself think him the dupe of those friends, of the unnamed member of his inner circle who had supposedly betrayed him in Thaton, of Tom and the American. Lynton couldn't force an ally to be loyal, but he could determine to believe in another's capacity for loyalty. And *she* could keep her faith: in his judgment, even if he'd fallen; in his allies. Perhaps the thing she could most convincingly offer Bo Moo was precisely the thing the Communists couldn't—the thing most impossible to convince another of, because it was defined by uncertainty: faith. True, Bo Moo and Lynton had broken faith with each other, but neither had—at least until now—lost faith in their people's original dream of democracy. Wasn't it true that she had reason to believe that America—that the West, that Will and Tom—would support them only if they refused to tangle with the Communists? She must tell Bo Moo of the American's proposed base, which Lynton had believed would facilitate their aid.

A distant splash drew her attention to the far side of the river. In the early moonlight, she glimpsed the silhouette of a man standing as if on the water: a soldier was paddling the raft this way.

Sunny quickly took the pot off the stand and kicked dirt into the fire, and they picked up their rifles and went out to the bank. When she looked down the shore, she saw that the colonel had emerged from the trees and was walking toward them at a slow pace, as if trying to put off reaching them.

By the time the colonel drew abreast of them, his breath coming fast, his eyes glimmering with uncertainty, the soldier on the raft had nearly arrived.

"He is ready to meet you," the colonel told her, seeming to apologize.

He and Sunny trudged into the water, each taking hold of the rope the soldier had cast out to them.

"I will hold it—I will hold it—" the colonel told Sunny, drawing the raft toward her with all of his might.

Sunny backed away and extended his hand to her in unspoken reassurance.

She moved, yet didn't take it. She had the sense that she might never stand again in this place. And she was keenly aware of the people whom she seemed to be leaving behind.

She couldn't know that her mother, ailing and bruised from the attack at her home, was at that moment walking toward her along the Gulf of Martaban, retracing the steps she had taken when she'd heard the rumor that ten-year-old Louisa had been slain. She didn't know that the boys, earlier that day, had scattered in the burning forest after Kyowaing's invasion. She would never know that Lynton's corpse, weighted with chains, had three days earlier been flown out over the gulf and dumped, so that, like a downed plane, it fell through the sky, plunged into the waters, and finally came to rest on the sea bottom. She couldn't fathom the atrocity she would witness four days hence, when, after she succeeded in convincing Bo Moo to reunify and called her men to her, Bo Moo would decide to punish ten of those men for having trusted Lynton. Nor could she imagine the harrowing way that nearly every one of those men would lose his poise, crying and swearing and beseeching someone—beseeching God—for mercy, while in the chaos, before the crack of the gunfire, Sunny, also seized, would find her with his eyes and motion for her to run, to spare herself the sight.

She couldn't know. She couldn't. Yet, as if for the last time, she held in mind those who had held her in turn.

"Take my hand," Sunny said.

"He's a Christian," the colonel added. She wasn't sure if he meant to remind or reassure her.

"I have faith," she told them.

She had the chilling notion that they were but souls in the abyss, without a god or a country or a man to defend them. And to banish the notion, she put her rifle in Sunny's outstretched hand.

"You can step onto the raft," he said gently. "It is safe."

But she waited, uncertain and trying to be brave, for one more moment on Burma's shore.

About the Author

Charmaine Craig is a faculty member in the Department of Creative Writing at UC Riverside, and the descendant of significant figures in Burma's modern history. A former actor in film and television, she studied literature at Harvard University and received her MFA from the University of California, Irvine. Her first novel, *The Good Men*, was a national bestseller translated into six languages.